This book is lovingly dedicated to our dear friends Richard and Rosie Skiver.

Thank you for so enthusiastically promoting our novels in your bookstore. We love you!

GALATIANS 1:3

As the Founder/CEO of NAVH, the only national health agency solely devoted to those who, although not totally blind, have an eye disease which could lead to serious visual impairment, I am pleased to recognize Thorndike Press★ as one of the leading publishers in the large print field.

Founded in 1954 in San Francisco to prepare large print textbooks for partially seeing children, NAVH became the pioneer and standard setting agency in the preparation of large type.

Today, those publishers who meet our standards carry the prestigious "Seal of Approval" indicating high quality large print. We are delighted that Thorndike Press is one of the publishers whose titles meet these standards. We are also pleased to recognize the significant contribution Thorndike Press is making in this important and growing field.

Lorraine H. Marchi, L.H.D.
Founder/CEO
NAVH

★ Thorndike Press encompasses the following imprints: Thorndike, Wheeler, Walker and Large Pr int Press.

Acknowledgment

We would like to pay tribute to the memory of Samuel Francis Smith who, at twenty-four years of age, wrote the great song "America" while studying for the ministry at Andover Theological Seminary in 1832. Millions of Americans have thrilled at those immortal words:

My country 'tis of thee,
Sweet land of liberty,
Of thee I sing:
Land where my fathers died,
Land of the pilgrims' pride,
From every mountain side
Let freedom ring!

Prologue

In the 1870s a group of French citizens celebrated the centennial of the American Revolution by commissioning the construction of a statue of "Liberty Enlightening the World." The statue was to be presented to the people of the United States to demonstrate the harmonious relationship between the two countries.

The statue, monumental in size, would be the creation of the talented French sculptor, Frederic Auguste Bartholdi, whose dream was to build a monument honoring the American spirit of freedom that had inspired the world.

In the United States, government leaders were pleased with the kind gesture, and set about raising the $300,000 needed to build a pedestal for the huge French statue, which would be erected on Bedloe's Island in New York harbor. Promotional tours and contests were organized to raise the money. During these fund-raising campaigns, American poet Emma Lazarus — the daughter of a prominent Jewish family in New York City — wrote the poem "The New Colossus" which was inscribed on the pedestal just prior to the statue's dedication by President Grover Cleveland on October 28, 1886.

Emma Lazarus's immortal words transformed the French statue of "Liberty Enlightening the World" into the American Statue of Liberty, welcoming the oppressed of the world within its borders to have opportunity to make their dreams come true.

"The New Colossus" on Miss Liberty's pedestal reads:

> Give me your tired, your poor;
> Your huddled masses yearning to breathe free,
> The wretched refuse of your teeming shore.
> Send these, the homeless, the tempest-tossed
>   to me,
> I lift up my lamp beside the golden door!

Castle Island in New York harbor served as the chief entry station for immigrants between 1855 and 1891, though it was diminutive in size. In order to enlarge the facilities for processing immigrants, New York authorities began considering another site in the harbor. Eyes shifted to Governor's Island, but that was already occupied by the United States Coast Guard. Attention turned then, to a larger island just a few hundred yards north of Bedloe's Island, where Lady Liberty held high her torch. (Bedloe's Island was later named Liberty Island.)

The choice island was originally called Kioshk, or Gull Island, by Native Americans in the 1600s; Gibbet Island in the early 1700s when criminals were hanged there from a gibbet or gallow tree; later Oyster Island because of its abundant population of shellfish. In the early 1780s, the island was purchased by wealthy merchant Samuel Ellis from whom it derived its present name. New York state bought Ellis Island in 1808 and used it as an ammunitions dump until June 15, 1882, when the immigration facility — built at a cost of $500,000 — officially opened its doors. From that time, Ellis Island was the lone entry station for immigrants, and remained so until 1943.

The hopeful message on the Statue of Liberty's pedestal has greeted millions of immigrants from countries across the seas who left their homelands behind in search of a better life in the United States of America.

According to the Statue of Liberty-Ellis

Island Foundation, today more than a hundred million Americans can trace their roots to ancestors who came into this country through Ellis Island. This means that approximately half of today's Americans are the offspring of pioneering ancestors who registered into the country through that immigration station which stands virtually in the shadow of the Statue of Liberty.

Martin W. Sandler, author of the Library of Congress's book *Immigrants* says, "Our cultural diversity is our greatest strength, for we are more than a nation. Thanks to those who dared to be immigrants, we are a nation of nations. It is a heritage of which we should all be proud."

American historian Oscar Handlin said, "Once I thought to write the story of the immigrants in America. Then I realized that the immigrants *were* America's story."

They came from many countries across the Atlantic Ocean. For many, the journey was treacherous, and the good life they came for was just a dream. For others, the sailing was smooth, and they prospered in the new land. Both kinds of people created the rich and diverse country we live in today.

They heard talk. About a place where all men were free. A place of compassion. But what about the cost? Not just money for the passage, but the emotional toll. For most immigrants, grandparents, aunts, uncles, cousins, and friends would be left behind. The same was often true of wives and children. The men would have to go alone and send for their families later. Many of the children, who came with their mothers later on, would see their fathers for the first time in months — sometimes years — in the shadow of the Statue of Liberty.

The immigrants were driven by pain and fear and hopelessness; by poverty and hunger; by religious persecution; or by the simple need to survive. These things they all had in common, as well as the hope of a better life.

They all shared a common destination: New York harbor.

They came with nothing but the clothes on their backs, a pocketful of dreams, a flimsy suitcase, trunk, or lidded woven basket . . . and some crumpled bills carefully stashed in pockets or purses. There are countless stories of new friendships and relationships that were begun while aboard ship or while waiting at the processing station to be approved by physicians and government officials to enter the country.

None who entered this new land and found their place within its borders did so without having their lives changed forever.

A Note from the Author

It is with great pleasure that we present this series of novels about America's immigrants. Together, we have walked the grounds of both Liberty and Ellis Islands and caught the spirit of those men, women, and children who left their homes in faraway countries, traversed the oceans, and came to the Land of the Free.

Passing through the same buildings on Ellis Island where they took their medical examinations and their verbal tests in hope of entering this country, we felt we could almost hear the shuffle of their weary feet, the murmur of voices, the laughter of children, and the crying of babies.

The walls of the buildings are covered with photographs of the immigrants, their faces displaying the intimidation they felt, yet a light in their eyes that showed the hope that lay within them for a better life in America.

The walls also bear quotations of remarks

14

made by the immigrants. One that was particularly humorous came from an Italian man after having been in this country for a short time: "When I came to America, I thought the streets were paved with gold. I found that they were not paved at all. I was especially surprised to find out that they wanted *me* to pave them!"

Those readers who know our other fictional series are fully aware that our stories are filled with romance, adventure, and intriguing plots designed to make the books hard to lay down. They are interlaced with Scripture that will strengthen and encourage Christians, and as always, the Lord Jesus Christ is honored and His gospel made clear.

Since the books in this series are about the people of Europe, which is comprised of many countries and tongues, and because a great number of them spoke several languages, we will not weary the reader by continuously pointing out what language they are speaking. We will simply give it to you in English.

It is our desire that the reader will feel as we did when we walked those hallowed halls, deeply impressed with the courage of those people who helped settle this land we call home.

Introduction

Involved in our story are the Cossacks, a Russian military force who were used extensively in the nineteenth century to suppress revolutionary activities. Dressed in impressive black uniforms that marked them as fearsome, they would punish anyone rebelling against the czar's regime — even peasants, if they did not pay their taxes. Punishment was always severe, even unto death if the Cossack leaders felt it necessary.

When a young man signed up as a Cossack, he was in for twenty years. The only way out was by death or a wound that was so severe he could no longer carry out his duties. If he deserted, he would be hunted down and executed.

Our story begins in the first week of January 1856. Since October 1853, Russia had been fighting England, France, and Turkey in the Russian Crimea, a peninsula linked with the mainland of Russia by the Perekop

Isthmus and bounded by the Black Sea on the south and west and the Sea of Azov on the north and east.

The Crimea covered an area of 10,400 square miles. Though there are many battlefields all over the peninsula, the heaviest fighting was at Sevastopal, the base of the Russian naval fleet.

South of the Crimea across the Black Sea is Turkey, where a military hospital has been set up in the coastal town of Uskudar. In charge of the hospital was nurse Florence Nightingale. Of British descent, Miss Nightingale, who was thirty-four years old at the time, organized a unit of thirty-eight women nurses for the Crimean War in 1854. By the war's end in 1856, she had become a legend, and during the war had been dubbed: "Lady of the Lamp."

Miss Nightingale was the founder of trained nursing as a profession for women and was known for her compassion and care for the wounded. She not only tended to the medical needs of wounded and dying soldiers of the British, French, and Turkish armies, but her compassion was extended to Russian soldiers who had fallen on battlefields and been left behind by the Russian army.

One

The howling wind was knifing out of the snow-laden hills to the north of the Crimean Peninsula in hard, hissing gusts, flinging needle-sharp snow crystals into Corporal Vladimir Petrovna's face. The sky was clearing after a night of snowfall, and the appearance of the midday sun did nothing to bring warmth.

Bellied down in the snow behind a fallen tree, the young corporal held his rifle in ready position, scanning the open area before him. Two of his comrades lay dead a few feet away, having gone down in a fierce shoot-out with the enemy forces, who now had pulled back into the thick woods on the west side of the clearing. He was now separated from the other Russian troops, who had withdrawn into the woods on the east side. He wanted to join them, but the distance to the protective timber was so great that if the Allied troops came out of the woods while he was plodding through the snow, they would catch him in the open and riddle him with bullets.

Vladimir's cheeks were red and chapped from many days of exposure to the harsh elements of this austere land. He pulled his fur cap down more snugly on his head and lifted his woolen muffler up tighter around his nose and mouth, trying to find a bit of comfort in the biting cold.

Keeping his eyes peeled on the west woods, Vladimir felt a deep longing for home and family. He let his tired mind wander to the warmth of the old farmhouse, and in his mind's eye, he envisioned himself sitting by the fireplace with his parents and siblings as he had done countless times before being inducted into the Russian army.

In the picture, he was sitting in his favorite chair with his feet on the tufted hassock, drawn up close to the fire. He could almost see the bright, dancing flames and hear the popping of the logs as the fire warmed his body.

With a start, Vladimir came back to reality as he peered through the windblown snow that skipped over the floor of the clearing and thought he saw movement at the edge of the west woods. The blowing snow made visibility poor, and at first he thought his mind was playing tricks on him.

Focusing closer on the edge of the woods, he saw people darting from tree to tree.

Suddenly, gunfire broke out. The Russian troops were charging out onto the battlefield, muzzles flashing fire, and the Allied soldiers were rushing out to meet them, rifles blazing.

If Vladimir was going to rejoin his comrades, it was now. Gathering his legs under him, he stood up and ran through the foot-deep layer of snow, heading for the Russian troops. Bullets were suddenly flying all around him, some of them plowing into the snow near his feet. He made a dive into the snow, and on his belly once again, he looked toward the enemy troops. The swirling snow cleared momentarily, and almost as if in slow motion, he lifted his rifle in numb fingers and carefully drew a bead on a uniform with the unmistakable markings of the Turkish army. The enemy soldier had spotted him, and was raising his rifle to take aim as he ran toward him.

Vladimir's weapon spit fire, and he felt a pang of sorrow as the Turk stiffened, dropped his rifle, and fell face down into the snow.

A half dozen Allied soldiers were coming toward him from the west woods. Vladimir worked the lever of his rifle, and fired into their midst. One of them went down, and at the same time, a small unit of Russian soldiers were charging at the others, guns blazing.

Vladimir jumped to his feet to join his comrades, and as he ran, from somewhere, more bullets began to hiss around him. There was a hot, searing pain in his right thigh, and he found himself plowing snow with his face as he went down. He lay there for a moment, with the thunder of battle pounding his ears and the excruciating pain of torn flesh and ligaments burning like fire in the wounded leg.

And then, it seemed that he was being sucked into a black, whirling vortex . . . and the pain was fading as was the light of day around him.

The western sky was aglow with the brilliance of the setting sun as Corporal Vladimir Petrovna felt himself being lifted out of the darkness back into his cold, frozen world. Instantly, he recalled the fierce battle that was being fought when he went unconscious. But now, there was complete silence, except for the whine of the wind. He was lying on his back. Putting his hands to his face, it felt like a stiff, ice-crusted mask.

Clawing at the coat of ice, he soon freed his eyes and mouth.

Struggling with his heavy eyelids, Vladimir finally got his eyes open, and found that he was covered with a thin layer of windblown snow. There was extreme pain in his right thigh. And then he remembered the sudden pain in the leg just before he fell facedown and the vortex swallowed him. He wondered how he ever managed to roll onto his back.

With effort, the young corporal raised his head and saw the lifeless bodies of both Russian and Allied soldiers strewn around him. They were also blanketed with a thin layer of snow.

His eyes then fell on the crimsoned snow next to his right leg. He could tell that he had lost a great deal of blood. However, as he reached down to touch the wound, he found that the cold air had stemmed the flow of blood. At least for the time being. He figured if he moved the leg it would start bleeding again.

Suddenly there was movement on the left side. Squinting, he was able to make out a band of Russian soldiers some fifty yards away, who were picking up two of their wounded comrades. He then noted four or five other wounded Russian soldiers who were slumped on the backs of horses, and by the obvious direction the group was headed, he knew they were about to head north to the Russian army camp. Looking around at the footprints and hoofprints in the snow, Vladimir realized that his comrades had already passed him by, thinking he was dead.

Panic tightened his chest. He attempted to raise up on his elbows, but found that he had not the strength to do it.

Head still elevated slightly, he drew a shuddering breath and tried to call out to them, but found that there wasn't even enough strength to do that. His head fell back in the snow. The numbing cold seemed to hold him in its grip like some giant hand. He knew the temperature was already no more than ten degrees. It would plunge far below zero when night fell.

The panic was on him again.

Gritting his teeth, Vladimir summoned every ounce of his strength and shakily raised himself to a sitting position. Clouds of vapor escaped his mouth and rode away on the wind as he looked closely at the fallen soldiers around him. There were two British soldiers some fifty feet away, who were breathing as they lay in the snow that was crimsoned beneath them. They were alive but immobilized by their wounds.

Vladimir looked back at the band of Russian soldiers. They were riding away, taking their wounded with them. He drew a deep breath, wanting desperately to call out to them, but dizziness washed over him like an ocean wave. He fell onto his back, fighting the dizziness, and rolled onto his side, gasping for breath.

A dark curtain was descending over him. Just before he passed out, a lovely face flashed onto the screen of his mind. "Sasha," he puffed. "My sweet Sasha. I . . . I will never see you again on this earth. I will die tonight. I . . . love you."

It was eleven-thirty that same night when one of the underground churches in southern Russia near the city of Kiev was holding its weekly secret meeting. Moving their meeting place from week to week among the homes of the farmers so as to elude detection by the Cossacks, they were in the home of farmer Olthan Kindranov and his wife. Farmer Vande Wendin, who had just become pastor, was preaching the sermon.

In the group of some thirty-five believers was seventeen-year-old Sasha Leskov, who was sitting next to her fifteen-year-old sister, Oksana. The girls were flanked by their parents, with Sasha seated next to her mother. Behind them sat Bakum and Margaret Petrovna.

The new pastor's message was designed to encourage his flock, who were deeply saddened because their previous pastor, Andrei Dolskan, had been arrested by the Cossacks and was executed. The Cossacks had somehow learned that Dolskan was a Christian and upon entering his farmhouse, had held Dolskan and his family at gunpoint while they searched for Bibles. Finding a Bible belonging to each member of the family, they confiscated them. Inside Andrei's Bible were some sermon notes, which told them that he was no doubt pastoring an underground church.

Being asked if this was so, Andrei told them it was. When they demanded that he tell them where his underground church met, he refused, knowing full well the edict passed down by Czar Alexander II. When found out, pastors of underground churches were immediately executed by the Cossacks unless they divulged the location of the church's meeting place, provided the Cossacks with the names of the people in their congregations, and publicly renounced their faith in Jesus Christ.

Andrei Dolskan had refused to give the

Cossacks the information they demanded and refused to renounce his faith in his Saviour. He was executed by firing squad in front of his wife and children. And because they refused to give the demanded information and renounce Jesus Christ, they were now in prison for life.

At the close of the sermon, Pastor Vande Wendin ran his gaze over the wan faces of his flock and closing his Bible, said, "We will go to prayer now, and as always, we will remember the three men of this church who are serving their country in the Crimean War. We must pray for God's protection over them even as we pray for ourselves in this time of great persecution against God's born-again people in Russia."

Wendin called on one of the older farmers to lead in prayer. As the farmer prayed for the three young soldiers who were members of the church, he wept.

Sasha Leskov's beautiful dark eyes pooled with tears at the mention of Vladimir Petrovna's name. Sasha and Vladimir had plans to marry when he came home from the war, but she lived with the fear that he would be killed in battle and their dreams of a future together as husband and wife would be shattered.

Malia Leskov heard her oldest daughter

sniffing as the farmer continued in prayer. Without opening her eyes, Malia took hold of Sasha's hand and gave it a squeeze. Sasha squeezed back. They could hear Margaret Petrovna sniffling behind them.

When the prayer was finished and the pastor had dismissed the service, the Leskovs and the Petrovnas huddled close. Margaret folded Sasha in her arms, kissed her cheek, and said with choked voice, "The Lord will bring Vladimir back to us, Sasha."

"Yes, He will," said Bakum Petrovna. "We have all prayed so hard for our Vladimir to come home to us safely."

"And we must believe it is going to happen," said Margaret.

Sasha wiped tears and said, "Oh, Mama Petrovna, I want to believe that, but I'm so frightened. Will this awful war never end?"

"It will if we pray hard enough, dear," Margaret said, smiling at Malia as she moved up, laying a hand on Sasha's shoulder.

Sasha turned and looked into her mother's eyes.

The members of the underground churches had to leave their Bibles hidden at home, lest they be stopped at any time by the Cossacks and their wagons or sleighs searched. Pressing a thin smile on her lips, Malia said, "Let me quote a verse for you, sweet daughter. First John 4:18. 'There is no fear in love; but perfect love casteth out fear: because fear hath torment. He that feareth is not made perfect in love.' "

"That's right," said Hegal Leskov, stepping close to his oldest daughter. "Sasha, dear, let God take away your tormenting fears and fill your heart with faith. With Him all things are possible."

"I know, Papa," said Sasha, "but sometimes my faith is so weak and small."

"You must ask Him to strengthen your faith, dear," said Hegal. "And according to Romans 10:17, faith comes to us from the Word of God. The more you study the Word and pray for greater and stronger faith, the greater and stronger it becomes."

Thumbing tears from her cheeks, Sasha nodded. "Yes, Papa. I know you are right."

Bakum took hold of Sasha's hand. With tenderness in his eyes, he said, "Margaret and I are so very much looking forward to the day you will become our daughter-in-law, Sasha. We must all trust the Lord to end the war soon and bring Vladimir home so plans can be made for the wedding."

Sasha smiled. Raising up on her tiptoes, she planted a soft kiss on Bakum's cheek.

"Yes, Papa Petrovna. We must trust the Lord to do that."

An hour later, at the Leskov house, Sasha hugged her parents and sister in the hall and went into her room to go to bed. She had just doused the lantern next to her bed and was snuggling down in the covers when there was a tap on the door.

"Sasha," came Malia's voice. "May I come in?"

"Of course, Mama," Sasha replied.

Malia entered, leaving the door open, and by the light that flowed in from the hall, she sat down on the edge of her daughter's bed and said, "I want to say it one more time, dear. 'There is no fear in love; but perfect love casteth out fear: because fear hath torment. He that feareth is not made perfect in love.' "

"Yes, Mama," said Sasha. "I must let the Lord put His perfect love deep in my heart."

Reaching under the covers and grasping Sasha's hand, Malia said, "Let's talk to Jesus."

Sasha gripped her mother's hand as Malia led them in prayer, praying for safety for Vladimir. She beseeched the Lord for a quick end to the senseless war then asked Him to fill Sasha's heart with His perfect love and to cast out her fear.

When the amen was said, Sasha once again thumbed away tears from her cheeks but this time a peaceful smile tugged the corners of her mouth.

Lying in the snow on the Crimean Peninsula, eighteen-year-old Vladimir Petrovna regained consciousness and opened his eyes to find himself staring toward a black, velvet sky with myriads of twinkling stars.

A frigid breeze was blowing. He knew he had never been so cold in all his life. He had gone on hunting trips into the Carpathian Mountains with his father on many occasions in the dead of winter, but he had never been this cold. He was surprised that he was still alive. Knowing the harsh, bitter Russian winters, Vladimir told himself that soon he would succumb to the cold. He would sink into a sleep from which he would never awaken.

His fingers and toes were numb. He wished his wounded leg was numb. The pain was still excruciating. He knew the enemy bullet must still be lodged in his thigh.

Once again his dulling mind went to Sasha, and he longed to see her lovely face and hold her in his arms.

Suddenly his thoughts of Sasha were interrupted by the sound of male voices. He cocked an ear in that direction. At first they seemed a great distance away, but the very sound of them helped to clear his mind and he realized they were close by.

With extreme effort, Vladimir raised his head and looked toward the sound of the voices. He saw men moving about on the battlefield, carrying kerosene lanterns. A closer look showed him that they were enemy soldiers, picking up their dead and wounded, and placing them on sleds. Some of them were working their way in his direction. He wondered if the two British soldiers that lay nearby were still alive.

Dizziness claimed him, and he laid his head back on the snow and closed his eyes. As the dizziness began to subside, Vladimir's heart thudded in his chest. The enemy soldiers were drawing nearer. He had been told by his military leaders that the British, French, and Turks were vicious in the way they treated their enemies. If they took prisoners, it was to torture them to death. Often if they found a Russian soldier wounded on a battlefield, they would just put a bullet through his head.

Moving his lips silently, Vladimir said, "Lord, let it be a bullet through my head.

Please don't let it be a slow, painful death."

Suddenly he heard one man's footsteps crunching in the snow, drawing close. He slitted his eyes and saw a ring of lantern light as the footsteps came to a sudden halt only inches away, and Vladimir heard him call out, "Hey, fellas! There's a Russian over here who's still breathing!"

Terror was something cold and sharp biting against the back of Corporal Vladimir Petrovna's neck.

Two

Corporal Vladimir Petrovna clenched his teeth as he heard more soldiers coming through the snow. When they stopped, a lantern was held close to his face as the sound of one more man met Vladimir's ears. There were three men standing over him. He knew by their uniforms they were British.

One man said, "Did I hear right? We have a Russian here who's still alive?"

"Yes, sir," said the man who held the lantern. "He's been hit in the right leg. Looks pretty bad."

Vladimir's heart was banging his ribs for fear of what lay in store for him as the man addressed as sir knelt down beside him, took a quick look at the blood-soaked leg, and said, "Sergeant Barrington, translate for me, will you?"

"Yes, sir," said Barrington, kneeling down on Vladimir's other side.

Vladimir noted the insignias on the officer's coat, and saw that he was a captain.

Surprised that the captain would want to say anything to him, he licked his lips and said, "I . . . speak English."

"Good," said the captain, meeting Vladimir's fearful gaze. "I don't think your comrades will be back tonight. You'll freeze to death before morning. That is unless you bleed to death first. That leg wound looks pretty bad. I know you have to be in a lot of pain."

Vladimir was puzzled. This British officer was actually speaking kindly to him. What is he going to do?

His question was answered quickly when the officer said, "With your permission, Corporal, we will take you with us and care for your wound."

Vladimir could not believe his ears. "I . . . I am your enemy," he said weakly. "You will help me?"

"You are the enemy," said the officer, "but you are still a human being. If we leave you here, you will die before morning. We will not take you against your will, but if you give us permission, we will take you with us and see that your wound is taken care of."

Vladimir was stunned. This kindness was totally the opposite of what he expected. His military leaders had painted a vastly different picture of how Russian soldiers would be treated if captured by the allied forces. "Sir," he said hoarsely, "your kindness is very much appreciated. Please take me with you."

The captain rose to his feet and said to his men, "Put him on the sled."

Two of the soldiers bent over Vladimir while the others held the lanterns. One of them said, "Corporal, we will do our best not to cause you any more pain than is necessary, but I want to warn you that it is going to hurt when we pick you up."

Vladimir clenched his teeth, steeling himself, and nodded.

When he was hoisted from the snow, a sharp pain lanced through his wounded leg, and a cry escaped his lips. He could hear the captain saying something about putting him on the sled, but the captain's voice seemed to be fading. He realized, as his head began to spin, that he was on the verge of passing out.

Vladimir struggled against losing consciousness as he felt himself being carried by the two enemy soldiers. He heard a horse snort, then his body was laid on something solid. The pain subsided some, and his head stopped spinning.

Moments later, Vladimir felt the sled moving over the snowpacked earth.

Opening his eyes, he noted that three wounded Allied soldiers were on the sled, and he saw other sleds nearby carrying Allied soldiers toward the shore of the Black Sea. Soon he could see the lights of a boat that was bobbing in the water just off shore. He wondered where they would take him and the wounded Allied soldiers.

When the sled came to a halt, Vladimir saw a small group of soldiers standing near the gangplank in a ring of lantern light. He could make out French and Turkish uniforms as well as British. They picked up stretchers and began to move toward the sleds. As they closed in, the captain met them, giving instructions as to who would go to which sleds.

Vladimir watched as some of the stretcher-bearing men drew up to the sled where he lay. One of them — a Turk — set eyes on him and said to the others, "We have a Russian here."

At that moment, the captain drew up and said, "Be very careful with him. That right leg is in bad shape."

"Yes, sir," said the Turk, and with the help of a French soldier, began lifting Vladimir from the sled. The movement sent a bolt of pain from his right thigh all the way through his body. Suddenly, the whole world seemed to be swirling around him, bringing a dark curtain. He could feel himself passing out . . .

It was a day in mid-April almost two years ago when Vladimir and Sasha had ridden together in one of the Petrovna farm wagons into the rugged hill country a few miles north of Kiev.

The midday sun sparkled off the Desna River's surface as Vladimir drew the wagon to a halt on the bank. The grass was losing its tawny look as the blades were turning green and tiny buds were visible, which would soon blossom into wildflowers.

Turning to Sasha, he smiled and said, "I'm so glad we could have this day together, my sweet."

"Me too," said Sasha, a look of sorrow in her eyes. "Tomorrow you will be gone, and in the uniform of the Russian army. Oh, Vladimir, my darling, it is going to be so hard. You will be sent to the Crimea to fight, and I will never know whether you are dead or alive." Her lips quivered. "I hate war. If only men could just live and let live. If only there didn't have to be armies and navies."

Vladimir folded her into his arms and held her close. Speaking softly into her ear, he said, "I will come home to you when the war is over, Sasha."

Clinging to him, she said sniffling, "I know this is your desire, my darling. But when your brother left for the Crimea, he told your parents the same thing. But . . . but Novalis will never come home, Vladimir. Never."

The mention of his brother's death brought a lump to Vladimir's throat. He held Sasha tight for a long moment, fighting the tears that were forming in his own eyes. When the lump began to diminish, he said, "Sasha, let me put it this way . . . if the Lord so wills it, I will come home to you when the war is over."

Easing back in his arms, Sasha nodded jerkily, wiped tears from her eyes, and said, "I'm sorry, Vladimir. I know I should trust the Lord more. Sometimes my faith is so weak."

"We all have that problem," said Vladimir. "Come on. Let's have that picnic lunch you prepared."

Hopping out of the wagon, Vladimir hurried around to Sasha's side and helped her down.

Soon they were sitting on the riverbank together, feasting on the luscious meal. With the music of the rippling water in his ears, Vladimir felt his heart swell in his chest as he set loving eyes on the girl he would one day make his wife. Sasha was pouring him a fresh cup of tea, concentrating on what she was doing. The brilliant sunlight caught the golden highlights in her light brown hair.

Sensing his eyes on her, she paused and looked up.

"I love you with all of my heart, sweet Sasha," he said with a smile. "I believe the Lord has made us for each other, and this is why I have to believe that when the war is over, I will come home to you, and we can become husband and wife."

Sasha's hazel eyes glistened with tears. "We must both believe this. It is this precious dream that will give us hope until the day you come home."

When the meal was over, Vladimir and Sasha stood on the riverbank for a long while, holding hands and talking of their future together.

Smiling up at him, she said, "Darling, before we head for home, I want to tell you something."

"Yes?"

"I . . . I have been thinking of names for our children."

He grinned, chuckled, and said, "Well, now, just how many children are we going to have?"

Staring off in the distance, Sasha appeared to be looking into the future. "I think four would be a good number — two girls and two boys."

"It would be nice if we could just pick what we want, but if the Lord gives us four children, it might be all boys or all girls. And again, He may not give us that many."

"I know, but just in case He does, and it's half and half, I would like for the girls to be named Zoya and Olecia. And I would like for the boys to be named Kadyn and Kievan."

Vladimir put an arm around her neck, pulled her close, and said, "I like those names. If the Lord gives us two girls and two boys, they will be named as you want."

Leaning her head on his shoulder, Sasha said, "Oh, Vladimir, I love you so much."

"And I love you so much," he told her.

Sasha and Vladimir enjoyed the rest of the afternoon together, then as the sun was lowering toward the western horizon, he helped her into the wagon and drove toward the Leskov farm.

As Vladimir pulled rein and halted the wagon at the front porch of the Leskov house, the door opened and Sasha's family emerged. When Hegal, Malia, and Oksana had told Vladimir good-bye, Hegal said they would leave the couple alone for their parting moments and ushered Malia and Oksana into the house.

The heavy-hearted couple stood beside the wagon, and both had tears in their eyes as they looked at each other. They embraced for a long moment, then Vladimir held her at arm's length and said, "I will go now. And God willing, my precious Sasha, I will return when the war is over."

She nodded, tears streaming down her cheeks. He planted a soft kiss on her lips, said, "I love you," climbed into the wagon as she returned the same words, and drove away, heading east.

When he reached the road, Vladimir pulled rein and hipped around on the seat. Sasha was still standing in the same spot. She waved, and he waved in return.

As he put the horses in motion again, he looked back at Sasha one more time. Behind her the fiery rim of the blood red sun dipped below the earth's western edge, staining the horizon a deep, glowing crimson.

For a brief moment the brilliant color hovered in a death struggle, then slowly bled away into the pale embrace of dusk.

As Vladimir's realistic dream of his last day with Sasha faded with the sight of her standing in the pale embrace of dusk, he became aware of the boat moving in the choppy water. There were stabs of pain in his wounded leg. He opened his eyes to see a British soldier bending over him, pulling his pant leg free of the wound and its dried blood.

Warmth was beginning its inroads into Vladimir's cold body, making him more acutely aware of the unbelievable throbbing pain in his leg. He clenched his teeth to keep from crying out.

The soldier noted that Vladimir had regained consciousness. He looked over his shoulder and said to someone Vladimir could not see, "Tell Captain Hamilton the Russian is conscious. He will need some water." Then to Vladimir he said, "Getting you into the warmth of the cabin caused one problem, Corporal. Your leg is bleeding again. The bullet is still in there. I'm going to clean the wound as best as I can, then do what I can to stop the bleeding."

Vladimir looked at him through pain-filled eyes, and mouthed a whispered "Thank you." His numb hands and feet were tingling from the warmth.

A French soldier rushed up with a canteen and handed it to the man who was working on Vladimir's leg. Pulling the cork, the British soldier placed the canteen to

Vladimir's lips, saying, "Here, Corporal. You need this."

Vladimir gulped down a few swallows, then suddenly realizing how thirsty he really was, he gulped down several more. After giving Vladimir his fill of water, the soldier laid the canteen aside and began cleaning the wound.

Vladimir did his best not to cry out as the cleaning was hurriedly done. He sucked in air through his teeth, but managed to keep from letting out even so much as a moan. The soldier began wrapping the thigh with a length of white cloth.

At that instant, Vladimir saw the familiar face of the British captain as he drew up, grasped a wooden chair, and sat down on the opposite side of the cot from the man who was bandaging the leg while pressing down to stem the flow of blood. "You passed out on us, Corporal," he said with a smile. "I'm glad you're back. Private Bachman here is pretty good with wounds. He will stay the bleeding until we can get you to the hospital."

Vladimir licked his dry lips. "Hospital, sir? You are taking me to a hospital?"

"Well, it isn't what you might generally think of as a hospital, Corporal. It's a military makeshift hospital. We have it set up in a storage building in the town of Uskudar on the northern coast of Turkey, near Istanbul."

"I have not heard of this medical facility, Captain," said Vladimir. "How long has it been there?"

"Since November, 1853. England's most beloved nurse brought thirty-eight nurses with her just a month after the Crimean War started and established the hospital in the storage building. Thousands of Allied soldiers' lives have been saved because of it."

"Would this be Miss Florence Nightingale?" asked Vladimir.

"Why, yes," said the captain, a bit surprised that a Russian would know about her. "How do you know her name?"

"My mother is British, sir. She has spoken of Miss Nightingale on a few occasions. It is because of my mother that I can speak English. Her maiden name was Wellington."

The captain's eyebrows arched. "Wellington as attached to Arthur Wellesley Wellington?"

"Yes, sir. General Arthur Wellington who defeated Napoleon at Waterloo in Belgium. He died four years ago, as I am sure you know."

"Of course. And your mother was related to him?"

"General Wellington was her uncle, sir. Her father's brother."

"Well, isn't that something? So you are half British."

"Yes, sir. My father met her when he was in London with his parents in the winter of 1833. They fell in love on first sight. Papa returned to England less than two months after he had met Miss Margaret Wellington and asked her to marry him. They married before leaving London, and he took her home to Russia."

"That's interesting, Corporal — I . . . I haven't asked your name."

"Petrovna, sir. Vladimir Petrovna."

The captain gripped Vladimir's right hand. "I'm Captain Robert Hamilton, Corporal Petrovna."

"I am happy to make your acquaintance, Captain Hamilton," Vladimir said, giving his hand a slight shake.

"There you are, Corporal," said Private Earl Bachman. "I've got your wound bandaged as securely as possible. I'm sorry we don't have anything to give you to relieve your pain."

"Thank you for the bandage," said Vladimir. "I can endure the pain, but without the bandage, I would soon bleed to death."

Bachman patted Vladimir's arm. "I'll check on you later." With that, he moved to a wounded British soldier on the next cot.

"We'll see that the bullet is removed as soon as possible when we get to the hospital," said Hamilton.

Vladimir frowned. "You mean as soon as possible after all the wounded Allied soldiers are taken care of, don't you, sir?"

"Not necessarily," replied Hamilton. "Miss Nightingale and her nurses give their attention to those soldiers who are wounded most seriously first, whether they are Allied soldiers or Russian."

Vladimir frowned again. "You mean other Russian soldiers have been brought here?"

"Oh yes. Many wounded Russian soldiers who have been left behind by their comrades have been picked up from battlefields all over the Crimea since Miss Nightingale established the hospital. Some died, but others lived and were sent back to their homeland."

Vladimir could not get over the kindness and compassion shown by the Allied people. It was so totally different than the way it had been presented to the Russian soldiers by their military leaders and the czar. Amazed at how he had been deceived, he thought about his own army. Russian soldiers would never help a wounded enemy soldier. They would leave them to die on the battlefields. Sometimes they would shoot them, just for the satisfaction of killing more enemy soldiers. They most certainly would not pick them up and treat their wounds — and even if they had enough compassion to do that, the wounded Allied soldiers would be the last to be tended to, no matter how serious their wounds.

Trying not to give in to the pain, Vladimir said, "Captain Hamilton, if I remember correctly, it is some three hundred miles across the Black Sea from the southern tip of the Crimea to the northern tip of Turkey."

"That's right. Which means it will take us some nine or ten hours to get to Uskudar. I wish we could get all of you wounded men there sooner."

Vladimir managed a weak smile. "This is still better than lying out there in the snow where you found me, sir."

Hamilton nodded. "So where do you live in Russia, Corporal?"

"My parents have a farm near the city of Kiev, sir. Do you know where that is?"

"I've seen Kiev on a map of Russia, but I don't recall where it is located."

"Kiev is in southern Russia between the Central Russian Upland and the

Carpathian Mountains, sir. We raise potatoes and sugar beets on our farm."

"And that's how your father makes his living? Farming?"

"Yes, sir."

The captain who was obviously in his late forties, asked, "How old are you, Corporal?"

"Eighteen, sir. I will be nineteen on April 12."

"And how long have you been in the army?"

"Since I turned seventeen. Under the czar's rule, all able-bodied young men are inducted into the army or navy when they turn seventeen. My . . . my older brother, Novalis, was inducted at seventeen years of age in February 1853. As you know, the war started in October of that year. Novalis was killed a month later in a battle at Sevastopal."

The mention of his brother's death brought tears to Vladimir's eyes. As he wiped them away while gritting his teeth against the pain in his leg, Captain Hamilton said, "I'm sorry about your brother, Corporal. And I'm sorry we don't have anything aboard to relieve your pain." He drew a deep breath, then added cautiously, "Would . . . would you be insulted if I prayed for you and asked God to relieve your pain?"

Vladimir's eyes lit up. "Captain, I would appreciate that very much."

Pleased at the Russian soldier's attitude, Robert Hamilton laid a hand on Vladimir's shoulder, bowed his head, and prayed for him, asking God to touch his leg with His own mighty hand, relieve the pain, and spare his life.

However, he did not stop there. He went on in his prayer to subtly preach the gospel of Jesus Christ to the young Russian soldier.

Eyes closed, Vladimir smiled to himself as Hamilton laid heaven and hell before him and made salvation's plan as clear and plain as possible.

When the captain closed his prayer in Jesus' name, he opened his eyes to find Vladimir smiling at him, his face beaming. Assuming the pain was beginning to ease, he said, "You are already hurting less?"

"It is a little better," said Vladimir, "but I am smiling because by your prayer, I know you are my brother in Christ."

Captain Robert Hamilton was stunned. A wide smile captured his face. Eyes shining, he said, "Corporal Vladimir Petrovna, you are a Christian?"

Vladimir nodded. "Yes! Born again and

washed in the blood of the Lamb!"

Hamilton shook his head in wonderment. "Praise the Lord!" he said as he leaned over and embraced him. "I'm so happy to know this."

Vladimir's pain indeed eased as the two men exchanged testimonies as to how and when they came to know the Lord Jesus Christ as their personal Saviour. Hamilton learned that Vladimir's parents were dedicated Christians, and had led both of their sons to the Lord when they were young boys. He also learned that Bakum and Margaret Petrovna were fully involved in the underground church.

Easing back on the chair, Hamilton said, "I know the underground church exists in Russia, Corporal, and my heart goes out to those faithful children of God who have to live in fear at all times that they will be found out."

"It is not easy, sir," said Vladimir, "but our love for the Lord keeps us faithful in spite of the danger. We figure that after what Jesus did for us at the cross, we must be faithful to Him and His cause."

"God bless you for that. I've never talked to anyone who is part of the Russian underground church before. This persecution starts with the czar, I understand."

"Yes, sir. It was pretty bad under Alexander I, but when Nicholas I succeeded him in 1825, it got worse. But it worsened even more when Alexander II became czar in 1855. He is an outspoken enemy of true Christianity and has sought to ban it from all of Russia. Anyone caught holding preaching or teaching meetings with the Word of God is severely punished. There is a law in Russia that no church is allowed in the country or its possessions except the Russian Orthodox Church, which is fully controlled by the government.

"The czar knows that the underground churches exist and has the Cossack soldiers continually in search of them. The churches meet in small groups of twenty to forty all over Russia and her possessions — in barns, sheds, and houses in the rural areas, and in stores, shops, and houses in the towns and villages."

"Do they meet on Sunday?"

"No, sir. They dare not meet on Sunday, for this is the day the larger number of Cossacks are patrolling on horseback and looking for any sign of a gathering. They only meet once a week late at night, and often change which day of the week they meet. They also change where they meet every week, too."

"Do these underground churches actually have pastors?"

"Yes, but secretly. Openly the pastor is a farmer, laborer, or a merchant."

"I see. Tell me this: Do the underground churches communicate with each other?"

"Indeed we do. In fact, you would be amazed at the clever way we have of communicating, so that any Christian who would be traveling anywhere in Russia or her possessions can find the pastors and their people so they can attend their secret services. By this excellent communication system, the pastors are able to keep an updated list of the existing groups. Many new underground churches are starting, and I'm sorry to say, sometimes they are caught by the Cossacks and arrested. The churches then are put out of business."

"You said a few minutes ago that the punishment is severe when they are caught."

"Yes."

"Just how severe?"

"Well, Captain, when the Cossacks catch an underground church having a service, they are brutal. At gunpoint, the adults and teens are commanded to renounce their faith in Jesus Christ or face life in prison. The pastors, however, are always executed. Usually right there in front of everybody."

"Oh, my. How awful!"

"Yes, sir. Sometimes when people in the congregation are facing the Cossacks' guns, there are those who because of their fear and dread of life in prison will renounce the Lord and be allowed to walk away. Of course their fear and dread are augmented because they know that so often those who are given life sentences for refusing to renounce Christ die 'mysteriously' in the prisons.

"The children belonging to those who refuse to recant their faith become wards of the government. Whatever property the people own becomes government property, which is sold to someone else. The czar and his cabinet split up the profits for their own pockets."

The captain scrubbed a palm over his face, shaking his head. "Corporal, this is the same kind of persecution those first-century Christians suffered. We read about them in the Bible, and our history books tell us of multitudes more who were martyred because they stood for Jesus and His Word."

Tears filled his eyes and he began to weep. "People who live in a free country like I do just don't realize what some of our brothers and sisters in Christ have had to suffer for their faith. Oh, Lord, help me to realize how easy I have it!"

Three

Mopping tears from his cheeks with the handkerchief, Captain Robert Hamilton said, "Corporal Petrovna, I knew the people of the Russian underground church were made to suffer when they were caught, but I didn't realize it was so bad."

"Most foreigners have no idea, sir," said Vladimir.

Hamilton sniffed and asked, "Do you want to go back to Russia when you are physically able? For all your government knows, you are dead."

"Oh yes. I must go back. Of course the army will keep me if my leg wound doesn't hinder me from carrying out my duties as a soldier. If the leg doesn't function properly, they will discharge me to return to civilian life. But either way, I must return for the sake of my parents and the girl I am going to one day marry."

A smile curved the captain's lips. "Oh, so there's a girl, eh?"

"Yes, sir," said Vladimir, adjusting the blanket that covered him and tucking it snugly under his chin.

"I'll hear about her in a moment. Tell me about your parents. Are they in good health?"

"As far as I know, sir. They are in their midforties now, and the last I knew, were doing fine. There is no letter service in the Russian army, so there has been no contact since I left home almost two years ago."

"I see. Something else I need to be thankful for. Our letter service is spasmodic, but at least we have it. I heard from my wife just a week ago."

"I'm glad, sir. It must be nice to be able to stay in touch. Tell me about your family. Do you have children?"

"Yes. Two. A son and a daughter. My wonderful wife, Beatrice and I are grandparents. Our daughter, Abigail, and her husband have a set of twins: Robert and William."

"And Robert was named after you."

"Yes. William is named after his other grandfather."

"I'm sure you enjoy those twins. And what about your son?"

"Emmett isn't married yet. He chose a

military career, like his father. He is in the Royal British navy."

"Mmm. I'm sure you're proud of him."

"I sure am. He is aboard ship just off the coast of India at Bombay, which you may know is under British control."

"Yes, sir. Where does your family live?"

"In Guildford, a small town just south of London."

"I see. Captain, I would like to ask you about your queen. I have heard that Queen Victoria is a Christian. Is this true? Mother left England three years before Victoria became queen, so she has no way of knowing."

Hamilton smiled. "It certainly is true. Queen Victoria has said publicly many times that her faith is in the finished work of Jesus Christ at Calvary — that she is going to heaven by God's grace, not her good works."

"Wonderful! Mother will be glad to hear this. It must be so nice to be under leadership like that."

"It most certainly is," said the captain. "Our queen shows so much love to her people . . . especially the men in her armed forces. Would you believe the blanket that is covering you was made by her?"

Vladimir's mouth sagged open. "You are joking."

"No, I'm not. Queen Victoria and her daughters — Vicky, who is fifteen and Alice, who is twelve — have been working together making blankets for the British soldiers in the Crimea. They also knit mittens and scarves for us."

"Well, isn't that something," Vladimir said, rubbing the blanket with his hands. "I can see why the British people love her so much."

"She is a special lady," said the captain. "Now, I want to hear about this young lady you are going to marry."

Vladimir's eyes lit up. "Of course. Her name is Sasha Leskov. She is the most beautiful girl in all the world and the sweetest, too. Her parents own a neighboring farm not far from ours. The Leskov family are Christians and part of the underground church."

"Are you and Sasha officially engaged?"

"Yes, sir. We have known each other since early childhood. We discovered we were in love just a few months before I was inducted into the army. We are mutually promised to each other, and I have received her father's permission to make her my wife when the war is over and I go home. Sasha will turn eighteen in May."

The captain leaned close and said, "I

can see why you are eager to go home, Corporal." He patted Vladimir's arm. "You are looking pretty tired. How's the leg?"

"It is hurting some, sir, but not nearly as much as before you prayed for me."

"Good. I've got to go see about some of my wounded men. You get some rest now."

At that moment, a British corporal drew up and said, "Excuse me, Captain. I don't mean to interrupt, but —"

"It's all right, Corporal," said Hamilton, rising to his feet. "I was about to tuck Corporal Petrovna in, anyway. He needs to get some sleep. What is it?"

"I thought you should know, sir, that Lieutenant Kemal just died. His Turkish comrades are quite upset. As you know, he was a real hero to them."

"I'll talk to them," said Hamilton.

"And, sir . . ."

"Yes?"

"One of the French soldiers is close to death. He is asking for you."

"All right. I'll see him first." The captain looked down at Vladimir and said, "You sleep, now."

Vladimir's eyes were droopy. He nodded and pulled the blanket made by the hands of Queen Victoria up tight around his neck.

He closed his eyes, and in less than a minute, he was asleep.

Almost instantly, Vladimir was dreaming of Sasha, seeing the two of them running across a sunny field of green grass and colorful wildflowers as they had done many times in days gone by. He reveled in her beauty and the brightness of her eyes as they stopped beside a rippling stream and she took hold of his hand and looked up at him. Her voice was sweet as she said, "Oh, Vladimir, I love you so much."

Vladimir was about to speak words of love to her in return when a loud, grating sound penetrated his dream.

He opened his eyes as the sound continued, and he realized it was one of the wounded soldiers in the boat crying out in pain. Two men were bending over him, trying to help him. Within a few minutes, the wounded man grew quiet, and Vladimir dropped off once more . . . this time to a deep, dreamless sleep.

Vladimir awakened when he felt himself jostled slightly on the cot, and opened his eyes. He saw sunshine streaming through the windows of the boat from a clear blue sky. Two British soldiers were standing over him. One of them held a stretcher. The other one looked down and said, "Sorry about shaking you a little there, Corporal. We just bumped the dock."

Vladimir blinked and rubbed his eyes. "You mean we're at Uskudar?"

"Sure are, and we have orders to get you to the hospital as soon as possible, along with the other eleven men who are seriously wounded."

Vladimir saw other soldiers with stretchers waiting to pick up the others. "There are only twelve of us who are considered in serious condition?"

"Yes. Five more died last night after you went to sleep."

"Oh. Wh-what time is it?"

"Almost noon."

Vladimir looked up to see Captain Robert Hamilton coming in from the deck. He drew up and asked, "How's the leg, Corporal?"

"Doesn't hurt like it did before you prayed, Captain," replied Vladimir, giving him a weak smile. "Sort of a dull ache."

"Good. These men will take you to the hospital as soon as the boat is secured to the dock. They'll take you in an army wagon. It's only about a five-minute ride. I'll look in on you shortly."

"All right. Thank you."

★ ★ ★

Florence Nightingale, who had turned thirty-six on her last birthday, was standing at the door of the makeshift hospital with two nurses flanking her as the wounded soldiers were being carried in on stretchers.

The other eleven soldiers who were considered to be the most seriously wounded were being carried just ahead of Vladimir. When the soldiers carrying him moved through the door, they stopped and the one in front said, "Miss Nightingale, we have a Russian soldier here with a bullet in his right leg. We picked him up on the battlefield at the southern tip of the Crimean Peninsula. He needs attention immediately."

Vladimir saw Captain Robert Hamilton coming through the door.

"All right," said Florence, "put him in that room at the back corner where we have kept the other Russian soldiers. We'll get to him right away." She was barely five feet tall and a bit portly. Her hair was swept back into a tight bun and like the other nurses, she wore a small white cap trimmed with lace.

Having heard Florence's words, Hamilton said, "Miss Nightingale, this Russian soldier doesn't need to be kept separated from the wounded Allied men like you were forced to do with the others. Corporal Petrovna will not cause any disturbances, nor stir up trouble as many of the other Russian soldiers have done in the past. He is a Christian and is grateful to us for saving his life."

"That's right, ma'am," Vladimir said softly. "I won't cause any trouble."

Florence smiled. "You speak English well, Corporal."

"My mother is British, ma'am. Her uncle was General Arthur Wellington."

Florence's eyebrows raised. "Oh, really?"

"Yes, ma'am."

"I'm glad to hear that, Corporal." Then to the stretcher bearers she said, "If you gentlemen will follow me, I will show you to Corporal Petrovna's bed."

Captain Hamilton followed.

Vladimir let his eyes roam from side to side as he was carried between two long rows of beds. The wounded British, French, and Turkish soldiers were a pitiful sight. Some were pale, thin amputees, having lost an arm or leg. Some had lost both legs. Some were blinded, while others had suffered various other kinds of head wounds. Others had taken bullets or shrapnel in their bodies. All of them were damaged to one degree or another for life.

Florence stopped the stretcher bearers at a bed between two wounded British soldiers and said, "Put him right here, gentlemen."

When the stretcher bearers had eased him onto the bed, Vladimir thanked them. As they were walking away, Captain Hamilton leaned over Vladimir and said, "I have to go now. I'll be gone a few days. You're in good hands here. I'll see you when I get back."

Managing a faint smile, Vladimir said, "Thank you for saving my life, Captain. Thank you for being so kind to an enemy soldier."

Hamilton laid a hand on his shoulder and smiled. "You wear the uniform of the enemy army, but you are not my enemy. You are my brother in Christ."

Florence Nightingale put a hand to her mouth and swallowed a lump that had raised up quickly.

Both the captain and the corporal had tears in their eyes as the captain walked away.

Florence stepped up and said, "I'll examine your leg, now, Corporal. What's your first name?"

"Vladimir, ma'am."

"All right, Vladimir," she said, picking up a pair of scissors from a small table next to the bed. "I'll try not to hurt you any more than is necessary, but I have to get a look at what we have here."

Vladimir experienced some pain as Florence cut away the bandage and pressed fingers around the wound to assess the damage. "The bullet is about two inches deep, Vladimir. It shattered some of the bone just above the knee. I'll do the surgery myself with the help of one of my best nurses."

"Thank you, Miss Nightingale," he said in a sincere tone.

She smiled at him, then called to a nurse who was passing by: "Edna, will you find Lara and tell her I need her right away, please?"

The nurse nodded. "Sure will."

Looking into the young Russian soldier's eyes, Florence said, "We will put you under with chloroform, Vladimir, then remove the bullet. Once the bullet is out, we will clean the bone fragments out of the wound and patch you up. You will be on crutches for a few weeks, then graduate to a cane. I am hopeful that in time, you will be able to walk without a cane, but —"

"But what, ma'am?"

"Well, I hate to have to tell you this, but you are going to walk with a limp for the rest of your life. Some of the damage is irreparable. I'm sure the Russian army will discharge you when you get home."

Vladimir sighed. "Well, Miss Nightingale, at least I'm still alive. If it hadn't been for Captain Hamilton and his men, I would already be dead."

"That's a good way to look at it," she said, then looked up to see the nurse she had sent for drawing up. "Lara, we have a Russian soldier here who needs a bullet taken out of his leg. I need you to help me."

"Of course," said the nurse, who was nearing fifty, and was showing a bit of gray at her temples. "Captain Robert Hamilton told me about him."

"I see," said Florence. "Corporal Vladimir Petrovna, this is nurse Lara Plekhanov."

Vladimir let a smile tug at the corners of his mouth as he looked up at Lara. "I knew you were Russian the moment I saw you, ma'am. I am happy to meet you."

"And I am happy to meet you, too, Corporal," said Lara, warming him with a smile.

Studying her face, he said, "You remind me a bit of my mother."

"Oh, really?"

"Mm-hmm. You look a lot like her in your eyes . . . and with your smile, you could be her sister."

"Well, I am honored, Corporal."

"Ma'am," said Vladimir, "how did you become a nurse for the Allied armies?"

"She can tell you all about it later," said Florence. "Right now, we need to get busy on this leg."

"Right," said Lara. "I'll tell you about it sometime after the surgery, when you feel like listening."

Six hours later, Vladimir came out of his chloroform-induced state of unconsciousness to find nurse Lara Plekhanov standing over him. She had a tender way about her, which he appreciated. "Is . . . is the surgery over?"

"Yes, and it went well. You should be up and on crutches in about ten days. Maybe two weeks. Are you hurting?"

Eyelids drooping some, he pulled his lips tight. "Yes. Feels like my leg is on fire."

Lara turned to the small table beside the bed, picked up a bottle of clear liquid and a spoon. Shaking the bottle vigorously, she removed the cork and poured the liquid in the spoon.

Vladimir asked, "What's that?"

"Morphine. Have you heard of it?"

"I have. It relieves pain."

"Right. It's mixed with water so it won't

be too potent, but still I can only give it to you in small doses. It will help considerably. Open your mouth."

Vladimir swallowed the morphine, made a sour face, then said, "You . . . remind me of my mother."

"Yes. You told me that. My eyes and my smile."

"Oh. Of course. I did tell you that, didn't I?"

"Well!" came a familiar voice. "I'm glad to see he is awake."

"He just came out of it, Florence," said Lara. "He's hurting, so I gave him a dose of morphine. I told him the surgery went well."

"My thanks to both of you," said Vladimir. "You have been so kind to me. How can I ever repay you?"

Lara chuckled. "Just get well so you can go home to Sasha. That will be payment enough."

Vladimir frowned. "H-how do you know about Sasha?"

Lara smiled. "You were talking to her for about ten minutes before you came to. I know she is the most beautiful girl in the world, and that you are engaged to be married."

Vladimir's pallid features tinted. "Oh."

"You need to relax now, Vladimir," said

Florence. "Let the morphine do its job."

Vladimir nodded, looked up at Lara, and said, "I still want to hear how you ended up being a nurse for the Allied armies."

"All in good time, soldier boy," she said. "Now do like the boss lady said and relax."

For the next two days, Vladimir Petrovna did little more than sleep. His body was extremely weak from loss of blood, both on the battlefield and during the extensive surgery. Each time he aroused from sleep, a nurse was there to administer the morphine-water mixture in small amounts.

Late in the afternoon on the third day since his surgery, he awakened and focused his eyes on the window directly across the aisle. Fat snowflakes were drifting down on a slight breeze in the bitter cold outside. The soldiers on both sides of him and across the aisle were sleeping.

His body felt stiff and cramped, and he gingerly moved his head and shoulders. He repeated the exercise again, then bravely moved his arms and his torso at the waist, stretching them to ease the stiff muscles.

Since that went well, he took a deep breath and moved the left leg, wiggling his toes. Bracing himself for what might come when he moved the right leg, he clenched his teeth and made a cautious movement. Pain shot through the wounded leg and into his upper body like a bolt of lightning, causing him to release a grunting sound. Tears filmed his eyes, but he quickly brushed them away, and moved the right leg again.

The pain was a little less intense this time. He breathed a sigh of relief. "Thank You, Lord," he said in a whisper. "At least there's feeling in it."

Vladimir was moving his arms and shoulders again when Lara drew up and said with a smile, "So . . . Sasha's future groom is awake and moving some."

Trying to return the smile, he said tightly, "Yes. Some."

"How is the pain? It's been long enough since your last dose. I can give you some morphine now."

"No, no," he said, lifting a hand in mild protest. "It's not too bad unless I move the right leg."

"Good. I'm going to get some hot broth for you. We need to start building your strength. We've only been able to pour a little broth down you when you were awake enough to swallow the morphine."

"I don't even remember," said Vladimir.

"I'm not surprised."

"But I am a little hungry. Hot broth sounds good."

Straightening his blanket some, she said, "Then hot broth it is."

"How long has it been since my surgery?" A frown crossed his brow and he touched a finger to a temple as he was trying to remember.

"This is the third day, and I'm glad I can honestly say that, all things considered, you are doing nicely. Now, I'll be right back with your broth. It will give you strength for sure." Lara gave him a bright smile and hurried away.

Once more, Vladimir began flexing joints and muscles that were stiff from inactivity.

Lara returned in a matter of minutes, bearing a tray with a steaming bowl of broth and a fragrant cup of tea laced with honey. "Here you go," she said in a cheerful tone, a smile lighting up her tired features. "Chicken broth."

Taking plenty of time, Lara spoon-fed her patient the hearty broth.

He was weary by the time the cup was nearly empty, and she helped him drain the cup.

Vladimir licked his lips. "Thank you, ma'am. That was very good. I feel better already."

"I'm glad. We'll get you well, my boy."

Vladimir grinned again. "Do you have time now to tell me how you came to be a nurse for the Allied armies?"

"Probably. I have to clean and dress your wound."

"All right. I'll listen while you do that."

As Lara pulled back the covers and began removing the bandage, she said, "First, Vladimir, I must tell you that I was informed by Captain Hamilton that you are a born-again child of God."

Vladimir smiled. "I sure am. And you must be also, or you wouldn't be talking to me about it."

She paused and looked him in the eye. "You're right." Then returning to her work, she said, "I was saved as a girl of twelve, Vladimir, at the same time my parents made professions of faith at an underground church in Bereznik. Do you know where that is?"

"Yes. In northwestern Russia. On the Northern Dvina River."

"You know your country well, don't you?"

"I believe so. Was Bereznik your home?"

"Yes."

"Is your family still there?"

"Ah . . . no. My mother died only three

months after becoming a Christian. Pneumonia."

"Oh."

"I'm so glad for the peace I have in my heart, knowing I will see Mother one day in heaven."

"Praise the Lord for that."

Continuing her work on the wounded leg, Lara said, "About a month after Mother's death, my father and I were in a service in the underground church, which was meeting that night in the back room of a clothing store in Bereznik. Suddenly the Cossacks burst in, waving their guns. Two of them quickly took our pastor from behind his pulpit and dragged him outside. A gunshot was heard, and everyone knew the pastor had been executed."

"Bless his heart."

"He has been in heaven almost forty years now. He is blessed, all right."

"For sure."

Applying antiseptic to the wound, Lara felt Vladimir wince. "Sorry."

"That's the way it has to be," he said softly. "Tell me what happened then."

"The Cossacks kept their guns pointed at all of us, and said everyone was to renounce their faith in Jesus Christ, or be sent to prison for the rest of their lives."

Vladimir was listening intently.

Lara began wrapping fresh bandage on his leg. "Two men and a woman renounced Jesus, Vladimir, but the others refused. One of those two men was my father."

"Oh no."

"Yes. I rushed to him, and weeping, begged him not to turn his back on the Lord. When he saw my tears, he was suddenly ashamed. He looked at the Cossacks and told them he had changed his mind. He recanted his renouncement. They laughed at him, took him out, and shot him."

"Oh, Lara, I'm so sorry."

"It was a horrible thing. Since I was only twelve, the Cossacks took me to a children's home in Bereznik. Less than a month later, I was placed in the home of a family right there in town. A man and woman in their late fifties. Rossos and Kazinka Lugvo. They were not Christians, but they treated me kindly, and in time, showed me love."

"I'm glad for that."

"Yes. As time passed, I witnessed to them of the saving grace of Jesus, but they would not listen. They feared even showing interest in Jesus Christ."

"I have seen many like that."

Tying the bandage in place gently, Lara said, "Three years later, when I was fifteen,

Rossos became quite ill. Kazinka was becoming arthritic, and was not able to do much for him. It fell on me to take care of him. But this was a blessing in disguise from the Lord, Vladimir, because in caring for Rossos, I found that I had a natural skill with medicine and caring for the sick. By the time I was eighteen, I was taking care of sick neighbors, and soon word had spread all over town about my work. I was approached by Bereznik's two doctors to work for them in their clinic. The doctors were brothers by the name of Plekhanov, and one of them had a son who was twenty-one years old. His name was Leopold."

Vladimir smiled. "And this was the young man you married."

"Yes. Leopold and I had known each other for some time, but it wasn't until I went to work in the clinic that he took a liking to me. He wanted to spend time with me, so when we were alone, I began to say little things to him about my faith in Jesus. Surprisingly, he showed genuine interest. He had heard the gospel as a boy from some neighbors who were in the underground church. The Spirit of God had planted the seed of the Word in his heart.

"In a short time, as I quoted Scriptures from memory when we had our talks, I was able to lead Leopold to the Lord."

"Wonderful!" said Vladimir. "Tell me more."

"I will as soon as I dispose of these soiled bandages," she said, walking away with them in hand. "I will be right back."

Four

Corporal Vladimir Petrovna adjusted his position slightly, feeling a stab of pain in the wound, and closed his eyes. He thought of home, of Sasha, and of his parents. He was glad the wound he had sustained would take him out of the army. Now, he and Sasha could concentrate on getting married.

Swift footsteps caught his ear and he opened his eyes to see Lara Plekhanov smiling at him as she drew up. "Sleepy?" she asked.

"I am feeling a little drowsy."

"All right. You take a nap, and we'll talk later."

"Oh no. Please. I want to hear how things developed between you and Leopold after he became a Christian. Then I'll take a nap."

"All right. Let's see . . . I stopped my story at the point where I had the joy of leading Leopold to the Lord, right?"

"Yes."

Moving to the foot of the bed, Lara worked at straightening the covers as she said, "Well, to make a long story short, Leopold and I married a few months later, and when we had established our home, I made contact with the underground church. Leopold and I began to attend. The pastor at that time was a man in his early thirties. His name was Andren Mrzlak. He was a clerk at a grocery store in Bereznik. The Mrzlaks had a nine-year-old son."

Finished with the cover adjustment, she stood over him once again.

"Just a few weeks after Leopold and I started attending the underground church, one night the Cossacks burst into the Mrzlak home, saying they knew he was the pastor of the underground church. They demanded that he give them the names of all his church members, threatening to kill his wife if he refused. The Mrzlaks' son had gone into the backyard on an errand for his father, and stayed hidden when he entered the house and realized what was happening.

"The boy heard his mother bravely tell the Cossacks they would not give them the names of any of the church members. A shot rang out, and his mother fell to the floor. His father scuffled with the Cossack leader, and again shots were fired. Pastor Andren

Mrzlak fell dead beside his wife. The boy slipped out the back door, ran to the house of neighbors who were members of his father's church, and told them what happened. The members soon learned that the Cossacks had somehow found out one member's identity, and when they arrested him and threatened torture, he gave them the name of the pastor and the names of some of the members."

"Did he give them your names, Lara?" queried Vladimir.

"Yes. But we were able to get out of Bereznik before they could catch us. We headed for England. It was in the dead of winter, and while we were making our way out of Russia, Leopold came down with pneumonia. He . . . he died shortly after we arrived in London."

"Oh, I'm so sorry."

Lara swallowed with difficulty, put fingers to her temples for a brief moment, then said, "It was very hard for me, Vladimir, but God gave me the grace to get through it. I told you I would make this story short. I went to work in a medical clinic in London, and several years later, I became acquainted with Florence Nightingale. When the Crimean war broke out, Florence needed nurses to go with her to

Turkey, so I volunteered, and here I am."

"I'm very glad you're here, Lara," said Vladimir. "I'm so glad the Lord crossed our paths. And I have to say again . . . you sure do resemble my mother."

Lara bent down, embraced him, and said, "Tell you what, Vladimir, I will just be a mother to you until you can go home to your real mother."

"I'd like that," he said, grinning again.

Reaching down, Lara lifted the young soldier's head and took the pillow. Fluffing it up, she said, "I'll do the motherly thing here. You take a nap now."

She placed the pillow back under his head, pulled the warm blanket up under his chin, patted his cheek tenderly, and hurried away.

Before she was out of sight, Vladimir was sinking into the most restful sleep he had had in weeks.

In less than two weeks, Vladimir was up and using crutches to move about the hospital. Moving from bed to bed as the days passed, he found most of the Allied soldiers congenial toward him, and on the third day he came upon a Turkish soldier who was a Christian. They were able to converse because Sergeant Lehman Kuchuck could speak Russian well.

On the third day since Vladimir had begun to move about on crutches, he was standing over Kuchuck, who lay in his bed. They were talking about the war and the toll it was taking on men in the Russian army as well as those in the Allied army.

Leaning on his crutches, Vladimir ran his gaze around the large warehouse-hospital full of wounded, hurting soldiers. "Lehman, war is so senseless. Nobody ever really wins."

"You are right about that," said Kuchuck. "But ever since early Bible days, men have been at war with each other."

"Yes, and the Lord Jesus said there would be wars and rumors of wars until He comes back to rule here on earth."

The sergeant nodded. "And I say with John at Patmos, 'Even so, come, Lord Jesus.'"

"Amen to that," said Vladimir.

Lehman looked up at his newfound friend and said, "You seem to be gaining strength every day."

"That I am. Getting around on crutches is not the most comfortable way to navigate, but it sure is better than lying in bed all the time, like you still have to do. The exercise itself builds strength."

"I overheard you talking to nurse Lara

yesterday," said Lehman. "You seem convinced that the Russian military will discharge you because of the wound to your leg."

"Yes. From what Miss Nightingale has told me, I will never be able to carry on the duties of a soldier again."

"Does this bother you?"

"Not in the least. I am very much looking forward to being with Sasha and getting our lives back on course. My thoughts continually travel to her and to my parents. I am eager to get home to them."

"I'm sure you are. How are those Russian soldiers they brought in last week doing?"

"I haven't been to the back room for a couple of days. Why?"

"Didn't Miss Nightingale say when you were well enough to travel, Captain Hamilton and his men would find a way to get you back to Russia?"

"Yes."

"I was just thinking that they would probably want to take all of you wounded Russians at the same time."

"I'm sure you're right. I may be here for a good while yet."

At that moment, Vladimir saw the double doors open and Captain Robert Hamilton enter, with several wounded men being carried in on stretchers behind him. Lehman turned his head to see what had drawn Vladimir's attention. "Oh. More wounded men."

Keeping his eyes on the line of stretchers coming through the door, Vladimir saw Florence Nightingale heading toward Captain Hamilton. He excused himself to Lehman and hopped toward Hamilton on his crutches. As he drew close, he heard the captain tell Florence they were bringing in twenty-seven wounded men.

Florence sighed, nodded, and said, "We've had forty-nine brought in by other Allied units in the past four days, but I assure you, Captain, we'll make room for these."

"I know you will," Hamilton said with sincerity. "Without you and your nurses, these men would all die."

Florence smiled. "That's exactly why we're here, Captain."

While Florence was calling for a nurse to direct the stretcher bearers to a section near the back of the building, Hamilton turned and smiled at Vladimir. "Well, dear brother, you are looking good. It's nice to see you."

"You too," said Vladimir. "It seems the fighting is still fierce on the Crimea."

"That it is," said Hamilton. "I wish this

horrible war would come to an end."

"Me too," came Florence's comment as she turned back, wearily brushing stray locks of hair from her brow. "We will do all we can to save the lives of these men, but there have to be great numbers being killed."

"There are," Hamilton said sadly. "Florence, you look awfully tired."

"I am a bit weary," she admitted. "All of my nurses are worn out. They have worked many a night through, doing surgery and patching up wounds by the light of kerosene lamps, getting no sleep at all."

Vladimir flicked an admiring glance at Florence and said, "Captain, she is stretching the truth a little. Actually, on most of those nights, this dear lady sent her weary nurses to bed, but stayed up all night and worked on the wounded men all by herself."

Florence blushed. "It is this Russian spy who is exaggerating, Captain."

While Hamilton was chuckling at her choice of words, Vladimir said, "Then, Miss Nightingale, why have the soldiers here in the hospital dubbed you the "Lady of the Lamp"?

Florence's features tinted again. "They all exaggerate."

Hamilton laughed. "I don't think so."

A warm smile spread over Florence's lips. "Men. They are such strange creatures. Well, gentlemen, I have work to do. I will see you later." As she spoke, she turned and walked away.

Vladimir and the captain chatted a couple of minutes, then Hamilton said, "It's good to see you improving so well. You take care, and I'll see you next time I'm back."

In the last few days of January, snow fell almost every day, and bloody battles continued to be fought all over the Crimean Peninsula.

On Saturday afternoon, February 2, Vladimir was standing beside Sergeant Lehman Kuchuck's bed. Lehman was sitting up in the bed, his back braced with pillows. They were talking with heavy hearts about the number of patients who had died in the hospital in the past week when the double doors of the building burst open and a smiling group of Allied soldiers came in shouting loudly in English, French, Turkish, and Russian that the war was over.

This immediately had the attention of everyone in the place. Some of the Russian soldiers who were kept in the back room stepped out, waiting to hear the details.

While the nurses and patients listened with happy hearts, they were told that government leaders in Austria had sent word to Russia's Czar Alexander II, threatening that if the Russians did not come to peace with the Allies immediately, the Austrian army would join with the Allied armies.

This was too much for Alexander, who knew the strength of the Austrian military. Yesterday, he formally accepted the Allies' peace terms. The long, bloody Crimean War was over!

Tears of jubilation were shed by soldiers and nurses alike — even the Russian soldiers.

Lara Plekhanov was standing beside Vladimir, who was leaning on his crutches. With tears streaming down her cheeks, she looked at a weeping Vladimir, wrapped her arms around him, and said, "Now there won't be any problem getting you back to Russia. You can go home to Sasha and your parents!"

Hearing Lara's words, Florence Nightingale embraced Vladimir. "I am so happy for you!"

"Thank you," said Vladimir. "Do you know when I might get to go home?"

"Well, as far as your wound, you can go anytime. You are doing well on the crutches.

I don't see why the other Russian soldiers can't go soon too. It will depend on Captain Hamilton and his boat. I'm expecting him to be here in two or three days. When he comes, we'll see what his plans are."

On Tuesday, February 5, Captain Robert Hamilton arrived with a few wounded soldiers from the last day of battle.

Vladimir was at Sergeant Lehman Kuchuck's bed when Hamilton came in. Lehman was telling Vladimir that Florence Nightingale had said he would not be able to travel for at least two more weeks. While watching Florence in conversation with Hamilton, Vladimir said, "It may be that long before Captain Hamilton can take the other Russians and myself across the Black Sea. I'll know shortly."

Hamilton was nodding as he backed away from Florence, turned, and headed for Vladimir. As he drew close, he smiled broadly and said, "Wonderful, isn't it, Vladimir? No more bloodshed on the Crimea!"

"It sure is," responded Vladimir. "Lehman and I were just praising the Lord that the war is over."

Hamilton greeted Lehman, then said to Vladimir, "Miss Nightingale was just telling me that you and your Russian comrades are well enough to travel by boat. If we take you to Sevastopol, can you get transportation from there to Kiev?"

"Yes, sir. I'm sure the Russian navy will work with the army to see that we get transportation to our homes."

"Fine. Then let's plan to leave at dawn on Friday. I'll see that your comrades are told."

"Sounds good to me."

Hamilton looked Vladimir square in the eye and said, "I can see it in your eyes. You're still having some pain in that leg, aren't you?"

"A little," admitted Vladimir. "But knowing I'm going home helps me to push the pain to the back recesses of my mind. I'm ready to go."

"All right. See you Friday."

Vladimir watched Hamilton walk away, then said to Lehman, "It's like a dream. I'm actually going home."

That night as Vladimir lay in bed with the sounds of other men snoring, he whispered, "Thank You, Lord. I'm going home."

Home, he thought. *What a beautiful word. Home.*

Suddenly a mental image was on the screen of his mind. He saw the farmhouse where he was born; where he had lived all of his life. His parents were standing on the porch smiling at him as he approached the steps. Just down the road a short distance, Sasha would be waiting for him. Sasha. Sweet Sasha.

For the next two days, Vladimir concentrated on getting his body in the best condition possible for the long trip home. Weakened from the amount of blood he had lost, as well as the extensive surgery and the rigorous exercise program he had put himself on, he knew that going home was the best possible medicine for him. Seeing his parents would do him a world of good, and holding sweet Sasha in his arms would bring healing to his war-torn body, soul, and spirit.

On Friday, dawn was a thin gray promise along the eastern horizon when Vladimir was making preparations to leave as his Russian comrades were being taken to the wagons that waited outside the hospital. Not wanting to disturb Lehman Kuchuck this early, he had told him good-bye the night before.

A small group of nurses collected around Vladimir to bid him good-bye. Captain Robert Hamilton stood by, waiting to escort him to the wagon.

Lara Plekhanov embraced him, and as she did, he said, "Thank you for your many kindnesses, Lara; especially for being a mother figure to me during my stay here."

"It has been my pleasure," she said and kissed his cheek.

Vladimir touched the spot on his cheek and said, "I will never forget you." He thanked the other nurses for treating an enemy soldier so well, then turned to Florence Nightingale who, like Lara, was blinking at tears, and said, "Miss Nightingale, thank you for performing the surgery on my leg, and for the wonderful care you have given me. If it weren't for you, I would have lost the leg. And . . . and thank you for setting up the hospital and being the leader of the nurses."

"It's what God wanted me to do," she said softly.

Vladimir embraced Florence and said, "Then please accept this Russian soldier's thanks for doing what God told you to do. Miss Nightingale, you are a very special lady."

"That she is," spoke up Captain Hamilton, smiling at her. "Miss Nightingale has become a legend to the people of England, France, and Turkey."

"Yes, and to the heart of this Russian soldier," said Vladimir, tears misting his eyes.

Florence, Lara, and the other nurses were wiping tears as Vladimir told them good-bye, and hopped along on his crutches beside Captain Robert Hamilton as they left the building.

The sky was a massive black dome spangled with white, twinkling stars as the boat drew up to the dock at Sevastopol. Russian navy men were in the dock house and emerged, carrying lanterns. Two of the wounded Russian soldiers explained to the navy officials that they had been picked up by Captain Robert Hamilton and his men on Crimean battlefields weeks before and taken to Turkey for medical treatment.

Using Vladimir as his interpreter, Hamilton asked the Russian navy officials if they would see that Corporal Petrovna was taken to his home near Kiev, and they assured him that he would be.

While Vladimir's wounded comrades were being helped onto the dock by the navy men, he turned to the captain and said, "Well, my brother, I've dreaded this moment, but it's time to say good-bye."

"We can at least have this moment in private," said Hamilton. "Let's go to my quarters. Tell your comrades you'll be out shortly."

When the two men were in Hamilton's quarters with the door closed, the captain blinked at his tears and said, "Isn't it amazing how on a war-torn battlefield far away from both of our homes, the God that we both worship and serve brought us together!"

His own eyes filmed with tears, Vladimir said, "He truly does have our lives in His control. Meeting a brother in Christ like I met you is like a cup of cold water to a thirsty man."

They embraced as Vladimir balanced on his crutches, and while they clung to each other, Vladimir said, "We will probably not meet again here on earth, but we will meet in heaven."

"Yes," said the captain. "In heaven."

A week later, a navy wagon pulled up in front of the Russian army post, which was located just outside of Kiev to the north a few miles. There was better than a foot of snow on the ground, and the evidence of traffic in and out of the post was all around. The sky was low and heavy, and the smell of fresh snow was in the cold air.

The wagon ride had been quite uncomfortable for Vladimir's wounded leg, and his face was pale and riddled with pain as he was ushered into the office of the commandant on his crutches and seated in front of his desk. General Philpin Smydstrup listened intently as Vladimir told him how he was wounded in battle, and how the Allied soldiers took him to their hospital in Uskudar, saving his life. He then explained that the British soldiers delivered him and several other wounded Russian soldiers to Sevastopol a week ago.

The general pulled at an ear. "I . . . I have to say this surprises me, after all we have been told by our military leaders of the cruelty of the Allied armies to our men."

"This is just not so, sir," said Vladimir. "They treated us kindly, and unselfishly shared medicine, food, and shelter."

Smydstrup drew in a deep breath, let it out his nose, and stood up. "I want our army physicians to examine you, Corporal. If you are no longer fit for military duty, you must be discharged from the army."

"I understand, sir," said Vladimir, feeling a secret thrill of joy rush through him.

Vladimir was escorted from the commandant's office to the infirmary by Corporal Vindh Lankhov, whom Vladimir had known since first taking his training at the Kiev army post. Lankhov kept a grip on him lest he fall in the snow as he hopped along on his crutches. Snow was starting to fall and the wind was picking up.

An hour later, in the presence of two doctors, Vladimir was given his honorable discharge papers by the commandant. As he placed the papers in Vladimir's hand, General Smydstrup said, "You have faithfully served your country, Corporal. May you live a long and happy life."

"Thank you, sir," said Vladimir, praising the Lord in his heart that he was out of the army.

"I have sent Corporal Lankhov to bring a sleigh," said the general. "He will take you home now."

Even as the general was speaking, the frost-lined windows revealed Lankhov pulling up in front of the office. Vladimir shrugged on his heavy coat, donned his fur cap, shook hands with the general and both doctors, then headed toward the door on his crutches. Corporal Lankov plodded through the snow and met Vladimir at the door. Before they stepped out into the wind-driven snow, Vladimir looked over his shoulder and smiled at the commandant and the doctors.

Lankhov closed the door and gripped Vladimir firmly as he helped him toward the sleigh.

As Smydstrup and the doctors watched them moving away, one of the doctors looked quizzically at the commandant and said, "General, I expected you to tell him about his father."

Smydstrup shrugged. "He will find out soon enough."

Outside, as Corporal Vindh Lankhov was helping Vladimir into the sleigh with the heavy snow pelting their faces, Lankhov said, "Maybe we should wait the storm out here at the post. I could take you home tomorrow or whenever it lets up."

"Please, Vindh," Vladimir said quickly, "I've waited so long for this moment. My parents will put you up for the night if you wish, and you can return to the post tomorrow or whenever the storm blows out. Papa has plenty of space in the barn for these horses. I really want to get home."

"I understand," said Lankhov. "I'll take you, in spite of the weather. General Smydstrup will understand if I don't get back tonight."

Vladimir smiled as he settled on the seat and wiped snow from his eyes. "I appreciate it. Thank you."

Lankhov rounded the sleigh, hopped into the seat and took hold of the reins. Squinting to see through the whirling snowflakes, he said, "You will have to help me head in the right direction and stay on the road."

"That will be no problem," said a relieved Vladimir. "I could almost negotiate this road with my eyes closed."

As Lankhov snapped the reins and put the team in motion, he said, "Vladimir, I am glad you survived the wound."

"Thank you. If it had not been for the compassion of the British officer and his men, I would not have survived."

Lankhov nodded but did not comment.

At the Leskov farm it was warm and cozy in the parlor. A cheery fire was crackling in the large fireplace, but a cold knot had formed in Sasha's aching heart as she stood at the parlor window, looking out at the snow-covered landscape.

The storm had abated some, but it was still snowing hard enough to obscure her vision of the road some sixty or seventy yards from the house. The gusty wind was rattling the window, and she hugged herself for warmth. Behind her, seated close to the fireplace was her mother, Malia, and her fifteen-year-old sister, Oksana.

Keeping her eyes fastened on the snowy scene outside, Sasha said, "Oh, Mama, the war has been over for almost two weeks, but there has been no word from Vladimir. He . . . he must be dead."

"Now Sasha," said Malia, "you must not give up. There are thousands of our soldiers returning to their homes all over Russia from the Crimea. It is going to take some time for the army to transport them. We have prayed for Vladimir's safety since he first went off to fight in the war. You must not give in to doubts now."

"We have had a lot of snow the past two weeks, Sasha," said Oksana. "This no doubt has slowed the army's wagons and sleighs in getting the troops home."

Still hugging herself and peering out the window, Sasha briskly rubbed her arms.

"Sasha, dear," implored Malia, "come away from that drafty window. You are going to catch a cold. And besides that, staring out the window is not going to bring him any sooner."

Sasha wiped tears from her eyes and still staring out the window, said, "Mama, if — I mean, when Vladimir does come home, it is going to be so awful for him."

"You mean when he goes into the house, and —"

"Yes," said Sasha, turning around and wiping away more tears. "He will enter that house and be in the surroundings where his father had always been. And . . . and he will have to face the fact that he will never see his father again on this earth. It had to have hit him hard when the army told him the terrible news, but just think what it is going to do to him to walk into the house and the barn and the sheds, where he and his father spent so much time together all of his growing up years. The memories will make him miss his father more than ever."

"Of course they will," said Malia. "It must have been devastating to him when he first learned about it, but at least he can be a great comfort to his mother. She needs him so very much right now."

As the army sleigh rocked and bumped along the road, Corporal Vindh Lankhov said, "I am glad the snowfall is easing up, Vladimir. I wish the wind would ease off, too. How much farther to your parents' farm?"

Wiping snow from his eyes, Vladimir looked around at the familiar surroundings. "Not far, now. Just about three more miles."

"We have made pretty good time then in spite of the weather," said Lankhov. "Since the snowfall is getting lighter, I won't need to ask your parents to put me up for the night. I can make it back to the post shortly after dark."

Pulling the fur collar up tight under his chin against the knife edges of the wind, Vladimir set his gaze on the intersection just ahead of them and said, "Tell you what, Vindh, take a left turn at this road right up here. I'll have you let me off at Sasha's place. It's about a half mile. I'll see her first, then go home. Sasha's father will take me. This way, you can head on back and get to the post before dark."

"All right," said Lankhov. "I appreciate that." He chuckled. "Besides, after what you told me about your beautiful Sasha, I would think you would really want to see her first."

Vladimir smiled at him.

The sleigh made the turn and headed in the direction of the Leskov place. They passed two other farms, then as the sleigh drew near the lane that led to the Leskov house, Vladimir's nerves tightened. He wiped snow from his eyes and rubbed his gloved hands together. His heart was banging his rib cage as he pointed to the lane and said, "Right here, Vindh. That's the house back there among the trees."

Vladimir licked his lips nervously. It had been so long since he had seen Sasha; she was going to be shocked when she saw him on crutches. He dreaded telling her that he would walk with a limp for the rest of his life.

Still at the window, Sasha rubbed her chilled arms while praying that the Lord would bring Vladimir home and day-dreaming about their future together.

"Sasha," said her mother, "come over here by the fire and warm yourself. That draft is cold."

Sighing deeply, Sasha started to turn away, when through the drifting snow, she caught a glimpse of a sleigh coming up the lane from the road.

She took hold of the curtain that hung on the window's side and stood rooted to the spot, her heart thundering in her ears.

Malia and Oksana saw Sasha stiffen and grasp the curtain, and Malia said, "What is it, dear?"

"Mama, there's . . . there's a sleigh coming up the lane."

Malia and Oksana rose to their feet and peered through the window.

"Mama," said Oksana, gripping Malia's arm, "do you suppose it's Vladimir?"

"We will find out in a moment, honey," said Malia, keeping her eyes on Sasha.

Holding her breath, Sasha unwittingly

squeezed the curtain with a death grip and watched as the sleigh drew up in front of the house. Snow had settled on the coats and hats of the two men in the sleigh. One of them hopped out, and at the same time, her line of sight zeroed in on the other one, who was looking at her. She released her pent-up breath and squealed, "Mama! Oh, Mama! It's him! It's Vladimir! Oh, thank God! It's him!"

Sasha's feet seemed glued to the floor. Looking down at her suddenly immobile feet, she mentally willed them to move, crying joyfully, "I can't believe it! I've waited so long!"

Finally her feet did her bidding and carried her swiftly toward the door.

Five

Sitting on the seat of the sleigh, a jittery Vladimir Petrovna looked through the falling snow as Corporal Vindh Lankhov hopped down. He saw Sasha standing at the window, gripping the curtain. She was saying something as she stared at him, but he could barely hear her voice. His heart was pounding.

She looked downward, said something else, then disappeared.

Seconds later, Sasha bolted through the door, crossed the porch, and dashed down the steps, crying, "Vladimir! Oh, my darling, it's you!"

She plodded swiftly through the snow toward the sleigh as Corporal Lankhov rounded the team and stepped up to help Vladimir out. Malia and Oksana were coming through the open door as Vladimir rose from the sleigh seat, smiling at Sasha.

Sasha skidded to a halt in the snow as Vladimir lifted up his crutches. "Oh,

101

Vladimir!" she gasped. "You've been wounded!"

As Lankhov took hold of him to help him out of the sleigh, Vladimir said, "Nothing life threatening, my sweet."

When Vladimir touched ground, he steadied himself on the crutches, then opened his arms to Sasha. She burst into tears as she hurried to him.

While the happy couple were embracing, Malia and Oksana were moving toward them. At the same time, Hegal Leskov was coming through the door. He had entered the rear of the house from the barn and heard the voices out front.

Sasha let go of Vladimir long enough for him to embrace her mother, sister, and father, then went back into his arms. Corporal Vindh Lankhov stepped close to the couple and said, "I will be going now, Vladimir."

Malia, though not at all comfortable in the presence of the Russian soldier, remembered her manners and said, "Corporal, may I offer you some hot coffee before you leave?"

"Thank you, ma'am," said Lankhov, "but since the storm has let up some, I want to take advantage of it. I need to get back to the post as soon as possible."

With that, Lankhov shook hands with

Vladimir, hopped in the sleigh, and drove away.

Malia rubbed her arms and said, "Sasha, bring Vladimir into the house before we all freeze to death!"

Sasha's brow furrowed as she walked alongside Vladimir while her father stayed on his other side to make sure he made it up the steps without falling. "Are you in pain?" she asked.

"I was," he replied, smiling, "but being with you has taken it all away."

She patted his arm. "Aren't you sweet?"

"No, just truthful," he said, chuckling.

As they stepped into the small area where the coatrack stood, Hegal began helping Vladimir out of his coat. Malia said, "Vladimir, you look so pale and weary. The kitchen stove is still hot from lunch. There is still some potato and sausage soup in the pot. How about a nice hot bowl of soup?"

"That does sound good," said Vladimir. "It has been some time since I had anything to eat."

Malia hurried into the kitchen ahead of the others, and Oksana was quickly on her heels.

Sasha and her father still flanked Vladimir as they headed toward the rear of the house, the crutches making their rhythmic thumping sound on the wooden floor.

"My boy," said Hegal, as he removed his own coat and hung it on a peg by the back door, "we didn't know about your leg wound, of course, but we have been praying daily since you left for the Crimea, asking the Lord to keep you safe. We have been eagerly looking for you to return since the war ended."

"Thank you for praying for me, sir," said Vladimir.

"I want to know all about this wound, Vladimir," said Sasha.

"The rest of us want to know too," said Hegal, "so you can tell us while you have your soup."

In the kitchen, Malia had slid the ever present coffeepot from the back of the stove to the front so it would heat up quickly, and was stirring the soup. Oksana poured coffee for everybody, and soon a steaming bowl of soup was placed before Vladimir. Between spoonfuls of soup and bites of dark brown bread, he told them the whole story of his being shot on the battlefield, of being picked up by Captain Robert Hamilton and his men, and of the bullet being removed from his leg by Florence Nightingale.

Taking a sip of coffee, he looked at Sasha, who sat beside him, and said, "I do have some bad news about my leg, though. Miss Nightingale said even when I can lay aside these crutches and the cane, which will come next, I will walk with a limp for the rest of my life."

Sasha touched his arm. "I'm sorry for this, darling, but if you are to walk with a limp, it doesn't change anything with me. I still love you and want to marry you."

Vladimir's lips curved into a wide smile. "Thank you."

"This wound should take you out of the army," said Hegal. "Have the army doctors looked at it?"

"Yes, sir. I have been given my honorable discharge. Sasha's future husband is a civilian again."

"Wonderful!" exclaimed Sasha. "I'm sorry about the wound, but I'm so glad to know you're out of the army!"

Reflecting on the story Vladimir had just told, Malia said to him, "It certainly was marvelous of the Lord to send Captain Hamilton to you, Vladimir — a born-again man."

"Yes. We really became close in the short time we had together," said Vladimir, pushing the empty soup bowl and bread plate back a few inches. "He is a fine man. Well, I hope you won't think me impolite to eat and run, but I am eager to see Mama and Papa. Mr. Leskov, could I impose on you for a ride home?"

The Leskov family looked at one another, eyes wide, and Hegal set quizzical eyes on Vladimir. "Y-you haven't been home, yet?"

"No, sir. I . . . I wanted to see Sasha so much I couldn't wait. I told Corporal Lankhov to let me off here, and I would have you take me home."

Hegal's features pinched. "Then . . . you do not know about your father?"

"What do you mean?"

Hegal ran his gaze over the faces of his wife and daughters, then settled it on Vladimir. "I . . . I hate to be the one to tell you this, but somebody has to."

Sasha took hold of Vladimir's hand as her father said, "Vladimir, exactly a week ago today, the Cossacks rode onto the Petrovna farm and arrested your father."

Vladimir's pupils darkened and his complexion drained to alabaster white. "Wh-why?"

"Do you remember a farmer who used to live down the road from your place named Georg Pushkin?"

"I don't remember him as far as what he looks like, no. But I've heard my parents talk about Georg and Letha Pushkin who used to be our neighbors. They live up north of Moscow near Petrozavodsk, on the shore of Lake Onega, if I recall correctly."

"Yes. Well, on the day before your father was arrested, he was in town, and ran into Georg. I think it's been about fourteen or fifteen years since the Puskins moved up north. Of course, your parents were saved just twelve years ago, so when your father had the opportunity to talk to Georg there in Kiev, he told him about becoming a Christian. From what your mother told me, Georg was showing interest in the gospel as your father talked to him. Neither man was aware that an off-duty Cossack in civilian clothes was eavesdropping nearby.

"The next day, six Cossacks rode up to the house and put your father under arrest."

Vladimir's heart seemed to freeze in his chest. For a moment there was dead silence, then he stammered, "Wh-what did they do to him?"

"They gave him a life sentence in the prison at Rybon. The only way he can ever be released is to renounce his faith in Jesus."

Sasha squeezed his hand. "Oh, Vladimir, I'm so sorry."

Vladimir squeezed back and said to the group, "Papa will never turn his back on the Lord."

"We all know that, son," said Hegal. "Bakum Petrovna is a true soldier of Jesus Christ. He will never retreat in the heat of this battle."

Vladimir licked his lips. "Is Vande Wendin still pastor of our church?"

"Yes," said Hegal. "And he and Mrs. Wendin have been spending time with your mother every day. Last Monday night at the meeting, Pastor Wendin preached a powerful sermon on our being soldiers for Christ, and he used your father as a shining example."

"I've got to go see Papa as soon as possible," said Vladimir. "Rybon is only thirty miles from here."

"They won't let you see him," said Hegal. "The day after he was taken to the prison, your mother had the Wendins take her there, but they would not let her see him. The prison superintendent, of course, does not know that Pastor Wendin is any more than a farmer. In front of the Wendins, the superintendent told your mother not to come back. He said coldly that she would never be allowed to see him, nor would the government ever advise her of anything about him. Even his death. I'm sure you would be told the same thing if you went to the prison. They won't let you see him."

Vladimir's face distorted. Anguish rode his voice as he said, "I must hurry home to Mama. She needs me."

"I will go hitch up the team to the sleigh," said Hegal, shoving his chair back and rising to his feet. "I'll take you home now."

"We will all take you home," said Malia.

"Yes," said Sasha, squeezing his hand again.

As Hegal was putting on his coat, he said, "Malia, while I'm at the barn, you need to tell Vladimir about the two widows from the church."

"I will," she said.

"Widows?" said Vladimir as Hegal hurried out the back door.

"You don't know Livadia Diglehev," said Malia, "but you know Darue Alpinz."

"Yes."

"Well, Livadia is in her late seventies as is Darue. They are staying with your mother so she won't be alone."

"I appreciate that," said Vladimir. "It is very kind of them."

Margaret Petrovna was at her kitchen cupboard peeling potatoes, knowing that when Livadia and Darue awakened from their naps, they would mildly scold her for starting preparations for supper without their help. But she had to stay busy. With Bakum in prison and Vladimir not yet home from the war, she kept her mind and body occupied lest she give in to the devil and his attempt to get her to doubt the goodness of the Lord.

When she laid aside a peeled potato and picked up another, Margaret glanced through the frost-edged kitchen window and saw that it was snowing hard again.

She was almost through peeling the last potato when she heard a horse blow at the rear of the house, and the soft pounding of hooves coming to a halt. Her heart lurched in her chest. She had been living in a constant state of fear since the Cossack soldiers took her beloved husband away. The Cossacks were so unpredictable. They might just return for her at any time.

Laying down the potato and the knife, Margaret inched up to the window and cautiously peered out into the storm. Though visibility was poor, she was able to make out a sleigh and the team that was pulling it. Knowing the Cossacks always came on horseback, she let out a sigh of relief. "Thank You, Lord."

There were people getting out of the sleigh, but she was not able to tell who they were. She moved to the door and opened it, letting a gust of snow-filled wind rush inside. Planting her feet against the wind, she called to the figures who were barely visible, "Come in, whoever you are!"

As they moved toward the porch in a tight-knit group, Margaret stepped aside to let her visitors in. She could tell that one of them was hobbling on crutches and was being supported on one side by a man and the other side by a woman.

Before she could tell who it was, a familiar voice penetrated the curtain of snow that thrilled her heart. "Mama, it's me! I'm home!"

Just as Vladimir reached the bottom step and planted his crutches on it, Margaret caught a glimpse of his face and the faces of Sasha and Hegal, who flanked him. "Oh, my boy! My boy!" she cried, and dissolved into tears as Vladimir hurried up the steps and folded her into his arms, letting the crutches fall to the porch floor unnoticed.

Hegal picked up the crutches and held them while mother and son clung to each other, sobbing, and Malia, Sasha, and Oksana topped the steps together.

Oblivious to the storm, Margaret eased back in Vladimir's arms and said, "How bad are you hurt, son?"

"I just took a bullet in my leg, Mama," he

said. "Come. Let's go inside before you freeze to death."

As they moved inside, Livadia Diglehev and Darue Alpinz appeared at the other side of the kitchen. Darue excitedly greeted Vladimir and introduced him to Livadia. Coats were removed, and when emotions settled to a degree, Margaret looked at her son through reddened eyes. "I'm sure the Leskovs have told you about your father."

Many more tears were shed as mother and son talked about Bakum's arrest.

Vladimir said, "Mama, Mr. Leskov told me about Pastor and Mrs. Wendin taking you to the prison to see Papa and what the superintendent told you."

"Yes," she sniffed, wiping tears.

"I want to see Papa. I will go to General Smydstrup. He approved my discharge, Mama."

"Discharge! Oh, praise the Lord! You are out of the army!"

"Yes, but I believe General Smydstrup will listen to me. I am going to ask him to use his influence to get me — as a medically and honorably discharged Russian soldier — into the prison to see Papa."

"That is a good idea, Vladimir," said Hegal. "I had not thought of that approach. It just might work."

"I am counting on it working," said Vladimir.

"I will pray to that end, son," said Margaret. "Now, I want to hear how you got that wound in your leg, and how the healing is coming along."

"Me too," said Darue. "You have lost weight, Vladimir."

"Probably a few pounds," he said.

"Let's all sit down in the parlor by the fire," said Margaret.

When everyone was comfortably seated, Vladimir told his story. Margaret broke down at times as her son told of lying wounded in the snow on the Crimea, and of being taken to the makeshift military hospital in Uskudar. She wept when she heard of the kind treatment he received at the hands of Captain Robert Hamilton and nurses Florence Nightingale and Lara Plekhanov.

"God is so good," said Margaret, dabbing at her tears with a hanky. "He is just so good. And just think . . . it was the famous Florence Nightingale who personally did the surgery on your leg!"

"Yes. And this Lara Plekhanov, Mama," said Vladimir, "she looks very much like you. And . . . and when I told her that, she said she would be a mother to me until I could come home to you. And she was. She treated me so good."

"I wish I could meet this dear lady so I could thank her," said Margaret. "So she really resembles me?"

"Yes. In her eyes and in her smile."

Margaret patted his arm. "Speaking of resembling someone, son, when you stepped into the light in the kitchen, I noticed how much more you look like your father. You have changed a lot in the past two years. The resemblance to your father is stronger the older you get."

"I see that, too, Mrs. Petrovna," said Sasha.

The others spoke their agreement.

Malia then turned to her husband and said, "Hegal, we need to head for home soon so the girls and I can get supper started."

Hegal nodded. "Before we go, we should let Sasha and Vladimir have a few minutes alone."

Margaret stood up quickly. "How about eating supper with us? Then Sasha and Vladimir can have their time together, and after that, you can go home with full stomachs."

"Oh, we don't want to impose on you," said Malia.

"It is not an imposition," Margaret said sweetly. "Come. Let us ladies go to the kitchen and get supper started. Hegal and Vladimir can stay here by the fire and talk."

A warm feeling filled the hearts of everyone when they sat down at the table for the meal. Margaret asked Hegal to offer thanks for the food. With heads bowed while Vladimir and Sasha held hands, Hegal prayed in a hushed voice, giving thanks to the Lord for the food, then wept as he praised Him for the safe return of their loved one.

When the enjoyable meal had been devoured, the two widows poured hot tea all around, accompanied by thick cream. Margaret placed a large plate of soft molasses cookies on the table.

Vladimir's eyes lit up. "Oh, Mama! My favorite cookies!" He picked one up, took a bite, closed his eyes while he chewed and swallowed, and said, "Mm-mm! This is what I have been missing since the day I left!"

Margaret stepped up behind him, squeezed his shoulders, and said, "Now that you're back, son, it will be my pleasure to cook your favorite things. That is, until you marry this girl beside you. Then it will be up to her."

"I will do it gladly, Mrs. Petrovna," said Sasha.

While the women were cleaning up the kitchen and washing dishes, and Hegal was once again seated in front of the fireplace in the parlor, Vladimir and Sasha were alone in Margaret's sewing room. Holding each other, they discussed their life together in the future and agreed they would talk soon about a wedding date.

Later, as the Leskovs were about to go out the door, Hegal said, "Vladimir, I will take you to the army post whenever you want to go."

"Is tomorrow morning all right?" asked Vladimir.

"Certainly. How about I pick you up at seven o'clock. That will get us to the prison by late morning, since we have to go to the army post first."

"I'll be ready. Thank you."

The winter sky was cold and clear the next morning as Hegal and Vladimir headed toward the army post. After a while, the exertion of pulling the sleigh warmed up the horses. Vaporous tendrils curled off their flanks and steamed from their nostrils in plumes.

As they glided over the glistening snow,

Hegal wanted to hear more about Captain Robert Hamilton and was very impressed with him as Vladimir went on about him.

"He must be a fine man," said Hegal. "I wish I could meet him someday."

Vladimir turned and smiled at him. "You will . . . in heaven."

General Philpin Smydstrup was leaning forward with his elbows on the desk top as Vladimir Petrovna stated his case. When the ex-soldier was finished, Smydstrup eased back in his chair and said, "Your father is in prison because of his stubborn refusal to renounce his faith in this Jesus Christ, Petrovna. I must tell you that I am very much opposed to Jesus Christ and the Bible. It is all nonsense as far as I am concerned."

Vladimir bit his tongue.

"However," the commandant went on, "because you were a faithful Russian soldier and you were wounded fighting for your country, I will write a letter for you to carry to Superintendent Konstin. The letter will strongly request that you be allowed to see your father."

Vladimir let a thin smile curve his lips. "Thank you, sir."

Prison superintendent Markov Konstin

read General Smydstrup's letter silently while Vladimir and Hegal sat in front of his desk. When he had finished, he laid the letter down and frowned. Konstin had a low forehead and a thick head of hair. The hair grew so low on his forehead that the frown lines plowed through it.

"Ordinarily," said Konstin, "no one is allowed to visit a prisoner who is kept in the cell block where your father is, but because you were wounded fighting for the motherland, I will allow you one visit . . . but only one. You will never be allowed to visit your father again. Do you understand?"

"I understand, sir," replied Vladimir, thanking God in his heart for the one visit.

Konstin's heavy jowl stiffened. "I remind you that your father, as a follower of Jesus Christ, is considered an enemy of the Russian government, and only upon renouncing his faith will he ever be released from prison. At this point, the fool has refused to do it."

Vladimir felt fire ignite inside him at the superintendent's use of the word "fool," but suppressed it. Losing his temper now would cost him the final opportunity to see his father in this life. He was glad that neither the commandant nor the superintendent had pressed him about having faith in Jesus

118

Christ since his father did.

Rising from his chair, Konstin said, "Mr. Leskov, you may wait in the small room right next to my office while this young man visits his father."

Both men stood up, and Hegal nodded.

Konstin stepped to the door, and seeing a guard passing by, told him to send Ivan Chikov to his office. Hegal laid a hand on Vladimir's arm and said, "You greet your father for me."

Knowing Hegal would like to send more of a message to Bakum, but could not because of the superintendent's presence, Vladimir said, "I will, sir."

Hegal left the office and entered the adjacent room.

Konstin stood in the open door of his office looking down the corridor until he saw the man he wanted coming toward him.

When Ivan Chikov drew up, he said, "You want to see me, sir?"

"I have Vladimir Petrovna here, Ivan. His father is Bakum Petrovna, who is in cell block five. Vladimir recently received an honorable discharge from the army, and brought a letter to me from General Philpin Smydstrup, asking that I allow him to visit his father."

"I see," said Chikov, giving Vladimir a bland look.

"You notice he is on crutches."

"Yes, sir."

"He was wounded on the Crimea. This is why I am setting aside the normal rule concerning prisoners in cell block five having no visitors. This will be the only visit I allow between them. Let them have half an hour."

"Yes, sir," said Chikov. "Come with me, Vladimir."

Chikov was silent as he guided Vladimir down the corridor with the crutches making their familiar tapping sound. They came to an iron door where a guard stood, and when Chikov explained where they were going, the guard unlocked the door, let them pass through, then closed and locked it again.

They passed through cell blocks number one and three, then crossed an open area and entered cell block number five. The sight of the place gave Vladimir the chills. His heart was heavy for his father.

Chikov guided Vladimir down a solid-walled corridor and stopped at another iron door, where a guard let them pass into a small area that had two glassed-in rooms with iron doors. The doors stood open. The rooms had windows, which allowed a full view into their interiors. There were two wooden chairs in each room.

Chikov gestured toward the room on the

left. "Go in and sit down," he said. "I will be back with your father shortly."

To Vladimir's surprise, Ivan Chikov closed the door, locked it, and disappeared.

While he waited for the guard to bring his father, Vladimir prayed, asking the Lord to help him to make the most of this final earthly moment they would have together.

He was wiping tears when he heard the key rattle in the door and looked up. He could see his father's right shoulder and arm as he stood behind Ivan Chikov. The door swung open, and Chikov took a step back, saying, "All right, Bakum, here's your visitor."

The moment Vladimir saw his father's face, he knew Chikov had not told him who had been allowed in to see him. Bakum's mouth flew open, and his eyes bulged as he gasped, "Vladimir! My son! Oh, my son!"

Instantly, Bakum was through the door, and father and son were in each other's arms, weeping. The crutches clattered to the floor.

"You have half an hour," Chikov said stiffly, closed the door, and locked it.

When Bakum Petrovna and his son had brought their emotions into control, Bakum held him at arm's length, glanced down at the crutches, then looked into his eyes and said, "You were wounded in the war?"

"Yes, Papa. But God was good. Only my leg took a bullet . . . not some vulnerable part of my body that would have killed me."

"Praise the Lord! I am so glad to see that you are still alive. We had no way of knowing."

"I know, Papa. Just as I had no way of knowing of your arrest and imprisonment."

Bakum bent down, picked up the crutches, handed them to Vladimir, and said, "Let's sit down."

When both were seated on the chairs, facing each other, Bakum said, "It is a hard and fast rule that no prisoner in this cell block may have visitors. These two rooms are here because this block used to hold men who had committed lesser crimes than murder and believing in Jesus Christ."

"So those are the only ones in this cell block now? Murderers and believers in Jesus?"

"Yes. They actually feel that we Christians are worse criminals than the murderers."

"How many other Christians are in here, Papa?"

"I have no idea, son. We are not allowed to mix with the other prisoners. From what the guards have told me, I know there are some born-again men in here, but I have no idea how many." Bakum shook his head in wonderment. "How did you manage to get in to see me?"

Vladimir explained his petition to General Smydstrup, and the letter that the general wrote to Superintendent Konstin. He told him that Hegal Leskov had brought him to the prison and sent his greetings. He then explained Konstin's firm dictum that there would never be another visit.

"Thank the Lord for making this one visit possible," said Bakum. "Is your mother all right?"

"She misses you terribly, Papa, but she is finding God's grace sufficient. Lavadia Diglehev and Darue Alpinz have been staying with her."

"Oh, that's good. They will be a lot of company to her."

"Yes. And Pastor and Mrs. Wendin come to see her every day as well as many of the church members."

Bakum managed a smile. "I knew they would. Now, tell me about your wound. Will you be all right?"

Vladimir told his father the whole story about Captain Robert Hamilton and his men, Florence Nightingale, Lara Plekhanhov, and his stay at the Uskudar hospital. He explained what Miss Nightingale had said about the limp he would have for the rest of his life, but showed a positive attitude about it, saying that Sasha had assured him it would make no difference to her.

Bakum said, "I am glad for your attitude about it, son. You will be all right."

"Of course, Papa. My greatest concern now is for you. It was such a shock to learn what had happened. If you had only known that Cossack was eavesdropping . . ."

"God knew, son. And that's all that matters. The lives of His children are in His hands. He has given me peace in this. At least I was able to sow the seed of the Word in Georg's heart. I'm trusting the Lord to bring both Georg and his wife to Jesus with it."

"Yes, Papa. I believe He will. But . . . but it's so hard to know that you will be in this prison for the rest of your life."

Bakum's features softened. "It's that, or renounce my faith, son. I cannot and I will not turn my back on my Lord and Saviour. I know this means that I will never see my wife and son again on this earth, but we will have eternity in heaven together. This life is so short compared to the next one."

"I understand, Papa. I wouldn't want you

to turn your back on the Lord. Just think of all those martyrs in the Bible and history who refused to renounce their faith in Jesus, doing as you are doing . . . not accepting deliverance."

They talked for a few minutes about John the Baptist, Stephen, and Paul, who were martyred because they stood for Jesus and would not compromise His truth. They talked about John Huss, Hugh Latimer, and Thomas Cranmer, whose lives were taken because they would not renounce their faith in Jesus Christ.

Tears glistened in Vladimir's eyes as he said, "Papa, ever since I learned about you being here in this prison for the rest of your life, I have been thinking of what the Lord Jesus said to the persecuted Christians in the church at Smyrna in Revelation chapter 2: 'Be thou faithful unto death, and I will give thee a crown of life.' "

Bakum was trying to swallow the lump that had risen in his throat.

"I'm out of the army now, Papa," Vladimir went on. "I will take care of Mama. In spite of this game leg, I will keep the farm going. And when we meet in heaven, Mama and I will watch the Lord place the crown of life on your head."

Bakum lowered his head, stared at the

floor, and said, "This dirt farmer doesn't deserve a crown, son. Only the one who went to Calvary's cross, shed His precious blood, and died for this guilty sinner deserves to wear a crown."

"This is true, Papa," said Vladimir, wiping tears, "but nonetheless, Jesus said He will give you a crown of life if you are faithful unto death. You are doing exactly that, so He will give you that crown at His judgment seat in heaven."

Bakum smiled thinly. "I know, son. But when He places that crown on my head, I will immediately drop to my knees, remove the crown, and lay it at His worthy feet. He is the one who deserves it."

Suddenly a key rattled in the door and it swung open. Two guards stepped into the room. "Time is up, Bakum," Ivan Chikov said crisply.

Bakum rose to his feet.

Using the crutches to raise himself to a standing position, Vladimir braced himself and put his arms around his father. Both began to weep.

"That's enough," snapped Chikov.

But still father and son clung to each other, tears flowing.

The guards roughly pulled them apart, and because of his bad leg, Vladimir lost his balance, dropped the crutches, and fell to the floor. Bakum helped him up, placed the crutches in his hands, and embraced him again.

Ivan Chikov clamped a strong hand on Bakum's shoulder. "You were given enough time to say good-bye. It's too late now."

Through his tears, Vladimir said to Chikov, "My father and I are not saying good-bye. It is only farewell for a little while. We have a promise of eternity together where there is no parting."

Chikov quickly whisked Bakum out the door and down the corridor, telling the other guard to take Vladimir back to the superintendent's office. With Vladimir looking back over his shoulder, the guard hurried him up the corridor the opposite direction.

As Bakum and Chikov reached the iron door to enter the area where Bakum's cell was located, a guard peered through the small window and opened the door.

Bakum turned around to take one last look at his son. At the other end of the corridor, Vladimir was still looking back. He waved at his father.

Bakum waved also, with tears streaming down his cheeks.

Chikov ushered Bakum to his cell. When

Bakum was inside, Chikov held the cell door, ready to close it, and said, "What did your son mean that the two of you have a promise of eternity together where there is no parting?"

Six

It was a subzero day in January 1886 as the lone rider turned off the road and pointed his mount down the lane that led to the Vladimir Petrovna farm. He could see hoof and sleigh tracks in the snow, which told him someone had left the farm sometime earlier that morning.

A brutal blizzard had lashed south central Russia the day before and didn't blow out until late last night. The horse plodded doggedly through the hip-deep mounds of powdery whiteness under a clear, sunlit sky.

Barny Kaluga let his slitted eyes travel across the frozen landscape to the old farmhouse, where billows of smoke lifted skyward from the chimneys, riding the morning's frosty breeze. Someone was still home. He told himself that Mr. Petrovna had probably taken Kadyn and gone to town. The fifteen-year-old boy loved to spend time with his father, and always accompanied him whenever he went into Kiev unless there were chores to do or there was schoolwork to be done.

Soon Barny hauled up in front of the house and dismounted. The porch and steps had been shoveled. As he climbed the steps, he smiled to himself. No doubt the shoveling job had been done by Kadyn, who was always quick to tackle a task he saw needed to be done. Like all of the Petrovnas, there wasn't a lazy bone in the boy's body.

Barny's heart picked up pace as he knocked on the door. The anticipation of seeing beautiful Olecia always made his heart pound.

Feminine footsteps were heard inside, and the curtain was pushed to the side. Barny saw that it was Olecia's older sister, Zoya. Smiling at him through the frost-edged glass, she opened the door and said, "Hello, Barny. It was nice of you to come by and see me. Please come in."

Barny, who was of medium build and stood three inches under six feet, chuckled as he stepped inside and said, "Well, no offense, Miss Zoya, but —"

"I know," she giggled. "Olecia is in the kitchen. Papa, Mama, and Kadyn have gone to town. I am working in the sewing room, so I won't bother you and Olecia if you want to talk."

Barny smiled, removed his gloves, stuffed them in the pockets of his heavy coat, and hung it on the coatrack. He took off his fur hat, hung it next to the coat, and said, "Shall I just go back, or do you want to announce my presence?"

"I'll take you back," said Zoya, who at twenty-one, was two years older than her sister.

As they moved down the hall and neared the kitchen, Olecia's voice met them as she called, "Zoya, did I hear a knock at the front door? Is someone here?"

"Yes," Zoya replied as she moved into the kitchen with Barny on her heels, "this young man said he would like to see you."

Olecia's face lit up as she saw the handsome Barny smiling at her.

"Hello, Barny," she said sweetly. "I'm glad the blizzard didn't get you."

"Not a chance," Barny chuckled. "I was born in Siberia. I can take all the wind and snow that comes my way."

"Well, I'll get back to my sewing," said the older sister. "Nice to see you, Barny."

"It was nice to see you too, Miss Zoya."

Wiping her hands on a towel and laying it on the cupboard, Olecia said, "You can probably tell by the aroma in here that I'm baking bread."

"Yes," responded Barny, sniffing the sweet scent. "The girl I marry must be able to make bread like that."

Without comment, Olecia gestured toward the large kitchen table. "Sit down, Barny. Would you like some coffee? It's hot."

"Thank you. I'll take some."

Olecia poured both of them a cup of coffee, set Barny's cup before him, then sat down across the table and smiled. Unable to pull his gaze from her, Barny drank in her beauty. Her dark brown eyes were like fathomless umber pools. Barny felt himself drawn into those depths, wanting to lose himself there forever. But he wondered if she would ever say she loved him. Would she ever be his?

Barny and his parents had moved to a neighboring farm some six years ago, and he had met Olecia shortly thereafter. Even then, he had felt drawn to her, but though she was kind to him and friendly toward him, she remained aloof. Two years ago, he had told her that he loved her, and he had told her many times since. She was always kind, but up to this day, had not said she felt the same toward him. He longed to hear her say it.

Barny sipped coffee, set the cup down,

and looking lovingly into her eyes. "And the girl I marry must not only be able to make bread like that, but she must have marvelous dark brown eyes just like yours."

Olecia's lovely features tinted. "Barny, I —"

"Olecia," he cut in, "I have to know. Don't you feel anything for me? Other than friendship, I mean. I have told you over and over that I am in love with you . . . but you have not responded. Please say you love me, too."

Olecia bit her lips. "Barny, I — I —"

He reached across the table, took her hand, and squeezed it gently. "You do, don't you? You do love me! For the first time, I can see it in your eyes. Say it, sweet Olecia!"

Olecia Petrovna's lips quivered as she met his gaze. "Y-yes, Barny. I do. I am so in love with you that it hurts sometimes. I so very much want to belong to you, but —"

"Oh. I know. It's because I am not a Christian, isn't it?"

"Yes. Barny, I have told you before that God's Word says a Christian should not marry someone who is not a Christian. It would never work. I have told you so many times what the Bible says about your need to be saved. Would . . . would you let me actually show it to you?"

"Well, I would, Olecia, but it goes against

the religion my parents have brought me up in."

"But you have admitted to me that your religion has given you no real peace about where you will spend eternity. You cannot say that you are going to heaven."

"I know, but —"

"You say you love me, Barny."

"I do love you."

"Then please let me show you what God's Word says about your need to be saved."

Barny ran shaky fingers through his dark hair. "All right. I'll let you show me."

Because the Bibles had to be well hidden in the Petrovna house in case the Cossacks ever came to make a search, Olecia left Barny at the table for the five minutes it took to get her Bible, then returned, and with love in her heart for him, opened its pages. She showed him scenes at the cross in the Gospels, explained why Jesus died as He did, then showed Barny passages that plainly said he was a guilty sinner before God like all human beings and in need of salvation and forgiveness. She showed him what Jesus said about hell in Mark 9 and Luke 16.

Carefully, Olecia showed Barny exactly how to be saved by putting his faith in Jesus Christ as his own personal Saviour, then looked at him and asked, "Do you have any questions?"

Scrubbing a nervous hand over his face, he said, "No. You have made everything very clear."

Cocking her head to one side, she saw his discomfort. "What's wrong, Barny?"

"Well, I . . . I have something to tell you. In fact, it's the main reason I came here this morning."

Olecia's brow furrowed. "What is it?"

Barny cleared his throat gently. "Olecia, I . . . well, I have signed up to become a Cossack."

Something cold settled in Olecia's stomach. "A Cossack? Why, Barny?"

"I . . . I just want to make something of my life. You know the prestige the Cossacks have in this country. They are considered special agents of the czar. The pay is excellent, too."

"But you have to sign up for twenty years."

"I don't mind that. I want to make it my career. I am to start my training tomorrow at Cossack headquarters, which is about a mile west of the army post. I can still see you once or twice a week while I'm in training. It will depend on where they place me once I'm in a Cossack uniform, how often I'll get home. Of course, the Cossacks who are married are always stationed as close to their families as possible."

Olecia lowered her head, stared at the table for a moment, then looked up at Barny, deep concern shaping her expression. "I . . . I so very much want to see you saved, but you couldn't be a Cossack and a Christian too. You know how the Cossacks are about Christians."

"Yes, but I promise you this, Olecia: Even as a Cossack, I will never let the government know that the Petrovna family are Christians and members of the underground church. I don't want anything to happen to you. And if you would change your mind about being a Christian and marry me, we could be so happy together."

"Barny, a person who truly knows the Lord doesn't change his mind about being a Christian. The only way you and I can ever let this love between us develop is if you become a Christian."

Barny was silent for a long moment, then said, "Olecia, I love you with all of my heart, but I can't give up the religion my parents gave me."

"I love you with all of my heart, too," she said, "but I cannot and will not turn my back on my Lord."

Moments later, Olecia stood on the front porch of the house with a shawl around her shoulders as Barny mounted his horse. Settling in the saddle, he said, "Then it is all right if I come by and see you whenever I can?"

"Of course. If you don't mind my preaching to you when you're here."

He smiled. "I can take that, just so I can be with you."

Olecia wiped tears from her cheeks as she watched him ride away. "Lord, I can't help how I feel about Barny. I'm not sure I can ever love anyone like I love him. But . . . You know I will not disobey Your Word and marry a man who is not a believer. Please. I've asked You for so long, now. Bring Barny to Yourself."

It was just after ten o'clock that night as Vladimir Petrovna was setting up chairs in the parlor of his house with the help of his son Kadyn, and Alekin Kolpino — to whom Zoya was engaged.

Limping on the leg that was wounded so many years ago in the Crimean War, Vladimir set two chairs in place and said, "Tell you what, boys, this has to be one of the coldest winters I've ever seen." He paused, smiled, and added, "Or maybe it's just because I'm getting old."

Alekin laughed. "Mr. Petrovna, forty-eight is not old."

Vladimir laid a hand on his shoulder. "Well, all I can tell you is that each winter my game leg pains me more, and I find it more and more difficult to get around like I need to."

Kadyn set a chair in place and said, "Papa, you know what Mama always says . . . 'A person who thinks young stays young.' "

"I know, son," said Vladimir, "but it's hard to think young when this old leg gives me pain."

Sasha entered the room, followed by her daughters. Hands on hips, she looked at her husband and said, "What's this I hear, Vladimir? You're thinking old again?"

Vladimir covered his mouth. "Oops! I didn't know you were close by."

"Even crippled children have pain in their legs at this time of year," said Sasha. "You mustn't let your leg make you an old man before your time."

"That's good advice, Papa," said Olecia.

"Very good advice," put in Zoya.

"All right, all right," said Vladimir, chuckling. "I am twenty years old again."

"That's better," said Sasha.

Alekin looked around at the chairs and the low-burning lanterns. "That's twenty-five chairs, Mr. Petrovna. You think it's enough?"

"For now, at least," said Vladimir. "This frigid weather may keep some folks home tonight. We can put up more if a larger number comes."

The Petrovna house was kept immaculately clean by Sasha and her daughters. There was a cheery fire in the fireplace, giving the parlor with its plain furnishings a mellow glow. The window shades were pulled down tight in the parlor so no one outside would be able to see the small congregation as they gathered for the service. Not wanting to draw attention to the house, the Petrovnas had only a few lanterns burning low in other rooms.

Alekin, who had been saved only a few months, looked around at the drawn window shades and said, "Isn't it sad that we have to hide to have our services? Mr. and Mrs. Petrovna, was it this bad when you were first married?"

"We had to hide back then too," said Vladimir, "but the penalty for meeting like we do is worse today than it was then. Today, when the Cossacks discover an underground church in session, instead of just executing the pastor and sending all the other adults to prison for life who will not renounce their faith in Jesus, they execute everyone who refuses . . . and the children are taken as wards of the government."

Alekin set his jaw and said, "My Lord died for me on the cross. By His grace, I will die for Him if it comes down to it."

Vladimir and Sasha smiled at each other. They were proud that Alekin was going to become their son-in-law. The wedding was set for April 8. Alekin worked at the lumber and hardware store in Kiev, and had already bought a small house in town. He was an orphan and had no siblings or other family.

At 10:30, farmer Nicolai Suvorov and his wife and children arrived. Nicolai, who was in his midthirties, had been pastor of the church for the past five years. He told the Petrovnas and Alekin that he did not expect more than twenty to attend the service. He knew of two families who had sickness, and the night was so bitterly cold.

Soon other families were arriving, and as they did, Alekin and Kadyn met them at the front of the house. After each family was safely inside the house, the two young men took their horses and sleighs inside the barn so if anyone should be moving down the road, they would not know a crowd was gathered there. So far, this small congregation felt very blessed that they had never been discovered. They were very careful as to when and where they met, for they were always on the lookout for the Cossacks.

When Alekin and Kadyn entered the house after placing the last of the horses and sleighs in the barn, Pastor Suvorov was pleased when he counted twenty-one in attendance. He was about to start the service when they heard horses whinny as another sleigh pulled up outside. A family of four came in and were welcomed by the others as Alekin and Kadyn hurried outside to place the team and sleigh in the barn.

The service was begun with prayer, and though they all wanted to sing some hymns, they dared not, lest they be heard from outside.

The pastor was just opening his Bible to begin preaching when they all heard horses whinnying and the sound of hooves crunching in the snow. Eyes widened as the people looked around at each other with fear evident in their eyes.

Somebody whispered, "Cossacks?"

Pastor Suvorov moved quietly toward the parlor window to look out, but before he could do so, the door opened and members Petr and Amana Noske came in. They had guests with them; a silver-haired couple who were strangers to the group. Pastor Suvorov had not expected the Noskes on such a bitter night, for they lived farther from the church than anyone else.

There was a unified sigh of relief as pounding hearts began to slow down. Alekin and Kadyn hurried outside to do their job.

The pastor stepped up to the Noskes and their guests and said, "You gave us a bit of a scare. We thought the Cossacks had come."

"I'm sorry we're late, Pastor," said Petr, peeling out of his coat. "We didn't mean to frighten you."

Suvorov smiled. "It's all right. I'm just glad you could make it."

As the Noskes and their guests were taking off their gloves, coats, and hats, Vladimir's attention was drawn to the silver-haired man. His face was vaguely familiar. But Vladimir could not place him.

The silver-haired man hung up his wife's coat and hat for her, and as he turned about, his eyes ran across Vladimir's face. Their eyes locked briefly, and Vladimir saw recognition in the man's eyes. He knew Vladimir, for sure.

The man was at least twenty years his senior. Where had he seen him? Vladimir asked himself. Who was he?

To Petr and Amana, Pastor Suvorov said, "Are these the people you told me about . . . the ones who have come to live on your farm?"

"Yes," said Petr, running his gaze around the group. "I want all of you to meet Ivan and Ridna Chikov."

The name meant nothing to Vladimir, but the man's face did, though he was sure it was much younger when he had seen it before.

"I was about to begin my sermon," the pastor said to Petr, "but before I do, I would like to tell the people about your guests." He turned to the group. "Everyone take your seats."

When the group was seated before him, Suvorov said, "I ran into Petr and Amana in town a few days ago, and they told me about the Chikovs. They are born-again people and have just moved to the Noske farm from Valday, which most of you know, is some two hundred miles northwest of Moscow. Ivan has been a guard at the government prison near Valday for almost thirty years. Prior to that, he had been a guard at the government prison near Rybon."

Suddenly it hit Vladimir. This man was the prison guard at Rybon who had led his father away to his cell the last time he ever saw him. And the pastor had just said Chikov and his wife were born-again people!

Suvoro went on. "The government forced Ivan to retire when he turned seventy, and through the underground church grapevine, he learned that Petr was looking for a hired man to help him on his farm. They got together, and the Chikovs now live on the Noske farm in the hired man's house."

There were some amens, and the pastor looked at the Chikovs. "We welcome you, dear brother and sister."

Sitting next to her husband, Sasha could tell he was tense. Suddenly Vladimir got up from his chair, moved to Ivan Chikov, and said, "You know me, don't you? I saw recognition on your face when you looked at me a few minutes ago."

Ivan smiled as everyone looked on, and said, "Yes. You are Vladimir Petrovna. I asked the Noskes about you. They said you now live on the farm your father had and are members of the same underground church. May I ask about your mother?"

"She died three years ago," Vladimir said softly.

"I'm sorry," said Ivan. "I would like to talk to you after the service."

Smiling, Vladimir said, "I would love that."

Suddenly, Vladimir realized that all eyes were on him. Blushing, he looked at Nicolai Suvorov and said, "I'm sorry, Pastor. I met this man at Rybon Prison thirty years ago, on the last day I ever saw my father alive in this world. I . . . I didn't mean to hold up the service."

The pastor smiled. "No need to apologize, Vladimir. This has to be quite a surprise for you."

Vladimir hurried back to his seat, sat down, smiled at Sasha, and whispered, "Maybe he can tell me something about Papa."

Tears formed in Sasha's eyes.

Pastor Suvorov opened his Bible again, and preached a Christ-exalting sermon of hope and encouragement from Isaiah 9:6–7. He directed their attention to the words in verse 6: "The government shall be upon his shoulder." He then pointed out the future tense: "shall be." He referred to 2 Corinthians 4:4, which calls Satan the "god of this world," reminding them that at present, there was murder, war, bloodshed, and the martyrdom of God's born-again people on earth because Satan was the god of this world.

He then took them to Revelation 19, showing them Jesus Christ coming to earth on the white horse to put the government of this world on His own shoulder. He showed them Satan ending up in the lake of fire forever in chapter 20 then took them back to Isaiah 9:6, emphasized that Jesus is the Prince of Peace, then pointed out that in verse 7 it says of Christ's government and peace there shall be no end. Jesus will establish His kingdom with judgment and justice "from henceforth even for ever."

In closing, the pastor told his hearers not to be discouraged nor to lose hope in the face of the persecution that was on them, but to believe God's Word. They had a great future ahead of them because they belonged to the Prince of Peace. Even though it did not look like it at the time, they were on the victory side. God's Word said so!

There were tears of joy as the sermon uplifted their souls, and the Christians vowed in their hearts to remain true to Jesus in spite of the persecution.

It was just after midnight when the service was over. Vladimir took Sasha by the hand and headed for Ivan Chikov, who was talking to Petr Noske. Alekin, Zoya, Olecia, and Kadyn followed.

Petr and Amana moved away from the

Chikovs and began talking to someone else.

Introductions were made, then Vladimir said, "My brother Chikov, I have only seen you once in my life. You were the guard who led me through the Rybon Prison to meet with my father in cell block number five. You took my father back to his cell the last time I ever saw him. Can you tell me anything about him?"

With a sad tone in his voice, Ivan said, "Bakum Petrovna died in Rybon Prison less than a month after you were there to see him."

Vladimir's face pinched. "Less than a month?"

"Yes."

Sasha took hold of her husband's hand.

Ivan saw the pain etched on Vladimir's features. He laid a hand on his shoulder and said, "But I have a wonderful story to tell you. I asked Petr a few minutes ago if I might have some time off to talk to you and your family. Would this be all right?"

A smile erased the pained look on Vladimir's features. "Oh yes. That would be good. Very good. When could you do this?"

"Petr said anytime."

"How about tomorrow?" asked Sasha. "Could you and Mrs. Chikov come here tomorrow afternoon then have the evening meal with us?"

"Why, of course," said Ivan, looking at Ridna.

"We would love that, Mrs. Petrovna," Ridna said, a wide smile spreading over her face.

"Excellent!" said Sasha. "If you could get here about three o'clock, Mr. Chikov can tell his story, then we can enjoy supper together."

"That will be fine," said Ivan.

When everyone was gone and all the chairs had been removed from the parlor, Olecia said, "Papa, I remember years ago that you mentioned about the last time you ever saw our grandfather Petrovna at Rybon Prison, but we've never heard any details. I would like to hear every detail."

"Me too," said Kadyn.

"We should all get to bed," said Vladimir. "Another time, all right? Alekin no doubt wants to head for home."

"I would like to hear it right now, sir," said Alekin.

"Me too, Papa," said Zoya.

Sasha chuckled. "I think you are outvoted, husband, dear."

It was nearly 2:30 in the morning when

every detail had been told and questions had been answered.

Alekin thanked his future father-in-law for telling the story, saying it helped him to know more about the stock Zoya came from and what made her the stalwart young woman she was.

When Alekin was gone, the Petrovna family headed for their rooms.

Lying in bed in the darkness, Sasha said, "What do you suppose Ivan has to tell us?"

"It has to be something to do with Papa," said Vladimir. "And I think maybe it has to do with what brought Ivan to Jesus."

Seven

The world around Kiev wore its white mantle proudly as dawn approached. Overhead, the stars winked out one by one, as if reluctant to let go of the night, and the rolling land, in its phantasmal majesty, awaited the amber benediction of the sun.

Even though the hour had been late when the Petrovna family finally slipped beneath the warm blankets of their beds, resulting in a relatively brief night, they were up before the sunlight crawled across the snow-covered land. There were daily chores for Vladimir and Kadyn to tend to at the barn while Sasha and her daughters worked at preparing the morning meal.

Excitement was in the air, and immediately after the prayer at breakfast, Olecia was the first to broach the subject. "Papa, what do you think the wonderful story is that Mr. Chikov is going to tell us?"

Vladimir was chewing his first bite of fried potatoes. He swallowed and said, "Your mama asked me the same thing before we went to sleep last night — or I should say, this morning. Since the subject was your grandfather Petrovna when Ivan brought up the wonderful story he wanted to tell me, I'm pretty sure it has to do with him. And I think we are going to hear that your grandfather had something to do with causing Ivan to become a Christian."

"I can't wait to hear it!" Kadyn exclaimed excitedly.

The others joined in, saying the same thing. Zoya added, "Alekin can't wait, either. He's going to be here by three o'clock if his employer will let him off."

Vladimir laughed. "Well, good! Since Alekin is going to be part of this family, he might as well learn all he can."

The excitement remained as Vladimir and his son returned to the barn to do some work on the farm implements, which would need repair and maintenance before spring plowing and planting time.

Inside the humble farmhouse, Zoya and Olecia made up the beds and cleaned house. Special attention was given to the parlor with extra sweeping, dusting, and polishing in preparation for their much-anticipated company. At the same time, Sasha was busy in the kitchen, setting bread to rise and rolling out dough for deep-dish dried apple pies.

The morning passed swiftly.

At noon, Vladimir and Kadyn came in, and Sasha had Zoya and Olecia warming up some leftovers from supper the night before for their makeshift lunch while she was busy at the oven.

Leaning over the open oven to check the venison she was cooking, Sasha said over her shoulder, "Vladimir, Kadyn, get your hands washed. We need to get you fed and out from underfoot here in the kitchen as quickly as possible."

Vladimir slipped up behind Sasha and put his arms around her just as she closed the oven door and stood up straight. Planting a kiss on her cheek, which was rosy from the heat of the oven, he said teasingly, "You certainly are in a twitter today, dear spouse."

"I have to be," she said. "I want things just right for the Chikovs when they eat with us this evening. You know I very much enjoy cooking and preparing for company, something I only get to do on a rare occasion, and I am going to enjoy it to the fullest."

The family sat down to eat, and within a quarter hour, Sasha inspected the plates of both males. "Looks like you gentlemen are about finished. I can hear the barn calling you."

Father and son rose from their chairs, still chewing. Vladimir moved to Sasha as he swallowed the final morsel, tweaked her nose, and said, "You hardly gave us enough time to gulp down our food, and now you are hurrying us out of the house again." The grin on his lips belied any gruffness in his voice.

Sasha stood up with a mock scowl on her face and hurried to the pegs where the coats and hats were hanging. She took down both Vladimir's and Kadyn's, handed them to them, and said, "Boys belong in the barn when the girls are preparing for company."

Olecia laughed and said to her sister, "Zoya, is this the way you are going to be when you and Alekin are married and you have company coming?"

"Sure," said Zoya, laughing. "Since the house Alekin bought in Kiev has a small barn, I'll have a place to send him to get him out of the house and from underfoot."

Father and son were buttoning their coats. Sasha put a hand on the posterior of each, and pushed them toward the door. "That's good, boys," she said, chuckling. "You can come in and make yourselves presentable for company about 2:30."

Vladimir looked at Kadyn, shook his head, and said, "Son, the Bible says it is better to dwell in the wilderness than with a contentious and angry woman. Let's get out of here and make the barn our wilderness!"

Everybody laughed, and father and son hurried out the door.

By 2:30, fresh baked brown bread and two spicy apple pies were cooling on the cupboard. The rest of Sasha's dinner was in the oven or on the back of the stove to finish cooking slowly.

Zoya and Olecia were setting the table with the best they had. Many pieces of china and crockware did not match, but the cloth covering the worn, scarred, round table was as white as the snow that covered the frozen ground outside the sparkling, sun-kissed windows.

Shortly before three o'clock, the Petrovna family — and Alekin Kolpino — gathered in the parlor. Vladimir and Kadyn had their hair combed and their faces freshly washed, and wore clean clothes.

Everybody was anticipating the arrival of their guests. It was bitterly cold outside, but a warmth glowed in the room, both from the fireplace and from each face as their eyes continually strayed to the window, watching for any sign of the expected company.

Suddenly Kadyn pointed toward the road. "There they are!"

The sleigh was moving steadily along the road and presently turned onto the lane that led to the house. Everybody waited at the door, and Kadyn was allowed the privilege of opening it as the Chikovs stepped up onto the porch.

The guests were welcomed warmly, and when their coats and hats were on the rack, Sasha and Vladimir led them toward the parlor. Ivan paused in the hallway, sniffed, and said, "Mm-mmm! Something back there sure does smell delicious."

"All in good time," said Sasha, chuckling. "Right now, we are anxious to hear your story."

Two chairs had been placed side by side for the Chikovs so the others could all sit and face them. Kadyn threw a couple of logs on the fire. Coffee was poured, then everyone sat down.

Ivan had their rapt attention as he began by telling of the day that eighteen-year-old Vladimir came to Rybon Prison on crutches with a letter from General Philpin Smydstrup. The letter, he explained, was directed to prison superintendent Markov Konstin, strongly requesting that because

Vladimir was a wounded war veteran with an honorable discharge, he be allowed to visit his father.

Ivan paused, looked at Vladimir, and said, "I notice you walk with a limp. Does the old wound still give you any pain?"

"There's some pain now and then," replied Vladimir, "but mostly it's just the inconvenience of the limp that bothers me. The bad leg, of course, is not as strong as the good one."

Ivan nodded. "I would like to say right here, Vladimir, that I owe you an apology."

"What for?"

"That day you visited your father, I was rude and brusque with both of you. Please forgive me."

Vladimir smiled. "You are forgiven."

"Thank you." Then he said, "When Bakum and Vladimir hugged each other at the close of their visit, not wanting to let go, I got rough with them. I curtly told them they had been given enough time to say good-bye. I used the word good-bye because it was positively the last time Vladimir would ever be allowed to visit his father."

Ivan looked at Vladimir. "Do you remember what you said to me?"

Misty-eyed, Vladimir said, "Yes. But you go ahead and tell it."

Eyes twinkling, Ridna said, "I just love this."

Ivan smiled at Ridna, then ran his gaze to Sasha and the others. "I will never forget it. Vladimir had tears on his cheeks as he said, 'My father and I are not saying good-bye. It is only farewell for a little while. We have a promise of eternity together where there is no parting.' "

The family and Alekin looked at each other, recalling those exact same words being quoted last night by Vladimir as he told them the story.

"Vladimir," said Ivan, "your words struck a chord somewhere deep inside me that day. When I was about to lock your father back in his cell, I said to him, 'What did your son mean that the two of you have a promise of eternity together where there is no parting?' At that very instant, two guards were drawing near us, and Bakum did not reply. When they had passed, Bakum told me he would like to explain his son's words, but it would take some time."

Vladimir thumbed unshed tears from his eyes. "That sounds like Papa. He would want to be thorough when he explained it."

"That's for sure," said Ivan. "I learned a little later just how thorough he would be. Anyway, Vladimir, your words that day to your father haunted me that night. I slept very little. You see, as a small boy, I had a grandmother whom I now realize was a Christian. She lived in the foothills of the Ural Mountains. I only got to see her a few times, but I remember one time when I was about six years old, my parents let me stay with her for a few days. She read the Bible to me, and talked about Jesus, heaven, hell, and eternity.

"Grandma died shortly after that, but the things she had told me stuck in my mind. I thought on them a lot. As the years passed, however, Grandma's words slipped from my thoughts and never came to mind anymore. That is until you said what you did to me that day before I took your father back to his cell. What Grandma had said to me long ago was vague by then, but was definitely related to what you said, Vladimir. That's why your words haunted me."

"I'm glad," said Vladimir.

Ivan took a deep breath, let it out slowly, and proceeded. "I worked the very next day so that I had about ten minutes alone with Bakum. He laid a foundation for his explanation about your statement by quoting Scripture that taught about man's fall into sin and his lost condition before God. He began explaining why God sent His only begotten Son into the world — but by then the ten minutes were up, and I had to move on.

"Two days later, I was able to get twenty minutes alone with him. He went on to explain why God sent His Son into the world, quoting Scripture as he went along. I was learning more and more about the Lord Jesus Christ. These sessions went on for almost three weeks with my periodically squeezing in fifteen to twenty minutes alone with Bakum in his cell. I clearly understood by then about heaven and hell as taught in the Scriptures, and that I was headed for hell without Jesus.

"Bakum had made the gospel clear, and this wicked sinner was under deep conviction about his lost condition. But I had not yet yielded to the Saviour. All this time, Bakum was not feeling well. He was having pains in his chest, and sometimes dizzy spells accompanied them."

Vladimir's jaw tightened. Sasha took hold of his hand.

"One day when I reported for work as usual, Superintendent Konstin called me into his office and told me I was being transferred to the government prison near Valday. This was on a Wednesday. Friday would be my last day. Ridna and I were living in a small house on the prison grounds — as did all the guards and their families. Konstin said we were to leave for Valday on Monday.

"Though I had not yet opened my heart to the Lord, I was very miserable, knowing if I were to die, I would go to hell. I tried to see Bakum alone that day, but I was not able to work it. I tried again on Thursday, but found it impossible. However, on Friday, I was able to spend almost a half hour with him. He was feeling poorly, but welcomed the opportunity to talk to me some more about being saved, and with joy, he led me to Jesus."

Vladimir's voice quavered as tears spilled down his cheeks. "Oh, praise God! Praise God!"

"Yes!" said Ivan. "Right after I received Jesus into my heart that day, I told Bakum about my transfer, and that I would not be seeing him again, since this was my last day. I explained to him that on Saturday and Sunday, Ridna and I would be busy packing all our belongings, so we would be ready to pull out early Monday morning."

"I suppose Papa was saddened to learn that you were being transferred," said Vladimir.

"He was. The first thing he said was that if I was not being transferred, he would tell me how to find the underground church at Kiev and become a part of it. But since I was being transferred, he told me there was an underground church near Valday, though he did not know who the pastor was nor any of the members. But he was quick to give me information on the underground church grapevine, which would make it possible for me to locate the pastor. He strongly urged me to do so as soon as possible after we arrived in Valday and to do everything I could to bring Ridna to the Lord. He explained that the church would provide me with a Bible."

Vladimir blinked at the tears in his eyes. "Papa brought so many people to the Lord over the years, Ivan. He was a true soldier of the cross."

"How well I know that," said Ivan. "He wouldn't have been in that prison if he hadn't taken his stand for Jesus. He paid a heavy price for his faith."

"And considered it well worth it," put in Sasha.

Ivan smiled. "Let me tell you about that last moment as I was about to leave Bakum's cell after he had led me to the Lord. I made sure no one was coming along the corridor, then hugged him. We both were weeping. When we let go of each other, I moved to the door, then stopped, looked back at him, and said, 'Good-bye, Bakum.' He shook his head and said, 'It is not good-bye, Ivan. It is only farewell for a little while. We have a promise of an eternity together where there is no parting.' "

By this time, everyone in the room was wiping tears and sniffling.

Ivan cleared his throat, wiped away tears, and said, "On that Monday morning, I went to Superintendent Konstin's office to report that Ridna and I were about to leave for Valday. Konstin told me they had found Bakum Petrovna dead in his cell on Sunday evening. They thought it was heart failure."

Vladimir choked up and his chest heaved heavily as he wept. Sasha patted his arm lovingly. Olecia rose from her chair, stepped to her father, and embraced him. Zoya and Kadyn followed suit. Vladimir smiled at his wife and children through his tears, then looked at Ivan and said, "It looks to me like the Lord's last job on earth for Papa was to bring you to the Lord. When that was done, He released Papa from the prison and took him to heaven."

"I agree," said Ivan. "When I was told that Bakum had died, I found myself wishing I knew where the Petrovna family lived so I could inform them of his death. But I had only a vague idea that their home was some-where near Kiev, and being a farm, it would take time to locate it, time I didn't have, for I had to get to the Valday prison as soon as possible."

"That is understandable," commented Vladimir.

Ivan explained how he followed Bakum's instructions when they arrived in Valday and found the underground church. "I talked to the pastor," he said, "and told him the story of Bakum Petrovna, why he was in prison for life, how he led me to the Lord and died two days later. The pastor knew there was an underground church near Kiev and offered to help me locate Bakum's family, but by that time, I was settled in my prison job and would not have a way to go to Kiev and meet the Petrovna family."

Ridna's face beamed as she said, "Only two weeks after we started going to the underground church, I saw the truth of the gospel and was saved in one of the services."

"Praise be to God," said Sasha.

Everyone was weeping by that time.

Thumbing tears from his cheeks, Vladimir told the group of the conversation he had with his father on that last day they were together about the crown of life the Lord would give him in heaven.

Sniffling and dabbing at her tears with a hankie, Ridna said, "What a glorious day that will be in heaven when Ivan and Bakum meet again! And . . . and —" She paused to get her breath. "And I will get to meet Bakum and thank him for leading my husband to the Lord, which resulted in my salvation! Oh, I want to watch as Jesus places that crown of life on Bakum's head!"

Sasha's cheeks were shining with tears as she said, "It will be even more glorious to observe as Bakum kneels down before Jesus and lays the crown at His feet!"

Everybody agreed, and this led to a discussion about heaven and God's beautiful city, new Jerusalem. Being a relatively new Christian, Alekin asked questions about the city. Vladimir got his Bible and read to him from Revelation chapter 21 while the others listened intently. He pointed out that the city's light was clear as crystal, and that in the great and high wall there were twelve gates of pearl. He read of the twelve foundations, then pointed out the massive dimensions of the city. Alekin was amazed at its size.

Vladimir then moved into chapter 22 and read about the river of life and the tree of life. "And listen to this," he said with elation in his voice. "Verse 3. 'And there shall be no more curse: but the throne of God and of the Lamb shall be in it; and his servants shall serve him . . .' Yes, we will serve our Lord forever and ever. Won't that be an honor and a pleasure!"

There were positive comments from the group, then Vladimir got a soft tone in his voice as he said, "But the best part of all is found here in verse 4: 'And they shall see his face . . .' Tears glistened in his eyes once again. "Do you hear that everybody? 'They shall see his face'! We are going to literally look into the face of the precious one who suffered and bled and died for us on the cross! Oh, it is going to be wonderful to see the faces of Papa and Mama again . . . and the faces of our saved loved ones, and the faces of dear Christian friends. But just think of it! We will actually see the face of our wonderful Lord and Saviour!"

Emotions were running high with the prospect of what lay in the future for the persecuted Russian Christians and tears were flowing again.

Alekin smiled through his tears and said, "And just think of it! In heaven, we won't have to fear that the Cossacks might ride up and shoot us down for being God's children!"

Suddenly, Olecia jumped up and fled

from the room, sobbing.

"Excuse me," said Sasha to the group as she left her chair. "Olecia needs me."

Alekin's brow furrowed. "Did I say something wrong, Mr. Petrovna?"

"I haven't told Alekin about Barny yet, Papa," said Zoya.

"What about Barny?" queried Alekin.

Vladimir saw the puzzlement on the faces of the Chinovs. "Let me explain," he said in a low tone. "Olecia has long loved a young man from a neighboring farm. His name is Barny Kaluga. We were not aware that she felt anything more than friendship for him until about a month ago, when she shared it with us. Barny, however, is not a Christian, so in spite of the love Olecia has for him, she has never allowed anything to develop between them. She has witnessed to him about Jesus many times, and even though he tells Olecia he is in love with her, he says he cannot go against his family's religion. They have remained on a friendship basis, and this family — especially Olecia — has prayed for Barny's salvation without ceasing.

"The reason Olecia jumped up and left the room is that just yesterday Barny told her he has signed up with the Cossacks and this very day is beginning his training.

Knowing how the Cossacks hate Christians, Olecia fears now that Barny will never be saved."

"She has tried to get Barny out of her heart," said Zoya, "but he is still there. She says she cannot help being in love with him."

"Mr. Petrovna," said Alekin, "I'm sorry for bringing up the Cossacks."

"You had no way of knowing it would upset her, Alekin," Vladimir said kindly.

Ivan said, "Vladimir, since Barny has joined the Cossacks, won't he feel obligated to report to them that this is a Christian family and part of the underground church?"

"He has assured Olecia that he will not do so. And I believe him."

Olecia had run to her room and closed the door. By the time Sasha opened the door and entered, she found the girl huddled on her bed, her face buried in a pillow, and sobs wracking her slender body.

Sasha eased down on the bed, laid a steady hand on her daughter's shoulder and said, "Let Mama hold you, sweetheart."

Olecia sat up and reached for her mother. Sasha gathered the trembling girl into her warm, comforting arms. She gently ran her hands over Olecia's dark, shiny hair while whispering, "Go ahead, honey. Cry it out. Then we will talk about it."

Sasha held her tight until the sobbing stopped and the trembling ceased. Easing back from her mother's embrace, Olecia looked into a face full of compassion and care.

"Sweetheart," Sasha said, brushing tear-soaked hair from her daughter's eyes, "our God is still in control, and He is able to rescue Barny from Satan's clutches and the wicked influence of the Cossacks. Barny still has a heart and mind of his own, and God — in His wisdom — knows how to reach him. The Lord loves Barny as He loves all lost sinners, honey. We have earnestly prayed for Barny to be saved. We must never despair; never give up hope of Barny seeing the truth and turning to Jesus to save him. You have given him the gospel over and over. We will continue to ask God to bring Barny to Himself. As our precious Bible tells us, there is nothing too hard for the Lord."

Olecia nodded, wiping a tear from the corner of an eye. "I know you're right, Mama," she murmured quietly. "If only I didn't love Barny like I do. As I've told you, I've asked the Lord to take the love away, so

I would just feel toward him like a friend — but I'm still in love with him. And because of this, my burden for him is heavier than if we were just friends. The burden has grown especially heavy since yesterday, when he told me he was joining the Cossacks. It's about to crush me."

Sasha placed firm hands on her daughter's shoulders and looked directly into her eyes. "Now, listen to me, little one. Psalm 55:22 says, 'Cast thy burden upon the LORD, and he shall sustain thee.' Don't ever put a limit on what God is able to do. Just cast your burden on Him, as He has told you to do, and let Him hold you up while He is doing His work on Barny."

As her mother's words penetrated Olecia's sorrowful mind, she felt the comfort of them. Nodding in agreement, she took Sasha's worn hands in her own and said, "Please, Mama, let's pray for Barny right now."

They bowed their heads close together as they sent their petition to the heavenly Father.

Eight

The clatter of gunfire echoed in a sharp staccato across the snow-laden Cossack firing range as a dozen trainees were firing revolvers for the first time in their lives. Some eighty years ago, the Russian government, under the direction of Czar Alexander I, had confiscated all firearms from the homes and businesses of private citizens. Thus, the trainees were inexperienced with guns.

Most of the trainees were missing their targets completely, but the instructors noted that three of them seemed to have a natural knack for the use of firearms and were hitting the targets.

Five Cossack unit leaders stood behind the trainees and observed the scene. Among them was Captain Lifkin Shanov, who was looking for one good man to add to his unit. The other leaders needed more.

Shanov's attention was drawn to a trainee who was drawing closer to the center of his target than the other two who were close.

One of the unit leaders pointed the trainee out and said to the others, "That young man has promise."

"He does," spoke up Shanov, "and if he does as well at hand-to-hand combat, I will use my seniority to lay claim to him."

The others smiled at him, and one of them said, "I do not blame you. If I had seniority here, I would lay claim to him even if he is not good at hand-to-hand combat."

On the firing line, Barny Kaluga finished firing the five rounds from his revolver, having hit the target every time and near centering it twice. The rule was that all trainees empty their guns then reload at the same time.

The trainee to Barny's right seemed to be having trouble with his gun and had Barny's attention. The hammer was eared back, but when he squeezed the trigger, the gun did not fire. An instructor was standing a few steps behind the line to the left. The trainee held the gun loosely, shaking it, and looked over his shoulder and said, "Sergeant Asmond, something is wrong with this revolver. The hammer is jammed. I don't —"

The gun fired, having slipped in his grasp, and the slug hummed past Barny's left ear, barely missing it. He reacted naturally by jerking his head to the side.

171

The instructor shouted at the trainee, up-braiding him for being so careless. He stomped up to him, angrily snatched the revolver from his hand and ordered him to report to the colonel's office immediately, saying he would be there in a moment. While the man walked away, shoulders drooped, the instructor said to Barny, "Private Kaluga, I am sorry. Are you all right?"

As cold as it was, Barny felt sweat on the back of his collar. He laid a palm over the ear. "I . . . I am fine, Sergeant," he said with a tremor in his voice. "The bullet came close but didn't touch flesh."

"Do you feel like continuing with the target practice? Your first lesson in hand-to-hand combat is next after everyone reloads and empties their guns one more time."

Still feeling the breath of the bullet on his left ear, Barny assured the instructor he would be fine. Inside, he was severely shaken from having come so close to death. Olecia's voice was echoing through his mind as she spoke of his need to be saved, and that if he died lost, he would spend eternity in hell.

Sergeant Asmond wheeled and headed for the colonel's office.

While the guns were being reloaded, Captain Shanov said to the other unit leaders, "I like that young Kaluga even better. Most trainees would have fallen apart to have come that close to death."

"You're right about that," said the man who stood closest to him.

As the firing commenced, Shanov wheeled and went to one of the instructors. "Sergeant Karnik, when the hand-to-hand lesson begins, I want you to pair off with that Private Kaluga. Put it on him real good. I want to see what he is made of."

"You don't want him hurt though, do you, Captain?" asked Karnik.

"If he puts up a good fight, a bruise or two will be good for him. No real damage, though."

"Yes, sir," said the muscular sergeant.

When the last shot was fired, Cossack Major Roban Mitlor ordered the young recruits to stand at attention. He addressed the near mishap for a moment, telling the trainees that they must have a healthy respect for firearms and be careful with them at all times. He then explained that the toughest branch of the Russian military was the Cossacks, and they were going to be trained thoroughly in hand-to-hand combat. In dealing with revolutionary uprisings and such serious problems, they needed to be adept at both the use of firearms and physical combat.

Mitlor went on to explain that in the first lesson of physical combat, each recruit would face off with an instructor and show him what he knew about the art. Each recruit would be graded, and the instructors would then know in what areas they needed the most training.

He suggested that in spite of the frigid air, they remove their coats. They would soon warm up as the lesson progressed. All recruits and instructors would be engaging at the same time.

Each instructor then approached his particular student as coats were peeled off and hats laid aside.

Barny's head bobbed as he saw the muscular Sergeant Boord Karnik coming straight toward him. Karnik was not a large man. He was only an inch or two taller than Barny, and outweighed him not more than ten pounds. It was his well-formed physique that intimidated other men. Over the years, Barny had been in fights with some of the toughest farm boys in the Kiev area, but only a couple of them were built anything like Karnik. He had, however, come out the victor even when those fights were over.

He had a flash of how close he came to being killed earlier, but quickly shook it from his thoughts. He was going to have to square off with the rugged sergeant.

Smiling at Barny as he drew up, Karnik said, "I have been assigned to you. I won't go easy on you. I want to see what you've got."

Barny nodded. "I'll do my best."

When every recruit had an instructor ready to begin the hand-to-hand combat and they stood facing each other in their shirtsleeves, Major Roban Mitlor explained that each instructor would decide how long his particular session would last, depending on how well the trainee did. He told them to make ready, and started the session by saying, "Go!"

Sergeant Boord Karnik took a fighter's stance, raising his fists to face level, and put them in motion. Eyes bright and lips pulled back into a toothy grin, he said, "All right, Private Kaluga, come and get me."

As Barny moved in, dancing on the balls of his feet in the snow, fists pumping, he took a glancing blow on the head and another on the shoulder as he backtracked. Karnik rushed him, but this time Barny fooled him by blocking a swinging right and stalling him in his tracks with a hard right to the jaw.

The sergeant staggered back, surprised.

He planted his feet, and as Barny came for him, he sent a piston-style punch toward his jaw. Barny ducked it, sent another blow to his jaw, and was about to take a step back when Karnik caught him with a solid punch. The impact of it sent Barny backpedaling.

Karnik glanced at Captain Shanov, who was watching intently. Karnik gave him a quick smile and made ready for Barny, who was coming in again.

Barny slipped past a swinging left and planted a solid punch on the sergeant's chin. Before he could step back however a powerful blow caught him on the jaw, and he found himself flat on his back in the snow.

Karnik stood over him. "Had enough?"

"Not yet," said a determined Barny Kaluga and jumped to his feet. The blow had stunned him a bit, and he was shaking his head to clear it.

Instantly Karnik bored in and swung an uppercut. Barny dodged it and retaliated with a punch that caught the sergeant on the ear. It was a stinging blow and sent streamers of pain through Karnik's head. He swiftly came back and struck the young recruit solidly on the chest then followed it with a chopping blow to the mouth.

Barny felt blood rush into his mouth and the brassy taste of it made him angry. He hadn't realized this was to be such a rough lesson. If that was the way it was supposed to be, all right.

Barny rebounded by striking the sergeant with a hammerlike blow to the jaw that rocked him. As Karnik staggered backward from the impact of the blow, surprise showed on his face. Before he could set himself, the young recruit bowled in and peppered him with powerful lefts and rights until he was flat on his back in the snow with Barny standing over him. Amid the roar that was resounding through his head, he heard Barny say, "Had enough?"

Suddenly a gruff voice said, "No more, Private Kaluga."

It was Major Mitlor.

Barny bent down, gave Karnik a hand, and helped him to his feet. "I'm sorry, Sergeant. I didn't know we were to hit each other so hard until you put blood inside my mouth."

Karnik wiped blood from his nose and said, "You don't have to apologize, Private Kaluga. I think you could give me some lessons!"

"You did well, Private," said the major.

"Real well," came the voice of Captain Lifkin Shanov as he drew up. "Major, I am officially requesting that Private Kaluga be assigned to my unit once he has finished his training."

"I will relay this request to the colonel, Captain," said Mitlor. "I am sure it will be granted."

Barny told Captain Shanov he would be proud to serve under him, then asked if he could go to the barracks so he could get the bleeding stopped inside his mouth. Given permission, he put on his coat and hat. As he plodded through the snow toward the barracks, he thought once again of how close he came to being killed earlier, and once more Olecia's loving words of warning about dying without Christ echoed through his mind.

At the Petrovna house, Sasha and Olecia returned to the parlor. Olecia's eyes were red and swollen.

"Is our girl all right, Sasha?" queried Vladimir.

"Yes. She's just having a hard time with her burden for Barny's salvation."

"I explained the situation to Ivan and Ridna."

Sasha had an arm around Olecia. "We just had special prayer for Barny. We asked the Lord to save Barny in spite of the fact that he is now a Cossack."

"Mama has been such a help to me," said Olecia. "She has taught me how to better trust the Lord for Barny to be saved."

Ridna set tender eyes on Olecia. "Bless your heart, dear. Ivan and I will be praying for Barny. If God can save people like us, who were so hard against the gospel, He can save a Cossack."

Olecia smiled. "Thank you for the encouragement, Mrs. Chikov."

"I will continue to pray for Barny too," said Alekin.

"Thank you, Alekin."

"I wasn't as hard against the gospel as Barny is," Alekin said with a chuckle, "but it still took a lot of prayer — as well as this family's faithful witnessing to me — to bring me to the Lord."

"I will keep praying earnestly for Barny, sister," said Zoya. "My life would have been so empty if Alekin hadn't become a Christian."

"I'll keep praying for him too, Olecia," said Kadyn. "I like Barny. I want him to be in heaven with us."

Olecia warmed her little brother with a smile. "Thank you, Kadyn. I just have to believe that the Lord will answer all of these prayers and do His work in Barny's heart.

He knows what it will take, so we can leave it in His hands."

"That's where it should be," said Ivan. Then he said to Vladimir, "I would like to hear how you and Sasha met, when you were married, and about the births of these fine children of yours."

Vladimir ran his gaze to his wife then said to Ivan, "Sasha lived on a neighboring farm. We met as children. By the time we were in our teens, we knew we were meant for each other. We were both in Christian homes and were brought up in the underground church. When I was forced into the army by the government in my late teens, Sasha and I vowed to each other that when the Crimean War was over, we would marry.

"When the war came to an end in February of 1856, I came home on crutches, as you well know, Ivan. With Papa in prison, I had to take over running the farm for Mama in spite of my bad leg. Sasha and I had to postpone our marriage plans. I had to work extra long and hard to keep the farm functioning and pay the taxes. This took up most of my time. The postponement lasted a little over four years. Sasha and I finally married in the spring of 1860. Mama was glad to have us take over the farm as husband and wife. She took one of the rooms at the back of the house and always helped with the cooking and housecleaning. So . . . we went on making our living raising sugar beets and potatoes."

"And the farm is doing well, I assume," said Ivan.

"Up until last summer, yes," said Vladimir. "I'll get to that a little later. Let me go ahead and tell you about the births of the children."

Ivan ran his gaze over the faces of Zoya, Olecia, and Kadyn. "Yes. I'm eager to hear about them."

"Me too," said Ridna. "These are such fine young people. I'm sure you are very proud of them."

"We are," chorused Vladimir and Sasha.

Vladimir went on. "It appeared after two years that we were not going to have any children. We prayed hard, asking the Lord to let us have a family. It looked worse after four years, then suddenly Sasha learned that she was with child. And let me tell you . . . there was great rejoicing in the Petrovna home!"

"I can imagine," said Ivan. "Ridna had to have surgery as a girl, which left her unable to bear children. We wanted them so very much, but it just couldn't be."

"But we can definitely imagine how you

two felt when you knew there was a baby on the way," said Ridna.

"We were so happy," Sasha said, glancing at her eldest.

"Zoya was born in the summer of 1865," said Vladimir. His eyes brightened. "And then we were blessed again. Olecia was born almost two years later, in late spring, 1867. And our third wonderful blessing came in the fall of 1871."

"That was your greatest blessing!" said Kadyn, chuckling.

Zoya laughed. "There might be room for argument on that!"

"For sure," agreed Olecia as she looked at her brother.

"Girls!" Kadyn said in mock disgust, looking at the ceiling and rolling his eyes.

"You asked about my mother last night, Ivan," said Vladimir. "I told you she died three years ago. It was pneumonia that took her."

"I'm sure you miss her terribly," said Ridna. "But now that she has had a glimpse of the face of Jesus in heaven, and is with your father, you couldn't wish her back."

"That's for sure," said Vladimir.

"Well, girls," said Sasha, rising to her feet. "It's time for us to head for the kitchen and get supper on the table."

"May I come and help?" asked Ridna.

"Of course," said Sasha. "We would love to have you."

"Kadyn and I have some cows to milk and stock to feed, Ivan," said Vladimir. "Would you like to come out to the barn with us?"

"Certainly," said Ivan.

Later, while the Petrovnas and their guests were eating supper, Ivan swallowed a mouthful of potatoes and gravy, took a sip of coffee, and said, "Vladimir, I just remembered that you were going to tell me about something that happened this past summer here on the farm that was a problem."

Vladimir nodded, swallowed, and said, "Yes. We had a serious blight on our sugar beets last summer. They did not produce well at all. The sugar beets are 75 percent of our crop."

"Oh. I'm sorry to hear that."

"Is this going to put you in a financial bind?" queried Ridna.

Vladimir exchanged glances with Sasha, shrugged, and said, "It is causing us some real concern, but we will make it through the winter, I'm sure. We are hoping things will be better this year." He took a sip of coffee. "Let's talk about the underground churches. Have there been new ones starting in northern Russia in the past year?"

"Just before we left Valday," said Ivan, "our pastor told the church he had learned of two new ones being established in nearby towns. We haven't heard of any others of late. How is it here in the southern part of the country?"

"I'm glad I can say there have been seven started in the past twelve months. Even though the government is so strong against real Bible-believing Christians, and the threat of being caught is worse than ever, still we are finding in witnessing to the common people, many are hungry in their souls and are willing to listen to the gospel."

"This falls in line with the way it went for the churches in the New Testament," said Ivan. "They flourished best when the persecution was the most severe."

"Right," said Vladimir. "And history tells us it was the same way as time moved on. The harder the enemies of Christ fought against God's people, the more they went after souls. They didn't buckle under even though their lives were in danger. They just kept doing God's work."

Alekin said, "I am a relatively new Christian. I love the Lord and want to stand for Him no matter what comes my way. How can I know if I would stand true to Him and to His Word if I knew my life was on the line?"

"Son," said Vladimir, "the strength to take that stand in the face of martyrdom would have to come from the Lord, but He can only give that kind of strength and courage to those who walk very close to Him in their daily lives. It is the Holy Spirit who lives in us, and only by His power can we stand against the kind of persecution our forefathers faced."

"Without the Spirit's power on us, we cannot stand," said Sasha. "We are too weak in ourselves. A perfect example is Peter in Luke chapter 22. When Jesus was arrested and taken to the high priest's house on the night before He was crucified, Peter sat down outside with the Lord's enemies. When they accused Peter of being a follower of Christ, he was weak and cowardly, and denied it three times. Yet in Acts chapter 2, on the day of Pentecost, when Peter was filled with the Holy Spirit's power, he stood before the very crowd that had called for Jesus to be crucified and courageously told them they were guilty of crucifying Him with wicked hands. The courage to do so came from the Spirit, who had given Peter His power."

"To be strong enough to face whatever persecution comes to us," said Vladimir, "we must spend time in prayer daily, and ask God to give us His power, so we will have the courage and strength to stand in the face of martyrdom if it comes our way. Without consistent prayer, we cannot possibly be strong in our Christian lives. We must also spend time in the Bible every day; not just reading it, but studying it. Revelation 1:3 says, 'Blessed is he that readeth . . .' and it is a blessing to read the Word of God. But 2 Timothy 2:15 says, 'Study to shew thyself approved unto God, a workman that needeth not to be ashamed, rightly dividing the word of truth.' It is the Christian who walks close to the Lord by spending time daily in prayer, and studying the Word to get it into their hearts who will stand in the face of persecution. The Word is the spiritual food that makes you strong, and the Spirit's power, which comes by prayer, is what gives you courage to stand for Him come what may."

"That is what I want," said Alekin. "If I am ever faced with having to deny my Lord or die, I want the strength and power to stand and choose death."

"The Bible has a classic example of this very thing," said Vladimir. "It's in the book of Acts. It's the marvelous story of Stephen, Alekin."

"And what a story!" said Ivan. "Every time I read it, my heart is touched deeply."

Sasha left her seat next to Vladimir, saying she would let Alekin sit next to him. Alekin thanked her, and moved to where she had sat. Sasha took Alekin's place next to Zoya.

Vladimir opened his Bible to Acts chapter 6, pointing to verse 8. "Look here, Alekin. 'And Stephen, full of faith and power, did great wonders and miracles among the people.' Notice Stephen is full of faith and power. Faith comes from the Word of God, Romans 10:17, and power comes from the Holy Spirit, Luke 4:14."

Alekin nodded thoughtfully.

Vladimir then read him verses 9 and 10, pointing out that the enemies of God and His Word disputed with Stephen over the Word of God, but that they were unable to resist the wisdom and the Spirit by which he spake.

"Alekin," he said, "this kind of wisdom only comes from being a student of the Word."

To demonstrate what he meant, Vladimir took Alekin into Acts chapter 7 and showed him all the Scripture Stephen quoted and referred to in his sermon to the unbelieving crowd. He pointed out how the power of the Word cut the crowd to the heart, and they gnashed on Stephen with their teeth. Jesus revealed Himself to Stephen from heaven at that moment, and when he told the angry crowd he could see Jesus standing at the right hand of God, they picked up stones and killed him.

"Do you notice here, Alekin," said Vladimir, "that in his martyrdom, Stephen never flinched. He stood true to Jesus to the last breath. But I emphasize, he had the courage and power to do it only because he was a man of prayer and a student of the Word."

Deeply impressed, Alekin said, "You have answered my question, Mr. Petrovna. Thank you."

Vladimir smiled, looked around at the others, then said, "Let me show you something really precious. When Stephen saw Jesus in heaven on the right hand of the Father, He was standing. See that?"

"Yes, sir."

Flipping pages, Vladimir stopped when he reached the book of Hebrews. "Look here, Alekin. Hebrews 1:3. It's speaking here of Jesus. In the middle of the verse, it says, 'When he had by himself purged our sins, sat down on the right hand of the Majesty on high.' Note the words: 'sat down.' See that?"

"Yes, sir."

"But when Stephen saw Jesus looking down at him from heaven, He was standing."

"Why, yes. He sure was! He was standing!"

"Why was He standing?"

Alekin rubbed his forehead. "I'm not sure, I — Oh! I know! Stephen was about to come to heaven, and Jesus stood up to meet him!"

The others applauded Alekin, and Vladimir said, "You are so right. Psalm 116:15 says, 'Precious in the sight of the LORD is the death of his saints.' When a child of God takes his or her last breath here on earth, Jesus stands up to meet them when they arrive in heaven!"

Tears were coursing their way down Alekin's cheeks. Looking heavenward, he said, "Dear Lord, if I should be called upon to die for my faith, help me to be strong in Your power and in Your Word like Stephen was!"

Nine

That night as Vladimir and Sasha Petrovna lay in the darkness under heavy covers, she said, "Thank you, Vladdie, for going no further with Ivan about our crop failure, and for not telling him that we have no idea how we are going to pay the taxes on the farm. If you had told him what we are facing, it would have appeared that we are feeling sorry for ourselves."

"That's why I limited the information," said Vladimir.

Sasha laid her head against his neck. "Oh, what are we going to do? The taxes are higher than ever this year, and they are due in just over two weeks."

There was only silence from Vladimir.

Sasha pressed her head tighter against his neck. "Vladdie?"

Vladimir sighed. "I would not mind paying taxes so much if they did something for the people of Russia. But it galls me when I know our tax money does nothing but make the czar and the men of his cabinet richer." He sighed again. "And it galls me even more when I think of what happens to a farmer when he can't pay his taxes by the date they are due. The vicious Cossacks come and arrest him — and he is never seen or heard from again. The farm is confiscated by the government, and the farmer's family is left homeless and destitute. It's horrible, Sasha. Just horrible."

"Yes," she said, her voice tight. "How did the government in this country become so powerful?"

"The people became apathetic back in the last century," he said. "The government leaders made all kinds of promises, and most everybody believed them. Slowly the government got out of the hands of the people into the hands of the greedy and nefarious political leaders."

"And look at the pitiful condition of this country now."

Vladimir was quiet for a moment, then said, "I have thought a lot concerning what we have learned about America. The people there are free. The government doesn't hold them in an iron grasp. They have to pay taxes, of course, but from what I've learned, the government leaders are good men who have compassion for the people. And comparatively, the taxes are not nearly as high as they are in Russia. In America, the taxes do not line the pockets of the government leaders. They are used to make things better for the people. If a man cannot pay his taxes because of hard times, they work with him on it. They do not have a militia take him out and execute him, then seize his farm and let his family starve to death without shelter."

Sasha drew a shuddering breath, pulled her head back and looked up toward his face in the pitch-black darkness as if she could see him. "I . . . I wish we could go live in America."

"I have entertained that wish, too," he said, "but there is no way we could even begin to pay the price for ship tickets, let alone all the other expenses involved."

"I know," she said dejectedly. "I know."

"Back to reality here," said Vladimir, "I will go to the tax assessor's office next week and explain to them what the blight did to our sugar beet crop. I will ask if I can pay a quarter of the tax bill and make it up next fall when we have harvested and sold our crop."

"Of course it is worth a try, but what if they are coldhearted about it and demand the money on tax day? I don't want the Cossacks to come and arrest you."

"We need to pray about it, sweetheart," said Vladimir. "Right now."

"Yes," Sasha said, reaching under the covers for his hand.

With their hands clasped together — as they so often did when praying — Vladimir began pouring his heart out to the Lord, asking for His help and guidance in the face of their tax problem. He reminded God of the penalty that would be exacted on him and his family if the taxes were not paid by the due date.

"Lord," he said in a strained voice, "I feel like David in Psalm 55, when his enemies were threatening him, and he cried out, 'Oh that I had wings like a dove! For then would I fly away, and be at rest.' If my family and I had wings like a dove, we would fly away to America and be at rest. But we don't have wings, dear Lord.

"And of course, neither did David. He spoke of his fearfulness and trembling, saying his heart was sore pained within him. He did the only thing he could do, Father. He said, 'I will call upon God; and the LORD shall save me.' And David was able to say in that very same Psalm, 'He hath delivered my soul in peace from the battle that was against me.' It was then that he said,

'Cast thy burden upon the LORD, and he shall sustain thee . . .' "

Warm tears were staining Sasha's cheeks as she thought of how she had used that same verse to encourage Olecia just a few hours ago.

"So Lord," said Vladimir, "Sasha and I are casting our burden on You. Please sustain us as You have promised. I will do what I can to try to reason with the tax assessor, but the results will be in Your hands."

Vladimir thanked the Lord for all of His wonderful blessings and closed in Jesus' name.

"Oh, Vladdie," said Sasha, sniffling, "I love you so much. You always make me feel better when you pray. I know the Lord will sustain us in this trial we are facing. Thank you for being such a faithful servant to Him."

Vladimir pulled her closer to him, kissed her forehead, and said, "I love you so much, my sweet."

With their hearts made lighter by giving their burden to the only one who was capable of shouldering it, they both slipped into a restful sleep.

The next morning, Vladimir and Kadyn headed for the barn to get the chores done while Sasha and the girls were preparing breakfast.

Father and son glanced at the rising sun on the eastern horizon, then let their eyes behold the cold, clear sky that arced overhead, deepening in hue and becoming a dark sapphire blue as it stretched toward the western horizon.

Half an hour later, the cows had been milked, and while Vladimir was turning them back out into the corral, Kadyn was in the loft, pitching hay down to the horses.

Just as Vladimir was closing the double doors behind the cows, a small door at the front of the barn opened, letting in a bright shaft of sunlight and the slender form of Olecia.

"We're almost ready to come in, honey," said Vladimir. "Your brother is feeding the horses right now."

"Breakfast isn't quite ready yet, Papa," said Olecia, "but Mama wanted me to come and tell you that Uncle Murom and Aunt Oksana are here."

"Oh? I didn't think they would be here for another couple of weeks."

Kadyn was making his way down the ladder from the hayloft as Olecia said, "They had to come to Kiev yesterday for some supplies. They stayed at the hotel last night, but wanted to spend a little time with us before they head for home."

"Well, I'm glad they're here, honey. Tell Mama we'll be in as soon as we finish up."

When Olecia was gone, father and son began spreading straw on the barn floor. Vladimir thought about Murom and Oksana Tambov's successful wheat farm some sixty-five miles west of Kiev. He wished he had done as well with his potatoes and beets as Murom had done with his wheat. Of course, Murom's farm was half again larger than Vladimir's and no blight had struck his crop.

"I'm glad your uncle and aunt could come by," Vladimir said to Kadyn. "It's been better than a month since we've seen them. I know how much your mama misses being close to her sister."

"She sure does, Papa," said the boy. "Mama is always so happy when she and Aunt Oksana can have some time together."

Within a few minutes, the straw had been spread. Father and son put the pitchforks away, picked up the milk buckets, and headed for the house. When they entered the kitchen, Murom and Oksana greeted them warmly, and after the milk had been poured through a strainer into a large lidded can and placed on the back porch to cool, everyone sat down for breakfast.

As they were eating, Vladimir asked how their underground church was doing, and received a good report. The church the Tambovs belonged to held their services in farm homes as did the one near Kiev. The group discussed the increasing danger of being a part of an underground church, but all agreed they would never give it up. They needed the preaching of the Word and the fellowship of other Christians.

When everyone had finished eating, Murom ran his gaze over the faces of the Petrovna family and said, "Actually, Oksana and I are here for more than just one of our normal visits. We have something to share with you."

Sasha could tell it was something important by the look in her sister's eyes. She was even more convinced of its importance when Oksana — who was seated beside her — reached over and took hold of her hand.

Murom cleared his throat nervously. "Oksana and I haven't said anything to you about it before, but we have been saving our money with a particular goal in mind." He paused, and took a deep breath. "We are going to leave Russia and move to the United States of America."

The Petrovna family could only stare in stunned silence at Murom. Oksana squeezed Sasha's hand and said, "We have had enough of the czar's oppression. We are going across the sea to begin a new life in that wonderful free country."

Sasha's lips quivered as she said, "I . . . I had no idea you were planning such a move."

"Neither did I," said Vladimir, rubbing the back of his neck. "Not that I can blame you, though. I wish we could go to America, too, but we don't have the money to make the trip."

Sasha ran her gaze from Murom to Oksana. "H-how soon will you be leaving?"

"We have sold the farm," said Murom, "and we must vacate it within four weeks. We plan to leave for the Netherlands in about three weeks, where we will board a ship for America. We will come back and see you once more before we leave."

Sasha's eyes misted as she rose from her chair, bent down, and put her arms around her sister. "Oh, Oksana," she said with a tremor in her voice, "you and I have always had such an exceptional closeness. It has been hard enough getting to see you only five or six times a year, but I can't imagine what life will be like with you living so far away."

Oksana kissed Sasha's cheek and put an arm around her shaking shoulder. "I'm sorry we had to spring this on you so suddenly. As Murom said, we have been saving money toward this end, but everything just fell into place so quickly. We hadn't even put the farm up for sale yet. One day a man came to our door and asked if we would consider selling the farm. When we heard the sum he was willing to pay for it, we knew the Lord had answered our prayers. It happened so fast, we are still trying to catch our breath. And there is so much to do before we leave."

Sasha's tears began spilling down her cheeks as they let go of each other. "I will miss you so much."

"Please don't grieve, sister," said Oksana. "Try to be happy for us."

A stab of guilt pierced Sasha's heart. "Oh, of course I'm happy for you. I wish we could go to America, too, as Vladimir has said. I'm glad the Lord is making it possible for you to get away from the oppression here." She dabbed at her eyes with the apron that was tied to her waist. "It's just that . . . just that I am going to miss you so much."

"We will both miss all of you terribly," said Murom, "but the Lord has opened this door of escape for us, and we must go."

"We understand that," said Vladimir.

"All of us understand, Uncle Murom," said Zoya. "If Alekin could go with us and we had the money to do it, I would be very happy to go to America."

"Me too," said Kadyn. "From what I have heard, America is a great place to live. And they don't have Cossacks, either."

Olecia's features compressed painfully. Sasha saw it, and knew what Olecia was thinking. If she went to America, she would never see Barny again.

"Well, Mrs. Tambov," Murom said to Oksana, "we had better head for home if we are going to make it before nightfall."

The Petrovnas put on their coats as the Tambovs were donning theirs, and walked out to the sleigh where the horses were swishing their tails and breathing clouds of vapor into the icy air.

Sasha embraced Murom and said, "You will come back and see us before you leave?"

"Oh yes. That's a promise. We wouldn't go without seeing you one more time. And Oksana and I talked about it. We may come back to Russia for a visit in three or four years."

"I hope so," said Sasha, then turned toward her sister, who was being hugged by Zoya.

Olecia and Kadyn had already hugged their aunt and were now hugging their uncle.

Sasha and Oksana embraced each other for a long moment, then with tears glistening in her eyes, Sasha said, "I will look forward to seeing you soon . . . before you leave for America."

"Yes. Soon," said Oksana.

Murom helped Oksana into the sleigh, then hurried around the front of the team and hopped in. Taking reins in hand, he put an arm around a teary-eyed Oksana and pulled her close to him. Snapping the reins, he clucked to the horses, and the sleigh began to glide over the snow.

A quivering smile broke through Oksana's tears and she waved to her sister and her family who stood in the barren, frozen yard of their meager farm.

Vladimir wrapped Sasha in his arms, and they stood with their children flanking them as they watched the sleigh disappear beyond a small hill.

Late in the afternoon that same day, Alekin Kolpino left the lumber and hardware store where he was employed and started down the street. He was almost to the corner where he would turn and head into the residential area where his house was located when he saw four black-uniformed Cossacks coming from the other direction on horseback. Suddenly one of them shouted and pointed toward a young man on the street, who had just come out of Joslun's Grocery. The Cossacks instantly put their horses to a gallop.

Alekin recognized the young man as Tonn Cumbro, who was employed at the grocery store and was a member of the underground church that met there in town. Tonn's employer, Kajer Joslun, was also a member of the underground church. Alekin and Tonn had talked a few times, each knowing that the other was a Christian.

Tonn stiffened and looked as if he were going to bolt, but the Cossacks drew their revolvers as they pulled rein, skidding to a stop. The leader, who was a young man himself, could be identified by the gold braid on his uniform. Alekin was within hearing distance when he stopped to observe, as many others on the street were doing. The leader warned Tonn Cumbro that if he moved a muscle they would shoot him down.

While Tonn was being held at gunpoint, the leader dismounted with a scowl on his face and told him they had a report that he was a Christian and was so bold as to carry a

Bible with him. They had come to confront him about it.

Alekin's heart went out to Tonn as the Cossack leader made him remove his coat. He then plunged his hand into Tonn's coat pocket and it came out holding a small Bible.

The leader shook the Bible in Tonn's face asking angrily if he knew the penalty for having a Bible in his possession. Quietly, Tonn replied that he did. The leader gave him the opportunity then and there to renounce his faith in Jesus Christ, and Tonn refused.

The leader angrily jammed the coat against Tonn's chest and told him he was under arrest. They put Tonn on a horse with another Cossack and rode away.

Alekin saw Kajer Joslun standing at the store window, weeping. As the people on the street began moving once more, Alekin went into the store. "Mr. Joslun," he said, "do you have any idea who might have known that Tonn carried his Bible in his coat pocket?"

"I do not," said Joslun, wiping the tears from his cheek. "Tonn loved to read his Bible during his lunchtime and when business was slow. He . . . he will die now. We will never see him again on this earth."

His heart heavy, Alekin nodded glumly. He patted the older man's shoulder, turned, and headed for home. As he walked briskly in the cold air, he thought of Stephen in Acts 7, and what Zoya's father had said: "Do you notice, Alekin, that in his martyrdom, Stephen never flinched. He stood true to Jesus to the last breath."

Alekin then recalled how Vladimir Petrovna had pointed out that when Stephen was about to die and go to heaven, Jesus stood up to meet him.

Almost blinded by his tears as he moved down the street, Alekin said, "Lord Jesus, I know You will be standing up to meet Tonn when the Cossacks execute him, for precious in Your sight is the death of Your saints."

The underground church service was scheduled on Tuesday night the following week in the home of farmer Theobold Engst and his wife, Nina.

The chairs were set up, and the potbellied stove was giving off welcome warmth as people began to arrive. Each family had placed their wagon or sleigh in the Engst barn.

Theobold and Nina, who were in their early sixties, were at the door to greet them and help them place their wraps in a small room off the hall across from the parlor.

Pastor Nicolai Suvorov, his wife, Katrina, and their three children were among the first to arrive, and moments later, the Petrovna family and Alekin Kolpino came in. On their heels, Parkum and Tsarina Wierenga arrived with their two small children. The Wierengas had missed the service the previous week because the children were down with colds.

Another family arrived, who always brought a forty-five-year-old widow, Elsa Muniz, with them. Elsa's husband had died of consumption three years previously.

Next to arrive were Petr and Amana Noske, along with Ivan and Ridna Chikov.

As the people mingled and talked, Tonn Cumbro's name was heard repeatedly.

Service time was set for ten o'clock, and by that time, forty-two people were there.

After prayer, Pastor Suvorov brought up Tonn Cumbro, explaining that Alekin had shared with him what he saw and heard. Suvorov told them that he had been in contact with both the pastor of the Kiev underground church and Kajer Joslun. Tonn indeed had not been seen nor heard from since the Cossacks arrested him and took him away.

Opening his Bible, Suvorov said, "In honor of brave and true Tonn Cumbro, I am going to speak to you tonight from Revelation 2:10 about the crown of life the Lord Jesus said He is going to give to those who are faithful to Him even unto death. Speaking to the persecuted saints in the church at Smyrna, Jesus said, 'Fear none of those things which thou shalt suffer: behold, the devil shall —' "

Suddenly the pastor was interrupted as the door burst open and six men in black uniforms barged in, waving their weapons. The Cossack leader barked loudly, "Everybody sit still and be quiet!"

Eyes were wide, and everyone in the group had a pounding heart. Zoya grasped Alekin's hand, as Sasha did with Vladimir. Olecia's gaze flicked from face to face among the Cossacks as Kadyn took hold of her hand, and was relieved to see that Barny Kaluga was not one of them.

The Cossack leader, who was older than the other five by twenty years, said, "I am Captain Oren Luchev, and I warn you . . . nobody move!"

While the other five men in black positioned themselves in a circle around the group, revolvers ready, Luchev stepped up to the pastor, who still held the Bible in his hand. "What is your name?"

"Nicolai Suvorov."

"And I suppose you are the pastor of this unlawful underground church."

Katrina Suvorov encircled her three children in her arms. The terror that she felt as she watched the wicked Cossack captain confronting her husband froze the current of her blood.

Nicolai Suvorov held his head high and his back straight as he looked Captain Luchev in the eye and said, "I am pastor of this church, Captain, but it is only unlawful with the Russian government. Not with God."

Luchev laughed wickedly. "God, eh? And I suppose you really believe that Bible in your hand is God's Word and speaks the truth."

Alekin's mind flashed to Tonn Cumbro, who no doubt had died because he would not renounce his faith in the Bible and its author. In his peripheral vision, he could see that Zoya's features were chalky white.

Their clasped hands were trembling, and Alekin knew his hand was shaking as much as hers.

Certain he was about to die, Suvorov said in a level voice, "Captain, I do believe this Bible is God's Word, and I assure you,

I believe every word of it from cover to cover."

"Now, Pastor Suvorov, you do not really believe that Jesus Christ was born of a virgin, do you? Anyone with good sense knows that such a thing is impossible."

Elsa Muniz's entire body was quaking. She leaned her head on the shoulder of the woman next to her and started sobbing.

The Cossack standing closest to Elsa aimed his revolver at her head and snapped, "Stop that blubbering, woman!"

Elsa stifled her sobs, looking up at him with terror-filled eyes.

Captain Luchev gave her a malignant look, then turned back to Suvorov. "I asked if you really believe that Jesus Christ was born of a virgin."

Holding the captain's gaze steadily, Suvorov said, "In your estimation, Captain, I do not have good sense, because I absolutely believe that my Lord Jesus Christ was born of a virgin. You say it is impossible, but nothing is impossible with God. And I emphasize that the virgin-born Son of God is the only hope for sinners like you and me to miss an eternal hell."

The Cossack captain threw his head back and laughed. "And I suppose you will tell me that this Jesus Christ died for you and me, then came back out of the grave."

"Exactly."

"Nobody comes back from the dead, Nicolai Suvorov," Luchev said coldly. "That is impossible."

"In your estimation, Captain," countered the pastor. "But you are wrong. My Saviour did exactly as He said He would do. Before He went to the cross, He said He would come back from the dead after three days and three nights."

Luchev drew a slow, deep breath, his eyes turning dark with anger.

The group sat frozen in their seats, eyes fixed on the two men.

Lips drawn back over his teeth, Luchev hissed, "You know the law, do you not? What does the law in this country say is supposed to happen to men like you who head up these nefarious underground churches?"

Suvorov's face was grim. "We are to be shot."

Pushing his face closer to Nicolai's the captain said, "Yes. You are to be shot un-less —"

"Unless I renounce my faith in my Lord and Saviour, Jesus Christ."

"Correct. And?"

Without hesitation the preacher said, "I will not do so."

"You will choose death instead?"

Nicolai's gaze flicked to Katrina. Her fear-filled eyes were fixed on him, and her face was pale. She had the children clutched tightly to her sides. He could feel the eyes of his people on him, waiting to see what he would say. Looking back at Luchev, he said evenly, "You can shoot me, sir, but you cannot kill me. In Jesus Christ I have eternal life, which no man can take from me. Your bullets will only transfer me from the land of the dying to the land of the living."

"So you are refusing to renounce your faith in this Jesus Christ."

Nicolai set his jaw and nodded. "I am."

The Cossack leader gave him a steely look. "All right. So be it. But first, we will find out how many in your congregation feel as you do."

With this, Luchev turned and faced the group. "The law of Czar Alexander III is that if you, as individuals, will publicly renounce your faith in this Jesus Christ, you may walk out of this building and live. You will be free to go. If, however, you choose to be as foolish as your leader, you will suffer the same fate that is coming to him. Who wants to renounce Jesus Christ and live?"

Nerves were strung taut and throats were dry.

Again Alekin's mind went back to the conversation at the Petrovna house a few nights earlier. Little did he know that he would be called upon to face martyrdom so soon.

Unknown to Alekin, the same thoughts were passing through the minds of every person who had been in on that conversation.

Ten

In the cryptic silence that gripped the room, Captain Oren Luchev's words seemed to echo and press against the eardrums of every Christian:

"Who wants to renounce Jesus Christ and live?"

The silence prevailed.

Luchev's hard-edged voice broke the silence. "I have no time to waste here! If there is someone who wants to walk out the door alive and free, you must stand up right now and renounce Christ!"

Suddenly Parkum Wierenga rose to his feet, his brow glistening with sweat. His breathing was rapid and shallow as he licked his lips with a dry tongue. "C-Captain, I c-can't let my wife die and my children become wards of the state. I renounce Christ, and I'm asking her to do so too."

"And what is your name?" asked Luchev.

"P-Parkum Wierenga."

Looking to the Cossack who stood closest

212

to him, the captain said, "Corporal, write it down for our record." Then to Parkum he said, "Spell your name."

When Parkum had spelled his name and that of his wife, the corporal held the pencil and paper as if he expected to write down more names.

The pastor and the rest of the people looked on in a numb hush.

Luchev swung his gaze to Tsarina, who was still seated, holding her children close to her. "What about it, woman? Are you going to join your husband and live? Stand up and declare yourself!"

Tsarina's arms and legs felt leaden. Her pulse raced as she let go of her children, grasped the back of the chair in front of her, and made her way to a standing position. "I . . . I renounce Christ," she said, her voice shaking so that her words could hardly be understood.

"Speak up, woman!" demanded the captain. "Did you say you renounce Christ?"

"Y-yes," she replied, trying to control her quivering body.

"All right. Mr. and Mrs. Wierenga, you may take your children and leave."

Again, there was a dead silence as the Wierengas hurried out of the parlor without looking at anyone and went in the small room to get their wraps.

The Cossack leader ran his gaze over the faces of the group, and was about to speak when Elsa Muniz stood up and in a hollow, tremulous voice said, "I . . . I renounce Christ."

"And your name?"

"Els— Elsa M-Muniz. M-U-N-I-Z."

The corporal wrote it down.

"All right, Elsa Muniz," said Luchev, "you may leave."

Elsa hurried out of the room, and could be heard speaking to the Wierengas as they were about to depart, asking if they would take her home.

Sasha's lips were quivering as she squeezed hard on Vladimir's hand and looked at him through a film of tears. His lips were drawn in a thin, colorless line.

The captain ran his gaze over the faces of those who remained and said, "Who else will do as these have done? They are walking free at this moment and will be alive to see the sunrise in the morning."

Silence.

Luchev frowned. "No one else? Am I to understand that this high percentage of you are willing to die by being shot, rather than renounce this Man called Jesus Christ?"

Still no one moved. The people were

looking around as if to give each other strength.

Zoya felt Alekin let go of her hand as he rose to his feet.

In his mind, Alekin was picturing the Saviour already standing to His feet at the throne in heaven as he said, "Captain Luchev, in the Bible there were Christians who chose death rather than to turn their backs on the Lord and His Word. History tells us of multitudes of Christians who were put to death because they stood for Christ. None of us want to have our lives cut short by a violent death, but as you see, the rest of us are not going to renounce the precious Lord Jesus who died for us on Calvary's cross."

Luchev's features took on a look of amazed disbelief. He slapped his leg, eyes bulging, and said, "Are you people going to let this young man speak for you? Do you understand what I have been telling you? The czar says you must be shot! Do you understand?"

Slowly, Ivan Chikov rose from his chair. Ridna's features were pale as she looked up at him.

"Captain Luchev," said Ivan in a steady voice, "it is you who do not understand. To know the Lord Jesus Christ as our personal

Saviour and have the peace that only He can give in an hour like this, means more to us than one more minute of earthly life. As our dear pastor has said, we have eternal life, which no man can take away from us. You can see that we are willing to die for our wonderful Lord Jesus. My word to you and these other men is that the day will come when you will face death in one way or another. You are not going to tell me that you will never die, are you?"

Luchev held his gaze in silence.

"You will go into eternity to face an angry God whose Son you rejected," Ivan said levelly, "and God's holy Word says you will suffer the pangs of the lake of fire forever. "You —"

"No, we won't, sir," cut in Luchev, the shadow of a smile twitching a corner of his mouth, "for you see, we are born-again Christians as yourselves. We are not Cossacks."

A shock wave ran through the group that was almost tangible.

Ivan blinked rapidly as if startled by a loud noise or awakening suddenly from a deep sleep. "Y-you are not Cossacks?"

"No. I used to be. That's why we have the uniforms. I put in my twenty years and chose to retire from the Cossacks three years ago. These young men are wearing uniforms I had collected over my twenty-year tenure with the Cossacks. I am sorry we have had to approach you like this, but it was necessary so we could find out if this church is made up of real Christians who love our Lord Jesus Christ and are willing to die for Him."

Relief began to replace the numbing shock the pastor and people were feeling. Nicolai Suvorov said, "You had to have come to know the Lord after you retired from the Cossacks."

"Correct. Let me explain that we are from the Kremenchuk area, some ninety miles south, toward the Black Sea. Three of these young men are my sons, and two of them are my sons-in-law. We had a large farm a dozen miles from Kremenchuk. There is an underground church in the area, and one day about six months after I retired, I was working alone, trimming some limbs in a tall tree. I lost my balance and fell about twenty feet. When I hit the ground, it knocked me out. A neighboring farmer was driving his wagon along the road and saw me fall. He picked me up and took me to our house.

"The neighbor's name is Gustav Weltmacht. To shorten a long story, Gustav is also the pastor of the underground church in that area, which meets on farms like you do here. While in our house that day, he talked to my wife and me about Jesus. After a few more sessions on the subject of salvation, he led us to the Lord. Our sons, daughters, and sons-in-law were all saved shortly thereafter, and we became part of the underground church."

"Praise the Lord for that!" said Pastor Suvorov.

There were several amens from the group.

"So your name really is Oren Luchev," said the pastor.

"Yes. And I used to be Captain Oren Luchev."

"And do I understand that you have moved to this area?"

"Yes. We recently sold the farm near Kremenchuk and bought a larger one just a few miles southeast of Kiev. My three sons are married too. All of the family lives on the farm, and we work it together."

"So you must have learned of this church through the grapevine."

"Yes. It took us a little while to find you tonight, but I am glad we did. You see, my family and I have been hearing about underground churches all over Russia that have been discovered by the Cossacks, and when

confronted with the firing squad if they refused to renounce their faith in Christ, the
majority renounced Him, and the minority
stood firm and paid for it with their lives.

"When we learned of this church through
the grapevine, it is the closest to our farm, so
it is the one we wanted to join. But we had to
make sure the majority of the membership
was made up of those who would take their
stand for Jesus and die rather than renounce
Him."

Suvorov ran his admiring gaze over the
group, smiled, then said to Luchev, "You
found out, didn't you?"

"Yes, and we are very pleased. Like I said,
we are sorry we had to approach you like we
did, but we could not think of any other way
to find out for sure. We had to give you the
acid test."

Still a bit in shock, Suvorov said, "Your
approach was indeed quite unusual."

Glancing toward the door where the
Wierengas and Elsa Muniz had gone moments earlier, Luchev said, "I hope you will
be able to help those people who left."

"I will try, of course," said the pastor.

"We need to know, Pastor Suvorov, if you
and your people will have us. We want to become part of this church because we know
you will stand for our Lord in the face of

persecution and death."

A smile broke over Nicolai Suvorov's face. "You are welcome as far as I am concerned." Then to the people: "How about you?"

Vladimir spoke up. "I say we need their kind, Pastor."

"Yes!" agreed Theobold Engst. "Because they are our kind!"

Other voices — male and female — spoke out their agreement.

"Thank you, my brothers and sisters," said Oren Luchev. "We will be proud to be a part of this church."

"How many children are in the family?" asked Suvorov.

"Five, and one on the way," said Luchev with a wide smile. "So you will have a healthy bunch added to your congregation."

The pastor smiled in return then said to the people, "I think it's time you folks come and meet these men personally and introduce yourselves."

"I'll feel better when they are out of those uniforms!" said one of the men.

There was laughter all around, and family by family, the people approached the six men and welcomed them, saying they were eager to meet their wives and children.

After Alekin and Zoya had greeted the men, she took him by the hand and led him away from the others. Looking up at him with shining eyes, she said, "Darling, I am so proud of you. Maybe you should change your name to Stephen!"

Alekin blushed. "Honey, the Lord gave me courage to stand up and speak as I did . . . but I am not worthy to wipe the dust off of Stephen's shoes."

Zoya smiled. "I have an idea the Lord might see it differently."

Shrugging his wide shoulders, Alekin said, "We'd better get back with your family."

As the young couple moved toward the Petrovnas, they heard Oren Luchev ask the pastor when and where the next meeting would be held. Suvorov told him, then explained how to find the designated farm from where they were.

The pastor then lifted his voice and said, "Folks, we need to have special prayer for Parkum, Tsarina, and Elsa. After we pray, the meeting will be dismissed."

On Monday of the next week, Vladimir Petrovna entered the outer office of tax assessor, Yelm Sukeava. He found three other farmers waiting ahead of him. The young man who sat at the desk looked up without smiling and said, "Yes?"

Glancing at the door behind the young man, which had the assessor's name painted on it in large black letters, he said, "I am Vladimir Petrovna. I have a sugar beet and potato farm. I need to see Mr. Sukeava."

"And what is your business with him?"

"I must talk to him about the taxes that are due a week from today."

The young man shook his head as if irritated and said with a sigh, "You said your name is Vladimir what?"

"Petrovna. P-E-T-R-O-V-N-A."

"All right. I will pull your file." Gesturing toward the waiting area where the other farmers were seated, the assessor's secretary said, "Take a seat over there. I will call you when Mr. Sukeava is ready to see you. It will be a while. These other men are ahead of you."

"I understand," said Vladimir, then turned and made his way to a vacant chair and sat down next to a farmer he had known for several years. "Hello, Rhuben. You here for the same reason I am?"

Rhuben nodded solemnly. "Blight. Sugar beets."

The two men discussed their predicament until they saw another farmer they knew come out of the inner office with a sad countenance. His face was drawn and his shoulders stooped as he shuffled out the door. Rhuben's name was called next, and Vladimir watched him enter the inner office with the secretary, who was carrying Rhuben's file.

When Rhuben came out less than ten minutes later, his face was colorless. He gave Vladimir a weak little wave of the hand and left in a hurry.

The next farmer was taken into the office, and came out after a few minutes, looking as hopeless as had Rhuben. The same thing was repeated once more some ten minutes later, then the young man picked up Vladimir's file off his desk and said, "All right, Mr. Petrovna, Mr. Sukeava will see you now."

Vladimir was ushered into the inner office by the secretary, who announced his name and handed the file to the tax assessor. The man reminded him of an English bulldog he had seen in London once.

Remaining in his chair behind the desk, Sukeava picked up Vladimir's file and said, "Be seated, Mr. Petrovna."

Sitting down in one of the wooden chairs in front of the desk, Vladimir waited quietly while the assessor read through the few papers in his file. When he had finished, he looked at Vladimir over the half-moon spectacles that rested on the rather blunt end of his bulldog nose, frowned, and said, "Mr. Petrovna, what is it you wanted to see me about?"

"The taxes on my farm, sir. You see, last summer the blight hit my sugar beet crop, which is the larger part of what I raise. The smaller part is potatoes."

"And?"

"Well, sir, with our crop sales way down because of the blight, I am not going to be able to pay the full tax amount when the taxes are due. I am here to ask for leniency on your part."

"Leniency."

"Yes, sir."

"Explain what you mean."

"Well, Mr. Sukeava, I am prepared to pay 25 percent of the taxes due, but I need to ask if you will allow me to pay the other 75 percent next autumn after my summer crop is harvested."

Yelm Sukeava scowled, the folds of his ample face making him look even more like an English bulldog. His voice was gruff as he said, "Mr. Petrovna, you know the law. On what basis do you ask that I allow you a crop year to pay 75 percent of the money you owe the sovereign government of Russia, which is due exactly one week from today? Are you a relative of Czar Alexander III or one of the men in his cabinet?"

Vladimir wiped a nervous palm over his mouth. "No, sir, I am not, but I had hoped that because I am an honest, law-abiding citizen of this country, you might show me a bit of understanding, since I am a victim of the blight."

"You and how many other dirt farmers?" spat Sukeava. "So you are a victim of the blight. This is no basis for leniency concerning your taxes."

Vladimir adjusted his position on the chair, leaned forward, and asked, "Might there be leniency on the basis that I am a war veteran? I fought for my country in the Crimean War and sustained a wound that I still carry today."

"Your leg?"

"Yes, sir."

"Mm-hmm. I noticed the limp when you came in. But let me say plainly, Mr. Petrovna, that your being a wounded veteran carries no weight whatsoever with this office. You must pay your taxes when they are due — and I mean all of them — or suffer the consequences."

Vladimir felt as if his heart had turned to lead. Slowly, he rose from the chair, turned, and silently limped away. Before he reached the door, Yelm Sukeava called after him, "Do not forget, Mr. Petrovna . . . tax day is one week from today."

Vladimir nodded, opened the door, and stepped out, closing it softly behind him.

Sasha was pacing the floor in the parlor when she looked through the window and saw her husband trot his horse down the lane. He did not look toward the house as he rode past it to the barn.

Moments later, Sasha stood at the kitchen door and watched him plod through the snow toward the house. She could tell by the slump of his shoulders and the look on his face that he had bad news.

When he came through the door, she rushed up and kissed his cheek. "I love you, no matter what happened at the assessor's office."

Giving her a good squeeze, he chuckled dryly and said, "It's a good thing, because Yelm Sukeava doesn't love me, for sure."

"I have some coffee hot. Let's sit down, and you can tell me about it."

Vladimir removed his fur hat and coat, hung them on the pegs by the back door, and sighed as he eased down on his chair at the end of the kitchen table. Sasha poured him a cup of coffee, set it before him, poured herself a cup, then sat down at the corner next to him. "All right, tell me what happened."

Taking a sip of the hot brew, Vladimir sighed, took hold of her hand, and told her the story.

When he finished, Sasha said, "Oh, Vladdie, what are we going to do?"

He took another sip of coffee, set the cup down, and said, "Sweetheart, we have prayed earnestly about this tax problem together, and in the face of what I was told by the assessor today, I can think of only one way to turn."

"Yes?"

"We . . . we will have to go to Murom and Oksana, and ask them to loan us the money to pay the taxes. Next year when the crop comes in, we can send the money to them in America."

Sasha drew a shuddering breath. "Vladdie, under normal circumstances, Murom and Oksana would lend us the money we need without hesitation, but they are about to make their journey to America. They might not have the money to loan."

Absentmindedly, Vladimir was turning his coffee cup in circles. "All we can do is try," he said hollowly. "There is nowhere else to turn. The Lord hasn't opened up any other way."

"I . . . I know. Then, it appears that He would have us approach my sister and her husband and ask if they can lend us the money. At this point, it seems to be our only hope."

Vladimir nodded. "We will leave a little before dawn in the morning."

"How much of this shall we tell our children?"

"Well, since they are fully involved in the problem, it is best that we tell them the whole thing."

"All right. How about we have a little family meeting before supper and Papa can tell them?"

At the Tambov farm, Murom came into the house for lunch, having spent the morning doing some minor repairs in the barn.

Oksana was at the stove, pouring hot potato soup from a pan into two bowls. "Just in time, sweetheart," she said, smiling at him. "Get your hands washed."

Moments later, they sat down at the table together, and when they bowed their heads, Murom said, "Dear Lord, we thank You for this food and ask that You bless it to the strength and nourishment of our bodies." There was a slight pause, then he added: "And, Lord, please keep Your hand on Vladimir, Sasha, and their family. We know You allowed the blight to destroy their sugar beet crop for a reason. They have said little to us concerning their financial status, but as Oksana and I have agreed, their situation could be serious. Please take care of them. You know what will happen to Vladimir if they are not able to pay their taxes. We trust them into Your care. We ask it in Jesus' name. Amen."

When Murom opened his eyes, he saw Oksana wiping tears with the tip of her apron. "Darling," she said, "could I talk to you about something?"

"Of course. And then there is something that I need to talk to you about."

"All right," she said, wiping more tears. "I . . . I have felt the Lord speaking to my heart ever since we visited my sister and her family last week. I have even awakened several times at night and it seemed He was impressing me about something."

Murom smiled. "Let me tell you what it is. The Lord has been speaking to you about our doing something big for Vladimir and Sasha. I mean something really big."

"Yes. I must talk to you about it."

"I said a moment ago there is something I need to talk to you about. Well, I believe the Lord has been impressing both of us with the same thing. Let's see if I'm right . . ."

It was a somber time at the Petrovna supper table that evening, even though Sasha had prepared a savory meal. The subject discussed before the meal had stolen the appetites of Zoya, Olecia, and Kadyn.

Picking listlessly at her food, Olecia said, "Papa, how could the government be so cold and unfeeling? How could that tax assessor be so mean? Aren't government officials human?"

"Sometimes they don't act human," put in Kadyn. "How would Yelm Sukeava like it if a blight would attack his body and he would be so sick that he couldn't work and he couldn't pay the taxes on his fancy house? How would he like to be taken out and shot?"

"It seems to me, Papa," said Zoya, "that there should be some consideration for a man who wore the uniform of the Russian army and will carry a wound for the rest of his life. Especially when his crop was hit with the blight — something over which he had no control."

"Those facts didn't phase him, Zoya," said Vladimir.

"It wouldn't be that way if we lived in America," Kadyn said, his jaw jutted. "From what I've been told, the people in America have a government that exists for the people . . . not the people existing for the government."

"I'm sure that is true, dear," said Sasha, "but there is no way we can afford to go to America."

Looking at her father with excess moisture in her eyes, Olecia said, "Papa, what are we going to do? I'm afraid."

"Your mother and I discussed this at length, honey," said Vladimir. "We feel that the Lord would have us go to your Uncle Murom and Aunt Oksana and ask them to loan us the money to cover our taxes. Next fall, after we have harvested our crops, we will send them the money wherever they are in America and pay them back."

Zoya frowned. "But with Uncle Murom and Aunt Oksana making their move to America, they may not have the money to loan you."

"Your mama and I discussed this, too, but we both feel that the Lord is telling us to go ask them for help. He hasn't opened up any other avenue where we can come up with the money."

Kadyn's young features were gray and downcast. "But Papa, what if there's a blight on the sugar beet crop again next year? And what if —"

"Son," said Vladimir, "we can't operate on what-ifs. Our God is not dead. He is still very much alive and will be very much alive next year. He still loves us and still cares what happens to us. He has allowed this present trial to come upon us for a reason, but He also knows how He is going to see us through it. He has the problem already solved. He has told us in His Word to ask, seek, and knock. Our responsibility in this trial, then, is to ask, seek, and knock in prayer . . . and to trust that He will take care of us. God will do right. However He sees best to resolve our problem, it will be the right way."

"Papa's right," said Olecia. "We are God's children, and He will take care of us. It is our responsibility to pray and trust Him, and it is His responsibility to solve this problem for us."

"Everybody in agreement with Olecia's assessment?" asked Vladimir.

The family all nodded their agreement.

"Good," said Vladimir. "We will have us a

prayer meeting right after supper. We will lay this time of trial and testing in the hands of the one who loves us and has the power and wisdom to solve all of our problems."

With this matter settled, they gained their appetites. As they began eating, Zoya looked at her parents and asked, "When will you be going to see Uncle Murom and Aunt Oksana?"

"We will leave shortly before dawn," said Vladimir. "I wish we could take all of you with us, but somebody has to stay here and take care of the place and feed the livestock."

"We will do that, Papa," said Olecia.

"And we will keep praying, too," said Kadyn.

"That's what we like to hear," said Sasha. "We have a wonderful God, and He is going to take care of us."

Eleven

The sun had gone down, leaving its golden spray of light on the snow-laden land as Vladimir Petrovna guided the team onto the Tambov farm and the sleigh glided over the frozen wheat fields. A stiff wind was hissing out of the north, sending swirling funnels of snow particles against sleigh and horses.

Sasha tightened the coat collar about her neck, snuggled a little deeper into the heavy bear skin blanket that covered them both, and said, "That fireplace is going to feel plenty good."

"It sure is," said Vladimir, glancing toward the barn where it stood some fifty yards to the rear of the house. "I see Murom coming out of the barn. Looks like he's got the milking done."

As the sleigh was drawing closer, Murom saw them and waved with his free hand while carrying the milk bucket in the other. Both waved back, and Murom hurried toward the house.

By the time Vladimir reined in at the back porch, Oksana was coming out the door with Murom.

"Sasha! Vladimir!" said Oksana. "It's so nice to see you! To what do we owe this pleasant surprise?"

"We need to talk to you," said Vladimir.

"Well, come on in!" said Oksana. "I've got supper on, and if Murom doesn't make a hog of himself, there will plenty for everybody!"

Murom laughed. "I'll try to suppress my appetite, dear wife of mine."

Vladimir and Sasha looked at each other and smiled.

"You go on in, too, Vladimir," said Murom. "Get yourself warmed up. I'll put the horses and sleigh in the barn and remove the harnesses."

After Vladimir and Sasha had soaked up some heat at the fireplace in the parlor, Murom came in from the barn, and the four of them sat down at the kitchen table to eat.

Murom led in a prayer of thanks for the food, and as the four of them began eating, he said, "Whatever you two want to talk to us about must be pretty important. We're listening."

"Well," said Vladimir, "it's about what the blight did to our sugar beet crop. Our funds are quite low. The taxes on the farm are due next Monday and we don't have the money to pay them. I went to the tax assessor yesterday and asked for leniency. He would give none. He said I must pay the tax bill in full on Monday, or suffer the consequences."

"This doesn't surprise me," said Murom. "I don't think our government knows what the word 'leniency' means. I'm glad Oksana and I are going to America."

"Sasha and I hesitated to come here and ask for a loan from you because you are going to America," said Vladimir, "but it seems we have no other option. Since my life is at stake, we must ask if you could loan us the money to pay the taxes. We will pay you back after we harvest our crops next fall. We . . . we really hate to ask, especially at this time, but —"

"Vladimir," cut in Murom, "as long as it is in our power to keep the Cossacks from getting you, we will do it." A smile curved his lips as he looked at Oksana. "Would you like to tell them?"

"I'll let you tell them," she said, gleeful light dancing in her eyes.

Vladimir and Sasha exchanged a puzzled glance, then Sasha said, "Tell us what?"

Murom swallowed the food he was

chewing and smiled again. "Our wheat crops have been more than excellent these past three or four years, so taking the trip to America is not crimping our finances. Besides, we also got a good price for the farm. The Lord has been dealing in our hearts separately about something, and just yesterday we got to talking, and it came out. We had both been thinking the exact same thing."

The Tambovs looked at each other, and Oksana's eyes welled up with tears.

Murom laid a hand on her arm, ran his gaze between Vladimir and Sasha, and said, "The other day when we were at your house and told you that we were going across the sea to begin a new life in America, you said, Vladimir, that you and Sasha wished you could go to America, too. Remember?"

"Of course. We have talked about it many times and agreed that we would love to go to America and get away from the pressure that is on us all the time by the government. Haven't we, Sasha?"

"Oh yes. Because in America, people are free. Even Christians. They don't have to have underground churches. They have freedom of worship and freedom to build their lives without government interference."

Meeting Vladimir's gaze, Murom said, "The reason you gave that you couldn't do it was that you didn't have the money to make the trip. Right?"

Vladimir's brows knitted together. "Yes."

"So if Oksana and I were to pay your way to America — I'm talking about the whole family — would you go with us?"

The Petrovnas looked at each other, astounded.

"The Lord laid this on our hearts separately," said Murom, "and we agreed that we want to do it. We will pay your travel expenses, and wherever we settle in America, we will loan you the money to put a down payment on a farm. Both families can have a fresh start for our lives in the land of the free."

Vladimir shook his head in wonderment. "Dear people, I . . . I don't know what to say. This . . . this is so overwhelming."

"To say the least," put in Sasha. "I'm at a loss for words."

"Just one word is all we want to hear," Oksana said, reaching across the table and taking her sister's hand.

Sasha looked at Vladimir.

He swallowed with difficulty and said, "Murom . . . Oksana . . . the answer is yes. I know I shouldn't be . . . but I'm amazed at how our precious heavenly Father has provided the way out of our predicament. As you well know, I was raised on that farm, and there is a great deal of sentimentality attached to it, but if we stay and can't pay the taxes, I will be executed, and Sasha and the children will lose it anyway. Besides, our dream of going to America — which we thought would never be possible — will now become a reality. I can hardly believe it."

Tears were flowing down Sasha's cheeks. "I can hardly believe it, either."

"I don't know how to thank you for being willing to do this for us," Vladimir said, choking on the words. He cleared his throat. "But . . . but we have to have an understanding about the money."

"What's that?" asked Murom.

"You must allow us to pay back the cost of the trip as well as the down payment, once we have our farm on a paying basis in America."

"Yes," said Sasha. "You must let us do that."

"All right, if it will make you feel better," said Murom. "You agree, Oksana?"

"Of course."

"Well, it's settled then," said Murom. "Let's finish supper, and we'll get down to business on when we should leave for America."

The foursome went back to eating. After a minute or so, Vladimir said, "We need to consider Alekin. I'm sure he is not about to let Zoya cross the Atlantic without him. He will want to go with us."

"Oksana and I talked about that," said Murom. "I was including him when I said I was talking about the whole family going to America with us. We will be glad to have him along. He and Zoya can get married in the land of the free."

"Sounds wonderful!" said Sasha. "And just think, Vladdie, our grandchildren will all be native-born Americans."

Vladimir gave her a lopsided grin. "I hadn't thought of that. Sounds good to me."

When supper was over and the two couples sat down before the fireplace in the parlor, Murom said, "All right. Let's talk about when we need to leave."

"If at all possible," said Vladimir, "we should head west before Monday. The tax assessment office will advise Cossack headquarters on Tuesday, I'm sure, that our taxes were not paid on time. Knowing the Cossacks as I do, I can tell you they will be sent to the farm immediately."

Murom chuckled. "By Monday, the

Petrovnas and the Tambovs will be high in the Carpathian Mountains. The Cossacks won't know where to look for us. If you can do it, you should be here so we can head west together early on Friday morning."

"This won't work a hardship on you?"

"Not at all," said Murom. "Everything is in order, here. We can go anytime."

"Good," said Vladimir. "We'll load the family sleigh tomorrow after dark and hide it in the barn. We'll leave the farm before dawn on Thursday and be back here about the same time we arrived this evening."

"Fine," said Murom. "That way we can get an early start toward the mountains on Friday morning."

Vladimir and Sasha waved to the Tambovs as the sleigh pulled away from the house in the cold embrace of dawn the next morning. The land about them seemed lifeless with ice and snow, and as they reached the road naked trees towered over them, whose jagged branches resembled skeletal hands silhouetted against the brightening sky.

In spite of the relentless north wind that assailed them, the Petrovnas had unspeakable joy in their hearts as they began their long journey home. Almost stunned into silence by what had transpired the night before, the couple rode together and did not speak for better than an hour. Both were silently praising the Lord for His goodness.

Finally Vladimir broke the silence, his breath coming out in small white clouds. "Sweetheart, of all the ways that I have pondered over and over in my mind how to rectify our situation, I never once considered going to America. There was no way we could pay for the trip, much less be able to purchase farmland when we got there. God, in His wisdom, already had the way planned for us. When I told our children God already had the problem solved, I had no idea it would be this! He never ceases to amaze me. How wonderful to be able to get out from under the oppression in this country and go to America!"

"Oh yes," said Sasha. "The Lord is so good. I'm very ashamed for the way I so often doubt Him. You would think that someday I would learn."

"Don't be too hard on yourself," Vladimir said, turning to look at her with a wide smile breaking across his face, reddened by the cold. "God always remembers that we are dust — as David wrote in Psalm 103. We are only human, and He forgives our frailties."

"Bless the Lord, O my soul," breathed Sasha.

"Amen."

Both lost in their own thoughts, the Petrovnas rode along in the gliding sleigh, planning the many things that needed to be done before Thursday morning.

Upon arriving home just after sundown, Vladimir and Sasha found that Kadyn had the chores done, including the milking, and the girls had supper almost ready. All three were eager to know the results of their parents' visit with Uncle Murom and Aunt Oksana.

Sitting them down in the kitchen, Vladimir and Sasha told them in brief of the offer they were given, that they had accepted it, and that they would be leaving for the Tambov farm before dawn on Thursday morning. By Friday morning, they and the Tambovs would be heading into the Carpathian Mountains on their way to the Netherlands.

Knowing their father's life was in danger, all three agreed that it was the only thing to do.

Eyes bright, Kadyn said, "Oh, Mama and Papa, what a wonderful thing it is that Uncle Murom and Aunt Oksana are going to do for us so we can go to America! It is just as you said, Papa, the Lord already had the problem solved. He told us in His Word to ask, seek, and knock — and we did. And look how He has answered us!"

By this time, Zoya's face was ashen and tears were in her eyes. "I, too, praise the Lord for what He has done, Mama, Papa, and I want to go to America as much as you do. But I cannot leave Alekin."

"Oh, please forgive us for not telling you earlier, honey," said Sasha. "We talked to the Tambovs about Alekin, and they said he is welcome to come along. They will pay his way, too."

"I'm sure he will want to go with us," said Vladimir. "Aren't you, Zoya?"

"Well, it will take him by surprise, but I think so. But, Papa, I can't go if he doesn't."

"Well, one thing for sure, Zoya, you certainly cannot stay here. The Cossacks would find you and punish you in my place."

Zoya closed her eyes and shook her head. "I hadn't thought about that, Papa." Then looking at her father, she said, "Will you take me to town right after supper so I can talk to Alekin about it?"

"Of course."

Olecia suddenly began to weep.

"Honey," said Sasha, "why are you crying?"

Tears spilled as Olecia said, "Mama, if we go to America, I will never see Barny again. I have prayed so hard for him to be saved, and even if he gets saved, I will never know it because I will be in America."

Sasha left her chair, bent over, and wrapped her arms around the weeping girl. "Honey, listen to me. It is all in God's hands. This whole family has prayed for Barny to be saved. But even if Barny does come to the Lord, this doesn't mean he is the man the Lord has chosen to be your husband."

Olecia choked on a sob and squeaked, "I could never love anybody but Barny. If the Lord doesn't have Barny for me, I will be an old maid!"

"Olecia," spoke up Vladimir, "as your mother just said, it is all in God's hands. You must trust Him to work His will in your life. Right now, it is very clear that it is God's will that the entire family go to America and begin a new life together. We cannot and we will not leave you behind."

Olecia sniffed, choked on a sob again, and said, "Papa, I want to go to America. I want to be with my family, but — but — Barny . . . I —"

"You have to leave Barny in God's hands, Olecia. There is nothing more you can do. Now, let's eat supper."

Snow was falling as Vladimir and Zoya drove away in the sleigh with its lanterns burning brightly. Sasha, Olecia, and Kadyn watched them through the parlor window until they were swallowed by the night, then Sasha said, "You two might as well go to your rooms and begin packing what belongings you are going to take to America. Remember: The sleigh has a limit as to what it can hold. We have to take along food to see us all the way across Poland and Germany to the Netherlands, and oats for the horses. I know it will be hard to leave so many things behind, but there is no choice."

As Olecia and Kadyn hurried off to their rooms, Sasha thought about what she had just told them. A heaviness came over her as she looked around the parlor and realized how hard it was going to be to leave so many of her own things behind.

She bit her lower lip. This was the only home she and Vladimir had ever lived in as husband and wife. They would be leaving all of their furniture behind. The sleigh couldn't hold much more than a few boxes of clothing and personal items. Sufficient food for the family and the horses would take up the most room.

Slowly, Sasha moved about the room, gazing at the furniture and the few paintings on the walls. While the firelight threw dancing shadows on walls and ceiling, she thought of the wonderful times the family had enjoyed in this room.

She lovingly caressed the sofa, the backs of the chairs, and the small tables that held the lanterns. At the bookshelf, she ran her fingers over the spines of the books, most of which were written in English and had been brought from England to Russia by Vladimir's mother.

Sasha stepped out into the hall and let her gaze touch the heart of the old farmhouse. A hot lump rose in her throat. All of her children had been born in this house. In spite of having to live as Christians in the threatening shadow of the government, it had always been such a happy place, filled with laughter and joy. Now it had to be left behind. A flood of sorrow washed over Sasha, and she began to weep.

The snow was falling harder when Vladimir and his oldest daughter arrived in Kiev.

Alekin was sitting close to the potbellied

stove in the parlor of his small house, reading his Bible, when the knock came on his door. His mind flashed to Tonn Cumbro as he jumped out of the chair and hurried to hide the Bible in a small hidden compartment underneath an old chest of drawers.

Surprised but relieved to see Zoya and her father, Alekin invited them in, asking what had brought them to town at that time of night.

Zoya explained that she had something very important to tell him and it couldn't wait till tomorrow.

They sat down by the potbellied stove, and Vladimir remained silent while Zoya told Alekin the whole story.

When she finished, Alekin took hold of her hand and said, "Zoya, my love for you is greater than anything other than my love for the Lord Himself. I certainly understand why your family must leave Russia in a hurry. I will gladly go to America with you. We will marry in America and build a new life together." Then to Vladimir he said, "Mr. Petrovna, it is very kind of you and your family to include me, and I will express my deep appreciation to Mr. and Mrs. Tambov for making it possible for me to go."

"We know how much you and Zoya love each other, Alekin," said Vladimir. "When

God moves in Christians' lives, everything works out for the best. Since we have to come this way to head for the Tambov farm, we will come by here on Thursday morning an hour before dawn and pick you up. This will give you time to pack. I'm sorry you won't be able to take much with you, but space in the sleigh is limited."

"I understand, sir. I won't take more than is absolutely necessary."

"What about the house, Alekin?" Zoya asked.

"There won't be time to sell it, so I will just have to leave it. Tomorrow I will tell my employer that I am quitting my job. I won't tell him why, nor where I am going. I know we mustn't leave any clues for the Cossacks."

"That's for sure," said Vladimir. "They may pick up our trail anyway, but if we are far enough ahead of them before they do, once we enter Poland we will be safe. The Cossacks would not dare to pursue us beyond the Russian-Polish border."

"Yes, sir. I know. And am I glad for that."

"Me too," said Zoya.

Vladimir rose to his feet. "Well, daughter, we'd better be on our way. We have to stop by the Suvorov farm and tell the pastor we are going to America."

Alekin assured them he would be ready to travel on Thursday morning. He asked them to tell the Suvorovs good-bye for him, then watched father and daughter drive away in the falling snow.

The Suvorov children were in bed asleep when Vladimir and Zoya entered the house. Katrina gave them hot tea, and the Suvorovs listened intently as Vladimir told them the story.

"Though we are sad to lose you," said the pastor, "please know that we understand why you must go."

"Yes," said Katrina. "We will be praying for you that the Lord will give you safety all the way. We hope you will be very happy in America."

"Thank you," Vladimir said, giving her a warm smile. Then he said to Suvorov, "Pastor, I would like to give you our milk cows and saddle horses, if you will take them."

"Why, of course. When would you like me to come and get them?"

"How about sometime tomorrow?"

"Fine. I'll get a couple of the men of the church to help me."

"It would be best if you take them on the road rather than through the fields. Just in case it has stopped snowing and they leave tracks, I don't want the Cossacks to be able to trace the tracks to you. The road is traveled enough that they wouldn't be able to follow you."

"That's the way we'll do it," said the pastor. "Now, let's have prayer together before you and Zoya go home."

When Vladimir and Zoya arrived home, the rest of the family was happy to know that Alekin was going to America with them.

Sasha had overcome her emotions, and no one in the family knew about the tears she had shed over leaving the house and its contents.

Vladimir went to Olecia, whose eyes were puffy from weeping, and took hold of her shoulders. "Are you all right, honey?"

Nodding in jerking movements, she said, "Yes, Papa. My heart is heavy about leaving Barny behind, but I know I must go with my family to America."

"That's my girl," he said, kissing her forehead. "The Lord has a plan for your life. We know He wants us to go to America. He will work out His plan in that new land if you will let Him."

"I will let Him, Papa. It is hard to leave, knowing I will never see Barny again, but you and Mama are right. I must leave Barny in God's hands."

Dawn was an hour away on Thursday morning as the fully-packed Petrovna sleigh pulled out of Kiev heading due west with Alekin Kolpino aboard, sitting beside Zoya. There were some four or five inches of new snow on the ground. The sky was clear and the moon was already down, but the stars were twinkling brightly in their black canopy overhead. The only light to guide the sleigh was the starlit whiteness that surrounded them. They were all bundled in layers of woolen clothing and covered with heavy blankets, and they found it difficult to move in the tightly packed sleigh.

Many mixed feelings accosted the Petrovna family as the sleigh whooshed across the fresh blanket of snow to the muffled sound of the pounding horses' hooves.

Tears were quietly shed as memories filled their minds, and they felt the pain in their hearts of leaving behind their dear friends in the underground church.

At the last possible moment, Sasha turned around on the front seat for one final glimpse of Kiev, and looked beyond it toward the place she had called home for so many years. A lump rose in her throat.

Though she couldn't see the farm, she imagined the little white house sitting forlorn in the midst of the vast frozen plain.

Brushing away the tears with her mittened hand, she once again faced forward, her mind resolute, and her eyes fastened on what lay ahead. Moving her lips silently, she spoke to the Father above: *Lord, we are Your children. You have provided this far, and I know You will not fail us. You understand that, being human, this new venture comes with a little fear and trepidation. Give my family and me peace as we make this journey. Thank You for making it possible for us to escape before the tax assessor sends the Cossacks to arrest Vladimir. Please keep us safe all the way.*

Laying a hand on her beloved husband's arm, Sasha said, "Any second thoughts now that we are on our way, Vladdie?"

"I won't say that I don't have some fluttering going on in my stomach, sweetheart. But no second thoughts. I know we are following God's leadership, and He will take care of us and supply our every need. What's that verse you have quoted sometimes about the daily benefits when things have gotten a little tight?"

"Oh. Psalm 68:19. 'Blessed be the Lord, who daily loadeth us with benefits, even the

God of our salvation."

"Yes. That one. Praise His precious name."

Releasing the reins from his right hand, Vladimir patted the hand resting on his arm, turned to look at her, and gave her a reassuring smile.

Twelve

By the time the sun peeked over the eastern horizon on Friday morning, the occupants of the Petrovna and Tambov sleighs had the majestic Carpathian Mountains in full view. They squinted into the glare that came off the towering, whitecapped peaks and lofty snowfields.

To alleviate the crowded condition of the Petrovna sleigh, Murom had offered to let either Zoya and Alekin, or Kadyn and Olecia ride in their sleigh. The engaged couple decided to take him up on it.

Over the years, Murom had made several trips over the Carpathians into Poland and across Germany. He also carried a map in case his memory should fail him at any time. The route he had chosen would take them over Kuwalt Pass, which was the least hazardous way to get to the other side of the mountains from his farm.

By noon the two sleighs were in the foothills, running side by side. Murom looked past Oksana to Vladimir and said, "In about another mile, the path will narrow, and one sleigh will have to follow behind the other. If it's all right with you, I will take the lead, since I've been over the pass before."

Vladimir chuckled. "I wouldn't have it any other way!"

"Me, either!" said Sasha, laughing. "Lead on, O mighty Murom!"

Everybody had a good laugh.

Sasha thanked the Lord silently that even though they were barely off the plain, already there seemed to be relief among all of them.

Soon they came to the narrowing of the path, and the Petrovna sleigh fell in behind the leader. Within a couple of hours, they had climbed past the foothills and found themselves in the high country, where the snow was exceptionally deep. As the Tambov sleigh topped a ridge, Murom pulled rein and lifted a hand to signal Vladimir to stop. The Petrovna sleigh slid to a halt. Both teams of horses puffed clouds of vapor into the frigid air as everyone looked around to see ridge after ridge left and right, each ending in cliffs whose sheer, rugged rock faces were coated with windblown snow.

"I think it's time to feed the horses," said Murom. "And maybe the people too."

Everyone agreed and piled out of the sleighs. While the men were pouring oats into the feedbags, the women took out bread and cheese from the supply boxes. As with the horses, when the meal was done, everyone obtained water by eating snow.

Soon they were on the move again, and as the Tambov sleigh moved out ahead of the Petrovna sleigh and headed down the steep slope in front of them, Sasha eyed the two tents that were rolled up and tied to the rear of Murom's vehicle. She was glad Murom had brought along the tents. They would better protect the travelers from the night winds.

As the sleighs touched the bottom of the narrow valley into which they had descended and started climbing again, Olecia's mind was on Barny Kaluga. It grieved her that she would never see him again on earth, but drawing strength from the Lord, she prayed once more that Barny would be brought to Christ.

The higher they climbed, the deeper the snow. The travelers chatted about things past and future while the horses bowed themselves into the harnesses and puffed out small clouds of vapor as the path grew steeper.

Hours passed.

The sun slid low in its arc toward the jagged peaks to the west. Green and bright in the late afternoon sunlight, the surrounding forests of spruce and birch stretched away toward the ramparts of higher mountain ranges. The spruce on the lower slopes of the mountains gave way to gulches of misty green alder that crept up the ridges all around the sleighs, then disappeared into the gray shades of rock ledges and windswept shale saddles.

Shadowed canyons gaped alongside the slanting slopes on both sides of the path. High above them, embedded in the mountainsides were scattered, dark pockets where the sun never reached. In contrast, between the pockets were blinding white pillars of snow-covered rock, flanked by hanging curtains of glacial ice. Far above this frozen scene were the loftiest peaks themselves, hard-etched towers looming like sentinels as they erupted into the icy blue skyline.

Once they were in the high country that day, the progress was minimal because of the deep snow and the steep, winding trail. When the sun had disappeared behind the peaks to the west, Murom led them off the trail into a rock enclosure that would offer some protection from the wind, which was now picking up.

As the weary travelers were stiffly climbing out of the sleighs, Vladimir stepped up to Murom. "What about building a fire so the ladies can cook us a hot supper?"

"Fine," said Murom. "We won't have to be careful about building fires until we know the tax assessor has found out you are gone. Once he knows it, the Cossacks will be sent to find you. Sukeava won't know you are not paying your taxes until he closes his office on Monday. At best, the Cossacks cannot be on our trail until Tuesday. We'll have a good head start on them by then. We're looking at six or seven days yet before we top Kuwalt Pass. That is, if we don't get any blizzards between now and then.

"The Cossacks may never find our trail, but we have to face the fact that they might. If they do, it will take them some time. Maybe several days. I'm hoping our head start will keep us far enough ahead of them that we will reach the Polish border before they so much as spot us. However, since they can travel much faster on horseback than we can with these heavily loaded sleighs, we will have to watch our back trail very carefully in a few more days."

The group had gathered close, and when Murom finished his words to Vladimir,

Sasha said, "All right, ladies. Let's get some food out of the sleighs."

"And while you're doing that," said Alekin, who already had an ax in his hand, "Kadyn and I will go chop some wood."

An hour and a half later, the night was dark around them as the group huddled close to the crackling fire, anticipating a hot, hearty meal. The aroma of potatoes, onions, and sausage, along with strong, black coffee made their mouths water. When Sasha told them the food was cooked and ready, the other women quickly helped her dish it up. Murom led in prayer, thanking the Lord for the food, and the hungry bunch began eating.

They discussed the long journey ahead, the storms they could encounter — especially in the mountains — and the possible threat of the Cossacks. While they ate and talked, gusts of icy wind fanned the burning embers of the fire, blowing sparks and ashes away into the darkness.

Kadyn looked across the flickering flames and said, "Uncle Murom, since there is a possibility that the Cossacks could pick up our trail, what are we going to do if they catch up to us before we cross into Poland? We don't have guns like they do."

"Our only earthly defense, Kadyn," said

Murom, "is to do as I said and watch our back trail very carefully. If we can see them coming, we will have an opportunity to hide." He took a sip of coffee. "I said this is our only earthly defense. More than anything, we need to be praying for God's protection."

"And that we will do," said Vladimir.

Alekin closed his eyes as a gust of wind blew smoke into his face, then opened them as the smoke was carried away and said, "We all knew we had hardships to face on this journey, but to me it will be worth every hardship we have endured when we set foot on American soil."

Everyone agreed.

Alekin kept his gaze on Murom and said, "So you think we can make it to the top of Kuwalt Pass in six or seven days if we don't encounter severe weather?"

"Yes. If we are hit with a blizzard or two, we will definitely have to hole up and wait till the weather clears."

"Hole up like in another place with high rocks all around like this, Uncle Murom?" asked Kadyn.

"Something better," replied Murom. "At the higher levels there are many caves in the sides of the mountains. Some of them are quite large. Many of them are inhabited by bears, so we will have to be careful when we pick them, but when we get to the level where we start seeing caves, we can sleep in them at night. We'll be out of the wind that way. And if we have a blizzard, we'll be where we can keep a fire going and stay warm."

"What about the horses?" asked Kadyn.

"Well, as I said, some of the caves are quite large. If we can find the larger ones, there will be room for the horses and the sleighs, as well as ourselves."

"That would be good."

"Uncle Murom," said Olecia, "will it take us as long to get down out of the mountains as it's going to take us to get to the top of Kuwalt Pass?"

"Well, again, it depends on the weather, but going down will be a bit faster than going up. Then, of course, as we travel across Poland and Germany, we will not have another mountain range like the Carpathians to climb. Germany does have lots of mountains, but our route to the Netherlands will not take us over any of them."

"So how long will it take us to make it to Rotterdam, darling?" asked Oksana.

"Well, again, it depends on the weather. We could have some severe weather anywhere in Poland or Germany which would force us to hole up. But let's say it's only some normal snowstorms in which we could keep traveling. Since we can only cover at best ten to twelve miles a day, we are looking at about six to eight weeks from the time we reach the Polish border till we arrive in Rotterdam, where we will take the first ship going to America."

Zoya sighed. "America. It sounds wonderful. I agree with Alekin: It will be worth every bit of this journey when we set foot on American soil."

Everyone nodded their agreement.

"Well," said Vladimir, "it looks like everyone has cleaned up their plates. I think we boys need to pitch the tents."

"And we girls will clean up," said Sasha as the group rose to their feet.

"We'll put the girls' tent on one side of the fire and the boys' on the other," said Murom. "And, of course, we boys will have to break up the night into three shifts so one of us is on watch at all times."

"But there are four of us, Uncle Murom," said Kadyn.

Murom grinned. "I guess I should have said we men will have to take shifts. Since you aren't a man yet, Kadyn, we'll let you sleep all night."

Kadyn shrugged and said, "Oh, well, I guess I'll have to wait a few more years before I'm considered a man."

"Be glad it's still a few more years, son," said Vladimir. "We all pass through our youth too fast as it is."

"That's for sure," said Sasha, moving up to Kadyn and putting an arm around him. "Mama wishes her little boy would just stay fifteen."

The boy's features tinted. "Oh, Mama," he said, rolling his eyes.

Everyone laughed.

By the time the tents were pitched and all of the bedding put in place, the moon rose in the sky, paling the stars around it, and the wind was picking up.

As they all gathered into the men's tent for prayer, Vladimir said, "I sure hope the weather holds good till we get over the pass."

"Me too," said Murom.

They had not bothered to take lanterns out of the sleighs, so the only light in the tent was from the fire, which had been fed more wood only moments before.

While the wind whistled around the tent, Vladimir led them in prayer, asking the Lord for safety as they continued their journey the next morning, and giving God thanks for His continual blessings.

Since their Bibles were in the sleighs and they were in near darkness, Vladimir suggested that they each quote a favorite Scripture verse. When they had finished, Vladimir said, "Even though the Cossacks may be on our trail in a few days, I believe we all have to say that there is already a measure of freedom among us."

"Amen to that," said Murom. "Amen to that."

"I'll put some more wood on the fire," said Vladimir. "We must all do our best to get what rest we can. We have a long, arduous journey ahead of us. I'll take the first watch. Who wants to be second?"

"I'll be second," said Murom.

"That makes me third," Alekin said with a smile.

Vladimir nodded. "All right. Murom, sleep tight. I'll be shaking you in a little over two hours."

With that the men went to their tent, and people in both tents made themselves as comfortable and warm as possible, huddled in their heavy coats and blankets.

Suddenly, everyone heard it. It rose, a strange, wild, mournful howl. Not the howl of a prowling mountain beast baying at the campfire or closing in on some helpless prey but the lonely wail of a wolf, full voiced, crying out the meaning of the mountains and the night.

"It's all right, everybody!" called out Murom. "Just a lonesome wolf doing what wolves do. Nothing to fear."

The relentless wind continued to whip through the rock enclosure, making the tent walls pop, but soon everyone except Vladimir Petrovna was fast asleep.

It was midmorning on Tuesday when eight Cossacks and tax assessor Yelm Sukeava rode into the yard of the Petrovna farm. The sky was clear and no snow had fallen in almost a week. There were hoof and sleigh tracks in the lane between the house and the road, as well as in the yard all the way back to the barn.

"The place looks deserted, Captain," said Sukeava as they neared the house. "No signs of life. There's no smoke coming out of the chimneys."

"Certainly a man like Vladimir Petrovna would know that if he is hiding somewhere we will find him," said Captain Lifkin Shanov.

"You would think so," said the tax assessor, dismounting. "I'll knock on the door. If I don't get an answer, we'll break the door down and investigate."

The Cossacks remained in their saddles, observing as Yelm Sukeava mounted the porch steps and banged loudly on the door. When he turned around, his face was crimson with anger. Eyes wild, he said, "Captain, tell three of your men to go out back and search the barn and outbuildings. Have the others break this door down and search the house."

Sukeava and Shanov followed the four Cossacks through the splintered door and waited in the parlor while they searched the house. The three men who had been sent to the barn and outbuildings came in, and Sergeant Waldo Kitmer said, "Captain, there are no animals in or around the barn, nor in the outbuildings. There is an old wagon in the barn but no sleigh and no harnesses."

"Looks like they have vacated the place," commented Shanov.

Sukeava was about to speak when the other men came in, and Corporal Victor Yarden said, "Captain Shanov, the house is definitely deserted. All the clothing is gone from the closets and there is no bedding on the beds nor anywhere else in the house. The kitchen cupboards are bare and so is the pantry."

Yelm Sukeava turned to Shanov and

hissed, "I want you to track them down and kill every one of them, Captain! I mean the entire family is to be shot! Vladimir Petrovna has defied the Russian government by refusing to pay his taxes and has fled to escape prosecution. They must be found as soon as possible!"

Shanov rubbed his chin thoughtfully. "My experience, sir, has been that when they flee this area to evade paying taxes, they leave the country by the shortest route, which is over Kuwalt Pass and down into Poland."

"Then get after them!" snapped the tax assessor.

"It might be, sir," said Corporal Yarden, "that they have gone to relatives or friends somewhere. They have to know that those mountains are very dangerous to travel at this time of year."

Shanov rubbed his chin again. "Relatives or friends, eh?" Turning to one of his men, he said, "Private Kaluga, were you not raised on a farm near here?"

Barny Kaluga was already getting a sick feeling in his stomach from what they had found at the Petrovna place. Nodding, he said, "Yes, sir. About two miles east of here, sir."

"Do you know the Petrovnas?"

There was a tightness in Barny's throat. "Yes, sir."

"Do you know them well enough to guess where they might have gone?"

"Well, sir, I —"

"Private Kaluga," cut in Sergeant Waldo Kitmer, "did I not hear you tell one of your fellow students at the training school that you were in love with the Petrovnas' youngest daughter?"

Barny blushed. "Y-yes."

"What's her name?"

"Olecia."

"Are you still in love with her?"

"Well, yes I am, but —"

"If you are that close to the family, you must have some idea where they have gone," said the captain, brow furrowed.

"I really don't, sir. You see, Olecia and I haven't been seeing each other for quite some time."

"But you're still in love with her?"

"Yes, sir, but things just haven't worked out between us. She considers us friends, but in her mind, there is no future for us as far as marriage is concerned. So I haven't been around here for quite a while."

"What about relatives?" asked Shanov. "Is there someone in Russia who might harbor them?"

"Well, sir, I know Olecia has an aunt and uncle somewhere in the country, but I have no idea where they live, or what their name is."

"Maybe the neighbors do, sir," spoke up Corporal Victor Yarden.

Shanov nodded. "All right, we will talk to the neighboring farmers on every side. If they cannot help us, we will just head for the mountains and Kuwalt Pass. Get on your horses. We'll divide up and talk to the neighbors."

"I will head on back to town, Captain," said the tax assessor, placing his foot in the stirrup. "I expect a report as soon as you have found the Petrovnas and executed them."

"You will have it, sir," said Shanov.

As Barny Kaluga swung into the saddle, his stomach felt sicker yet.

He hoped with everything that was in him that they would not catch up to the Petrovnas, wherever they had gone.

When each of the chosen neighbors had been interrogated, the Cossack unit rendezvoused in front of the Petrovna house. Last to draw up was Sergeant Waldo Kitmer, and every man noticed the broad smile on his face. "Anyone else get the name of Mrs.

Petrovna's sister and husband?" he asked.

"No, we didn't," said the captain. "Tell us."

"Well, those neighbors you sent me to, the Zieglans, told me that Mrs. Petrovna's sister is married to a man named Murom Tambov, and they have a large wheat farm about sixty-five miles due west of here."

"Ah, now we're getting somewhere," said Shanov. "We will return to the post, pack our traveling gear, and head out immediately. The Petrovnas are probably seeking refuge at the Tambov place."

Barny Kaluga's heart felt like it had turned into cold lead.

It was almost dark as the eight black-uniformed men drew rein at the spot where the lane that led to the large farmhouse met the road.

"This is the place, all right, Captain," said Sergeant Kitmer. "Exactly as that farmer we talked to back there on the road described it. There are lights in the windows of the farmhouse and smoke is coming from the chimneys."

Barny Kaluga never felt so helpless in all of his life. What was he going to do if Olecia and her family were in that farmhouse?

Shanov let his gaze follow the double set

of sleigh tracks that came from the Tambov farm, crossed the road, and headed across the fields due west. "Looks like somebody left here and headed straight for the mountains," he mused aloud. "Let's go see what the Tambovs have to tell us."

When the farmer responded to the knock and opened the door, his eyes widened at the menacing sight of the men in black uniforms and tall fur hats who stood on his porch.

"May I help you, gentlemen?" the farmer said. The strain in his voice betrayed the intimidation he felt.

"Mr. Tambov, I am Captain Lifkin Shanov," said the leader. "I want to ask you some quest—"

"Oh, I am not Murom Tambov, Captain," said the farmer. "I bought this farm from him, and my wife and I moved in only a few days ago. My name is Selo Nastova."

Shanov turned to Barny. "Did you ever see your young lady's uncle and aunt?"

"No, sir," said Barny, relieved to know the Tambovs had gone elsewhere. He thought of the double set of sleigh tracks they had seen at the road. Had the Tambovs and the Petrovnas indeed headed for the mountains? "I never saw them, sir."

Setting stern eyes on the farmer, Shanov said, "Do you have something that would identify you as Selo Nastova?"

"Yes. How about the bill of sale between myself and Mr. Tambov?"

When the captain had seen the bill of sale, he said, "I see you bought all of their furniture. Did the Tambovs tell you where they were moving?"

"No, sir. They never mentioned it. They were gone when we moved in here last Sunday. I have no idea where they went."

"Would you know if they were traveling in two sleighs?"

"I saw evidence of that here in the yard when we moved in, Captain, and I recall that they only had one sleigh in the shed out back when we looked at the place with the prospect of buying it."

Shanov nodded. "All right. Mr. Nastova, I am going to have my men search the house, barn, and outbuildings before we leave. As far as I know, you are telling the truth when you say the Tambovs were gone when you moved in on Sunday, but I must satisfy myself that they are not here."

"Whatever you say, Captain." Nastova scrubbed a nervous palm over his face. "Did the Tambovs do something wrong?"

"We're not sure yet. All right, men, let's

273

get our search over with."

Thirty minutes later the Cossack unit paused at the snowpacked road, which was now vaguely illuminated by the shimmering stars overhead. The double set of sleigh tracks were barely visible as Shanov eyed them and said, "Mr. Nastova said the Tambovs only had one sleigh, and that he had noticed the evidence in the yard that there had been two sleighs when the Tambovs left the farm. It is quite obvious that someone was traveling with them. I would say it was the Petrovnas, wouldn't you, Private Kaluga?"

Barny's tongue was sticking to the roof of his mouth. "Well, it could be, sir, but we really have no proof it was them."

"It's them, all right," Shanov said levelly. "I can feel it in my bones. The Petrovnas and the Tambovs are leaving Russia together, and they are no doubt going over Kuwalt Pass. We must catch up to them. The Tambovs will be executed, also, for helping the Petrovnas flee from the government authorities."

Barny's blood ran cold.

The Tambovs and the Petrovnas — along with Alekin Kolpino — found the travel slow and laborious as they made their way higher into the mountains through the deep snow. Often they had to stop and dig through snow that was piled too deep for the horses to get through, or to remove tree limbs that had fallen across the trail.

Only twice had they met up with travelers who had come over Kuwalt Pass on their way to the eastern plain. The second time was when a small avalanche had covered the trail where it was only a dozen feet wide on the edge of a sheer precipice, and men on both sides were shoveling snow to clear it.

As the sleighs inched their way higher, Alekin and Zoya talked about their future together and agreed that even though they might not be able to marry by the date they had set in April, it would be worth it to live in the land of the free and raise their family there. On Tuesday night they slept in their first cave, and found it much warmer than sleeping in the tents out in the open. The cave had been too small to include the horses, but they were tied so they could keep their heads in the mouth of the cave.

At midmorning on Wednesday they reached a plateau and found a shallow valley stretched out before them beneath a cloudless, sunlit sky. Beyond the valley stood the highest peaks where Kuwalt Pass would eventually lead them to the other side of the mountains.

Murom pulled rein to give the horses a breather and scanned the valley with squinted eyes. As Vladimir drew his sleigh up beside the Tambov sleigh, he said, "How many days do you estimate to the top of the pass?"

Murom thought on it a moment. "Well, we didn't do as well as I thought we would because of the snow depth and the time we lost digging through that avalanche. I think we're about four to five days from the top of the pass."

Vladimir twisted on the seat, looked at their back trail, and said, "This could mean if the Cossacks are coming, they might catch up to us sooner than we first thought."

Murom nodded solemnly. "Yes. We'll need to start looking over our shoulders in a couple more days. The Cossacks are crafty and intelligent, and they are great trackers."

Olecia pictured Barny in a black uniform and wondered where he might be stationed by now. She whispered another prayer for his salvation. Sitting beside her in the family sleigh, Kadyn could not make out what she said, but he felt sure she was praying for Barny.

"Well, let's move on," said Murom. "At least we'll make better time while we cross this valley."

Thirteen

Traveling was smooth across the floor of the broad valley which presented the Petrovnas and the Tambovs with frozen lakes to veer around as they aimed toward the high trail that would lead them to Kuwalt Pass.

On both sides of the valley were giant cliffs, standing inscrutable and silent with gleaming snow cornices on their lofty crests.

The wind whipped across the valley for the rest of the day, and just before darkness closed in on them the travelers pitched their tents on the edge of a frozen lake in a thick stand of junipers. The wind howled around them and plucked at the tent walls all night long, making everyone think about the cave they had used the night before and wish they had another one like it.

When they climbed aboard their sleighs the next morning, the sky was clear and the temperature below zero. Frigid blasts of wind picked up fallen snow along the trail, tossing it in the faces of horses and travelers.

As the white silence pressed in around the occupants of the sleighs, they huddled beneath their blankets and thought of summertime with its warm breezes, colorful wildflowers, and green grass.

It was almost noon when they reached the west side of the valley and once again began to climb the steep trail. Always trailing the Tambov sleigh, Vladimir found himself turning to look behind periodically as if he could almost feel the breath of a relentless Cossack unit on the back of his neck.

Olecia's heart was heavy as the sleighs continued on, knowing she was moving farther and farther from Barny. She would not know until she got to heaven if her prayers had been answered and Barny had been saved. So far, she was successfully covering the pain of her heartache from the others.

When the sun was lowering toward the mountaintops ahead of them, heavy clouds were beginning to prowl over the jagged peaks like beasts of prey, and the wind was growing stronger. Murom twisted in the seat with Oksana beside him and called back, "Looks like there's a storm coming! Everybody keep your eyes peeled now. It's time to make camp. We've got to find a cave."

Hardly had the words left his mouth when

Kadyn called from the rear seat of the Petrovna sleigh, "Uncle Murom! There's one right up there ahead of you!"

Murom looked back to see where the boy was pointing, as did everyone else. He then followed the boy's extended finger off to the right about fifty yards ahead, and saw the gaping black hole in the side of the mountain.

"Good, Kadyn!" called Murom. "We'll check it out!"

Moments later, when both sleighs had come to a halt in front of the cave, Murom hopped out and said, "Everybody sit tight till I make sure there aren't any big black bears hibernating in there."

"Darling," said Oksana, "I wish you had a gun. I don't like you going in there without some protection."

Murom chuckled. "Only the military and the police have guns in Russia, honey. I'll be fine."

"I'll go in with you," said Vladimir, hopping out of his sleigh and picking up an ax from the rear compartment.

Alekin reached behind him, grasped Murom's ax, and said, "I'll come too."

When the three men stepped into the mouth of the dark cave, they halted as a deep rumbling sound met their ears, coming from somewhere farther back. Murom put a vertical finger to his lips to make sure Vladimir and Alekin remained silent. They listened a few more seconds, then Vladimir whispered softly, "It's a bear, all right. Let's back out very quietly."

As the trio drew up to the sleighs, Murom said, "Sure enough. There's a bear sleeping in there."

Sasha sighed. "I'm sure glad he's asleep."

"Me too," said Vladimir.

The heavy clouds that were coming over the peaks to the west were getting darker, and beginning to swirl violently under the pressure of the high winds. The clouds had swallowed the sun.

"We've got a healthy storm coming in," said Murom as he climbed back in the sleigh. "Let's hurry. We've got to find a cave with no big hairy occupants."

They had been in motion less than ten minutes when Alekin leaned forward and said, "Murom, there's a cave just up ahead. See it? It's back off the trail to the right about twenty yards."

"I see it," said Murom. "Tell Vladimir."

Before Alekin could get turned around to call to him, Vladimir said, "We see it. Let's hope it's unoccupied."

When the sleighs halted near the mouth

of the cave, Kadyn said, "Hey, it's really big! If it's as deep as it looks, we can put the horses and the sleighs in there too!"

"Well," said Murom, "if there aren't any bears in there, we'll take refuge from the coming storm and wait it out."

Axes were in the hands of Alekin and Vladimir once more as the three men went into the cave.

At the same time Vladimir, Murom, and Alekin were entering the cave, some three hundred yards back down the mountain the Cossack unit was following their leader up the snow-laden trail. Two pack horses carried food for men and animals, along with each man's canvas-wrapped bedroll.

Barny Kaluga was thinking about Olecia and her family. Captain Lifkin Shanov was brilliant at tracking, and he was sure the tracks in the snow were those of the Petrovna and the Tambov sleighs.

I have to do something, Barny told himself. *I cannot let my comrades execute the girl I love, nor her family. But I am only one man. What can I do?*

His thoughts went back to the times Olecia had talked to him about his need to be saved and the passages she had shown him in the Bible. He had tried to keep the

Scriptures from sticking in his mind, but to no avail. Over and over, Barny had experienced unwanted mental pictures of hell and of facing God in judgment as a rejecter of Jesus Christ; he found them frightening. He had even had nightmares about it and awakened in the night in a cold sweat. He had also experienced mental pictures of God's Son hanging on the nails of Calvary's cross for Barny Kaluga's sins.

As the snow crunched under the horses' hooves and the massive storm built in the west, Barny told himself he had been a fool to go against God, His Word, and His Son. But what could he do? Olecia told him many times how to be saved, but he was not sure he understood it enough to actually approach the Lord about it.

At that moment, the Cossacks were approaching a small cave alongside the trail, and Corporal Victor Yarden, who was riding next to their leader, said, "Captain, I suggest with night coming on and that storm blowing in, that we take refuge in this cave."

"Not yet, Corporal," replied Shanov. "We must press on for a while." He pointed down at the tracks left by the two sleighs and their horses. "See how the cut of the sleigh runners in the snow is still sharp?"

"Yes, sir."

"Barely disturbed, yet we have a stiff wind."

"Yes, sir."

"Note that the imprints made by the horses' hooves are still sharp, also. This means they are not far ahead of us. We must keep going. If we can catch up to them before dark, we can get the execution over with and head for home in the morning."

Shanov's mention of execution turned Barny's insides to stone.

At the mouth of the cave, the women and Kadyn waited in the sleighs, watching the boiling clouds and hoping Vladimir, Murom, and Alekin would soon emerge and tell them the cave was unoccupied.

The three men had only been gone about five minutes when they came out of the cave, smiling through their fur-lined hoods. The smiles told the others that it was not occupied.

"We've got the best hotel in the Carpathians," Murom said as they drew up. "The cave actually has two sections. The section at the rear has firewood already piled up. There have been other travelers in there recently. We can keep the horses and sleighs in the front section, so they will be sheltered from the storm when it hits."

"Wonderful!" said Sasha.

"Amen!" said Oksana. "Since we don't know how long the storm will last, at least we'll be out of it."

"We already started a fire back there," said Vladimir. "There's a crack in the ceiling of the cave, and it lets the smoke out. Let's go ahead and carry the bedrolls, blankets, and food inside, then we'll put the horses and sleighs in."

Down below, with the wind blowing harder and the churning clouds growing darker, the Cossacks topped a rise with a sheer cliff on the left side of the trail. To their right a towering snow-covered mountain loomed skyward. One of them pointed ahead and cried above the howl of the wind, "Captain! Look!"

Every eye focused on the two sleighs that were stopped in front of a cave at a slightly higher level about two hundred yards ahead of them. People were moving about the sleighs and carrying items into the cave.

A smile curved Captain Lifkin Shanov's cold lips. "It has to be them!" he said gleefully as he turned around and unbuckled a saddlebag. Taking out a telescope, he put it to his eye and quickly focused on the people moving about the sleighs. Motioning to

Barny, he said, "Private Kaluga, come here."

Barny drew his horse up beside the captain. "Yes, sir?"

Shanov handed him the telescope. "I can clearly make out the faces of those people up there. Take a look and see if some of them are the Petrovnas."

As Barny took the telescope in his gloved hand, fear clawed at his insides like a wild beast. While the captain and the other men watched with keen interest, he raised the tube-shaped instrument to his eye and pointed it at the scene in front of the cave. The powerful lens bit into the two-hundred yard distance and pulled it into view.

The first face he recognized was that of Olecia's brother, Kadyn, who was in one of the sleighs handing blankets to a man. When the man turned to carry the blankets into the cave, Barny recognized Vladimir Petrovna. At the other sleigh were a man and woman he did not recognize, but he knew who they were. The woman bore a strong resemblance to Olecia's mother. They were Oksana and Murom Tambov. Moving the telescope toward the mouth of the cave, his heart lurched as he focused on Olecia. Beside her, emerging from the cave, were Zoya and Alekin. The lens seemed frozen on Olecia's pretty face. He licked his lips as the captain said, "Well?"

Lowering the telescope with the taste of fear like copper in his mouth, Barny held his voice level. "It is not the Petrovnas, Captain. All of those faces are strange to me."

Sergeant Waldo Kitmer moved his horse up beside Barny. Looking at Shanov, he said, "I believe Private Kaluga's heart is blinding his eyes, sir. You heard him admit he is in love with Olecia Petrovna."

A frown penciled itself across Shanov's brow. "Yes. But Private Kaluga is a sworn Cossack, Sergeant. He would not lie to me."

"Oh? Well, tell him to give me the telescope and let me take a look. I know what Vladimir Petrovna looks like. I have met him on a few occasions."

The wind was blowing harder, its whine piercing the air. Barny's pulse was a pounding sledgehammer in his temples.

"Give him the telescope, Private Kaluga," said Shanov.

Taking the extended instrument from Barny, Kitmer put it to his eye and ran the lens from person to person. He started over again, focusing on the men, but still he could not find Vladimir Petrovna. Then suddenly there was movement at the mouth of the cave, and Vladimir was emerging while saying something to a woman who walked beside him.

A fiendish grin curved Kitmer's mouth as he lowered the telescope, looked at Barny, and said, "Private Kaluga, you are a liar! I just saw the face of Vladimir Petrovna."

Captain Shanov said, "Sergeant, are you absolutely sure?"

"Yes, sir. There is no doubt about it. One of the men up there is Vladimir Petrovna."

Suddenly the air was filled with a thick curtain of blowing snow. The storm had struck, and the Cossacks could hardly see each other. The horses danced about, whinnying.

Shanov gasped and spat, "Private Kaluga, you're under arrest! Sergeant Kitmer, disarm him!"

Reflex came alive in Barny Kaluga. While Shanov's command to Sergeant Kitmer was still coming from his mouth, Barny wheeled his horse and charged blindly back down the trail, galloping along the edge of the deep canyon.

The captain gasped again and shouted, "Shoot him! Shoot him!"

There was no time for the Cossacks to pull their rifles from the saddleboots. Revolvers were whipped from holsters and sharp blasts repeatedly cut through the snow-filled, wind-whipped air. Suddenly Private Kaluga's horse stumbled, peeled over the edge of the sheer precipice, and disappeared, taking his rider with him.

As the fierce wind carried away the powder smoke from the muzzles of six revolvers, one of the men shouted, "They went over the edge of the canyon, Captain!"

"Yes, I saw it!" Shanov shouted above the roar of the storm. "Kaluga's dead now, that's for sure! It's a long way to the bottom of that canyon!"

"What are we going to do, Captain?" asked Sergeant Kitmer.

Brushing snow from his eyes, Shanov raised his voice so all could hear. "It's too far to the cave where the Petrovnas and the Tambovs are. This storm is too fierce for us to try going up there. We must hurry back to that cave we saw down the trail a little while ago. If we don't find shelter, we're in trouble!"

"Lead the way, Captain!" shouted one of the men.

Bending his head against the force of the wind, Captain Shanov slowly urged his mount forward and was quickly flanked by Sergeant Waldo Kitmer and Corporal Victor Yarden. The others followed. The seven Cossacks carefully made their way down the trail with the blinding fury of the blizzard at their backs.

It took quite some time to reach the spot where Barny Kaluga and his horse had gone over the edge of the canyon, and it could barely be seen as they slowly moved by it.

Kitmer spoke through the shrill whine of the wind. "I suspected Kaluga might be a problem on this chase, Captain. He just seemed to be caught up with that Petrovna girl. It didn't surprise me when the dirty traitor lied about not recognizing anybody up there at the cave."

"Well, he got what was coming to him," said Shanov. "It would have been more pleasant standing him in front of a firing squad, but we probably put several bullets in him, anyway. If he wasn't dead before his horse went over the edge, he sure is dead now."

In the large cave, Kadyn Petrovna was adding logs to the fire in the rear section under the directions of his mother, while Zoya was getting food ready to be cooked. Olecia had brought in a bucket of snow and was setting it close to the fire so it would melt and give them water to make coffee.

In the front section, Murom, Vladimir, and Alekin were unhitching the horses from the sleighs. The fury of the storm had hit just after they had moved teams and sleighs inside.

While unbuckling the harness, Vladimir glanced outside and said, "The Lord is good to us, gentlemen. We would really be in trouble if we had to pitch our tents in that blizzard and try to sleep tonight."

"That's for sure," said Murom as he unhooked his harness from the double tree. "I'm very thankful for this cave. I wish we could just take it with —"

Murom's words were cut off by a sudden series of rapid reports that sounded from somewhere outside above the loud whine of the wind.

"What was that?" said Alekin, letting a strap of harness hang loose on one horse while moving toward the mouth of the cave.

The other two men followed, pausing to flank him where he had stopped. The wind-driven snow was hitting the ground at their toes.

"Sounded like gunfire to me," said Vladimir. "I remember hearing similar sounds when fighting in blizzards on the Crimea. Hard to tell, though, the wind being so loud."

"But why would there be any gunfire up here in the mountains?" asked Murom.

"Only the military and the police have guns. Hunters in Russia have to use bows and arrows."

"Military . . ." Vladimir said, his voice trembling. "Cossacks?"

Abruptly from behind them, Sasha said, "Vladdie, what were those crackling sounds? We heard them back there."

"We were just trying to figure them out ourselves," said Vladimir. "I was telling Murom and Alekin that it sounded like gunfire to me. You know, like when I was fighting in the midst of blizzards on the Crimea."

Laying a hand on his arm, Sasha said, "Did I hear you say something about Cossacks?"

By this time, the other three had drawn up.

"Cossacks?" said Zoya. "What about Cossacks?"

"Are they out there shooting at us, Papa?" asked Kadyn.

The mention of Cossacks quickly surfaced Barny Kaluga in Olecia's mind.

"No, they're not shooting at us, son," Vladimir said to Kadyn. "Uncle Murom and I were just saying that nobody in Russia has guns but the military and the police. The police have no reason to come into the mountains, but the Cossacks do. Us."

"But no bullets came our way, did they, Papa?" asked Zoya.

"No," said Vladimir, shaking his head. "It must have been something else. Maybe the wind was breaking some trees down. You know how green trees pop when they split."

"Could be," said Murom. "The sound only lasted a few seconds."

"And you didn't hear it again?" asked Oksana.

"No."

"Well," said Sasha, "by the time you men finish removing the harness from the horses and get them fed, supper will be ready."

Soon everyone was sitting around the fire, enjoying the hot meal.

"Papa," said Kadyn, "I was thinking about the Cossacks. Could they possibly have picked up our trail and be close to us by now?"

Vladimir chewed the food in his mouth, swallowed, and said, "I suppose they could, son. We did get slowed down digging through some of that deep snow, you know. And they can travel on horseback a lot faster than we can with the sleighs."

"The Lord isn't going to let them catch up to us, though, is He?"

"Of course not," said Vladimir. "He is

going to take us safely to America."

Kadyn smiled. "They don't have anything like Cossacks in America, do they, Papa?"

"They sure don't."

"They have military forces, Kadyn," said Alekin. "Army and navy, both. And they have a special corps they call the marines. They are trained for military service on both sea and land, so they can fight alongside either navy or army. But in America they don't have a military group like the Cossacks who go around punishing the citizens and executing them if they can't pay their taxes."

"That's good," said the boy. "I'm really going to like it in America."

"We all are, son," said Sasha. "It will be so wonderful to live free and make a new life for ourselves without having to fear carrying our Bibles and going to church on Sundays. There are no czars to worry about and no Cossacks."

Kadyn's eyebrows arched. "No czars? Who runs the country?"

"In America, Kadyn," spoke up Murom, "they have a man they call their president, and a large group of men they call the United States Congress who work with him to run the country. Right now, their president's name is Grover Cleveland."

"Oh," said Kadyn, nodding.

Vladimir sipped coffee and said, "New subject. Murom, do you have any particular place in mind where we might settle in America?"

"Not really. I have heard of several farming areas that sound good. I figure when we get to America, we will stay in New York City for a while. I'm sure we can come by information there about the rest of the country."

"Sounds good to me," said Vladimir. "I'm eager to get there."

"We all are, Papa," said Zoya.

On a snow-covered ledge some fifty feet below the edge of the precipice, Barny Kaluga found his left leg cramped and numb beneath the horse's weight. The Cossack bullets had hit the bay gelding, wounding him, but missing Barny. The deep snow on the ledge had cushioned Barny's fall. He was unhurt.

In the vague light that was left, he could see blood oozing from the horse's wounds. The gelding was breathing hard. Barny knew he was in a great deal of pain. He glanced at the butt of the rifle protruding from the saddleboot. If he could just free himself, he could get the rifle in hand. Then shaking his head, he told himself that even if he could get the rifle loose, he couldn't use it to shoot the animal and put him out of his misery. He had heard the snorting of the Cossacks' horses overhead only moments ago, and knew the Cossacks were moving back down the trail. No doubt Captain Shanov and his men were heading back to the cave they had passed earlier. If he used the rifle to shoot the horse, the Cossacks would hear the shot.

His first problem, he knew, was to get himself out from under the weight of the animal. His next problem would be to somehow climb back up to the trail and make his way to the cave where the Petrovnas and the Tambovs were taking refuge from the storm.

But getting to the cave would not be possible till morning. Night was crowding in on him. He could feel the dropping bite of the temperature. Somehow he had to survive the night.

The gelding nickered, lifted his head, and laid it back down. Barny raised up as best he could and patted him. "I'm sorry, boy. I know you're hurting. Right now I have to get this leg out from under you."

While the wind-driven snow swirled around him and darkness closed in, Barny clenched his teeth and struggled to free his leg from beneath the horse's heavy body. At first it was like his foot was fastened to the snow, but after a while he felt it come loose a little. The struggle went on for what seemed to be hours, but finally the leg was free.

Breathing a sigh of relief, he groped his way to a standing position and checked to make sure his revolver was still in the holster. It was.

What now? he thought. *I can't see my hand in front of my face. Somehow I must keep from freezing to death.*

The horse nickered again. Suddenly Barny knew he had one chance to make it. He knelt down beside the gelding, patted his neck, and said, "You have to stay alive, boy. The only way I can make it through this night and not freeze to death is for your body to keep me warm."

Feeling about in the darkness, Barny loosened the saddle and removed it from the horse's back. He removed the rifle from the saddleboot and pushed it up close to the horse's body to keep it as dry as possible. He would need it in the morning.

A blast of icy wind buffeted him, pelting him with snow. He tugged the furry coat collar up tight around his neck and pulled his fur hat down tighter over his ears. *This wind is a killer*, he thought.

Barny's lungs were aching from the freezing air. A layer of ice was forming on his eyebrows. The snow was no longer melting when it hit his face. Removing one glove, he rubbed his palm over his brows to rid them of the ice. He put the glove back on and rubbed his thighs to get the circulation going. He flailed his arms and found them growing numb too. His whole body felt numb. He ran in place to stir the circulation in his feet and legs. He kept it up until he was breathing hard and his lungs felt like they were on fire.

Lying down in the snow next to the horse's back, he snuggled up close and said, "You've got to stay alive now, boy. If you die, I die. Please stay alive so you can keep me from freezing to death."

Barny could feel the gelding breathing as he pressed himself against the only source of heat he had. His stomach growled. He was hungry, but there was nothing to eat. His only hope was to make it through the horrible night and climb up to the trail when he had some daylight. The Petrovnas would give him shelter and food.

He pictured Olecia there in the cave and tried to imagine what she would do when he appeared, asking for help. She would be surprised to see him, that was for sure.

Feeling warmth from the horse's body, Barny told himself he was going to make it. He had to. When the storm was over, the Petrovnas and the Tambovs had to move on and Barny Kaluga had to do something to keep the Cossacks from catching up to them.

Fourteen

After a restless night of turning from side to side in an attempt to soak up as much of the gelding's warmth as possible, Barny Kaluga awakened with the scream of the wind in his ears. He was facing the horse, nestled as close as possible to him, but his body was trembling.

Removing a glove, he laid a palm against the animal's smooth hide. It was cold. He slid the hand to the belly, which he had felt heaving each time he had awakened in the night. There was no movement.

Barny opened his eyes. Light was coming now, pale gray through the blizzard's shroud.

He pushed back from the gelding and struggled to his feet, brushing snow from the front of his fur hat and shaking his shoulders in an attempt to dislodge the snow from the back of his coat. The steam clouds of his breath were instantly carried away by the wind as he looked down at the gelding's head. The dull eyes were staring into nothingness.

"Well, thanks, boy," he said. "At least you stayed alive long enough to keep me from freezing in the night."

Bending his head against the fury of the storm, Barny bent over and picked up the rifle from where he had left it next to the horse's body.

He checked once again to make sure the revolver was still in its holster, then picked up the saddlebags and brushed away the snow that covered them. Opening the left saddlebag, he took out a leather strap that was made to be attached to the rifle and fastened it in place. He took spare cartridges from the saddlebag, stuffed them into his coat pockets, then hung the rifle on his back.

Barny let his gaze flit across the face of the canyon and upward to the edge where the trail ran. "There has to be a way to get back up there," he said aloud, squinting to peer through the blizzard. Suddenly his eyes stopped where a narrow shelf ran in an upward curve from the far end of the ledge where he stood, around to the right, and out of view. The shelf was no more than two feet wide and was packed with snow. He could also make out the uneven shapes of rocks protruding beneath the snow. He hoped the rocks were embedded in the solid body of the shelf, and he hoped it went all the way to the top. And even if it did, the climb was going to be dangerous. One slip and he would fall into the depths of the canyon.

He took a deep breath and let it out in a slender cloud that was quickly carried away by the wind. There was only one way to know if the shelf found its way to the top. He would have to climb it and see.

Approaching the spot where the narrow shelf joined the ledge, Barny told himself there would only be one way to do it. He would have to crawl and use the rocks to steady himself. That is, if the rocks were socketed into the shelf.

Dropping to his knees in the deep snow, he adjusted the rifle that was strapped to his back, tightened the revolver in its holster, and began crawling. He was glad for the snow beneath his knees, for he could tell the floor of the shelf was strewn with small, sharp stones.

Carefully making his way along the shelf, Barny could see the yawning chasm to his right in his peripheral vision. What he could make out from the corner of his eye was enough. He would not venture a glance into the canyon.

Soon he was at the spot that had curved out of sight from the ledge. As far as he could tell with the blizzard half blinding him, the shelf went all the way to the trail above him. However, it was much steeper from this point on.

As Barny crawled upward, making sure each time that he was anchored solidly before moving on, he noticed there were periodic spots where small shrubs grew out of the face of the sheer wall of the mountain. The blizzard beat on him unmercifully as he continued his climb. His knees were getting sore, but he forced himself to ignore the pain. He had to make it to the top and get to the cave before the Cossacks decided to hazard the steep climb up the trail and execute the Petrovnas and the Tambovs.

"Olecia, I love you," he said while straining every muscle. "I can't let them kill you!"

The wind was relentless as it drove snow into his face, but determined to make it, Barny crawled on. He reached a spot where a large, pointed rock stuck its head up in front of him, as if to block his path. He would have to work his way around it, for its slanted base spread from the wall of the canyon to the edge of the shelf. It was so shaped that it was impassable on the side next to the sheer wall. He would have to inch his way around the rock on the canyon side.

Brushing the snow off the rock's sharp peak, Barny gripped it with both hands and began working his way around it. For the moment he was forced to let his only security be the grip he had on the rock while his legs dangled dangerously over the edge of the shelf.

Suddenly one hand slipped. He gasped as he clung to the rock with the single hand while struggling to gain a double hold again. For a split second, it seemed he would never make it, but finally he was able to grip the tip of the rock and work his way to the other side. When he had the shelf under him again, he sucked hard for air and wiped snow from his eyelashes.

It took him a couple of minutes to get his breath, then he began crawling again. Suddenly a powerful gust of wind slammed him head on, lifting him off his knees. He felt himself slipping toward the edge of the canyon and desperately clawed at a patch of shrubs. His gloved hands found a twisted limb, but it started to pull loose.

"No!" he cried and clawed furiously for something solid. His fingers suddenly closed around seemingly more sturdy limbs, and they held his weight as his legs once again were dangling precariously over the edge of the canyon. But how long would the limbs maintain their hold?

The fierce wind was like a giant hand, attempting to pull him loose and hurl him into the canyon. He felt a kernel of hopelessness twist in his stomach.

Suddenly the limbs seemed to loosen their hold in the mountain's side.

Fighting the panic that was thickening in his throat, Barny did something he had never done in his life. "Oh, dear God!" he prayed. "Help me! Please, God! Help me!"

Teeth clenched, Barny clung to the limbs and gasped out another prayer for help while struggling to get himself back up on the shelf before the limbs broke loose.

And then . . . almost miraculously, there was a break in the wind. The brief respite allowed him to swing his legs onto the shelf's edge unhindered, and he was able to pull himself all the way up. Once again the wind was buffeting him unmercifully.

On his knees and elbows, Barny labored to catch his breath and thought of what would have happened if he had fallen into the fearsome maw of the canyon.

He would now be in hell.

This made his blood chill, even worse

than the literal cold that was all around him. Summoning all his strength, he began his crawling climb again through the wind-whipped veil of snow. Another quarter hour brought him to the top, and to make sure he was safe, he crawled a few more feet, then lay there on flat snowy ground, the breath sawing in and out of his lungs.

Pushing up on his hands and knees, he said, "Thank You, God! Thank You!"

With effort he leaned into the savage wind and made his way to his feet. Looking around him, then down the trail, he saw no tracks, nor any other sign of the Cossacks. He could almost hear them cursing his name in the cave below. Pivoting to face the wind, he looked up the trail and said, "I'm coming, Olecia."

Determined to make it to the cave, Barny braced himself against the storm and headed up the trail. From time to time he had to pause and face away from the fierce wind long enough to catch his breath, then resume his climb. His heart lurched in his chest when through the maelstrom of driven snow, he caught a glimpse up ahead of the winking firelight flickering around the rim of the cave's mouth.

The sight of the cave provided impetus to his legs, and he was almost running as he made his way toward it.

Inside the cave, breakfast was over, and Vladimir was reading Scripture to the group around the fire at the rear of the cave while the blizzard howled outside.

His intention was to read Psalm 40 in its entirety, and after pausing to comment on verses 1 and 2, he went on: "And he hath put a new song in my mouth, even praise unto our God: many shall see it, and in fear, shall trust in the LORD. Blessed is that man that maketh the LORD his trust, and —" Vladimir's head came up, and he looked toward the mouth of the cave.

Everyone else was looking that way, also.

"Did you hear what I did?" said Vladimir.

Sasha swallowed with difficulty. "I . . . I thought I heard a voice calling your name."

"That's what it sounded like to me," said Murom. "But —"

The haunting cry came again — the faint sound of a voice calling Vladimir's name seemed to ride the wind to every ear.

Murom jumped to his feet. "It must be —"

"Cossacks!" gasped Olecia.

"I don't think so," spoke up Alekin. "Cossacks wouldn't give any kind of warning. They'd just burst in here, guns ready, and start shooting us down. I don't know who that is out there, but the Cossacks would definitely not take this approach."

"But who in these mountains knows Papa?" asked Zoya. "And how would they know he is in here?"

The cry rode the wind into the cave again: "Vladimir Petrovna-a-a-a!"

"I don't know who he is," said Vladimir, stepping to the woodpile and picking up a stout piece of wood, "but we're about to find out."

Dashing to the woodpile, Murom picked up a log and said, "I'm going with you."

"Me too," said Alekin, going for a length of wood.

"I'll come, too, Papa," said Kadyn.

"All right, son." Then to the others he said, "You ladies stay here."

Fear showed in Sasha's eyes as she huddled her daughters close to her. Oksana joined them.

Within seconds the men were out of sight, and the wind carried the indistinct voice once more as it called Vladimir's name.

"Who could it be?" Oksana said in a hoarse whisper.

No one ventured a reply.

The frightened women clung to each other and waited breathlessly.

Several minutes had passed when the men

appeared with a snow-covered figure walking between Vladimir and Murom. The women tightened their grip on each other when they saw through the snow that clung to the man and recognized the black Cossack uniform.

With obvious relief in his voice, Vladimir said, "Look who we found out there!"

The Cossack's face was obscured in shadow until they drew up to the fire.

The women were stunned at the sight of him. But none as much as Olecia. When she saw his face, the shock hit her chest like a hammer. *My mind is playing tricks on me!* she thought, her face as white as the snow that covered him. She blinked, drew a short, sharp breath, and took a tentative step toward him.

Reaching for her, he said softly, "Olecia . . ."

"Barny!" she cried, rushing to him and taking hold of his gloved hands. "It really is you!"

"And has he got a story to tell us!" said Vladimir. "He gave us a short version out there. We want to hear all of it!"

"Not until we thaw him out," said Sasha. "Barny, you look half frozen."

"I think I am, Mrs. Petrovna," he said, bending his blue lips into a thin smile.

Olecia looked into his eyes. "Barny, are the Cossacks on our trail?"

"He will explain it all, Olecia," said her father. "But as your mama said, he needs to thaw out first. And, Sasha, he hasn't had anything to eat since yesterday morning."

"All right," said Sasha. "You sit down here by the fire, Barny, and get thawed. I'll fix you some of what we had for supper last night."

As Vladimir and Murom were taking the rifle from Barny's back and removing his snow-crusted coat, he commented that as soon as he could get warmed up and get some food in his stomach, he would tell them the whole story.

Olecia took Barny's hand and said, "Come. Sit down here close to the fire."

They eased down by the fire together, and Vladimir, Murom, Alekin, and Kadyn joined them. Barny leaned close to the flames and held his open hands so the heat could quickly warm them.

Zoya and Oksana helped Sasha prepare Barny's meal, and soon he was forking stew into his mouth, eating thick slices of bread and ham, and taking huge gulps of steaming coffee.

The hot meal and warmth from the fire slowly began to thaw him, leaving his body feeling warm at last. All the while Olecia watched him closely, satisfying herself that he was all right.

As Barny was mopping his plate up with a slice of bread, Olecia said, "I told you I would pray for you every day, Barny, and I have done just that. I had given up hope that I would ever see you again, but look what the Lord has done. He has almost literally dropped you in our laps."

Barny gave her a lopsided grin.

A smile tweaked the corners of her mouth. "The Lord is so good, Barny. Sometimes I'm just stunned at how He works."

Barny thought of his narrow escape on the snow-laden shelf in the canyon. "Yes. Me too."

This was more than Olecia had ever been able to get Barny to say about the Lord. It thrilled her heart.

There was a dead silence then.

Kadyn broke it by saying, "Tell us the story now, Barny."

Sasha took the plate and eating utensils from Barny's hands, then sat down with the rest of them.

While the blizzard continued to howl outside the cave, Barny told them how sick he felt at heart when he found himself in the Cossack unit that had been assigned to find the Petrovnas and execute them. He explained how Captain Lifkin Shanov led his Cossacks as they followed their sleigh trail to the Tambov farm, then followed both sleighs into the mountains.

He went on to tell the Petrovnas and the Tambovs how they were spotted by the Cossacks from the lower level on the trail yesterday when they were unloading items from the sleighs in preparation to enter the cave. He told how he had lied to Captain Shanov when asked if he recognized any of the faces through the telescope and of his being put under arrest when Sergeant Waldo Kitmer identified Vladimir.

Vladimir wiped a hand over his eyes and shook his head. "Kitmer knows me, all right. His brother, Mykah, owns a grocery store in Boyarka. Mykah has bought his potatoes from me for years. Waldo has been with him a few times when he has come to pick up a load of potatoes."

"I see," said Barny. "Of course I had no idea there would be a man in the unit who knew you. When Kitmer told the captain he knew you and that I had lied, I knew I was in trouble."

Barny went on to tell of his attempt to escape on his horse, the guns that were fired at him, and how he and the horse went over the edge of the cliff. He explained about the ledge and how the deep snow had cushioned his fall. The horse was hit with bullets, but the animal had lived long enough into the night to keep him from freezing to death with the warmth of his body.

Barny smiled as his listeners made comments at this point on how God had watched over him. He went on then to tell them about his precarious climb off the ledge on the narrow shelf, and how close he came to falling to his death in the canyon. Again there were comments on God's watch care over him, and as before, Barny agreed.

"So the Cossacks think you fell to the bottom of the canyon and are dead," said Murom.

"I'm sure of it," replied Barny. "They didn't even bother to look over the edge."

"Well, it's a good thing they think you're dead, Barny," said Vladimir, "or they would be coming after you with a vengeance."

"Without a doubt. They consider me a traitor."

"Do you have any idea where they are now?" asked Zoya.

"Yes. In our climb up the trail — shortly before we spotted you we passed a cave. I heard them moving back down the trail a few minutes after my horse and I had landed on the ledge. I'm sure they were heading for the cave. They are taking refuge from the storm there. This is why you must get back on the trail as soon as the storm breaks. They will be coming after you."

"I expect that," said Vladimir. "We will move out the minute the storm is over."

Olecia looked at Barny with concern in her large, dark eyes. "What about you? What are you going to do?"

"You can come with us," Vladimir said before Barny could reply. "You dare not show your face in Russia again."

Barny let a grim smile curve his lips. "I want to tell all of you what went on in my mind when I almost fell to my death in the canyon. From what Olecia has shown me in the Bible, I knew if I had fallen, I would have been in hell. This was foremost in my mind."

Tears filled Olecia's eyes.

Looking at her, Barny said, "So many times you talked to me about being saved. So many times you read to me from the Scriptures about salvation."

"Yes," she said, thumbing at the tears as they started down her cheeks. "Barny . . ."

"Yes?"

"God spared your life for a reason. He wanted to give you another opportunity to be saved. What are you going to do with that opportunity?"

Barny took hold of her hand. "I've been such a fool to reject Jesus Christ when you tried so hard to get me to open my heart to Him. Indeed, He has been so good to spare my life. Olecia, I want to take advantage of the opportunity. I want to be saved."

More tears rushed to Olecia's eyes. "Oh, Barny. Oh, Barny."

Vladimir reached for his Bible. "Then let's take care of that matter right now."

While the group sat silently praising God in their hearts, Vladimir read several verses regarding salvation to Barny and answered the few questions he had. Vladimir then helped the young ex-Cossack as he unashamedly called on Jesus to save him. Olecia embraced him, weeping for joy while the others rejoiced in what God had done.

When each person in the group had welcomed Barny into the family of God and emotions had settled down, Vladimir said, "Barny, you know better than we do how Cossacks think. Since they are down there in that cave, fully aware that we are up here . . . what will they do? How can we escape them?"

Barny was quick to reply, "They will come for you when they have the slightest break in the storm. You have already said you would be ready to pull out the moment the storm breaks. Your only hope is to be on the move as quickly as possible. They can travel faster on their horses than you can with those sleighs, so you must get the jump on them and stay ahead of them till you're across the Polish border."

"That's not going to be easy," spoke up Alekin.

"You're right," said Murom, "but we are going to do it anyhow."

"That's the spirit!" said Vladimir. "We know what we have to do, and together we will do it!"

There was a spirit of optimism in the group as Sasha said, "Barny, you look like there is still some chill in your system. You stay by the fire. The men have to go attend to the horses and we ladies need to do some cleanup around here. We'll excuse Olecia so she can stay by the fire with you."

While the blizzard continued to rage outside and the others were occupied in various places within the cave, Olecia placed a blanket over Barny's shoulders and sat down beside him. Kadyn had just put more logs on the fire and they were cracking and popping from the sudden heat.

Taking hold of his hand, Olecia said, "Oh,

Barny, there are no words in human language to tell you how glad I am that you got saved! I've . . . I've prayed so hard . . ."

"I know you have. I was such a fool to turn my back on Jesus." He squeezed her hand. "Thank you for all those times you talked to me and told me the gospel story. Thank you for all those Scriptures you read to me and quoted. I could never get them out of my mind."

"That's the way God's Word works, Barny. On its own pages, it is likened unto a two-edged sword that pierces to the very core of our being."

Barny nodded. "I can testify to that." Then turning to look deep into her dark brown eyes, he said, "Olecia, I still love you."

The brown eyes went misty.

Tightening the grip on her hand, Barny said, "I could never love anyone else like I love you."

The mist grew heavier and began to spill down Olecia's cheeks. "Barny, darling, I still love you too. In fact, when we were talking about going to America, I told my family I could never love any man but you. I told them I would just be an old maid."

"Really?"

"Really. But I'm so thankful that you are

going to America with us. We can have our lives together, after all."

Barny smiled and squeezed her hand again.

The storm lasted another day. While the hours passed, Olecia spent a great deal of time with Barny, helping him with his new Christian life by showing him many passages of Scripture that would bring spiritual growth and answering the normal questions that arose in the mind of a newborn child of God.

Late in the day the sky cleared. They all stood at the mouth of the cave and watched the last light of the sun fade over the snowcapped peaks to the west.

Adjusting his fur cap, Vladimir said, "We will pull out at the first hint of dawn in the morning."

"The going will be pretty slow since the snow is so deep," said Murom. "But we'll still get a good jump on the Cossacks. It looks even deeper down the trail." He turned to Barny. "I've been meaning to tell you that Oksana and I will pay your way across the Atlantic. You're not carrying much money, are you?"

Barny looked at him blankly, then said, "Ah . . . no, I'm not."

When Barny said no more, Vladimir moved closer to him, a slight frown lining his brow. "You are going to America with us, aren't you, Barny? I don't think I've heard you say for sure."

Olecia was standing a few feet away, beside her sister. Barny glanced at her. Uneasy about the way he was looking at her, she said, "You really haven't said for sure, but you are going with us, aren't you?"

Barny's features turned a bit pale. He cleared his throat nervously, put his glance on Vladimir, then on Sasha. "Mr. and Mrs. Petrovna, Olecia knows that I have been in love with her for a long time. I am more in love with her now. I would like nothing more than to marry her now that I am a Christian and qualify to do so." He swallowed hard, cleared his throat again, and said, "However, I cannot go to America with you."

Everyone was stunned. Especially Olecia, who showed her utter astonishment as her eyes widened and she said, "Why not? Why can't you go with us?"

Voice level, Barny said, "The Cossacks will be coming. I appreciate the optimism all of you have shown in believing you can get enough of a head start on them to keep them behind you until you cross the Polish border. But . . . but your optimism isn't realistic. There is no way you can outrun them. They will be on you in a very short time, unless . . ."

"Unless what?" queried Murom.

"Unless I stay behind and hold them off with my rifle and my revolver when they come up the trail. You will never make it over the pass, much less to the Polish border, if I don't."

"No!" blurted Olecia, rushing to him and throwing her arms around him. "No, Barny! I love you! You must go with us!"

Holding her close, Barny closed his eyes and said, "Olecia, my love, I have known in my heart what I have to do since before I even made it up here to the cave. I have spent every minute I could with you since then, wanting to enjoy it to the fullest." He eased back in her grasp and looked into her fear-filled eyes. "Olecia, unless I stay behind and hold them off as long as I can, there will be no chance for any of you. I will unleash my guns on them from ambush at a high spot and take out as many as possible. The confusion of bullets flying and some of them falling out of their saddles will give the rest of you time to get away. I have enough ammunition to take them all out. And I will, if they stay in one spot for very long. And as deep as the snow is, this is very probable."

"No!" sobbed Olecia. "You're just one man. They will kill you!"

"Not before I at least take out enough of them to buy you time," Barny said, his face grim.

Shaking his head, Vladimir said, "Barny, we can't let you do it. There has to be another way."

"Mr. Petrovna, there is no other way. If you people had guns, we could ambush them together and no doubt put them all out of their saddles, but the only weapons among us are my rifle and pistol."

Vladimir scrubbed a hand over his eyes. "There has to be something else we can do."

"Right!" said Murom. "There has to be!"

"We could hide, Papa!" said Kadyn.

Vladimir sighed. "We can't hide two sleighs, four horses, and all of us too, son."

"Then we'll have to find a way to fight them," said Alekin.

Murom's features were bleak. "What with? Tree branches? Snowballs? They would mow us down in seconds."

Tears were running down Olecia's face. Wrapping her arms around Barny, she sobbed, "No! I can't let you do this! I want us to have our future in America together."

Cupping her face in his hands, Barny said, "That's what I want too, sweet Olecia. But there is a band of Cossacks down the trail who have been sent to execute you and your family. They will also kill your aunt and uncle and Alekin. I wish there was some way we could have our lives together, but no one has been able to come up with a solution for this predicament. I must stay behind and ambush them. At least, I will save every life here, including yours. My love for you has no boundaries, Olecia. I don't know how else to say it without sounding heroically hollow, but I am willing to give my life to spare yours."

Olecia's sobbing grew more intense as she clung to Barny crying, "No! No!"

Fifteen

Sasha Petrovna's lips were quivering as she beheld the heartrending scene. Moving up beside her sobbing daughter, she laid a hand on her shoulder and drew a ragged breath. She tried to speak, but nothing would come.

Barny's hands released Olecia's face and his arms slid around her as she continued sobbing as if her heart would shatter into tiny pieces.

Alekin and Zoya were clinging to each other, as were Murom and Oksana. Murom also had an arm around Kadyn's shoulder. The boy's head hung low.

Vladimir stood in silence until Olecia's sobbing became soft sniffles as she remained in Barny's arms and Sasha kept a hand on her shoulder. His features set in a somber, haunted mask, Vladimir laid a hand on her other shoulder and said, "Olecia, Barny is right. We have no chance against the Cossacks unless he holds them off. We have no guns, or we would stay and fight them with him."

Barny's head lay against Olecia's, and she could feel him nodding his assent to what her father was saying. "But Papa," she said, her voice quivering, "there are too many of them. He may get two or three of them when he starts shooting, but the others will dive for cover and shoot back. They will kill him."

Vladimir patted her shoulder. "Barny understands what he is facing, honey. If he doesn't do battle with the Cossacks, all of us will die. I wish it could be different, but we've discussed it, and there is no other way to do it. I have no words to speak my admiration for him."

Olecia sniffed, still clinging to Barny. "Oh, Papa, I prayed so hard that Barny would be saved. The Lord sent him here so we could lead him to Jesus. Why . . . why would He let him be killed?"

Vladimir was trying to think of how to answer her when she said, "I don't understand. We have loved each other for so long, and now that Barny's saved we could have a life together, a home, children. I can't let him do this thing."

"Olecia," said Barny, "there is no choice. I have to deter the Cossacks to save your life and the lives of these others."

She eased back in his arms and met his gaze. "Barny, I am staying with you. I can fire your revolver at the Cossacks while you use your rifle."

Barny shook his head. "No. I can't let you do it."

"Olecia," said Sasha, "you have never fired a gun. You might not hit any of them. You would be wasting Barny's bullets. He can do much more damage with those bullets than you can."

Tears rolled again as Olecia blurted, "Then I will just stay and die with him!"

"No, Olecia," said Barny. "I won't let you throw your life away. I want you to go to America and have a long, happy life."

"But I don't want to live if I can't have you!" she sobbed.

"I love you for feeling this way, precious Olecia," said Barny, "but I will not let you stay here and die."

"I haven't fired a gun since the Crimean War, Barny," said Vladimir, "but I'm sure the feel of it would come back to me. I'll stay and fight them off with you."

Sasha's body tensed, but she could only look at her husband with fear-filled eyes.

"I can't let you do that, Mr. Petrovna," said Alekin. "I have never fired a gun, but

I'm sure I could hit some of those Cossacks. I'll stay with Barny."

"No, Alekin," said Murom. "I will stay with Barny. You must make it to America with Zoya."

"I appreciate these offers," said Barny, "but I am going to do this alone. You are all going to be in those sleighs when they pull out in the morning. There is no need for anyone but me to stay behind."

Quietly the group moved back to the rear of the cave and stood close to the fire. Olecia clung to Barny, sobbing, but after a while, finally gained control of her emotions. She was sniffling when Vladimir said, "I watched a lot of my comrades die in the war, but I have never faced anything like this. Barny, I — I'm so sorry. Sasha and I have known for a long time how Olecia felt about you. She has prayed all this time for you to be saved so the two of you could marry and have your lives together. I have to admit that I don't understand why the Lord would let circumstances work together that would bring you to Him, then let you be placed in such a position that you must sacrifice your life to save the rest of us. Please don't misunderstand me. I'm not accusing God of doing wrong. I just don't understand this situation."

"I don't understand it either, Vladdie," said Sasha, clinging to his arm. "Why would the Lord allow this predicament, with no way out but for Barny to die fighting off the Cossacks?"

"I can't say that I understand, either," spoke up Murom, "but one passage of Scripture comes to my mind. Isaiah 55:8–9. 'For my thoughts are not your thoughts, neither are your ways my ways, saith the LORD. For as the heavens are higher than the earth, so are my ways higher than your ways, and my thoughts than your thoughts.' "

"Yes, darling," said Oksana. "Our little finite minds cannot begin to fathom God's thoughts. We are in a position here that we must trust our heavenly Father's ways, and not question Him."

"But we can pray, can't we?" said Kadyn. "We should ask the Lord to somehow let Barny stop the Cossacks but not be wounded or killed."

"That would take a miracle," said Olecia. "Those Cossacks are fierce fighters. When Barny opens fire on them, he won't be able to shoot fast enough to take them all out. They will leave their saddles in a hurry and take cover. He will be outnumbered."

"Kadyn is right, though," said Vladimir.

"Let's have a prayer meeting, and ask the Lord for just such a miracle."

All agreed and knelt together in a circle around the fire as Vladimir led them in heartfelt prayer.

That night, when all were in their bedrolls near the crackling fire, Olecia was lying next to her parents. Raising up on an elbow, she glanced at Barny and found him looking at her. Holding his gaze for a moment, she turned and said, "Papa, could I have a few minutes to talk to Barny alone?"

"Of course, honey," responded the heavy-hearted father.

Putting their coats on, Barny and Olecia moved to a quiet corner in the cave and sat down. The light of the flickering fire danced on their faces as Barny put a strong arm around her and pulled her close.

"B-Barny . . ." she said haltingly, "I . . . I just wanted to tell you that if . . . if in God's higher thoughts, He chooses to let you go home to heaven tomorrow, I —" She choked up, then swallowed the lump in her throat. "I want you to know that I will never marry anyone else. I love you so very much that I could never marry another man."

Barny squeezed her tight. "Sweet Olecia . . . it is all in God's hands. I will accept whatever He chooses to do. I must save your life. And, of course, the lives of the others. I love you the same way, my darling. If it was the other way around, I could never marry another woman. You are the one and only love I will ever have."

They mingled their tears as they shared a tender kiss, then returned to the others, lying in their bedrolls. As yet, no one had been able to fall asleep.

As the night passed, Olecia was barely able to sleep. She was wide awake when her father rose from his bedroll better than an hour before dawn and called for everyone to get up.

Sasha soon learned that no one felt like eating. Convincing them that they needed something hot before going out into the frigid air, she talked them into drinking some robust hot tea laced with honey, but even then, they had to force it past the lumps in their throats.

Dawn was barely a hint of gray in the eastern sky when the sleighs were fully loaded and ready to pull out. The group gathered around Barny, and Vladimir led them in prayer one more time.

Olecia waited while the others embraced Barny, each one trying to find the appropriate words. Then while they were climbing into the sleighs, Olecia moved up to him, tears running down her cheeks.

Barny took hold of her hands and said, "Please, Olecia, my love . . . have a happy life. God has blessed me so much by letting me know you and love you all these years. Your sweet witness to me has brought me to salvation, and . . . and the Lord has given me this opportunity to save your life. Maybe this is the only thing He has for me to do in this world. And if so, it's all right. I was thinking while lying awake last night, that possibly God is sparing you in this way because He has greater things for you to accomplish for Him. This gives me a little part in it."

Olecia blinked at her tears. "Oh, Barny, I can't . . . I can't —"

"Let me do this for you out of a grateful heart, Olecia. God has been so good to me, not only in giving me salvation, but in letting me have your love. Please don't feel sorry for me. Just use the life the Lord has given you for His honor and glory."

With hot tears streaming down her ashen face, Olecia placed her hands on his cheeks. Running her gaze over his beloved face, she tried to memorize every nuance of it and hide it deep in her heart. Rising on tiptoes, she placed a soft kiss on his lips. Their tears mingled as they held each other close.

Both of them heard the sound of the sleighs moving past them to the outside.

"I love you so much, my precious," Barny whispered in a choked voice.

Her warm breath on his ear, she said, "I will never stop loving you. You are my only love." With that, Olecia turned and hurried toward her father's sleigh without looking back, for fear that another glimpse of Barny would make it impossible to leave. As she climbed in among the blankets, Murom snapped the reins and put his sleigh in motion. Vladimir did the same, and the heavily loaded sleighs moved silently across the deep snow toward Kuwalt Pass.

It was all Olecia could do to keep from turning around to look at Barny. Staring straight ahead where stars still twinkled in the heavens above the mountain peaks, she saw nothing but the face she had committed to memory and had buried with her love in the depths of her heart.

As the sleighs headed up the steep trail, Barny swallowed back a rush of tears that were threatening to overwhelm him. "Good-bye, my love," he said with quivering voice. "If never on earth again, I will see you in heaven."

He watched the sleighs until the trail bent, taking them from view in dense timber, then looked down the trail the other direction. It was barely light, but there was no sign of the Cossacks.

"I'll be ready for you when you do come," he said grimly and returned to the cave to get his rifle.

Down the trail, Captain Lifkin Shanov and his men were busy digging their way through a huge drift the wind had piled in front of the cave's mouth. Having no shovels, they had to dig with broken tree limbs and their gloved hands.

Sergeant Waldo Kitmer plowed snow with both hands like a madman. Since they first entered the cave, Kitmer had paced and fumed with fury boiling inside him toward Barny Kaluga.

Captain Shanov watched the sergeant exert himself in the snow until he had to stop and catch his breath. Stepping up to him, Shanov said, "You might as well settle down, Sergeant. You can't take your vengeance out on Private Kaluga. He's dead."

"I . . . know," said Kitmer, sucking hard for air, "but it'll make . . . me feel better . . . when I've punished those . . . people in the sleighs for being friends of the dirty traitor.

The reason I'm digging so hard is . . . because I don't want them to . . . get away."

"We'll catch them," said the captain, grit in his voice. "And when we do, I am going to personally kill every one of them while you men watch."

"Come on, now, Captain," said Kitmer. "You can't take that privilege all to yourself."

Shanov's face crimsoned. "I can't? Who's in charge here?"

While working, the other men were listening to the conversation. One of them said, "Sergeant, what difference does it make if Captain Shanov executes them? They will still be dead, won't they? Come on now. The faster we get this snow out of our way, the sooner we'll catch up to those two sleighs."

At the higher level, Barny Kaluga picked up his rifle in the cave and checked the loads. He was glad for the extra cartridges in his coat pockets. He checked the loads in the revolver once more, and patted the full cartridge belt.

Moving back outside, he found the eastern sky growing lighter. Standing knee deep in the snow, he glanced down the trail, but still there was no sign of the Cossacks.

He looked the other direction and fixed his gaze on the spot where he had last seen the sleighs. "Dear God," he said with a tight throat, "please take care of my darling Olecia. If . . . if You see fit to let me die at the hands of the Cossacks, I ask, please, that You allow me to detain them long enough that the Petrovnas and the Tambovs may escape their cruel clutches. Please help me to do this task whatever the cost. Thank You, Lord, for the brief but precious time I had with Olecia. It was so very special. And if I must die to give her freedom, I will do it with a willing heart. There was more love packed into those few moments than some people ever experience in a lifetime."

Wiping away tears that were threatening to freeze on his face, Barny looked heavenward. "Lord, one more thing. I ask that sweet Olecia be able to find love with a good Christian man, even though right now, she doesn't believe she can ever love anyone but me. I want her to have a full and happy life in America."

Barny's attention was drawn to the east, where the brilliant top rim of the sun was crawling over the lower peaks. The sky was as clear as crystal. He stamped his feet and worked his arms to keep the circulation going and sent another glance back down the trail. There was still no movement, but he knew the Cossacks would be coming shortly.

After staring at the snow-covered trail for another moment, he looked back to the west and let his gaze settle once more on the last spot where he had seen the sleighs. The gnaw of loneliness stretched through him, then was replaced by the dread of what was coming with the Cossacks. His hand tightened on the rifle. He felt a weight growing in his chest like thickening lead.

Taking a deep breath, Barny let it out in clouds on the freezing air and said, "Well, I'd better get situated."

He looked around for an advantageous spot where he could fire down on the coming enemy. His attention was drawn to an outcropping of rock about sixty or seventy feet above, slightly to the west of the cave. "That's it," he said aloud. "Perfect."

Studying the situation, he saw a way to get to it, but before heading that direction, he glanced once more up the trail. The tracks of both sleighs lay in absolute silence. Every minute the distance between Olecia and himself was growing greater. His heart felt like it would explode into a million pieces.

Moving away from the mouth of the cave, Barny strapped the rifle on his back and began his climb to the outcropping, but with the latest storm, the snow was deep. He had to scrape it away little by little in order to gain solid spots for his hands and feet.

When he was about halfway up, he was balancing on a slender rock with his feet while brushing snow from a cone-shaped rock so he could get a good grip and move up higher. Suddenly his feet slipped, and he found himself falling helplessly. When he hit bottom, he tumbled a few feet in the whiteness. Wiping snow from his eyes, he worked his way to a standing position, glad for the cushion the blizzard had left him.

He was cleaning snow from the muzzle of the rifle when he heard a horse whinny down the trail, followed by another. His heart pounded his rib cage as he hastened to begin his climb again.

Higher up the trail the sleighs climbed steadily in the light of the rising sun as the horses trudged through the deep snow.

Olecia was sitting in the rear seat of the Petrovna sleigh beside her mother. Kadyn was in the front seat with his father. The Tambov sleigh was directly ahead, maintaining a distance of no more than thirty feet.

Olecia was staring straight ahead, blankly.

Sasha took hold of her daughter's gloved hand. "Sweetie, you haven't said a word since we left the cave. Would it help to talk about it?"

Lips quivering, Olecia looked at her mother. "What's to talk about, Mama? All I can say is, I wish I had stayed behind to die with Barny. I will never love anyone but him."

Sasha tightened her grip on Olecia's hand. "I can relate to how you feel. When your father and I were promised to each other and he was away in the Crimea fighting in the war, I feared, of course, that he would be killed. I used to tell the Lord that I would never love anyone but Vladimir Petrovna. I told Him if He ever meant for me to be a wife and mother, He would have to bring Vladdie home to me. Otherwise, I would live my life out as a spinster. I know the kind of thing that is going through your mind right now."

"But Papa came home to you," said Olecia, staring straight ahead again.

"Yes, because it was God's will, honey. Please remember that the Lord loves you, and He has a perfect plan for your life. It is hard for you to understand this right now, I know. But you were saved by faith, and you must walk by faith. You must trust your heavenly Father and let Him work out His will in your life."

The bitter cold had frozen the tears on Olecia's eyelashes. She brushed the ice crystals away, and taking a deep, shuddering breath, tried valiantly to calm herself but with little success. Sniffling, she said, "But, Mama . . . why did the Lord let me love Barny so much and even see him saved, then allow this horrible thing to happen? My life can never be happy without Barny."

Knowing how much Olecia's young heart was aching, Sasha prayed for wisdom then said, "I understand that right now you cannot possibly imagine loving someone else. But remember, precious daughter, that our God does all things well. And in the Psalms, He told us He will perfect that which concerns us. Time is a powerful healing element, and you must trust the Lord to do what is best for you, even if it takes a while for Him to show you His will for your life. Our finite minds cannot begin to comprehend the mind of God, but to question His wisdom is a sin."

Olecia's eyes remained blankly staring straight ahead.

Moving closer to her, Sasha put an arm around her daughter, fighting her own tears. "God alone can see our future, and even though right now we are very confused by all of this, one day in His own good time He will make it plain to us. For now you must put your complete trust in Him and let His grace and peace heal the pain in your shattered heart."

Olecia laid her tired head on her mother's shoulder, burying her face in the fur collar of her coat. Sasha stroked her head lovingly as Olecia murmured pleadingly into her mother's warm embrace, "Help me, God. Please help me."

The sleighs continued to climb steadily higher. After a while, Olecia sat up and dried her tears. Sasha held her hand under the blanket.

From time to time, Olecia turned and looked back as if it would bring Barny back to her. But there was only the steep trail, lined with snow-laden trees and snow-covered mountains.

With the sound of whinnying and snorting horses coming from down the trail, Barny scrambled upward breathlessly, trying to reach his vantage point before the Cossacks put in an appearance.

Finally reaching the outcropping, he panted for breath while he took the rifle from his back and flattened himself on the snow. Working the lever, he jacked a cartridge into the chamber. He heard a horse snort again and within seconds the unit of black-uniformed riders came into view.

Captain Lifkin Shanov and Sergeant Waldo Kitmer were in the lead, with the others following single file. Corporal Victor Yarden was first behind them. All of them had rifles in hand.

"Lord, help me," Barny whispered. "The lives of those people in the sleighs depend on what I do right here."

He shouldered the rifle, drew a bead on Captain Shanov's chest and squeezed the trigger. The sharp report of the rifle sliced through the quiet morning air, echoing across the mountains, as Shanov stiffened, then peeled out of the saddle. Instantly, Barny worked the lever and fired again. His target this time was the sergeant, but as with the other men, Kitmer was diving into the snow and the slug missed him.

Barny got off another shot, taking out Corporal Yarden. The other Cossacks were burrowing themselves in the deep snow while attempting to locate the shooter. The horses were dancing nervously and making fearful sounds. Pale plumes of breath streamed from their wet black nostrils.

When Barny fired the fourth time, his

bullet barely missed a Cossack, but by this time they had located him and unleashed a barrage of gunfire. Lying flat, head down, Barny heard the bullets chipping rock just above him and felt the pieces showering him. He raised his head slightly, poised to return fire when he had the chance. A slug chipped rock on the edge of the outcropping and splattered his face.

Blinking against the rock particles, he fired again, then had to duck once more as bullets chewed into rocks all around him. "Please, God," he breathed, "help me to hold them off till Olecia and her family can get away."

Suddenly, Barny heard a deep rumbling sound shuddering the air like summer thunder. He raised his head to look around, but had to duck in a hurry as more bullets came his way.

Higher up in the mountains, the sleighs were stopped while Murom, Vladimir, Alekin, and Kadyn were struggling to move a huge fallen evergreen tree from the trail.

In the rear seat of the lead sleigh, Zoya turned and looked at her sister. "Are you all right, Olecia?"

There was a slight pause as Olecia drew a quivering breath. Nodding, she said, "As good as can be expected."

"You just hang in there, sweetie," Oksana said from the front seat. "The Lord has His hand on you. Everything is going to be —"

Oksana's words were suddenly cut off by the distant sound of gunfire coming from the lower level behind them. The heads of the men whipped around to look that direction as the sharp cracking noises continued to echo and reverberate across the mountains.

Everyone was frozen in place.

Olecia's eyes were wide as she stared downslope into the dense, snow-laden forests, her hands trembling. Sasha quickly grasped them.

The gunfire went on for another minute or so, then stopped abruptly.

All was still.

As the silence prevailed, Olecia's stomach cramped painfully. Grief came swooping like a gruesome dark bird into her heart, and she cried, "Barny's dead! They've killed him! They've killed hi-i-im!"

The men hurried from where they stood as Sasha wrapped her arms around Olecia. Oksana and Zoya jumped out of the lead sleigh and hurried to the grief-stricken girl. As the group gathered close, Zoya jumped in the sleigh, and along with her mother, embraced Olecia as she wailed repeatedly that Barny was dead.

Olecia's prolonged loud wailing covered the distant rumbling sound at the lower elevation. The attention that came from her mother and sister soon quieted her.

When there had been no more gunshots for three or four minutes, Vladimir removed his fur cap. Face pallid, he said, "God bless Barny's memory. He died a hero, trying to save our lives at the cost of his own."

The others were nodding, fighting their own emotions.

Replacing the cap on his head, Vladimir said, "The Cossacks will be coming. We must hurry on."

The men quickly finished their task of removing the tree from the path, and tears were on every cheek as Murom and Vladimir snapped the reins, putting the sleighs in motion once again.

Every heart was a heavy lump as the realization of what Barny Kaluga had done fully penetrated their saddened minds.

Sixteen

With Captain Lifkin Shanov lying dead in the snow, Sergeant Waldo Kitmer took charge by calling to the men. "Get as deep into the snow as you can! The shots are coming from up high. Anybody see the ambushers?"

The horses were dancing nervously, kicking up snow and neighing shrilly.

Corporal Victor Yarden was prostrate in the snow a few feet to Kitmer's left. Raising his head slightly, he lifted a hand, pointed a finger in the direction of the outcropping, and started to speak, but another shot pierced the air and Yarden let out a grunt as the slug found its mark. His face fell into the snow.

One of the horses bolted and headed down the trail and another followed. The others, though frightened, stayed with their riders.

Another shot rocked the air, this time just missing one of the men, and another pointed up to the outcropping. "Sergeant! Up there!"

Every man pointed his rifle in the direction of the shooter and unleashed a barrage of gunfire. Bullets chipped rock, and as they worked the levers of their rifles to fire again, Kitmer saw a head lift up and was shocked when he saw the face.

One of the men fired at the man on the ledge, hitting rock. The ambusher fired again and had to duck as the other Cossacks unleashed hot lead at him.

When the men were working the levers of their rifles to fire again, one of them said, "There's only one man up there, Sergeant."

"I know," said Kitmer. "Did any of you get a look at his face?"

All shook their heads as they shouldered their weapons, ready to fire again. They were stunned when Kitmer said, "It's Barny Kaluga!"

"Kaluga!" gasped one of them. "Are you sure?"

"Yes, I'm sure! I got a good look at him for a second or two, but it was enough. It's Kaluga, all right. You men keep firing at him. I'm going to work my way around the bend down there and find a way to get up on that ledge above and behind him. From that perch, I'll be able to get a good shot."

Kitmer rose to his feet and dashed down the trail, zigzagging so as to make himself a difficult target as he ran. The men were aiming at the edge of the outcropping where

Barny was situated, ready to commence firing again when suddenly they heard a deep rumbling sound that shuddered the air. They looked up at the steep mountain slopes above them to see a massive avalanche of snow sliding toward them at unbelievable speed.

"The gunfire did it!" shouted one of them as he sprang to his feet and started running.

The others jumped up, too, horror showing on their faces. They knew they were not going to make it. The horses were screaming, eyes wild, as they danced about, not knowing which way to run.

Thirty yards below them, Waldo Kitmer was bounding down the trail in the white depth when he heard the rumbling above him and paused to look up. What he saw lanced terror into his heart. It was like the entire world had suddenly become a tumbling mountain of snow, throwing up a fine spray above its churning, sliding mass as it descended on him at breakneck speed. For an ageless moment, he stood frozen in place. There was nowhere to run.

The avalanche was going to engulf him.

His heart was a wild beast in his chest, trying to claw its way out.

Just as he released a jagged breath from his lungs, the pressure wave hit him. In its sudden vacuum of air, his eardrums popped, sending a jolt of pain through his skull.

Behind the pressure wave was a gigantic thundering wall of snow. When it hit him, it picked him up, carrying him toward the edge of the canyon. The roar was deafening as a white cloud inundated his senses, filling his mouth, and knocking off his tall fur hat. He felt himself tumbling head over heels. Instinctively, he flailed his arms and kicked with his legs.

Suddenly he was falling through space in a maelstrom of snow . . . down . . . down . . . down.

From his high perch, Barny Kaluga watched in awe as the avalanche rolled down the sides of the mountains, missing him by no more than twenty yards. He saw the Cossacks and their horses engulfed helplessly in the sliding white death as it buried them in its wake, carrying some of them into the vast depths of the canyon.

When the last of the sliding snow had come down, there was a heavy silence. Barny closed his eyes and said, "Thank You, Lord. You let the gunfire vibrate the air and shake the snow loose. The Petrovnas and the Tambovs are no longer under the Cossack threat."

Running his gaze over the scene below, he estimated that the Cossacks and their horses that were still on the trail were buried under at least twenty feet of snow. No man or animal could survive in that depth.

Strapping the rifle on his back, Barny began his descent down the treacherous snowy face of the rock wall. "Olecia," he said with ecstasy, "I'm coming, darling! I'm coming! We'll have our new life together in America!"

Slowly and carefully he moved down, slipping and almost falling twice.

When he was some thirty to forty feet above the trail, his feet suddenly slipped, pulling his hands loose from their grip on a jagged, rocky lip. As he was falling, his head struck a jutting piece of rock, sending fiery streamers through his brain. He landed in the soft depth of snow with a black tide lapping at the edges of his vision.

Moaning, he rolled over and tried to raise his head. A wave of dizziness washed over him, and suddenly he was floating on the surface of a swift river toward the edge of the world. He felt himself go over the edge into a void, still and dark.

When Sergeant Waldo Kitmer regained consciousness, he felt himself in a cramped, uncomfortable position, lying on his back. Coldness was seeping into his bones. Where was he? What had happened?

Suddenly it all came back to him. The traitor firing from the rock ledge. Captain Shanov lying dead in the snow. His own legs carrying him down the trail. And then . . . the avalanche!

Of course. It was only natural. Gunfire in a mountainous area like this right after the storm had loaded the steep slopes. He had to be buried beneath tons of snow. But he could breathe!

Kitmer opened his eyes, expecting only darkness. Instead, there was faint light just above him. And a gray granite surface of smooth rock around him. He was in a hole of some kind. It wasn't deep. The hole was partially covered by the root end of a large fallen tree. The tree had kept the heavy, sliding snow from filling the hole. If he could get on his feet, his head would be out in the air.

Struggling to put his cold limbs into motion, he managed to get on his knees. Then pressing his palms against the walls of the hole, he rose up, twisting his body past the tree, and thrust his head through the snowy opening and looked around. The sun was halfway up the eastern sky in its morning arc. He could see the edge of the trail high above him to the north, but was surprised to find a gentle slope reaching toward the trail, where the avalanche had carried him over the edge. If he had been fifty feet farther up the trail when he went over, he would have gone to his death in the depths of the canyon.

With a little more effort, Kitmer was out of the hole, standing almost hip deep in the snow. He put his hand to the holster to make sure he still had the revolver.

It was gone. Lost in his fall.

He no doubt had dropped the rifle when the avalanche hit him. It was buried somewhere under tons of snow.

Kitmer's whole body was quivering. He thought of the cave higher up the trail where he had seen the two sleighs and the people through the telescope. It would be much warmer in the cave. He was sure the Petrovnas had headed up the pass by daylight that morning. It would take him most of the day to do it, but Kitmer told himself he must reach the cave before dark.

As he plodded his way up the slope toward the trail, he thought of Barny Kaluga. He figured the traitor was probably buried in the avalanche, but found himself wishing Kaluga were alive. He would love to get his hands on him . . .

Barny woke from red dreams of Cossacks,

gunfire, bullets chipping rock around him, and the deep rumble of sliding snow.

But there was only silence. There were no Cossacks. They were buried in the avalanche, he recalled.

His head was throbbing, and every pulse beat sent blades of pain stabbing through it. He sat up in the snow, removed a glove, and put a hand to the knot on the side of his head where it had struck the protruding rock when he fell. There was clotted blood where the skin had split, but it wasn't bleeding at all now. Probably the cold air.

The pain caused faint sprays of twinkly yellow and white lights in the blackness behind his eyelids. There was so much pain, Barny wondered why he had even regained consciousness. He was surprised that his head was clear. Maybe it was because his whole body felt like it had been buried in ice for a hundred years. He was cold all the way to the marrow of his bones.

With effort he made it to a standing position. Pulling the revolver from its holster, he found the cylinder packed with snow. Breaking it open, he cleaned out the snow, made sure the cartridges were dry, and dropped the revolver back in the holster. Taking the rifle from his back, he checked the muzzle and found that it had not picked up any snow. Hanging it on his back again, he looked up toward the cave where the Petrovnas and the Tambovs had been, and headed toward it.

Plodding up the slope, he shuddered at the chill that was attacking his joints and muscles. His breath puffed out in cones of frost as he flailed his arms vigorously in an attempt to create some heat in his upper body. He was looking forward to building a fire in the cave.

Little more than a half hour had passed when Barny reached the mouth of the cave. His head was aching something fierce as he paused to look at the world of white around him before going inside. The only sign of life in the brilliant light of the late morning sun were three gray squirrels skittering across the trail, racing toward the dense forest.

Pressing his temples to help relieve the pain, he moved into the dusky cave and to the place where the wood was piled and the fire had been built before. Suddenly it struck him that he had no way to light a fire; but just as suddenly, his eye caught a gleam of red embers and a thin thread of smoke.

"Oh yes!" he said jubilantly as he removed the rifle from his back and laid it aside. "Thank You, Lord! You kept it burning for me!"

Stepping to the woodpile, he gathered some small pieces and carried them to the blackened spot on the cave floor. Kneeling, he laid them over the red glow, then blew on the embers. When he had the small pieces burning, he placed larger ones on the fire and smiled as they quickly turned black and burst into flame.

Soon the fire was blazing and giving off welcomed heat. Barny sat down, opened his coat to soak up the warmth, and held his palms toward the flames.

While his hands tingled from the heat, he thought about Olecia and the others. "Lord," he said, "You have let me survive thus far, for which I praise and thank You. But how am I ever going to catch up to the sleighs? I don't see how I can ever make it on foot. But there is no other way to do it. I need Your help. Please help me."

As the warmth of the fire slowly seeped into Barny's seemingly frozen bones, a lassitude stole through his weary body. His head began to drooped and his heavy eyelids closed.

Instantly, he jerked his head upright, blinked, and rose to his feet. Moving away from the fire, he briskly paced the rear part of the cave to shake off the drowsiness. *I mustn't fall asleep. I can't waste any time. I'm about thawed out now, and I need to keep moving on. I must somehow catch up to the sleighs. I have to let Olecia know I'm alive!*

He started toward the fire to soak up a little more heat before leaving, and a wave of dizziness assaulted his senses. He staggered, groped for the wall of the cave, and steadied himself with both hands pressed against it. When the dizziness eased some, he went back to the fire and carefully lowered himself to the ground. He shook his head gently, trying to clear away the rest of the dizziness. Pain shot across his brow and set up a pounding inside his head. A low moan escaped his lips as he clasped his head with both hands.

"What am I going to do, Lord?" he whispered. "I . . . I'm too weak to leave the cave and walk any distance in the deep snow. With my head pounding the way it is, I could collapse, pass out, and freeze to death. Olecia would never know I survived the battle with the Cossacks. Please, Lord. I'm a new Christian, and I don't even know how to word my prayer. I'm asking that You will help me to somehow catch up to Olecia so we can have our lives together and serve You."

The drowsiness he had felt earlier was on him again. His head drooped as before, and his eyelids felt like they were weighted with sand. He could fight it no longer. Lying down on the hard floor of the cave, he inched closer to the warmth of the fire. Making a pillow of his hands, he placed his aching head on them and was immediately asleep.

When the sun was at its apex in the crystal blue sky, the occupants of the sleighs were bustling about in the snow with the highest peaks in view to the west. The women were making lunch over a fire while the men were clearing away snowpacked, wind-blown brush that was entangled with trees on both sides of the trail, blocking it completely.

While stirring a pot of steaming broth, Olecia let her gaze drift into the dense forest on the north side of the trail and saw something move. She started to call to her father when she saw the movement again and focused on a large male wolf, his mate, and five pups who were trotting through the timber, single file.

The horses began to whinny and bob their heads. The men turned to look at them, and Olecia said just loud enough for them to hear her, "It's a family of wolves, Papa." She pointed at them with her chin. "Right over there."

The women glanced toward the wolves.

The male wolf paused, causing the others to do the same. He looked straight at Olecia for a brief instant, then tossed his head and led the mother and her pups over a ridge, running effortlessly, with powerful, limber muscles.

When the wolves had disappeared, Sasha said, "Whew! The way the horses were acting, I thought they might run away."

"They would have if the wolves had come this direction," said Vladimir.

Moments later, the group was standing around the fire, holding their bowls, and eating the broth. Sasha noticed the sadness that had come over her youngest daughter's features. Looking at her across the fire, she said, "Olecia, what's wrong, honey?"

Every eye went to the girl as she said, "Oh, just the wolves."

"What do you mean?" asked Vladimir.

"I didn't mean to show it, Papa. I'm sorry."

"What is it, honey? Did the wolves frighten you? Are you worried that they will come back?"

"No. That's not it."

"What then?" asked Sasha.

Olecia sighed. "It's just that . . . well, both the male and the female had their mate.

And . . . and they had their little ones."

Nodding, Sasha said, "And you were thinking that you will never have a mate and little ones because Barny is gone."

Olecia bit her lower lip, trying not to cry. "That's exactly what I was thinking."

"God knows He created you with the natural desire to be a wife and mother, honey. Since it can't be as Barny's wife, it doesn't mean it can't be as the wife of the young man He has all picked out for you."

Olecia knew she had already stated too many times that she could never love anyone but Barny. Biting her lip again, she dipped her spoon into the bowl and sipped the hot broth.

Vladimir and Sasha exchanged sad glances.

To change the mood of the moment, Murom pointed up the trail and said, "Just about two more days and we'll be going over the pass. America, here we come!"

"That's right, Uncle Murom!" said Kadyn, trying to help put a happy note in the air. "America, here we come!"

After struggling up the trail through the deep snow, Sergeant Waldo Kitmer approached the mouth of the cave. His body was quaking from the cold, and he had to bite down hard to keep his teeth from chattering. He had seen the smoke rising from the rocks on the mountainside above the cave.

Halting at the cave's edge, he carefully peered in. He could see the spot where the horses had obviously been kept. He quickly saw that there was another section of the cave farther back. Who was there to keep the fire burning? The traitor, maybe?

Desperate for warmth, Kitmer flattened his back against the wall of the cave, and inched his way inward. Soon he was close enough to see the shadows of the flickering fire dancing on the walls and ceiling. Holding his breath, Kitmer moved in farther. Suddenly he saw the form of a man lying on the earthen floor next to the fire and stopped. The man was asleep, breathing steadily.

Kitmer crept closer. When he could make out the black Cossack uniform, he grinned wickedly. It was Barny Kaluga. The traitor had fallen into his hands!

Careful not to make a sound, Kitmer moved closer. He saw Kaluga's holstered revolver on his hip, and only an arm's length away lay his rifle. Eyes fixed on the rifle, Kitmer thought that all he had to do was get his hands on that rifle! *I can lever a cartridge into the chamber quickly, and shoot the dirty traitor before he wakes up. That is . . . if there are cartridges in the gun. Maybe Kaluga used them all up while he was shooting at his ex-comrades from the rock ledge . . .*

Barny rolled his head, making a soft moaning sound, then settled down again.

Kitmer took off his gloves and stuffed them into his coat pocket.

Maybe the best thing would be to slide the revolver out of the holster, and — Wait a minute! That's too dangerous. Why not pick up one of those logs over there on the stack and bash him on the head? That would take care of him.

Moving cautiously, Kitmer made his way to the woodpile and closed his fingers around a stout log about three feet in length. As he lifted it off the stack, the movement caused two other logs to shift position, making a clattering sound. Kitmer's heart thudded in his chest as his head swung around. He waited to see if the sound had penetrated Kaluga's ears. There was no movement.

On the floor, Barny had indeed heard the clatter at the woodpile. Something . . . or someone was in the cave! Without moving his head, he slitted his eyes and saw the form of a man in a black uniform moving toward him, holding a log at one end with both hands. It was Sergeant Kitmer! How did he survive the avalanche?

Barny tensed, every nerve going wire tight.

Smiling to himself, Waldo Kitmer thought of the reward the colonel would give him when he returned to Kiev with the body of the traitor who had killed Captain Lifkin Shanov. When he stood over Kaluga, he gripped the log tightly and raised it high so as to bring it down with full force on the traitor's head.

Suddenly, Barny's feet shot out, kicking Kitmer's legs out from under him, toppling him to the floor. Quickly, Barny raised up on his knees and clawed for the revolver on his hip. Surprised but well-trained in hand-to-hand combat, the sergeant let go of the log and sprang at Barny, who had the gun out of the holster and was bringing it up.

Before Barny could cock the hammer, Kitmer slammed into him, grabbing for the gun. Barny was able to keep Kitmer's fingers from closing on the revolver but not from grasping his wrist. As both men struggled for control, they worked their way onto their feet. Grunting and hissing through clenched teeth, they staggered about the rear section of the cave, at times almost stepping into the fire.

At one point, Barny had Kitmer back-stepping, and in a quick move he planted his foot behind him, tripping him. They crashed to the floor, with Barny on top. Kitmer still had his grip on the wrist of Barny's gun hand, but having the edge because he was on top, Barny used his weight to bear down with the gun, and with a quivering movement, brought the muzzle to bear on the enemy's face. Kitmer's eyes bulged as he looked down the barrel.

As Barney was struggling to ear the hammer back, he could feel Kitmer's breath against his face. Straining. Trembling.

Suddenly Kitmer's knee came up against Barny's rump solidly, throwing him off balance. In the same instant Kitmer flipped on his side, raised up, and shoved Barny down. Barny used his free hand to make a fist and pop his adversary solidly on the nose. This watered the sergeant's eyes, temporarily disturbing his vision, which gave Barny time to regain his balance, but Kitmer was trying desperately to get a grip on the gun and wrest it from Barny's hand.

Seconds later they were on their feet

again, face to face. Barny jerked his gun hand violently in an attempt to break Kitmer's hold, and at the same time, Kitmer happened to be forcing his arm in the same direction. Suddenly the revolver slipped from Barny's fingers, sailed through the air, hit the dirt floor with a thud, then skidded out of sight into a dark corner.

Moving swiftly, Barny bent over, and with both hands, grasped the nonburning end of a log that lay in the fire. He swung the flaming end at Kitmer, who dodged the blow in the nick of time. Barny swung again and Kitmer jumped back, barely out of the log's reach. Barny rushed him, swinging it again, the flame hissing like a serpent. Again, Kitmer leaped back, but hardly had his feet under him when Barny went after him again, swinging the log with deadly force.

The contest continued, with Kitmer backing up while trying to figure out a way to counter effectively. Barny's white-knuckle grip held the flaming log with grim determination as he rapidly backed his opponent into the front section of the cave, and within seconds, they were outside the cave, standing in the snow.

Kitmer feinted a forward move just after Barny had swung. In his attempt to counter,

Barny slipped in the snow and went to one knee. Adeptly, Kitmer kicked the log from his hand and it sailed away, dropped into the snow with a hiss and was gone.

The sergeant ejected a howl of victory and lunged for his man. Barny was up, feet planted, and cracked him on the jaw with a powerful blow. Kitmer went down and Barny waited for him to get up, fists pumping.

In a rage, Kitmer clambered to his feet, shaking his head to clear away the cobwebs, and lunged at his enemy. Barny chopped him another one on the jaw, but it was only a glancing blow. Kitmer stumbled slightly, then whirled and charged, head down. Barny's feet slipped a bit when he was trying to set himself to punch him again, and Kitmer slammed into him full force. They went down in the snow, and now it was a wrestling match.

They rolled over and over in the snow, toward the edge of the canyon. One was on top, pounding his opponent, then the other. One of Kitmer's blows stunned Barny momentarily, which gave the Cossack the time he needed to close his hands around Barny's throat. As the fingers closed Barny's windpipe, Barny rammed a thumb into Kitmer's left eye. He howled and let go to put a hand to the damaged eye.

Barny threw him off, sprang to his feet, and cracked him solidly on the jaw. Kitmer sprawled on his back, but managed to evade Barny as he sprang at him. In seconds, both men were on their feet, swinging fists again. Kitmer was blinking at the blood that was coming from his damaged eye. He ejected a wild yell and charged.

Sucking for air Barny planted his feet, timed it just right, and kicked him savagely in the midsection. Kitmer went down, rolled over, and started to get up. Barny moved in and backhanded him, following it with a solid punch. Kitmer dived for his legs and quickly brought him to the snow-covered ground.

Gasping for air and spitting snow, Barny twisted loose from his grasp and swung a fist at Kitmer's jaw but missed. His head was pounding like it had before, from cracking it on the rock protrusion. Kitmer lunged at him, swinging his own punch, but also missed. For a moment, the two tiring men lay in the snow, staring angrily at each other, their breaths raking through them, making a raw sound.

Then suddenly the sergeant was up on his hands and knees, crawling at Barny, teeth bared. Barny shoved himself up, dived at him, and slammed his elbow into his mouth. Both men went down. Barny jumped on Kitmer, and gripping each other, they rolled closer to the edge of the canyon, plowing through the snow. They slid to a stop less than three feet from the precipice.

Panting, Kitmer growled, "I'm going to kill you, traitor!" As he spoke, he was staggering to his feet.

Barny rose to meet him.

The two panting men fell into each other, weary arms trying for a hold and not succeeding. Summoning strength from somewhere deep within himself, Barny pushed away from him and drove a fist into his stomach. Kitmer buckled, then swung at Barney's jaw. When the fist went harmlessly past his face, Barny had to think about it to get the strength to raise his right arm, but he managed to do so and punched him on the nose.

Kitmer took a step back, then lunged for his opponent. He got a hold on him, then wrestled him into the snow. They rolled over once, and suddenly both men peeled over the edge of the canyon. They landed on a narrow, protruding ledge some thirty feet below, sinking a foot into the snow.

The Cossack was on the lip of the ledge with the yawning canyon behind him. Mindful only of the man he was eager to kill, he rose up and planted his feet in the snow. As Barny stood up only an arm's length away, Kitmer swung at him with all his might. His feet slipped, sending him off balance, and suddenly he fell backward over the lip of the ledge and ejected a terrorized scream as he fell some eight hundred feet to the canyon's rocky bottom.

Gasping for breath, Barny watched until Kitmer hit bottom, then searched for a way to climb back up to the trail. He noted that to his right, there was a large spot of rock on the ledge that had been blown clean by the wind. Above it were small rocky shelves, also blown clean that he could use for climbing.

Taking a deep breath, he prayed for strength and started the climb. His feet slipped a few times for lack of space on the shelves, but he was able to keep a secure hold with his hands each time and move up steadily. He was about ten feet from the top when a foot slipped. His weight started down, and he tightened his grip on a shelf, but it wasn't enough. He fell all the way back to the ledge and landed on his back where the rock was bare.

The breath was knocked out of him. He lay there, gasping for air, suddenly aware of sharp pains lancing through his lower back. His head — already pounding from his previous fall — began spinning, and the dark void he had experienced before enveloped him.

Seventeen

Barny Kaluga's first sensation as he was regaining consciousness was the sharp knives of pain stabbing him in the small of his back.

The sun was slanting downward in its trek across the sky.

With great effort, Barny rolled on the ice-crusted rock ledge and sat up. There was a tingling in his legs that he had never felt before. His head was still throbbing, and he felt a bit dizzy. Crawling to the wall of the canyon, he pulled himself to a standing position. When the weight of his body settled on his legs, the tingling sensation was replaced with a numb feeling, which puzzled him. He was afraid if he tried to climb up to the trail, he might fall again, but he had to take the chance. He would freeze to death on this ledge if he stayed here tonight.

Forcing his legs to function, he began his climb. Sheer determination brought him to the trail after nearly three quarters of an hour. Exhausted and experiencing a throbbing headache, he lay in the snow to catch his breath and allow what strength he had left deep inside him to flow into his weakened limbs.

While lying there, he scooped snow into his mouth. Soon he felt strong enough to trudge through the snow to the cave. He still had a headache, but the throbbing had ceased. Once again on his feet, he grimaced at the pain in his back as he forced his numb legs to carry him. He stumbled and fell twice, but within a few minutes, entered the cave.

As he made his way slowly toward the rear section, he thanked the Lord for the cave and the protection it gave him from the elements. As fast as his cold, cramped hands would permit him, he added logs to the glowing embers and soon had a roaring fire going.

Making his way to the dark corner where his revolver had gone during the struggle with Waldo Kitmer, he found it next to the wall and picked it up. Sliding it into his holster he returned to the crackling flames.

Hovering over the fire, Barny said aloud, "What I wouldn't give for some warm quilts." He was amazed at the hoarseness of his voice. He decided it was because he had let his throat get so dry. He would eat some more snow later.

"Right now," he said, "I've got to work the numbness out of these legs." Bending at the waist, he started at his ankles and vigorously rubbed his legs all the way to his hips.

This effort caused his head to throb again and his lower back to complain from the movement. Pressing the heels of his hands to his temples, he said, "Dear Lord, I'm Your child, now so I'm in Your care. I'm almost afraid to lie down and sleep, but I must. I . . . I'm so weary."

He rubbed his thighs again, dropped to his knees, then lay down as close to the fire as possible. "Lord," he said, pulling the coat collar up around his ears, "please keep watch over me . . ."

And with these words he drifted off to sleep.

When Barny awakened, his stomach told him it had been a long time since he had eaten anything. There was no food in the cave. This would necessitate leaving the cave to find something to eat.

He found his legs still quite numb as he stumbled his way outside, rifle in hand. The sun was setting, filling the western sky with golden light.

It was dusk when Barny returned to the cave carrying two dead squirrels. He would cook one on a stick tonight and save the other one for morning. He would also eat more snow.

While Barny Kaluga was hunting squirrels in the golden light of the setting sun far below, the two sleighs were nearing the top of Kuwalt Pass. Murom pulled his team to a halt near a dense stand of blue spruce trees, and as Vladimir was pulling rein behind, Murom stood up and said, "Looks like there aren't any caves up this high. Let's make camp over here in the trees."

While the men were setting up the tents and the women were preparing supper over a fire that Kadyn had built, Sasha's attention was drawn to a large sled coming down the trail from the crest of the pass. She pointed it out to the other women, then called to her husband, "Vladimir, someone's coming!"

Glancing at Sasha, Vladimir saw her looking up the trail to the west and quickly focused on the sled, which was about eight feet wide and some thirty feet in length. It was being pulled by a team of four horses with two men in the seat.

By this time, Murom and Alekin were

looking at the sled. "Loggers," said Murom.

"Sure enough," said Vladimir. "Must be planning to cut their trees on this side of the pass."

"Let's go speak to them," said Vladimir. Turning toward the women, he called, "Sasha, we're going to give a friendly greeting to the loggers. We won't be long."

"Invite them to eat with us if you want to," she called back.

Vladimir nodded, then joined Murom and Alekin as they headed toward the trail. Quickly, Kadyn was running to catch up to them.

When the three men and the boy raised their hands in a friendly gesture to the loggers, the driver pulled rein, and smiling, said, "Hello. Making camp for the night, I see."

"Yes," said Vladimir. "We're on our way west, and we'll be glad to get over the pass tomorrow."

The sun was down over the high peaks when Vladimir and the others drew up to the campfire.

"They didn't want to eat with us, Vladdie?" said Sasha.

"Well, they thanked us for the invitation, but said they wanted to take advantage of the daylight that is left to get farther down the trail. They're from a little village called Stoyville down low on the other side of the pass. Since the government has restrictions where they can cut timber at different times of the year, they have to get their timber over here right now. They have to go lower before they can start dropping trees, and want to get an early start in the morning."

Sasha nodded. "I can understand that. Supper's ready. Let's eat."

After supper the travelers huddled around the fire as the last vestige of daylight was fading and shadows of the pines encroached darker and darker around them. A cold breeze fanned the fire, whipped up flakes of white ashes, and moaned through the trees. The wild howl of a wolf was heard, coming from somewhere in the forest, and the sky became a fascinating black dome spangled with white stars.

They talked about the loggers, who had introduced themselves as Tito Tkachev and Lysen Glikman. Both had families: Tkachev with four children, and Glikman with three.

"Did you tell them about us, Papa?" asked Olecia. "I mean, where we are going, and why?"

"No, we didn't. They were in a hurry to move on, so we bid them a quick farewell.

They will no doubt meet up with the Cossacks who are on our trail, and we agreed after they moved on that the less they know, the better."

"I wonder if Barny was able to take some of them out before they killed him," said Alekin.

Olecia felt a lump rise in her throat at the mention of Barny's death but did not let on.

"No way to know," said Murom. "I wish we did. It would help to know how many are following us."

"Well," said Vladimir, "since by this time tomorrow night, we'll be a good distance down on the other side, maybe we'll be able to stay ahead of them till we're safe in Poland."

"We've prayed hard to that end," said Zoya. "I just know in my heart we'll make it."

"That's right," Oksana said, patting Zoya's arm. "Our God can handle the Cossacks."

The next day, Barny was still experiencing a great deal of pain in his back, and his legs continued to go numb on him at times. He was able to bag more squirrels, giving him the needed substance for his body.

That night, while lying next to the fire, he

374

said, "Lord, I know so little about how You work in the lives of Your children. And You understand this. I'm in a really bad situation here. In a couple more days, I'll be out of firewood. I have no ax to supply more. I . . . I'm asking You to somehow provide me a way out of these mountains soon, and to make it so I can catch up to Olecia and her family. There is no way I can do it on foot, especially now, with this back injury and my legs going numb so often."

He prayed for God's hand on the Petrovnas and the Tambovs as they continued their journey over the pass and down the other side, asking the Lord to get them safely across the border into Poland. He was asking again for help in catching up to them as he fell asleep.

The sky above the jagged, windswept Carpathian peaks to the east was changing from pink to gold as Tito Tkachev and Lysen Glikman dropped their first tree. Dawn had brought a stiff wind, which only grew colder and more menacing as they continued their work.

Four hours later they were guiding the team down the trail. There were a half dozen huge trees on the sled, and their eyes searched the forests on both sides of the trail for another good place to cut more timber. They huddled in their fur coats with hats pulled down low as the wind knifed out of the north in hard, hissing gusts, hurling clouds of fallen snow and needle-sharp particles of ice at them.

Shuddering, Glikman rubbed his gloved hands together briskly. "I wish we could get out of this wind for a little while. My bones feel like they're frozen all the way through."

Tkachev, who held the reins, turned and looked at him. His face was like a stiff, ice-crusted mask. "A little break from it would feel good, that's for sure." Looking back to the trail ahead of him, he sighed. "But I guess we won't know real warmth till we get home, and —"

As Glikman turned to see what had cut off his friend's words in the middle of a sentence, Tkachev pointed ahead, saying, "Look, Lysen! Smoke!"

Trying to make out where he was pointing, Glikman said, "Smoke? Where?"

Shaking the pointing finger, Tkachev said, "See that cave? There's smoke coming out of those rocks above it, back to the left a little."

"Oh! Yes!"

"There has to be someone in the cave.

Maybe they would let us thaw out a bit at their fire."

"Let's go!"

Barny Kaluga was lying next to the fire, dozing, when he was suddenly awakened by a voice calling from the mouth of the cave. "Hello! Is there someone in here?"

Laboring to his feet with pain stabbing his lower back, Barny picked up his rifle and jacked a cartridge into the chamber. He could hear footsteps as the voice came again, obviously closer, asking if someone was in the cave. He raised the muzzle when two men entered the rear section. "Hold it right there!" he commanded sharply.

They drew up quickly, eyes widening at the sight of the Cossack uniform.

"Who are you?" asked Barny, steadying the rifle on them.

"We're lumbermen from a village called Stoyville, sir," said Tkachev. "It's on the other side of the mountains. My name is Tito Tkachev, and my friend, is Lysen Glikman. We're cutting trees where it is allowed by the government. We saw the smoke from your fire. The wind is fierce out there, and we're about frozen to the bone. We would like to warm up by your fire before we start cutting again, if . . . if that would be all right."

Lowering the rifle, Barny said, "Sure. Come on over by the fire."

A look of relief showed on the faces of both men as they moved up, yet Barny could read the touch of fear in their eyes as they began warming themselves. "We really appreciate this, sir," said Glikman.

"I'm happy to share the fire with you," said Barny. "You . . . ah . . . seemed a bit startled when you saw this uniform."

The lumbermen looked at each other, then Tkachev said, "Well, we don't mean any offense, sir, but —"

Barny smiled. "I understand, Mr. Tkachev. I know the Cossacks instill fear in the hearts of the Russian citizens." As he spoke, he set the rifle down, leaning it against the wall. "Let me explain that I am no longer a Cossack, though I am still clad in this uniform. I was Private Barny Kaluga. Now I am just plain Barny Kaluga."

Puzzlement showed in the eyes of the lumbermen; then Barny began telling his story. As he did, he saw them slowly relaxing. When he came to the part about his staying behind to hold off the Cossacks so the Petrovnas and the Tambovs could escape them, Tkachev and Glikman told him of meeting up with the two sleighs near the top of Kuwalt Pass. They explained that neither Vladimir Petrovna nor Murom Tambov had given them any information about where they were going or why.

Glad to hear that Olecia and her family were all right and still on the move, Barny went on to tell Tkachev and Glikman about his fall and the injury to his back. He then explained that he wanted to catch up to the Petrovnas and the Tambovs so he could go to America with them, but he knew he could never do it on foot.

Tkachev looked at his friend and said, "We must help him."

"I agree," said Glikman.

Then Tkachev said, "Barny, we have a strong dislike for the czar and his atrocities against the Russian people. We especially do not like the Cossacks, who carry out these atrocities. And you understand why."

"Yes."

"You took a stand against the Cossacks at the risk of your own life. We appreciate that. Lysen and I will take you with us to our village as soon as we can cut down enough trees to fill our sled. We should be ready to go day after tomorrow. Will that be all right?"

Barny smiled. "It sure will! I don't know how to thank you!"

"No need," said Lysen. "We are glad to do it for you. We want you to catch up to that young lady so you can have your life together."

"Do you know where Stoyville is?" asked Tkachev.

"I believe so," said Barny. "Isn't it about halfway between Kuwalt Pass and the foothills of the mountains?"

"Yes. We have a doctor in Stoyville. You need to let him check your back."

"I'll do that," said Barny. "I'm having a great deal of pain."

That night as Barny laid beside the fire in the cave with his two new friends sleeping close by, he thanked the Lord for answered prayer. Truly, God had worked in His own magnificent way to provide him transportation to a doctor. Barny had no doubt the Lord would provide the way for him to catch up to Olecia and her family.

By the end of the next day the lumbermen had felled their trees and loaded them on the sled. At dawn the following morning the huge sled pulled away from the cave with Barny sitting on the seat between Tito Tkachev and Lysen Glikman.

Four days later the sun was shining down from a cold afternoon sky when Stoyville came into view, nestled in a small valley. Smoke lifted from the chimneys of buildings in the business section and from the houses that surrounded it. People moved about in the streets, on foot and in horse-drawn vehicles.

The lumbermen had explained to Barny that Dr. Edin Parda was a retired army doctor and held disdain against the czar's government as did most of Russia's citizens. They knew the good doctor would be glad to treat a man who had turned against the Cossacks, though he still wore the uniform.

"We'll leave you with Dr. Parda while we go unload our timber," said Lysen. "As soon as we are finished, we'll be back."

Soon the sled was drawn to a stop in front of the doctor's office. Both men ushered Barny inside and were glad to see that Dr. Parda was between patients and had a moment to talk to them.

The silver-haired physician listened intently as Tito told him Barny's story and of the fall that had injured his back. He smiled at the ex-Cossack, saying he could not blame him for wanting to get out of the country and go to America.

The lumbermen took their leave, and after Dr. Parda had attended to the next scheduled patient who came in, he took

Barny into the back room. There he had him remove his clothing, put on a backless gown, and lie facedown on the examining table.

After a complete examination of Barny's back and legs and asking many questions about his pain and numbness, he had him sit up on the table with his legs dangling over the side. Parda rubbed his chin and said glumly, "Barny, it will be impossible for you to catch up to your young lady and her family anytime soon."

Concern showed in Barny's eyes as he said, "It's that bad, Doctor?"

"I'm sorry to say that it is, son. You have a very serious injury to the vertebrae and the discs in your lower back. I must fit you with a brace, and you must wear it at least two months. For the first month you will have to stay completely off your feet. If you are healing well by the end of the first month, you can use crutches to get around. Except for when you're bathing, you must wear the back brace all of the time."

Barny's brow furrowed. "Two months? That long?"

"At least. I will watch you closely. It may take longer. But you definitely cannot travel until the brace comes off."

"But, Doctor, I —"

"Barny, listen to me. If you don't do as I say, you could end up losing the ability to walk. Is that what you want?"

"Of course not. But, Doctor, I have no place to stay. I saw an inn down the street a ways, but I don't have much money on me. There is no way I could stay there."

The aging physician rubbed his chin thoughtfully. "I will explain your situation to Tito and Lysen when they return. Possibly one of them could keep you in his home. I would take you, but my wife is quite crippled with arthritis and wouldn't be able to help you."

Barny shook his head. "Doctor, I don't want to be a burden to either Mrs. Tkachev or Mrs. Glikman. There must be some other way."

"Well, before we go any further with it, let me talk to Tito and Lysen first. Right now, I must get your brace fitted."

Dr. Parda took Barny into a small private room and went to work to fit him with a stiff leather brace. He had to leave him at one point to take care of patients who had appointments.

While lying on a table, Barny said, "Dear Lord in heaven, I had no idea my injury was this serious. I thank You that You have let me live to come this far, but now I am stuck here for at least two months. I cannot go to Olecia. I have no way of letting her know that I am still alive. I . . . I am sure that by the time I am able to travel, the Petrovnas and the Tambovs will already be on their way to America. Please, dear Father, don't let her fall in love with some other man. Somehow I will have to get to America and find her. You sent Tito and Lysen to bring me this far. Please provide the way for me to go to America and find Olecia."

Dr. Parda returned to the small room after about an hour and finished fitting Barny with the brace. He was helping him get dressed when he heard the front door open, and excused himself. A few minutes later, Parda came in and had Tito and Lysen with him.

Barny had managed to finish dressing but his shoes still lay on the floor.

Smiling at him, the doctor said, "You did quite well, Barny. Of course there is no way you could put your shoes on. The brace will not let you lean over."

"I'll put his shoes on him," said Lysen, kneeling before Barny.

Tito laid a hand on Barny's shoulder and said, "Dr. Parda explained about the brace and that you would be wearing it for at least two months."

Barny nodded solemnly.

"I told them that even after the brace comes off," said Parda, "you will not be able to travel for about two weeks. It will be at least the first part of April before you can travel."

"He also told us you need a place to stay, Barny," said Tito. "My wife and I have a larger house than the Glikmans, so we will take you into our home. We have a spare bedroom. You will be our guest. We will see that you don't starve to death too."

Barny grinned at him. "Tito, don't you think you'd better talk to your wife first? She may not want a houseguest who can barely get around."

Tito chuckled. "I know Marita, Barny. When she hears your story, she will want to take you in."

"Yes, she will," said Lysen, rising to his feet. "My Naska would take you in, too, if we had another bedroom."

"All of you are very kind," said Barny. "And thank you for putting my shoes on, Lysen."

"My pleasure. Tito and I discussed your situation after Dr. Parda told us about the brace and all. Once Dr. Parda says you can travel on a sled or in a wagon, we will take you across the border into Poland and find someone there who will help you get across Poland to Germany. We know some people in a couple of the Polish border towns. After you get to Germany, you should be doing better and it will be up to you to get yourself to the Netherlands and to Rotterdam."

"I'll find a way," Barny said, giving him a crooked grin.

Pinching the collar of Barny's black shirt between his fingers, Tito said, "Something else, my friend. Tomorrow, I am going to take your measurements and buy you some new clothing so you can get rid of this Cossack uniform."

"I don't have enough money in my pocket to do that," Barny said, looking up to meet Tito's gaze.

"No matter, my friend. I said I am going to buy you some new clothing. I want you to understand that you will owe us nothing for the food you eat at our house."

"Your kindness is overwhelming, Tito," said Barny, "but I'm telling you right now that when I get to America and start earning money, I am going to repay you for your kindness."

Tito laughed, patted Barny's shoulder, and said, "We'll see about that!"

"We sure will," Barny said, grinning at him again. "We sure will!"

Eighteen

On Monday, March 29, the Petrovnas, the Tambovs, and Alekin Kolpino pulled into Rotterdam as the sun was lowering in the west. They had made good time in spite of the heavy snows they had encountered in both Poland and Germany. There was still deep snow on the ground in the Netherlands.

Having been to Rotterdam on two other occasions, Murom had explained to the group when camping the night before that the city lay some nineteen miles east of the North Sea, to which it was linked by a canal called the New Waterway. Prior to the latter part of the nineteenth century, all shipping in and out of Rotterdam was done on the Nieuwe Maas River, which flowed along the southern tip of the city on its way to the North Sea.

In the seventeenth century, when the discovery of the sea route to the Indies gave great impetus to commerce and shipping, Rotterdam expanded its harbors and docking accommodations along the Maas. By midnineteenth century, sea travel and commercial shipping was at an all-time high. Between 1866 and 1872 the New Waterway was dug to accommodate larger steamships.

As Murom drew his sleigh to a halt in front of the Dutch Arms Hotel and Vladimir pulled up behind, Olecia felt a painful twinge in her heart as she tried to imagine what it would have been like if Barny had lived and was going to America with her. The travelers had agreed that to hold costs down, the men would stay in one hotel room and the women in another. They were able to get adjacent rooms, and when the men had placed the women's luggage in their room, Murom ran his gaze over their weary faces and said, "We men are going to take the horses and sleighs to a nearby stable for safekeeping until time for all of us to embark for America and we sell them. We'll be back in a little while and take you ladies downstairs to the restaurant for supper."

Oksana kissed his cheek and said, "That sounds good, darling. In the meantime we'll unpack what we need."

Sasha smiled at Kadyn. "If you don't want to go with Papa, Uncle Murom, and Alekin, son, you can stay here with us."

Kadyn's features tinted slightly. "That's all right, Mama. We men need to stick together."

Zoya laughed and said to Olecia, "Our little brother is growing up. He already thinks like a man."

Olecia grinned, looking at Kadyn, and said, "You'll always be a little boy to me."

The other men were filing out the door. Kadyn playfully made a face at Olecia, crossing his eyes, then hurried into the hall, closing the door behind him.

Sasha, Zoya, and Oksana laughed, and Sasha said, "Just think of what you would have missed, Olecia, if Kadyn had never been born."

"Oh yes! I would have missed those faces he makes at me!"

Everyone laughed again; then Sasha picked up her valise and laid it on one of the beds. She looked around the room and said, "Aren't these beds wonderful? After being cramped in the sleighs and sleeping in caves and the tents for what seems like an eternity, we can finally sleep in real beds. And isn't it going to be fabulous to take a real bath? Just think, girls . . . a hot bath and a soft bed!"

"Mmm!" said Olecia. "I can hardly wait."

"Me too!" said Zoya.

"And me, too!" put in Oksana. "Well, let's get unpacked."

While all four were taking the necessary things out of their valises, Oksana said, "Sasha, I think you should enjoy the first bath when we come back from supper."

"Oh no," said Sasha. "You can go first. The girls and I will argue over who gets to be second."

"I insist you be first," said Oksana. "My nieces and I will talk about who will be second, third, and fourth."

"Let's just go by age, Aunt Oksana," said Olecia. "You will be next after Mama, then Zoya, then me."

The three agreed, then Olecia said, "Mama, you are outvoted. You get the first bath."

Sasha sighed, rolled her eyes, and said dreamily, "It sounds like a little bit of heaven, girls."

The group enjoyed a delicious meal together in the hotel dining room, talking about the long journey ahead of them as they would sail down the North Sea into the English Channel and across the Atlantic Ocean to America. Murom explained that the men would go to the docks together in the morning and he would book passage for them on the first available ship to America.

When they were finished eating, they lingered over steaming cups of strong black tea and talked about the hard journey they had just completed. Sasha put a hand to her mouth, trying to stifle a yawn.

Zoya was quick to say, "Mama, since you are going to bathe first, you go on up to the room. I'll go to the desk and have your hot water sent up."

"I will take care of ordering the hot water, Zoya," said Vladimir, rising from his chair. Then to the others he said, "I will be back shortly to have another cup of tea with you."

Sasha covered another yawn, excused herself from the table, and walked away with her husband. Vladimir paused at the desk to order the hot water, then accompanied Sasha to the bottom of the staircase. Kissing her cheek, he said, "I will see you in the morning. Sleep well, my love."

"I will, dear. And you too. Please send the girls up soon. We all need to get to bed early."

Conversation at the table had turned once again to the future they were all anticipating when Vladimir returned and sat down. Almost an hour passed; then Oksana said, "Well, girls, we need to go upstairs so we can get our baths too."

The men walked them up the stairs and after Murom and Oksana, and Alekin and Zoya had taken a minute to say good night, the women entered their room.

A single lantern was burning and Sasha was already in bed, fast asleep, with the covers up to her chin. All three paused and looked down at her freshly scrubbed face and her silky black hair, which was still slightly damp, lying in ringlets on her flawless brow.

Zoya smiled at the other two and whispered, "Even if she wasn't my mother, I would still believe she is the most beautiful woman in all the world."

"Me too," whispered Olecia.

"Who could argue with that?" said Oksana, her own gaze lingering on her beloved sister.

The next morning Rotterdam's docks were bustling with activity as Murom, Vladimir, Alekin, and Kadyn entered the ticket office of the Dutch Ship Lines. Three of the agents behind the counter were each busy with customers. The fourth, whose nameplate identified him as Hoek Van Tilburg, smiled as they approached him and spoke in Dutch, saying, "Good morning, gentlemen."

Murom knew Dutch vaguely, but since Great Britain was so close, and many of the Dutch people knew English, he decided to try what he had with the desk clerk at the hotel. "Do you speak English, sir?"

A smile broke across the clerk's friendly, fifty-year-old features.

"Why, yes, I do. But you and your companions do not look like Englishmen."

"We're Russians, sir," said Murom, throwing a thumb over his shoulder at Vladimir, "but this gentleman's mother was English. He has made sure everybody in the family can speak English."

"Well, I don't know Russian," said the clerk, smiling, "so let's stay with English, and I won't have to call an interpreter from the back room."

"Good enough," said Murom, then introduced Vladimir, Kadyn, and Alekin to him. "What we want, Mr. Van Tilburg, is to book passage to New York harbor in the United States of America for eight people. Kadyn here is the youngest. The others are women, all adults."

"Oh," said the clerk, the smile draining from his lips, "I am sorry, but it will be some time before I can put you on a ship to America."

Murom frowned. "Why is that?"

"Well, Mr. Tambov, the United States customs authorities have put a temporary hold on immigrants coming into their country. So many immigrants have gone to America from all over Europe, Africa, and the Caribbean, that the customs people at Castle Island have had to hold many ships in New York harbor for weeks before they could check them through."

Disappointment showed on all four Russian faces.

Van Tilburg cleared his throat uneasily. "The United States government has put a limit on how many ships can enter New York harbor from each country. The next ship from Rotterdam will leave here on June 15 and the next one will leave on August 12. I'm sorry, Mr. Tambov, but both of these are booked full."

Murom nodded, his features grim. "Well, sir, what is the first date you can book for us?"

"There is a ship scheduled to leave here on September 10. I can book you on that one with no problem. It will arrive in New York harbor approximately October 26, depending on the weather at sea."

Murom nodded. "What about if you have cancellations on the June or August ships? Could we get our names on a list of some kind?"

"I can put your names on both lists, Mr. Tambov," said the clerk. "But there are many people ahead of you already. I doubt there will be enough cancellations to get you on either ship."

Murom turned to Vladimir. "It looks like we don't have any choice. We'll just have to stay in Rotterdam until the September ship goes."

"Looks like it," said Vladimir.

"We'll have to find something less expensive than the hotel until we go in September."

"Of course. We'll have to find work, too, if possible. We're looking at better than five months."

"Ah . . . Mr. Tambov . . ." said Van Tilburg.

Murom turned to look at him. "Yes, sir?"

"There are eight of you, correct?"

"Yes. We four, plus my wife, Mr. Petrovna's wife, and his two daughters. His oldest daughter is engaged to Mr. Kolpino here."

"Well, sir, it so happens that the house next door to where my wife and I live just came open for rent. It is a small house, but maybe you can make it work. I can direct you to the house. The owner lives right across the street from it. I'm sure the rent will be much less than what it would cost you to stay in a hotel for all that time."

"Let's look into it," said Vladimir.

"All right," Murom said, pulling out his wallet. "Let's purchase the tickets for the September ship; then we'll go talk to the owner of the house."

When the reservations were made and the tickets purchased, Hoek Van Tilburg gave them directions to the rental house and to the house of its owner.

As the foursome stepped out of the ticket office and walked along the dock, Murom laid a hand on Vladimir's shoulder and chuckled as he said, "Tell you what, old pal . . . I'll be glad to let you have the honor of breaking the news to the women."

Vladimir put a smile on his lips and said, "Thanks."

All four had a good laugh.

In their room at the Dutch Arms Hotel, the women were sitting on the beds and discussing what they figured life in America was going to be like. There was a mixture of emotions. On one hand, they were excited about their new homeland, but on the other, there was much fear and trepidation.

"It will be so new and different from what we are accustomed to," said Oksana. "Even the food will taste strange to us, I'm sure."

"It shouldn't take us too long to get used to the food in America," said Sasha. "Wherever we end up, the climate will probably be something that will take some adjustment. I wish we knew where we are going to settle there."

"The Lord will lead us where He wants us to live," said Oksana.

"I've done some reading about America," said Olecia. "On the West Coast is a place called California, which sounds wonderful."

"I've heard about the mountains in California," said Zoya. "They call them the Sierra Nevada Range. They are supposed to be quite beautiful."

"I wonder if they are as towering and majestic as Russia's Urals and Carpathians," said Oksana.

"In my reading," said Olecia, "I found that the tallest mountains in the United States are the Rocky Mountains. They are east of California about a thousand miles. They have something like fifty-three peaks over fourteen thousand feet. There's nothing that high in Russia."

Sasha said, "We probably won't end up in any mountain ranges since we have to farm for a living. We will need level land to do that." A shallow frown furrowed her brow.

"I . . . I'm going to miss our homeland in some ways — especially our Christian friends in the underground church. Our neighbors, too. But won't it be glorious to have the freedom to worship and serve the Lord openly without fear of reprisal, imprisonment, or execution?"

"It sure will," said Oksana. "We'll be privileged to carry our Bibles anywhere we want, and won't have to hide them anymore. I will miss the old country, as you said, Sasha, and our friends. But our lives will be across the wide ocean where we can enjoy deliverance from the strong oppression under which we have suffered all these years."

A calm peace filled the hearts of the women and the discussion returned to their new country, with renewed hope of a better life.

Soon the men returned, and Vladimir broke the news of the five-month delay in embarking for America. Like the men, the women were disappointed, but with the dream of a new life in the "land of the free" still fresh in their hearts, they all agreed that it would be worth the wait.

Murom then explained about the rental house they had looked at. They found that it was simply too small for eight people, but the landlord had told them of another house about the same size that was for rent on the next street, less than a block away. Murom had rented both houses, and invited Alekin to stay with him and Oksana.

They moved into the houses the next day. Within a week, they had found a good Bible-believing church, and the men — including Kadyn — had found temporary employment to help their financial situation. Murom had put aside what he believed was enough money to take care of their plans for purchasing a farm in America, and down payment for a farm for the Petrovnas, and he would not touch it for anything else.

On April 5 in Stoyville, Tito Tkachev waited in the office while Barny Kaluga was being examined by Dr. Edin Parda.

In the examining room, Parda finished checking Barny's back and legs and sighed, saying, "You can put your clothes on now."

Raising himself to a sitting position, Barny frowned. "Is there a problem, Doctor?"

Parda took a few seconds to choose his words. "Barny, as I've told you all along, there is some healing in your back, and you're definitely walking better, but —"

"But what, Doctor?"

"Well, I wish you would wait another month before you try to travel. Give your back more time to heal first."

"I can't, Doctor," Barny said flatly.

When both men stepped into the office, Tito rose to his feet, looked at Parda, and said, "So, how is he doing, Doctor?"

"The healing process is coming along fine, Tito," Parda replied with a trace of strain in his voice. "However, I have advised him not to travel for another month. He needs to give the discs and vertebrae more time to heal."

Tito set his eyes on Barny. "So, what's another month?"

"Plenty," said Barny. "I can't wait any longer. Olecia and her family may already be on their way across the Atlantic Ocean toward America. The longer I wait, the farther they will get from me. Finding them in America is going to be difficult, for sure . . . but the more time that passes, the harder it will become."

Tito nodded, then said to Parda, "Doctor, I have a sledge. Would it help Barny if I took him on the sledge to my friends just across the Polish border?"

"Since the sledge is much heavier than a regular sled, it would be best, of course. And since he insists on going, please do use the sledge. But Barny, you are not quite halfway down this side of the mountains. You could still face bad weather — even blizzards — in Russia, Poland, and Germany till the end of May. When Tito leaves you in Poland, you will probably not have a sledge to ride on for the rest of your journey. No doubt it will be a sled or a wagon, and your body will feel every bump. If you are jostled severely, you could end up never walking again."

Barny looked dismally at the floor, rubbing the back of his neck.

"And let me warn you of something," said the doctor. "Don't try to ride a horse. Bouncing on a horse's back could undo the work I have done on you. If you have to provide your own transportation anywhere along the line, purchase yourself a sleigh or a wagon, depending on how much snow is on the ground at the time."

"Doctor," said Tito, "Lysen and I haven't told Barny yet, but we have pooled some money to give him so he can do just that."

Surprise showed in Barny's eyes. "Tito, I don't expect you to do a thing like that."

"We know it," said Tito, smiling. "But we're doing it anyhow."

In his heart, Barny said, *Thank You, Lord. For sure, You are looking out for me.*

Tito took out his wallet. "Also, Doctor,

Lysen and I have come up with the money to pay you for your services to Barny."

Parda was instantly shaking his head and holding up a palm. "No, Tito. Put your money away. This is my part in helping this young man to leave Russia and go to America."

"But, Dr. Parda," said Barny, "you can't —"

"Oh yes, I can. As I said, I wish you would wait another month to go, but I also understand about the young lady. Go with my blessings, Barny."

Barny thanked the doctor sincerely, and as he walked outside with Tito, he saw once again that God was taking care of him.

That evening, the Tkachevs had the Glikman family for supper in honor of Barny Kaluga, who would be leaving the next day.

While they were eating, Tito said, "Barny, Lysen and I will have the horses harnessed to the sledge and be ready to go at sunrise in the morning. If all goes well, we will have you out of the mountains in three days and be on our way on level land toward the border. As we told you, we are sure our Polish friends will help you get to the German border."

Barny smiled. "I wish there was some way

I could repay you people for what you have done for me."

Marita said warmly, "Barny, all we want for payment is for you to find Olecia and have a happy life in America."

"Thank you," he said, tears misting his eyes. "Thank you."

The three men pulled out of Stoyville as planned the next morning under a clear, cold sky. Barny was thankful for the padding Tito had put under him and for the heavy sledge, which made the trip down the steep trail much more comfortable.

At noon they pulled into a mountain village called Nunscow. Tito tied the team to a post in front of a clothing store and indicated a small eating establishment a few doors down where they would eat lunch. Barny walked awkwardly between them as he had to do since his fall.

When they came out an hour later, their stomachs comfortably full, Barny's attention was drawn to two men in black uniforms and tall fur hats who were talking to three townsmen in the street near Tito's sledge. When he stiffened and halted, Tito and Lysen both asked what was the matter.

Pointing with his chin, Barny whispered,

"Cossacks. See them?"

"We do," said Tito.

"Their units always stay close together," said Barny. "There are at least four more somewhere nearby."

"Do you anticipate a problem?" asked Lysen.

"I . . . I guess not. My first reaction was to keep them from seeing me. But these Cossacks can't have any idea what happened on the trail since all the men in that unit are dead."

"Let's just get on the sledge and leave this place in a hurry," said Tito.

The Cossacks continued to talk to the townsmen as Barny, Tito, and Lysen were drawing up to the sledge. In a casual manner both Cossacks happened to look their way.

"I know the one on the left," Barny whispered as they stopped with the sledge now between them and the Cossacks. "We were in training camp together. His name is Nadin Akhmatova. If he recognizes me, I'll tell him I'm out of uniform because I'm off duty."

Tito ejected a chuckle and said in a low voice from the side of his mouth, "That won't be a lie. You are off duty. Forever."

Akhmatova's brow puckered as his line of sight strayed to Barny's face.

"He recognizes you!" breathed Lysen.

Before Barny could make a move, Akhmatova's revolver was out of his holster and aimed at him. "Stay where you are, traitor Barny Kaluga!" bawled the Cossack. "Get your hands in the air!"

Barny's revolver was in the sledge under the blanket that had covered him. Strictly by reflex, he ducked low, grabbed the revolver, and remained out of Akhmatova's line of fire by darting along the board sidewalk and using the first saddled horse in front of the sledge team as a shield. Pain lanced through his back and legs, but he ignored it.

People on the sidewalk and in the street were trying to get away before the inevitable shooting started. Tito and Lysen ducked behind the sledge, knowing there was nothing they could do.

Nadin Akhmatova said to his comrade, "Turve, go around on the other side of the horses! I'll stay here. One of us will get him!"

From his vantage point, Barny drew a bead on Turve as he came toward him and fired. Turve went down with the slug in his shoulder, breathing hard, and unable to move.

Women were screaming and men were shouting as the street became a bedlam of confusion. Akhmatova fired twice at Barny, barely missing the horse and sending the bullets through a store window, shattering the glass. The sledge team whinnied and reared at the sound of Akhmatova's gun. Traffic was jamming up in the street as sleigh and wagon drivers pulled rein and tried to turn around.

Akhmatova fired twice more at Barny, but missed. But this time the double roar of his gun was enough to cause the sledge team to bolt. They charged into the street and were stopped abruptly when they slammed into a pair of wagons that blocked their path.

Four other Cossacks came running from up the street, but couldn't get through the traffic jam, which extended to the front walls of the buildings on both sides of the street. People on the board sidewalks, frozen in panic, were unwittingly blocking the Cossacks from getting through.

One wagon got turned around, but had to stop when another slammed it. Nadin Akhmatova had to dive for safety when the wagons collided and found himself rolling in the snow.

Barny took advantage of the moment. The horse that had become his shield belonged to one of the Cossacks. Stiffly he mounted the horse with pain shooting up his back and galloped down the street away from the traffic jam. He wished he could have said something to his friends, but his life was at stake.

Lying in the snow themselves, Tito Tkachev and Lysen Glikman watched Barny gallop to the next intersection and make a quick turn. As he vanished from view, Lysen said, "I hope he makes it."

"Me too," said Tito.

By the time the Cossacks could get through the traffic jam, Barny was out of sight, and it took only a moment for them to discover that he had taken a Cossack horse.

The captain in charge of the Cossacks commanded the people to pick up his wounded man and take him to the doctor, then called for his men to mount up. The Cossack whose mount Barny had taken jumped on the closest horse tied to a post. Nadin Akhmatova was in the saddle quickly and began asking the people which way the man went. Hating the Cossacks as they did, the people gave a variety of directions they saw the man go.

The angry Cossacks had no time to lay punishment on the people. The captain told them to spread out and find the fleeing Barny Kaluga.

Barny had no idea how the Cossacks had learned about the incident on the trail, but he knew the unit would search for him with dogged determination, and the first thing they would expect him to do was get as far away from the village as possible. He decided to fool them.

While riding swiftly down a quiet street where traffic had sufficiently tracked up the snow, he noted that nearly every house had a barn behind it. He picked a small, unpainted barn, and rode around to its backside. Still trying to ignore the pain, he slid from the saddle and quickly led the gelding inside the barn. There were no other animals in sight, for which he was glad.

Breathing hard, Barny put a hand to the small of his back and thought of Dr. Parda's warning about riding a horse. He shrugged, patted the horse's neck and said, "I'll put you over here in this stall, boy. We won't stay very long. Just until I think it's safe to ride on down the trail."

Suddenly the door at the front of the barn rattled and swung open. A bowlegged, silver-haired man with deep wrinkles in his face looked at Barny and said, "I saw you ride up and go behind the barn, young man. Why did you bring your horse in here?"

"How do you feel about the Cossacks,

sir?" Barny asked bluntly.

"They are a bunch of heartless brutes who dance on the czar's strings and torment decent people. That's what I think of them."

"Good. Then let me tell you a story . . ."

When Barny had finished his story, the old man said, "Well, Barny Kaluga, since you are no longer a Cossack, you're welcome here. My name is Otto Gagarin. Take the saddle off the horse and let's go in the house."

"Oh no, sir. Thank you, but it's best that I stay here in the barn. If the Cossacks catch you harboring the man they consider a traitor, they will kill you and possibly your family."

"I'm a widower, son," said Otto. "I live alone. I will take that chance in order to help you. Besides, there is no heat in the barn. The nights are still very cold. You would freeze to death out here."

When Barny could find nothing else to say, Otto laid a hand on his arm. "Come on. Take the saddle and bridle off the horse. I don't have any livestock anymore, but I still have some grain."

Ten minutes later, Barny followed Otto into the house, looking every direction for any sign of the Cossacks. When the door closed behind him, he felt safe.

As he was taking his coat off, his gaze fell on a well-worn Bible lying on the kitchen table. It was open and a pair of spectacles lay beside it. Apparently Otto had been reading it when he saw him ride up to the barn.

Hanging the coat on a peg, Barny placed his hat next to it, and said, "I see you've been reading my favorite Book, Mr. Gagarin."

Otto's eyes lit up. "That's your favorite Book, is it?"

"Yes, sir. Let me ask you — do you believe that Book is the Word of God?"

"Indeed I do, son. Every jot and tittle. Have you been born again?"

"I sure have. I received the Lord Jesus Christ as my own personal Saviour not very long ago. You remember, I told you about wanting to catch up to Olecia Petrovna? She and her family are on their way to America."

"Yes."

"Well, it was Olecia who first told me about Jesus, and how He had died for my sins at Calvary. It was when I caught up to them at that cave on the trail to Kuwalt Pass that they led me to the Lord."

Taking Barny by the arm, Otto said, "Come. Sit down here at the table. I'll heat up some coffee and you can fill me in on all the details."

When Barny had told the Christian gentleman the full story, Otto was deeply touched. He leaned on his elbows, looked Barny in the eye, and said, "I want to help you. First thing, I'm going to walk into the center of the village at sundown, when the Cossacks have to give up the chase for today, and see what I can learn about their pursuit of you."

"This is very kind of you, sir," said Barny. "When you're there, if you should see a sledge that might belong to my friend Tito Tkachev, will you let him know where I am?"

"Certainly, son."

"He and Lysen have probably headed back to Stoyville, but if they haven't, I must see them and thank them properly for all they have done for me."

"If they are there, you may rest assured that I will bring them to you," said Otto.

Nineteen

The sun was setting red in the west when Otto Gagarin arrived at the village center and saw three Cossacks off their horses and huddled in conversation while looking up and down the street. The insignias worn by one man told Otto he was the captain.

People moving by eyed the black uniforms warily. By that time, everyone in town knew about the shooting incident, and hopes were high that the young man who had dared defy the Cossacks had made good his escape.

Otto looked around for a sledge, but there was none in sight.

Soon he saw two Cossacks riding into the village, one from the south, and the other from the north. Otto moved up reasonably close to the spot where the Cossacks were huddled, but not close enough to draw attention. When the final two dismounted and told the captain they had not seen any sign of Barny Kaluga, the captain said angrily,

"Men, we cannot let that traitor escape!"

"How are we going to track him, Captain?" said one of them. "There are countless tracks in the snow on every side of the village. It is impossible to tell which ones are his."

"We will resume our search tomorrow morning," said the captain. "We must spread out even farther. Sooner or later, we will find his trail. And when we catch him, he will die!"

At the Gagarin house, Barny Kaluga hurried to the front door when he heard Otto stamping snow from his shoes on the porch.

When the old gentleman came in, Barny said, "So what did you find out, Otto?"

Otto told Barny what he had heard the Cossacks say, including the words of the captain.

"Did you see the sledge?" asked Barny.

"No. Your friends must have done as you said and headed for home."

"I can't blame them for that. As far as they know, I rode out of the village, intending to get as far from here as possible."

Otto took off his coat and hat. "I would say, son, that before those Cossacks give up finding you, they just might search every house and barn in the village. I have an idea how to get you out of here and on your way safely."

"I'm listening," said Barny, following him to the rear of the house where he hung up his coat and hat.

The silver-haired man turned and faced him. "My neighbor next door has a large sled and a good team of horses. He will lend me sled and team, no questions asked."

"Yes?"

"As soon as it's completely dark, I will bring sled and team over to my barn, and we'll load that Cossack horse on the sled. The next village down the trail west of here is Whipna. Some sixty, seventy miles. We'll go down the trail that direction by moonlight. The sled tracks will fool the Cossacks when they take up their search again in the morning. They'll be looking for the tracks of a lone horse. I'll take you nine or ten miles, so you'll have a good head start on them in case they decide to keep looking in that direction, anyhow."

Barny met his gaze and said softly, "I appreciate this, Otto."

"I'm happy to do it. Now you're going to need more help, son. It's still a long way to the Polish border. There is an underground church in Whipna, and I know some of the members. My best friend there is Alfredin

Cherny. After we eat some supper, I'll write a letter to Alfredin for you to give him. In the letter I'll explain to him that I am trying to help a Christian brother escape the country for his life's sake. I know Alfredin will help you get down out of the mountains, across the plains, and into Poland."

A smile curved Barny's lips. "The Lord has been so good to me, Otto. I didn't even realize it when I felt drawn to your barn, but He was guiding me."

Otto chuckled. "That's the way He works."

"So I'm learning. And not only did He lead me to you, but now, through you, He is leading me to Mr. Cherny."

After Otto and Barny had eaten supper together, Otto packed food into a small cloth sack for Barny's journey, then sat down and wrote the letter to Alfredin Cherny and told Barny how to find the Cherny house in Whipna. Otto then went to his neighbor and moments later, drove the sled into the yard. Barny had the Cossack horse bridled and saddled. He had placed his revolver in the saddlebag and tied the food pack to the saddle. They put the horse on the sled and headed down the trail just as the moon was putting in an appearance.

★ ★ ★

The three-quarter moon bathed the snow-laden mountains in creamy white under a partly cloudy sky. Otto Gagarin drew the sled to a halt and said, "This is the spot, Barny. I'll let you off here and head back home."

Otto stood in the snow while Barny led the horse off the sled. Draping the reins on the saddle, Barny stepped to the man, hugged him, and thanked him for his help.

Cuffing Barny's chin playfully, Otto said, "When you find that girl, tell her I'll look forward to meeting her in heaven."

"I will," said Barny. "When we meet up there, we'll never have to say good-bye again. God bless you."

"You too. I'll be praying for you."

With the letter to Alfredin Cherny in his coat pocket, Barny mounted the horse with fiery streamers of pain lancing his lower back and settled in the saddle. He waved to Otto as the man snapped the reins, turned the sled around, and drove away.

The pain was excruciating as Barny headed the horse down the trail. He understood better than ever why Dr. Parda told him not to ride a horse.

Some two hours passed, and as the horse plodded through the snow, Barny's pain was so bad, he told himself he had to get out of the saddle for a while and rest.

But where?

The temperature was near zero, and there was no place to find warmth. Gritting his teeth, he kept riding. He tried to keep his thoughts on Olecia, but at times the pain was so severe, he could think of nothing else.

Another hour passed. The pain continued, and he was getting dizzy. His vision became distorted, and under the night sky, the earth around him seemed to undulate, like a stormy ocean heaving up and down.

Gripping the saddle with his free hand, he blinked and tried to clear the dizziness from his head. *If I pass out*, he thought, *I'll fall from the horse and freeze to death before morning.*

A cloud was just beginning to drift across the moon when Barny spotted a small building at the edge of the forest about a hundred yards down the steep, snow-covered slope. Nudging the horse to put him in a trot, he endured the added pain, trying to keep from passing out. As he drew close to the building, he saw that it was an old shack. There were no other buildings around.

Suddenly, off to the right, he caught a glimpse of movement among the trees . . . like the wisp of a shadow. Was the dizziness causing him to imagine things?

Sitting still in the saddle, Barny cautiously looked about him. The pain in his back would not permit him to turn very far right or left. He looked back into the forest, but this time, there was no movement. The moon was fully covered by the cloud at that moment, but another glance at the shack in the obscure light showed him it was old and weather-beaten, and small dark holes were visible in the roof. However, to Barny Kaluga at that moment, it looked like a palace.

He dreaded the sheer torture that would be his in the process of dismounting, and paused to raise his eyes heavenward. "Please, Lord, help me. Don't let me pass out. I need to get inside that shack."

Getting a good grip on the pommel, he took a deep breath, clenched his teeth, and in one agonizing movement, lowered himself toward the ground. As his feet touched the deep snow, his knees buckled, and he grabbed the saddle to keep from falling. A cry escaped his lips as severe pain knifed through the small of his back then shot down both legs.

Suddenly he found himself sitting in the snow. In agony he rolled onto his knees and tried to get up, but fell down again. He decided he would have to use a stirrup to pull himself up. At the same time, the horse swung his head, looked toward the deep shadows in the forest and nickered. Barny thought he detected fear in the nicker.

He got a firm hold on the stirrup, and with effort brought himself to a standing position. The pain had brought tears to his eyes and they slid down his pale cheeks. His head was spinning. He must get inside the shack.

Tying the reins to a small birch tree, Barny struggled to release the small sack of food from the back of the saddle. Clutching the sack close to his chest, he made his way laboriously toward the door of the shack, wiping the moisture from his cheeks. He stopped in his tracks when the horse nickered again, and at the same time he saw a flitting shadow among the trees.

Suddenly the gelding ejected a shrill whinny, reared, shaking his head and pawing the air. The movement put stress on the thin birch as the reins tightened.

Then Barny saw them as they hunkered low in the shadows, growling. His eyes widened to circles of astonishment.

Wolves! Hungry. Slavering. Wanting horseflesh.

The horse cried again, and wheeled, snapping the tree in two as he bolted and galloped across the clearing toward the forest on the south side of the trail. The wolf pack went after him.

Barny moaned as he watched the chase in the light of the moon, which was now free of the cloud. Soon the gelding topped a rise and disappeared with the growling pack close behind. "Lord, what am I to do now?" he asked, his voice breaking. Heartsick, he turned his attention back to the shack. He knew the wolves would eventually wear the horse down and kill him.

Breathing raggedly, he put a hand to the latch and was glad to find that it was not locked. Moving inside, he closed the door, and by the moonlight flowing through the dirty windows, he could see a stove, a small cupboard, four tattered canvas cots, four wooden chairs, and an old table.

Barny had seen shacks like this before. They were once used by lumbermen many years ago before the government changed the rules for cutting timber.

Laying the cloth sack on the dusty table, he shuffled painfully to the cupboard. Opening its doors, he found dusty old tin plates, cups, bowls, pots, pans, and eating utensils. His stomach was growling with hunger, but the discomfort in his back over-ruled his need for food. His head bobbed

420

when he saw a couple of old blankets on the bottom shelf.

Though it was somewhat warmer inside the shack than outside, it was still very cold. Weary and racked with pain in his lower back, Barny took out the blankets, shook the dust from them and eyed the cots. Moving to the closest one, he found it in such bad shape that if he laid on it, his weight would rip right through. Soon he found that all four were unusable, so he laid down on the dirt floor and wrapped the blankets around him. With his head down, the dizziness began to subside.

"Dear Father in heaven," he whispered, "I'm in deep trouble again. I need Your help. It's a long way down to Whipna."

In a little while the blankets had him warm and the pain in his back eased. With his mind on Olecia, he soon fell asleep.

Startled, Barny Kaluga opened his eyes. Sunlight was shining through the south window of the shack. He hadn't meant to sleep this late. Something had awakened him. Something that startled him. What was it?

And then it came again.

Horses neighing.

Cossacks!

His heart thundered in his chest as he

threw off the blankets, rose to his feet, and stumbled to the south window. Immediately he saw five Cossacks riding their horses down the snow-laden trail in bright sunshine, and one of them was pointing to the shack. It was Nadin Akhmatova!

Barny's mind was racing. There was no place in the shack to hide. His footprints and those of the horse were plainly visible in the snow outside the front door. Somehow the Cossacks knew what he had done back on the other side of the mountains and would enjoy taking the life of a traitor.

By reflex, Barny's hand went to his side for the holstered gun. But it was not there. He had put it in the saddlebag.

In spite of the cold, Barny felt sweat on his brow and running down his back. The Cossacks were drawing near, eyeing the shack and pointing to the tracks in the snow by the front door. His heart was pounding so hard he could feel it throughout his body. There was only one door in the shack. If he crashed through the back window, they would hear it.

Keeping himself hidden, he peered cautiously past the edge of the window.

"He's in there, all right," said the captain, dismounting. "Let's get him!"

The other men left their saddles.

"Let me do it, Captain," said Nadin Akhmatova, whipping out his revolver with a wicked leer on his face. "Nothing would give me more pleasure than to put hot lead through the heart of that traitor."

The captain laughed. "All right. You go in first, but we'll be right behind you."

Barny began backing across the floor as footsteps crunched in the snow. In that brief moment before his back touched the wall, he couldn't even utter a prayer. The terror in him was so strong it stopped his breath like a seizure.

The latch rattled and the door swung open, letting in a stream of sunlight that threw the shadows of the intruders on the floor.

Barny's jaw slacked and his mouth flew open.

Instead of the Cossacks, it was Olecia and her family! Olecia was first through the door. "Oh, Barny, you're alive!" she cried as she dashed to him, arms open wide.

Stunned, Barny took her into his arms. In spite of her parents being there, he kissed her soundly, then held her at arm's length and said, "Olecia, my sweet! I love you! I love you! I love —"

Suddenly Barny found himself sitting up on the floor of the shack, the breath sawing in and out of him, and blinking his eyes. There was only pale moonlight filtering through the windows. "Oh, Olecia!" he gasped. "It was so real! But I do love you! I love you with all of my heart."

He gasped again, drew a sharp breath, and said, "Please, Lord, don't let her go to somewhere in America where I can't find her!"

With the strength in his body sapped more than ever, Barny lay back down and snuggled into the blankets. He could hear the wind whining around the eaves of the shack and rattling the door. The dream had been so real that it took him some time to get back to sleep.

When Barny awakened at sunrise, his first thoughts were of the dream and of holding Olecia in his arms.

Then his predicament hit him. The horse was gone. He had very little food, and he was a long way from Whipna. If the Cossacks were coming his way, he dare not be caught inside the shack. For a brief moment he relived the terror of the dream when he thought the Cossacks were coming through the door. Shaking it from his mind, he faced the facts. He must brave the cold, ignore the pain in his back and legs, and walk down the trail to Whipna.

Moving to the table, Barny sat down on a chair and opened the cloth sack. The wind was growing strong outside and beginning to howl like a fierce beast. Gulping down a chunk of bread and a hard piece of cheese, he tied the sack again, and forced himself to his feet. Pain shot through his back. A cry of anguish escaped his cold lips, but he told himself he mustn't let the pain stop him. He tied the cloth sack to his coat belt, rolled up the blankets placing them under his arm, and stepped out into the howling wind.

When the wind buffeted him unmercifully, it took an immense effort of will to force himself to plod down the trail. But plod he did. He paused long enough to bend down and pick up a fistful of snow. Moving on, he ate the snow, enjoying the moisture it provided.

Within a couple of hours, Barny found himself entering a shallow canyon with a barren wilderness of snowcapped peaks on both sides. There were rocky ledges and outcroppings along the canyon walls, inscrutable, dark, and silent, and snow cornices on the jagged crests of the walls.

In those grim surroundings, Barny kept

moving . . . his thoughts divided between Olecia, who was somewhere ahead of him, and the Cossacks who could be coming up behind him.

From time to time his legs grew weary, and the pain in his back became almost unbearable. He had to move off the trail and find a place to sit down, preferably out of the wind. After allowing himself a brief respite, Barny moved on, praying that the Lord would see him through this ordeal.

The sun was setting as Barny moved out of the canyon, and as he stopped to survey what lay ahead of him, he saw seemingly endless miles of rugged country ahead. The cruel wind still assaulted him. He thought about turning around and finding some secure spot in the canyon to spend the night but decided against it. He had another hour or better before dark. He had to keep moving while he had sufficient light.

When twilight was coming on, Barny moved into the forest on the north side of the trail, hoping to find a place that would shelter him from the wind. He had only walked a short distance beneath the towering, wind-tufted pines when he found a large fallen tree. He could tell by its weather-beaten bark that it had been there for quite some time. He smiled when he saw that it was partially hollowed out on one side. This would be his bedroom for the night.

Quickly he ate a few bites of bread and cheese then a fistful of snow. This done, he wrapped himself in the blankets and took refuge in the hollow of the tree for the night.

The warmth of the blankets helped the pain in his back to ease. Barny talked to the Lord, asking Him to give him the strength to continue on the next day and to let him find Olecia and make her his wife. A short time later he fell asleep, thinking about the girl he loved.

Barny's sleep was dreamless, but he awakened at one point in the deep of the night. He opened his eyes and looked around him. The pallid moonlight made long shadows of the trees, and the wind still moaned.

The ex-Cossack awakened at sunrise and rolled out of the tree. He ate his ration of bread and cheese, capped it off with a mouthful of snow, and painfully trod his way westward.

After a long, steep decline on the trail for most of the morning, Barny came to a level stretch where a wind-swept frozen lake offered him some smooth walking. Letting his eyes take in the lake, he saw it glistening like silver, and sparkling with the sunlight reflecting from millions of frozen crystals.

He left the trail and walked the lake until midday. When he reached the west edge of the lake, he found himself some three hundred yards from the trail. He was once again on rugged land where the snow was deep. As he plodded toward the trail, he found that the snow covered a mass of small boulders. It was treacherous walking, for he couldn't tell as he took each step whether his feet would fall upon a snow crust that would hold him or plunge him hip-deep into the crevices between the boulders.

Soon he was on the trail again and moving west. He had to stop periodically and stamp his feet and clap his hands together to fight off frostbite. He had hoped to meet up with someone on the trail who might offer help, but finally told himself nobody would be traveling the trail till the spring thaw came.

That night Barny found a small cave, for which he thanked the Lord. He wouldn't have a fire, but he would be sheltered from the relentless wind.

The sun was lowering in the western sky on the fourth day since Barny had told Otto Gagarin good-bye and watched him drive away on the sled in the moonlight. He had run out of bread and cheese on the third day and was growing weaker by the hour. New snow had fallen the night before, which made it more difficult as he plodded toward the sunset.

He was glad for one thing. After the new snow fell, the wind had diminished to a slight breeze.

Squinting into the fiery brilliance of the sun, Barny told himself he had to be nearing Whipna. *Maybe tomorrow,* he thought.

His back was shooting pain. His knees were feeling watery and there was a dull, throbbing beat behind his eyes. Suddenly he stumbled and fell. His strength was almost gone. As he struggled to rise, the breath plumed out from his mouth and nostrils like steam from a boiling kettle.

He made it to his feet, took several faltering steps, and fell again. "Please, God," he said as he fought his way to a standing position once more, "give me the strength to make it to the village."

Barny Kaluga had staggered another hundred yards or so when he fell again. Raising up on his knees in the snow, he looked around for someplace to spend the night. He was too weak to go any farther.

Suddenly his attention was drawn down the trail straight ahead of him. Rooftops! He could make out the outline of the village against the sunset. "Oh, thank You, Lord!" he gasped. "I've made it to Whipna!"

The sight of the village put impetus into Barny's legs. He was on his feet quickly and staggered toward it as fast as he could go. When he reached the edge of the village, he heard the happy laughter and chatter of children. He was looking around, trying to spot them when his back began to spasm and his legs gave out.

Once again he found himself lying in the snow. The sound of children playing was still in his ears while he was trying to get up. Pausing on his hands and knees, he spotted them in an open field off to his right some thirty or forty yards. At the same time, he saw a boy running toward him. Barny's arms gave out, and he fell flat.

Keeping his eyes on the boy, he whispered, "Thank You, Lord. I'll get help, now."

As the boy drew up, Barny estimated him to be about twelve or thirteen years of age.

Kneeling down beside him, the boy said, "Are you sick, mister?"

"N-not what you would call sick. I . . . I injured my back, and I have a hard time walking. But I've been traveling for days. D-do you know a Mr. Alfredin Cherny, who lives here in the village?"

The boy smiled. "Yes, sir. My name is Bartyn Cherny. Alfredin Cherny is my father."

"Your father? Oh, thank the Lord." Reaching into his coat pocket, he drew out the folded paper. "Bartyn, this is a letter to your father from Otto Gagarin in Nunscow."

"I know Otto, sir. He is a good friend of my father's."

"My name is Barny Kaluga. The letter is about me and some help I need from your father."

"It isn't far to our house, Mr. Kaluga," said the boy. "I'll help you. We can be there in a few minutes."

Bartyn helped the weary man to his feet, and with Barny's arm slung over his shoulder, they moved down the street while the children continued to play in the field.

When they reached the front porch of the Cherny house, the boy helped Barny over the threshold, closed the door, and called, "Papa! Mama! I have someone here who needs our help!"

There was no response.

"They must be at the neighbors' house, Mr. Kaluga," said Bartyn. "Let's get you in here by the fireplace, then I'll go get them."

Bartyn guided Barny into the parlor

where a crackling fire greeted him, then helped Barny out of his coat, took his hat, and laid them both over the seat of a chair. Pulling a chair up close, he said, "You sit right here and get warmed up. I'll be back in a few minutes."

The boy hurried toward the parlor door, then stopped, wheeled, and said, "If it's all right with you, Mr. Kaluga, I'll take Otto's letter and show it to Papa so he can read it before he sees you."

"Sure. It's there in the coat pocket."

Bartyn hurried out with the letter in his hand.

The warmth of the fire was like a dream to Barny. It had been so long since his body had been warm. He was soaking up the welcome heat when he heard voices at the rear of the house, then footsteps coming up the hall. Seconds later, Bartyn entered the room, followed by the rest of the family. "Mr. Kaluga, this is my father, Alfredin; my mother, Weldina; and my sister, Ludmilla. She's sixteen."

The family drew up close, eyeing their guest with compassion. Barny's matted hair was sticking to his forehead. He looked up at them with eyes red rimmed and bleary with pain and exhaustion. Smiling, he said, "I am very glad to meet you."

Letter in hand, Alfredin moved close, smiled down at him, and said, "Welcome to our home, Barny. You are our brother in Christ, and let me assure you . . . we will do everything we can for you."

"I appreciate that, sir," Barny said sincerely.

"Otto's letter has given me only limited information. When you get warmed up good, we want to hear the whole story."

Weldina drew up beside her husband. "Barny, my philosophy is that most problems can be helped with a hot meal. It is almost suppertime. Ludmilla and I will go prepare it while you sit here and thaw out."

When mother and daughter were gone, Alfredin said, "According to the date on Otto's letter, you have been traveling for four days. Have you walked all this way?"

Barny explained about the Cossack horse, the shack, and the wolves.

"So you have walked almost the entire distance from Nunscow."

"Yes, sir."

"With back pain."

"Yes."

"I imagine your feet are about frozen."

"Well, they do feel like ice cakes."

Kneeling down in front of him, Alfredin said, "Let's get these shoes off."

Removing the shoes, he rubbed Barny's feet briskly with his big, strong hands. The sudden warmth was almost as painful as the freezing cold at first, but gradually the stinging sensation eased, and relief flooded his pale features.

As Alfredin was putting Barny's shoes back on him, Ludmilla came in and announced that supper was ready. Father and son walked their guest down the hall and into the kitchen, which was rosy with warmth and alive with delicious aromas.

Prayer was offered before the meal by Alfredin, in which he asked the Lord to give them wisdom so they could help Barny in every way possible. When he closed the prayer, Alfredin asked Barny to tell them the whole story.

As Barny ate his first real meal in many days, he explained to the Chernys about Olecia and her family, of his battle with his former Cossack comrades to buy time for their escape, and of the events that led up to his meeting Otto Gagarin.

At last, replete with a tasty meal and the blood flowing warmly through his veins, Barny sighed and said, "That was wonderful, Mrs. Cherny."

"I'm glad you enjoyed it," Weldina said, her eyes sparkling with joy.

Alfredin smiled at him and said, "Otto pointed out in his letter how important it is that you see a doctor."

"Yes," Barny said, nodding.

"Well, just in case some Cossacks show up here looking for you, we'll disguise you so nobody in the village knows what you really look like except the Chernys and Dr. Vatmin. He is very much opposed to the czar's ways and laws and will never disclose that he has seen you if the Cossacks question him."

"I'm glad to know he can be trusted," said Barny.

"And now," said Weldina, rising from her chair, "it is time our guest is shown to his room so he can wash up and get to bed. Come, Barny. I'll show you to your room. Alfredin, dear, will you bring that pan of hot water on the stove?"

"I'll help you walk, Mr. Kaluga," volunteered Bartyn.

"I'll start cleaning up the table," said Ludmilla.

When Barny was ushered into the guest room, the first item to draw his attention was the bed. His entire body yearned to slip under the covers and get a good night's rest.

Alfredin poured the steaming water into a basin where Weldina laid soap, washcloth, and towel. "There you go, Barny," he said. "We'll leave you now so you can wash up and get to bed. Weldina will have a good breakfast for you in the morning."

"How can I ever thank you people for your kindness?" asked Barny.

"No need to worry about that," said Weldina. "As brothers and sisters in God's family, it is a joy to help each other. God has sent you to us, so we will give you the help you need. We are honored to have you in our home."

Tears welled up in Barny's eyes. "I am the one who is honored, ma'am."

When the door was closed, Barny stood for a long moment, running his gaze between the steaming basin and the inviting bed. The bed almost won the contest, but he knew he would sleep even better if he washed up first.

Twenty

After breakfast the next morning, Alfredin and Weldina Cherny dressed Barny Kaluga in an old coat and slouchy hat as Ludmilla and Bartyn looked on.

Alfredin said, "Now, Barny, pull the hat low and the coat collar up so your face is exposed as little as possible. You need to walk with stooped shoulders and shuffle along like an old man."

Barny chuckled. "I don't have to put on a shuffle, Mr. Cherny. Walking is pretty hard for me, anyway."

"Well, hopefully, Dr. Vatmin will be able to do something about that. Barny, I want you to know that Weldina and I have instructed our son and daughter here what they are to do if the Cossacks should show up in the village and ask them about you. They are to pretend as if they are a bit dull mentally. When the Cossacks see this, they won't bother with them any further."

"That's a good idea," said Barny.

Bartyn chortled. "Well, Ludmilla won't have to put on. She actually is a bit dull mentally!"

The girl sank her fingers into Bartyn's hair and messed it up good. "I may be mentally slow, little brother, but I still know how much it upsets you to get your hair messed up when you have it combed so pretty!"

Hair standing on end, the boy gave her a mock scowl. "Now I have to go comb it again."

Ludmilla giggled. "No, you don't. You can just go the rest of the day looking that way. Some bird will come along and decide your hair would make a good nest!"

Barny laughed. "Does this kind of thing go on all the time?"

Weldina snorted, "All the time!"

"Well, Barny," said Alfredin as his own laughter died out, "we'd better get going."

Weldina, Ludmilla, and Bartyn watched out the parlor window as Alfredin drove away in their wagon with Barny sitting beside him. Barny was bent over with hat tilted low over his forehead and collar pulled up.

Dr. Ludwig Vatmin was a small, wiry man of fifty, with a touch of gray in his thick black hair. He listened intently as Alfredin told him Barny's story, giving only the necessary details.

The doctor set kind eyes on his new patient and said, "Barny, I will do everything I can to make you well. Let's go in the back room. I want you to tell me exactly what you feel in your back and legs and what Dr. Parda told you. I want to know what he did to treat your problem, then I'm going to give you a thorough examination." Then to Alfredin he said, "I will let you know when you can come in. Since you have taken him into your home, and he is dependent on you, I want you to hear my diagnosis."

"Fine, Doctor," said Alfredin. "I'll be right here."

Almost an hour had passed in the back room when Dr. Vatmin finished the examination and fitted Barny with a new leather brace. He sighed and said, "You can put your clothes on now, Barny."

While Barny was dressing, Vatmin said, "Son, I have to be honest with you. You are in bad shape."

Barney frowned as he buttoned his shirt. "You mean worse than when Dr. Parda treated me?"

"Much worse. He was right when he told you not to ride a horse. From what you have told me Dr. Parda said and did, your back is in worse condition now. But it doesn't stop there. Your many days without sufficient food, exposure to the severe weather, and pushing your body beyond its normal limits to make it to Whipna has left you on the verge of a complete physical breakdown. You can travel no farther until you have had a long rest."

"How long, Doctor?"

"Several months."

Barny's countenance fell.

The doctor patted his shoulder. "I know this means that you will definitely not catch up to your young lady and her family before they embark for America — if they haven't already done so — but if you do not rest and take the treatments I am going to schedule for you, you could end up a cripple for the rest of your life. Your overall health is also at stake."

"But, Doctor, I —"

"The choice is yours, of course. You can move on if you want to, but you had better think it over very carefully." Turning toward the door, Vatmin said, "I'll call Alfredin in."

Barny was on his feet, buckling the belt around his middle when Alfredin came through the door with the doctor, who was already telling him the same thing he had told his patient.

While Vatmin continued his explanation, Barny gravely weighed his options. Feeling deep disappointment that his physical condition had deteriorated, and being told by the doctor that he should prolong his travel plans, he thought of Olecia and wrestled with the idea of moving on.

When the doctor came to the part about his advising Barny to stay in Whipna and rest for several months, Alfredin looked at Barny and said, "You must do as Dr. Vatmin says."

Barny ran splayed fingers through his hair, set his eyes on Vatmin, and said, "I've made it this far under deplorable conditions, Doctor. I can continue on."

"Oh, you can for a while, son, but eventually your abused body will give up on you. And like I said, you could end up a cripple for the rest of your life. Alfredin already told me out there in the office that you are welcome to stay in his home until you are in the proper condition to travel. The wise thing for you to do is to stay here and rest until you regain at least the greater measure of your health and strength before you travel on. You must give your back and legs a chance to heal."

Face pinched, Barny shook his head. "Mr. Cherny, I deeply appreciate the offer to stay in your home all of this time, but Olecia and her family are probably already at sea, heading for New York harbor. I've asked the Lord to let me catch up to them before they go somewhere that I can never find them. The United States of America is a big country."

Alfredin laid a hand on Barny's shoulder. "You're trusting God to help you find Olecia wherever she goes, aren't you?"

Barny met his gaze. "Yes."

"Well, if you have to stay here until Dr. Vatmin says you are in the proper condition to travel, can't the same God still help you to find her?"

Barny drew a deep breath, let it out slowly, stared at the floor for a long moment, then looked up at Alfredin, and said, "You're right, my friend. The Lord will always know where Olecia and her family are." Then to Vatmin he said, "And you are right, Doctor. I must let my body heal before I make that long trip across Poland and Germany to the Netherlands . . . and then to America."

A happy smile made the doctor's eyes twinkle. "I'm glad you are going to take my advice. I certainly don't want you to end up crippled."

"Me, either." Then he said to Alfredin:

"When it's God's time for me to go, I will do so. Because I'm His child, He has my future in His hands. I will do as Dr. Vatmin says and concentrate every day to healing my body, so that when I do find Olecia I will present her with a healthy man to be her husband."

The doctor smiled, his eyes twinkling again. "Smart thinking, my boy. Smart thinking."

"You want to set an appointment for him to come back for treatment, don't you, Doctor?" said Alfredin.

"That I do. Let's look in the appointment book."

As Alfredin was driving Barny back to the house in the wagon, Barny said, "I want to thank you for your kind hospitality, Mr. Cherny. I will also express my appreciation to Mrs. Cherny."

"It's our pleasure, my friend," said Alfredin. "We are glad to do it. Weldina and I talked about it before going to sleep last night. We both felt sure the doctor would tell you to postpone your travel for a while. Now, when the doctor says you are well enough to move on, I will take you to Poland. We have Christian friends in a town called Lublin, which is just over fifty miles from the border. Their names are Henryk and Lena Penricki. We have visited them many times over the years. They have a wonderful church, and we always enjoy the services. They don't have to go underground to have preaching services as we Russians do."

"I hope someday things will change in Russia," Barny said.

"Yes. Me too. Anyway, I'm sure the Penrickis will have Christian friends in Poland who will help you get to Germany, and no doubt there will be others who will help you get across Germany to the Netherlands and to Rotterdam."

"The Lord has been so good to me, Mr. Cherny," said Barny. "He has so marvelously shown this young Christian that He can take care of him. I know He will provide the way for me. I know He works through the prayers of His children. I would appreciate it if you and your family will pray that whenever the Lord allows me to go to America, that He will help me to find Olecia quickly."

"We most certainly will," Alfredin assured him. He paused briefly, then said, "Weldina and I talked about how much we would love to take you to the services in our underground church, Barny, but if other people see your face, it will endanger you if the

Cossacks come and start questioning the people of Whipna about you. Someone could become frightened and let it slip that they have seen you."

"I understand," said Barny. "Though I would love to attend the services, I don't want to put God's people in a bad position, either."

As the weeks passed, Barny Kaluga stayed inside the Cherny house except when Alfredin took him to the doctor. Each time, Barny wore the disguise.

One afternoon in the second week of May, Alfredin came home from work and put the horses and wagon in their small barn. As he walked toward the house, enjoying the warm sunshine and the sound of birds singing in the trees, he saw Weldina smiling at him through the kitchen window.

Weldina met him at the door, kissed him, and said, "Did you have a busy day?"

"Very," he replied as they stepped into the kitchen. "Barny taking his nap?"

"Yes. He lay down over two hours ago. He should be getting up soon."

Alfredin looked around. "Where are the children?"

"I sent Bartyn to the grocery store to pick up some things for supper. Ludmilla is visiting her friend, Melisa Heinle. She is trying to win the confidence of Melisa and her parents so she can invite them to church soon."

"Bless her heart. She'll get them there."

At that moment, a sleepy-eyed Barny Kaluga entered the kitchen, covering a yawn.

"Well, there's our houseguest," said Alfredin. "Get a good nap?"

Barny smiled. "Sure did."

"Well, that's what the doctor ordered. I think you're looking better every day."

"I'm feeling better every day," said Barny. "Maybe it won't be too long until —"

Suddenly they heard the front door of the house open, followed by rapid footsteps. Bartyn bounded into the kitchen holding a grocery sack, eyes bulging. "Papa! Mama! Barny! Cossacks are in the village!"

"Oh no!" gasped Weldina.

"Are they here because of Barny?" asked Alfredin.

"Yes. They're talking to people, giving them Barny's name and description and asking if they have seen him. I heard one man tell another man that there are about three dozen of them!"

Barny's face lost color.

"Some of them were talking to people in front of the store," the boy said, placing the sack on the cupboard. "When I came out, they asked me if I had seen Barny. I did what you told me to do, Papa. I put a dull look in my eyes and acted like I couldn't understand what they wanted to know. It worked. They let me go real quick."

"I'm proud of you, son," said Alfredin.

"Me too," said Weldina. "You did real good."

"You sure did," said Barny. "I know how they work, though. They'll search every house and building in the village."

"We have to be prepared, Barny," said Alfredin. "We'll hide you in one of the —"

The sound of the front door opening again cut off Alfredin's words. Ludmilla came running into the kitchen, gasping, "The Cossacks are in the village looking for you, Barny!"

"We know, honey," said Weldina. "They questioned your brother."

"I didn't tell them a thing," Bartyn said quickly.

Turning to Alfredin, the girl said, "What are we going to do, Papa? The Cossacks are searching houses and barns in the next block, and they're coming this way."

"I had started to tell Barny we would hide him in one of the closets, when you came in."

"The best one would be the hall closet," said Weldina. "It's the largest one in the house. We could put him up on the high shelf and cover him with that loose clothing up there."

"That's what I had in mind," said Alfredin.

"Wouldn't it be safer to get him out of the house, Papa?" asked Bartyn.

"Not with that many of them in the village, son. It's not safe out there anywhere on the streets. We've got to hide him in the closet."

Barny shook his head sadly. "I'm sorry to bring this trouble on you. If the Cossacks find me, all of you will be punished for harboring me."

"We'll trust the Lord to keep them from finding you," said Alfredin.

"God's people have to look out for each other. Let's get things ready so we can act quickly when they come."

The pile of loose clothing was removed from the shelf and laid on the floor. Alfredin explained that when the time came, he would put Barny on his shoulders and lift him up to the shelf. Once he was positioned on the shelf, they would hide him beneath the pile of clothes.

While Weldina and Ludmilla went to the

kitchen to start supper, Alfredin and Barny sat down in the parlor with the shades drawn. Bartyn volunteered to be the lookout on the front porch until suppertime.

When the meal was ready, Ludmilla entered the parlor and said, "Time to eat."

As the two men were rising from the chairs where they were sitting, the girl said, "I'll go tell Bartyn to come in."

Ludmilla was almost to the front door when it opened abruptly, and Bartyn came in, eyes wide, announcing that the Cossacks had just appeared at the nearest corner on their block, on their side of the street, and were knocking on the door of the first house.

Weldina had heard Bartyn's words and said, "Alfredin, while you're getting Barny on the shelf, I'll remove his place settings from the table. Hurry! Let's have the rest of us at the table eating supper when they knock on the door!"

When Barny was on the shelf, covered with the pile of clothing, Alfredin said, "I left a few pieces dangling to give it a normal appearance. Just don't move. Stay absolutely still and breathe as shallowly as you possibly can."

"I will," came Barny's muffled voice.

When the closet door clicked shut, Barny was enveloped in total darkness. In a soundless whisper, he said, "Dear Lord, it will take Your own mighty hand to deliver me from this situation. You know my heart. Of course I want to live and one day be reunited with Olecia . . . but right now, more than anything, I don't want this precious family to suffer because they have taken me in. Please spare them any harm."

Some twenty minutes passed. Barny's body jerked when he heard a loud knock on the front door of the house, and his heart thundered in his chest. Listening intently, he heard the muffled sound of footsteps approaching the door, then a gruff voice. He couldn't make out what Alfredin was saying in return, but within seconds, there were heavy footsteps in the house spreading every direction.

As the sounds of the house being searched assaulted his ears, Barny struggled to keep his jarred nerves in check. Suddenly he heard the closet door swing open. His scalp prickled and cold chills attacked his backbone like tiny needles of ice.

He heard the Cossack rummaging through the clothes that hung on the rack below him. Then, there was movement as an exploring hand ruffled the pile of clothing that covered him. He could hear some of the pieces falling to the floor.

A deep voice said from outside the closet, "Anything?"

"I wish there were," the man in the closet said in a flat, sepulchral tone. "I would like the privilege of executing that traitor with my bare hands."

"Wouldn't we both?" said the other man. "Let's go. Maybe he's in the next house."

When the closet door clicked shut, Barney ran his tongue around a dry mouth and used a piece of clothing to mop sweat from his face.

Voices rumbled for a few seconds, then the front door of the house opened. The sound of heavy footsteps followed, then came the pleasant sound of the door being closed. Barny took a deep breath and held it.

He released it when Alfredin opened the closet door and said, "All clear. They're gone."

Alfredin helped Barny down from the shelf, and the Cherny family embraced him while praising the Lord together.

By the end of June Barny was walking almost normally, and Dr. Ludwig Vatmin told him he was on the mend. In another seven or eight weeks, he would be well enough to travel.

On a warm day in the last week of August, Alfredin guided the wagon around the house and pulled rein by the front porch. It was an emotional moment when Barny told Weldina, Ludmilla, and Bartyn good-bye.

Running his tear-dimmed eyes over their faces, he said, "I can never thank you dear people enough for risking your own lives to save mine and for the marvelous hospitality you have shown me all these months."

Weldina hugged him tight, then taking hold of both his shoulders and looking him in the eye, said, "Barny, we are family. As God's children, we must care for each other. It was our duty and our privilege to help you." Tears were making tracks down her cheeks. "We may never see you again on this earth, but there is a far better day coming when all of God's people will be together."

Barny embraced her again, then did the same with Ludmilla and Bartyn, and climbed into the wagon.

Telling his family once more that he loved them and would see them in a few days, Alfredin put the horses into motion.

"Godspeed, Barny!" called Weldina, waving.

He smiled and waved back.

Alfredin and Barny arrived in Lublin, Poland, as scheduled, and soon one of Alfredin's friends had Barny in a wagon that would take him into Germany.

By the end of the first week of September, Barny was on a horse given to him by his new Christian friends, and was halfway across Germany, heading due west.

On September 15, the Petrovnas, Alekin Kolpino, and Oksana Tambov were standing on the dock amid a large crowd of people, most who were going to board the Dutch Ship Lines vessel, *Willem Bilderdijk.* Many in the crowd were there to tell friends and loved ones good-bye who were going to America.

"Papa," said Kadyn, awed by the size of the massive ship, "what does that name up there mean . . . *Willem Bild— Bild—*"

"*Bilderdijk,* is how you say it, son," said Vladimir. "I think it's a man's name, but I don't know who he might be."

Oksana was keeping a sharp eye toward the ticket office, where Murom had gone to get the tickets validated. When she saw him emerge from the office, she said, "Kadyn, here comes Uncle Murom. Maybe he knows who Willem Bilderdijk is . . . or was."

Murom was smiling as he threaded his way through the crowd. As he drew up, he said, "All right. We're all set. We'll be boarding in about ten minutes. We still have cabins 34 and 35 on the second deck."

"Uncle Murom," said Kadyn, "the name of our ship is *Willem Bild— Bild—*"

"*Bilderdijk,* son," said Vladimir.

"That's it," chuckled Kadyn. "Uncle Murom, do you know who that might be?"

Murom smiled. "I didn't until I went in the office just now. A passenger from Poland asked one of the ticket agents about the name of the ship. It's named after a famous eighteenth-century Dutch poet."

"Oh. A poet."

"Yes. Well, we might as well move on up toward the gangplank and get ready to board."

A half hour later, the Russian immigrants had boarded the ship and placed their belongings in cabins 34 and 35, and were standing at the railing on the second deck taking a last look at Rotterdam. Smoke was billowing from the two huge smokestacks, and soon the gangplank was lifted into place on the ship. The mooring ropes were loosened from the dock posts by dockworkers. A moment later, there was a sharp blast from the ship's whistle and a roaring rush of water at the rear of the vessel as the passengers felt the great power of the engines throb through the decks beneath their feet.

Suddenly Vladimir pointed down to the dock and said, "Look! It's the pastor and his family and some of the people from the church! They must have misunderstood us when we told them Sunday what time we were leaving."

"Well, all we can do now is wave to them," said Murom.

The Tambovs, the Petrovnas, and Alekin waved their arms and called out to their Christian friends, who finally were able to find them and waved back. The pastor cupped his hands around his mouth and shouted something, but it was indistinguishable.

"He's probably telling us he's sorry that they were late," said Sasha.

"I'm sure he is," said Vladimir, waving exuberantly.

When the ship was out of the dock, people began to leave the rails and head for their cabins on levels two and three or down the stairs into the belly of the vessel, where they would travel in steerage.

Zoya watched the larger numbers heading down the stairs, and said, "My heart goes out to those poor people who have to travel in steerage."

"Mine too," said Sasha. "It is very crowded down there, from what I hear. They have no privacy at all."

"I learned in the office that there are 556 passengers on the ship," said Murom, "and over 400 of them are in steerage."

"Praise the Lord we were able to afford second-class accommodations," said Oksana.

"Amen," said Olecia.

After a while, the *Willem Bilderdijk* was in the middle of the English Channel, heading toward the open sea. Sasha said, "Well, girls, we might as well go to our cabin and unpack some things."

"We boys ought to do that, too," said Vladimir.

As everyone in the group was turning around to enter their cabins, Olecia said, "Mama, I'll be there shortly. I . . . I just need a few minutes alone."

"Sure, honey," said Sasha. "I understand. You come when you're ready."

When both cabin doors closed, Olecia made her way along the rail until she could see past the stern of the ship and get a clear view of Rotterdam. In her mind's eye, she looked past the city, all the way to the Carpathian Mountains.

The afternoon was warm and the stiff breeze toyed with her long, black hair. As she gripped the rail, a haunting loneliness came over her and tears filled her eyes. "Oh, Barny," she said with quivering voice, "my life will never be complete without you. But . . . but we will have eternity together in heaven, my darling."

Olecia choked up, swallowed tears, and used a handkerchief to dab the moisture from her cheeks. "Lord," she said in a low voice, "I don't understand. Why do I still hurt so in my heart and miss Barny so much? I'm so fearful about my future. I know I shouldn't be, but I am." Even as she spoke, the stiff breeze carried her words away.

Suddenly a passage of Scripture came to her . . . one she had hidden in her heart shortly after the sleighs had left the cave where she had last seen Barny alive. The sacred words of Psalm 121 made their careful way into her troubled mind:

I will lift up mine eyes unto the hills, from whence cometh my help. My help cometh from the LORD, which made heaven and earth. He will not suffer thy foot to be moved: he that keepeth thee will not slumber. Behold, he that keepeth

Israel shall neither slumber nor sleep.

The LORD is thy keeper: the LORD is thy shade upon thy right hand. The sun shall not smite thee by day, nor the moon by night. The LORD shall preserve thee from all evil: he shall preserve thy soul. The LORD shall preserve thy going out and thy coming in from this time forth, and even for evermore.

With those words of calm assurance echoing in her heart, Olecia told herself she could face the future, knowing that the God she served would keep her in His faithful loving care.

Looking back at the diminishing outline of Rotterdam through the tears that dimmed her eyes, she watched the city grow smaller and smaller until it was swallowed in the mists that were now rising from the deep blue water.

Twenty-one

It was midmorning on the seventh day at sea, and the Atlantic was a deep blue with sunshine dancing on the mildly rippling waters. A warm breeze wafted across the ship, and the happy laughter of the children from steerage filled the air as they played games on the main deck.

Vladimir Petrovna had enjoyed the journey so far, and while the rest of the family was occupied in their cabins, he decided to take a walk about the ship as he had done every morning for the past six days. He had met several interesting people on his walks and was eager to meet some more.

Only once since leaving Rotterdam had Vladimir been up to the third deck, which housed the first-class cabins. After chatting with an elderly couple from Russia who were on their way to New York City to join family members who had gone there a year previously, he left the second deck and mounted the metal stairs to the top level.

As he walked slowly along the railing, speaking to people who were sitting on deck chairs, he glanced up to the bridge and saw Captain Ernst van Deuningen looking down at him. They had met and talked on a few occasions. The captain, who was accompanied by two ship's officers, waved in a friendly manner. Vladimir smiled and waved in return.

Captain Ernst van Deuningen was a tall, bearded Dutchman with wide shoulders and a barrel chest. Vladimir felt he could command a ship with physical presence alone. He and his officers all wore neat white uniforms resplendent with gold braid and insignia.

The captain said something to his officers, then wheeled and entered the pilot's cabin. Vladimir resumed his casual stroll, and after speaking to a young couple sitting on deck chairs holding hands, he came upon a well-dressed, middle-aged man with silver creeping into his thick, blond hair. The man was reading a German newspaper. He looked up and smiled as Vladimir drew near.

Knowing the German language well enough to converse in it, Vladimir stopped, smiled in return, and greeted him in German.

"And good morning to you, sir," came the reply in English. Then the man chuckled, shook his head, and said it in German.

"Oh," said Vladimir, "you know English."

"Yes. I have lived in the United States for twenty years and am much more used to speaking in English."

Bending over, Vladimir extended his hand. "My name is Vladimir Petrovna. I am Russian."

As the man met his grip, he said, "I am Max Hillgruber, Mr. Petrovna. I was born in Frankfurt, Germany, but my wife, Marlena, and I migrated to the United States in April of 1866. How is it that you know English?"

"My mother was British."

Hillgruber chuckled. "Well, that would do it." Gesturing to the empty chair next to him, he said, "Please sit down."

"Thank you," said Vladimir.

As Vladimir was easing onto the chair, Hillgruber said, "I was just in Frankfurt to visit an ailing relative. Marlena was not able to come with me. She is having some health problems of her own."

"Oh. I'm sorry to hear that."

"Nothing really serious. Just a flare-up of a lung problem she developed when she was in her teens."

"I see. So where do you live, Mr. Hillgruber?"

"My home is in Grand Forks, Dakota Territory, which is ninety miles south of the Canadian border. Grand Forks is on the confluence of the Red River and the Red Lake River on the Minnesota border."

"I understand that is cold country in the wintertime."

"It sure is. Very much like Russia."

Vladimir smiled. "Well, I guess I would feel right at home there."

"You sure would."

"And what do you do in Grand Forks, Mr. Hillgruber?"

"I'm in the retail clothing business. Hillgruber Clothiers. Actually I have a total of fourteen stores. The main store is in Grand Forks. The other thirteen are located in cities both in Dakota Territory and the state of Minnesota. The clothing business is a family tradition among the Hillgrubers. It was my Uncle Max — after whom I was named — that I just visited in Frankfurt. It was he who financed my venture to America when I was in my midtwenties so I could realize my dream of carrying on the family tradition in America."

Vladimir smiled and nodded. He had figured the man was wealthy just by the way he was dressed. The fact that he was traveling first class was a bit of a hint too.

"So what about you, Mr. Petrovna?" asked the German. "Are you migrating to America?"

"Yes, sir. I was raised on a potato and sugar beet farm near Kiev."

"Oh? Southern Russia."

"Yes. And except for my military service during the Crimean War, I have been a potato and sugar beet farmer, myself."

"Mm-hmm. And you have family on board with you?"

Vladimir told him about Sasha, Zoya, Olecia, and Kadyn, then explained about Murom, Oksana, and Alekin, saying they were moving to America to begin a new life.

"So where are you going to settle?" asked Hillgruber.

"We haven't decided yet. We plan to stay in New York until we can learn the best areas in the United States to raise potatoes and sugar beets, then make our decision."

The German's eyebrows arched. "Well, my friend, you are looking at a man who lives in potato and sugar beet country. There are others, of course, but let me encourage you to seriously consider coming to the Grand Forks area. Both of those products grow well there, and farmland is plentiful."

Smiling, Vladimir said, "Well, because of your recommendation, I will talk to my brother-in-law about it."

"Good!"

"Let me ask you something."

"Of course."

"Do you know if there are any Bible-preaching churches in the Grand Forks area?"

By the way Hillgruber's pale blue eyes widened, Vladimir knew he had surprised the man by asking such a question. His features contorted slightly as he said, "There is one in Grand Forks, but I have never been to it."

Vladimir started to say something, but Hillgruber cut him off by saying, "I don't attend church of any kind, Mr. Petrovna. I am a student and follower of the renowned German philosopher, Friedrich Wilhelm Nietzsche. I'm sure you know he is an impassioned critic of the Bible and of that segment of Christianity that believes the Bible is God inspired and the only basis for spiritual truth and guidance."

"I know about Nietzsche," said Vladimir.

"Well, like him," said Hillgruber, "I consider myself a confirmed infidel."

Vladimir knew that Nietzsche's nefarious philosophy had been making inroads into Russian thought for several years, declaring that the fools who followed the "Jesus Christ idea" were victims of a slave morality and a herd mentality. He recalled Pastor Nicolai Suvorov standing before the church a couple of years ago with a popular widely-read German publication in his hands that had been published in Russian. The headlines declared: "GOD IS DEAD!" In the front-page article, which was written by Friedrich Wilhelm Nietzsche, God's death was called the "greatest event of recent times."

Nietzsche's article went on to assert emphatically that when God died, this left man alone in the universe and limitlessly free to live as he wished without restrictions that had been laid down in a sacred book called "the Bible."

Vladimir cleared his throat gently. "I know about Nietzsche's teaching, Mr. Hillgruber. Many Russians have begun to follow it. But I must tell you that God is indeed alive. I have come to know Him personally through His Son, Jesus Christ. Jesus did die on Calvary's cross, but three days and three nights later, He came back from the dead, just as He had declared He would.

He is alive and looking down at us at this moment from heaven. He saved my soul when I received Him as my own personal Saviour as a youth, and when I die, I know I'm going to heaven to be with Him forever."

Hillgruber licked his lips. "Mr. Petrovna, I mean no insult to you, but Friedrich Nietzsche has taught me that Jesus Christ is only part of the Bible fairy tale."

Vladimir managed a friendly smile. "Nietzsche is wrong, Mr. Hillgruber. If you will give the living God the opportunity to make Himself known to you, He will do it. But on His terms. By faith in His infallible Word, which is no fairy tale."

"Mr. Hillgruber?" came the voice of a white-uniformed crew member.

Both men looked up.

"Yes, Garold?" said the German. "Are you finished?"

"Yes, sir. I had to put new screws in the legs of the bed to anchor it more securely to the floor. It won't tilt and rock with the motion of the ship anymore."

"Thank you. I appreciate your getting right on it."

"It's my job, sir," said Garold, walking away. "If you have any more problems, please let me know."

"I surely will," said Hillgruber, rising from the chair and folding the newspaper.

By this time, Vladimir was on his feet. Hillgruber said, "Well, Mr. Petrovna, it's been nice talking to you. I've got to get back to my cabin. And give some serious thought to settling in the Grand Forks area."

"I certainly will, Mr. Hillgruber. I'll talk it over with my brother-in-law and the rest of the family and let you know."

"Good. I'm in cabin number 4. I'd like to know what they think about it. And when we meet the next time . . ."

"Yes, sir?"

"You can call me Max."

A wide grin spread over the Russian's face. "All right. And you can call me Vladimir."

"Vladimir it is. See you later."

When Vladimir returned to the second deck, he found his group standing at the railing in front of their cabins, looking out across the vast body of water that surrounded them. The Atlantic remained clear and sapphire blue, the surface calm. The breeze was still soft and warm.

"Well, there you are, darling," said Sasha. "Did you make some new friends again this time?"

Vladimir laughed. "Well, you might say

467

that. I met a wealthy German man up on the top deck, and we had quite a talk."

"Wealthy?" said Murom. "Now that's the kind of friends to make. Is your new friend migrating to America?"

"He already did. Twenty years ago. His name is Max Hillgruber. He owns a string of clothing stores in the state of Minnesota and in Dakota Territory. His home is in Grand Forks, Dakota Territory, just across the border from Minnesota. He asked me to talk to all of you about seriously considering settling there. He told me that farmland is plentiful, that sugar beets and potatoes grow well there, and the climate is a great deal like Russia's climate."

Murom's eyes lit up. "Well, we really do need to seriously consider it. I'd like to talk to him."

"I can arrange that," said Vladimir, "but there is one thing about Max Hillgruber that I need to explain."

"What's that?" queried Murom.

"He is a student and avid follower of Friedrich Nietzsche."

"Uh-oh," said Zoya. "Are you sure he wants us to live near him, Papa? Did . . . did you tell him we are born-again Christians?"

"I briefly gave him my testimony. He told me he doesn't believe the 'Bible fairy tale,' but we stayed civil to each other. He is expecting me to let him know about our thoughts concerning the idea of settling in the Grand Forks area. And he did tell me there is a Bible-preaching church in Grand Forks."

"This is sounding better all the time," spoke up Alekin. "Maybe the Lord let you meet him in order to guide us to Dakota Territory."

"Could be," said Vladimir. "And I'd like to bring him to Jesus in the process!"

"Well, Papa," said Kadyn, "you gave him your testimony. The Lord can sure use it to convict his heart."

The next day the Petrovnas, the Tambovs, and Alekin Kolpino climbed the stairs toward the top deck together under another clear, blue sky. With the bowsprit of the *Willem Bilderdijk* pointed westward as gracefully as the arched neck of a magnificent stallion, the ship glided smoothly over the water. Beyond the stern the churning propellers left a whitened wake gleaming in the sun.

When the group reached the third level, Vladimir looked around at the passengers who were seated in deck chairs and standing at the railings. "He's not on deck at the moment, but since he asked me to let him know everybody's reaction to the Grand Forks idea, I'll go knock on the door of his cabin and see if he's there."

Just as Vladimir turned to head for the cabin, he saw the German come out the door. When Hillgruber saw him, he smiled and hastened toward him.

"That's him," said Vladimir, pointing with his chin.

"He does dress nicely," said Oksana.

As the blond man drew up, still smiling, he said, "Vladimir! It's nice to see you again."

"You, too, Mr. Hillg—"

"It's Max, remember?"

Vladimir touched his temple with his fingertips. "Oh. Yes, of course." He introduced Max to the rest of the group, then said, "I talked to them yesterday about the Grand Forks area, and we are giving it some serious thought. Murom wanted to ask you some questions about the area."

"Certainly," said Max. "Let's all go over here, collect us some deck chairs, and sit down."

When the group was seated, Murom asked Max about the kind of rainfall the area had, as well as snowfall in the winter. He asked about irrigation and water rights, the price of land, and about marketing their crops.

Each question was answered to Murom's satisfaction. He thanked Max for the information, and looking around at the others, said, "This may very well be God's way of showing us where we should settle."

"I think so," said Oksana.

"Me too," said Vladimir. Then he said to Max: "We are going to earnestly pray about it. I'm sure the Lord will give us an answer before we finish the journey."

A bit off balance at the mention of prayer, Max forced a smile. "Well, I'll certainly be happy if you decide to make the Grand Forks area your home. I guarantee you will like it there. And believe me, you will make a good living raising potatoes and sugar beets."

Murom laughed. "And here I am a wheat farmer. Oh well, I guess I can learn to produce potatoes and sugar beets."

"You won't need to," said Max. "Wheat is also a main crop in our area."

A smile broke across Murom's face. "Oh, really?"

"Yes. Really."

Looking at Oksana, Murom said, "I'm getting a better feeling about Dakota Territory all the time!"

A week later, Vladimir was walking the lower deck on another beautiful day when he came upon Max, who was just finishing a conversation with a deckhand who was swabbing a section of the bow. Turning from the man, Max said, "Hello, Vladimir. You and your family enjoying the trip?"

As they walked together toward the starboard railing weaving among the crowd, Vladimir said, "We sure are. So far the weather has been wonderful."

"Well, let's hope it stays that way. I've been across these waters a few times when it wasn't so good."

"I've been told it can get treacherous when severe storms come up."

"For sure," said Max as they drew up to the railing. "Any decision yet on settling where I live?"

"We're still praying about it. And I might add that so far everyone is feeling stronger in that direction every day."

Vladimir noted the sour look that settled in Max's eyes at the mention of prayer. He was about to bring up the subject of salvation again when he saw Max's eyes take on a different look as he saw a man coming toward him, smiling.

"Max!" the man said, hurrying to him

and extending his hand.

Speaking in German, Max said, "Hagen! I haven't seen you since I was visiting in Frankfurt . . . what was it? Four years ago?"

"It sure was!" said his friend as they pumped each other's hand. "How have we been on the ship this long and not seen each other before?"

Max shrugged. "Big ship. Almost six hundred people. I'm sure there are people yet that neither one of us has seen."

Hagen laughed. "Well, I'm sure you're traveling up there in first class. Vera and I are here on the main deck in third class. We don't mingle with the upper crust that much."

It was Max's turn to laugh. Then he said, "Oh! Hagen Richter, I want you to meet a new friend of mine. From Russia. I met him a few days ago. Vladimir Petrovna."

Vladimir and Hagen shook hands, greeting each other warmly, then Vladimir said, "Max, I'll let you and Hagen have some time together. See you again soon."

Just as he was walking away from Max and his friend, Vladimir's line of sight fell on two familiar faces in the crowd. Totally unprepared to see Ivan and Ridna Chikov aboard the ship, he stopped dead in his tracks, unable to believe his eyes. They were angling his direction while talking to each other but had not yet seen him.

Hurrying toward them, he excused himself as he bumped into other passengers, and as he drew near them, he called out, "Ivan! Ridna!"

It was the Chikovs' turn to stop dead in their tracks. Surprise showed on both faces.

"Vladimir!" Ivan gasped, opening his arms wide. "We thought you would already be in America!"

Vladimir embraced Ivan, then Ridna. When he stepped back from Ridna, she said, "I can't believe we've been on this ship all this time without running into you or somebody in your family before now."

Vladimir smiled, echoing what he had heard Max say only moments ago. "Big ship. Almost six hundred people. It's possible, all right."

Vladimir quickly explained the delay he and his family had experienced in Rotterdam, then asked about their being on the ship.

"We've had enough of the czar's atrocities," said Ivan. "We're going to America to start a new life. Ridna has relatives in New Jersey, and we're going there to live."

"Well, isn't this something?" said

Vladimir. "My family is going to be plenty surprised to see you."

"Can you take us to them right now?" queried Ridna.

"I was just going to suggest that. We're on the second level."

As Vladimir led the Chikovs across the deck toward the stairs, Ivan laughed and said, "No wonder we haven't run into any of you. We poor folks have a cabin here on the main deck. We don't mingle with the elite up there on the higher level."

"It's only because of Sasha's sister and brother-in-law that we're up there," Vladimir said. "If it had been what we could afford, we'd be down in steerage."

When they reached the second level, Vladimir spotted his group sitting in deck chairs and led the Chikovs to them. Zoya and Alekin were not with them, having taken a walk together, but the reunion was sweet between the Chikovs and the rest of the Petrovnas, and Vladimir introduced Ivan and Ridna to Murom and Oksana.

Moments later, Zoya and Alekin returned from their walk and were pleasantly surprised to find the Chikovs.

When they all sat down to talk, Ivan asked if they had a place picked out where they were going to live in America. Vladimir told them about his meeting Max Hillgruber on the third level several days ago, and of Max's encouraging them to settle in the Grand Forks, Dakota Territory area.

"We have been praying earnestly about it," spoke up Murom, "and we all have peace in our hearts that the Lord is leading us to go there."

"Wonderful," said Ridna. "I'm so glad for you."

Vladimir then told the Chikovs about Max being an infidel and a follower of Friedrich Nietzsche and how he had given Max his testimony.

He asked Ivan and Ridna to be praying for Max, saying that he was going to talk to him some more about Jesus and give him enough Scripture to really cut his heart and bring him under conviction of his need to be saved.

Ivan and Ridna assured Vladimir they would be praying.

On the night of October 1, Sasha was reading Scripture to her daughters and her sister at bedtime, and while she was reading, they heard the wind begin to buffet the ship.

Sasha stopped in the middle of a verse, looked up, and said, "We haven't had that kind of wind since we were in the Carpathians."

"Could be a storm blowing in," said Oksana.

Sasha went on reading and by the time she closed her Bible, the ship was pitching to and fro and rocking from side to side. Sasha laid her Bible down and went to the cabin's porthole. Cupping her hands at the sides of her face, she peered out and said, "I can see by what lights are shining from the ship that there are whitecaps on the water. It looks like they're three and four feet high."

When the women prayed together, each one asked that if a storm were brewing, the Lord would keep them safe. They included Max Hillgruber in their prayers, asking God to bring him to salvation, and thanking Him that He had used Max to show them where they were to settle in America.

By morning dark clouds covered the sky, and the whole surface of the ocean had been set in furious motion. The pitch and sway of the *Willem Bilderdijk* made it difficult for the passengers to stay on their feet as they came to the dining rooms for breakfast.

The Petrovnas, the Tambovs, and Alekin Kolpino left their adjacent cabins, and gripping the rails, descended the stairs to the main deck.

Vladimir and Murom helped their wives toward the dining room of their choice, while Alekin helped Zoya, and Kadyn steadied Olecia.

While they were attempting to eat, with beverages spilling and plates sliding on their table, Captain Ernst van Deuningen entered the dining room. Shouting above the roar of the wind, he told everyone in the room that they were facing a fierce storm. He wanted them to return to their places as soon as they had finished breakfast. Everyone in steerage was to go below and all others were to stay in their cabins. He warned of the danger they faced while moving on the decks and told them not to leave their quarters unless it was absolutely necessary.

Having said this, the captain hurried out to make his way to the next dining room.

By the time the Petrovnas, the Tambovs, and Alekin left the dining room to head to their cabins, the wind was slamming the ship with hurricane force and there was a driving rain. With the ship tossing and bobbing in the troubled sea, people were terrified, having a hard time walking, standing up, or being heard as they struggled to get to their quarters. Many — especially the elderly — were being helped by the crewmen.

When Vladimir's group neared their cabins, he shouted above the storm for them all to go into the men's cabin so they could pray together.

Once safely in the men's cabin, they used towels to dry their faces, then sat on the beds with the howl of the wind in their ears and prayed aloud one by one, asking the Lord to stop the storm.

When it was Kadyn's turn, he said, "Lord Jesus, You were on a ship one day with Your disciples when a storm hit like this one. The wind was strong and the waves beat into the ship. The disciples were scared, just like we are now. You told the wind to stop blowing and told the sea to be still. We need You to stop this storm for us. Please?"

Suddenly the roar of the wind ceased.

Everyone in the bobbing cabin opened their eyes and looked at each other.

"I can't believe it!" said Alekin. "The wind quit blowing!"

"Of course it did, O ye of little faith," said Kadyn, secretly astonished himself.

Everybody laughed.

The ocean was still rough, but within an hour the clouds had broken up and the sun was shining. Much praise was given to the Lord by the little group, and Kadyn Petrovna was very encouraged in his prayer life.

The next morning, the sea was still somewhat choppy under a sunlit sky as Vladimir Petrovna and Ivan Chikov were walking together on the main deck. Vladimir spotted Max Hillgruber standing at the rail on the port side and whispered from the side of his mouth, "There's Max! I'll introduce you to him."

When they drew up, Max smiled at Vladimir and was introduced to Ivan. Vladimir explained that Ivan and his wife were friends of his family from Russia, and how surprised they were to find them aboard ship.

Max grinned. "Like Hagen Richter surprised me."

"Yes, sir. Just like that," said Vladimir. "Max, you asked me to let you know when we had made our decision about settling in the Grand Forks area."

Max's eyebrows raised. "And have you decided?"

"We have. We are going to follow your advice."

"Good! I'm glad to hear it. And Vladimir . . ."

"Yes?"

"I want you and your family to feel free to call on me if there is ever anything I can do for you."

"I appreciate that," said Vladimir.

Looking at Ivan, Max said, "Have you two known each other for a long time?"

The two Russians grinned at each other, then Ivan said, "For many years. I'll let Vladimir tell you the story."

Happy for the opportunity, Vladimir told Max how he and Ivan met at the Rybon Prison so many years ago when his father, Bakum Petrovna, had been arrested and sentenced to a life term for refusing to renounce his faith in Jesus Christ.

Before Nietzsche's disciple could comment, Vladimir said, "Max, my father would not turn from his faith in Jesus because He is real. He is not part of a fairy tale."

Calmly, Max said, "I don't mean to offend you, but I don't believe that Jesus Christ was any more than a mere man who lived and died like all other mere men."

Vladimir said, "Max, you are wrong. The Bible says when God brought His Son into the world, He said, 'Let all the angels of God worship him.' Jesus is no mere man. Scripture also says, 'In this was manifested the love of God toward us . . .' That's talking about the entire sinful human race,

Max. 'In this was manifested the love of God toward us, because that God sent his only begotten Son into the world, that we might live through him.' It goes on and says, 'And we have seen and do testify that the Father sent the Son to be the Saviour of the world.' "

"That's right," said Ivan.

"Max," Vladimir said, "the sentence of eternal death is on this sinful human race. We need a Saviour to save us from the wrath of God, and we need a Saviour who can give us eternal life. That Saviour is God's virgin-born Son, the Lord Jesus Christ."

Max shook his head. "This may be all right for you, but not for me."

"Are you telling me that you will never die?" pressed Vladimir.

"Of course not. Everybody has to die."

"Well, the Bible says there are two deaths."

Max frowned. "What?"

"There is physical death. The one you just spoke of when you said everybody has to die. That's the first death. But there is a second death if you die physically without Jesus as your Saviour. God calls it the lake of fire, which is hell in its final and eternal state. Today when unbelievers physically die, they go directly into the flames of hell.

One day they will be brought out of hell to face the Judge of the universe at His great white throne. There the books will be opened, Max. God has kept a book on every human being, listing all their sins committed on earth against Him. They will face Him there, with those sins on their record. Another book that will be opened is the Book of Life. He will show those Christ-rejecting sinners that their names are not in the Book of Life.

"Revelation 20 tells about it, and says they will be cast into the lake of fire. Verse 14 says, 'This is the second death.' Verse 15 says, 'And whosoever was not found written in the book of life was cast into the lake of fire.'

"God sent His Son to pay the price for the sins of the world, Max, and Jesus did just that when He willingly died on the cross of Calvary and shed His precious blood. This is the gospel message: 'How that Christ died for our sins according to the scriptures; And that he was buried, and that he rose again the third day according to the scriptures.'

"Jesus is alive, Max, and if you die without Him as your Saviour and your sins washed away in His blood, you will burn in hell for centuries. Then one day you will be brought out of hell to face Him and your record.

From there, you will be cast into the lake of fire, where you will burn forever but never go out of existence. But you don't have to. Jesus said, 'Repent ye, and believe the gospel.' "

"That's right, Max," said Ivan.

"But I don't believe any of this," Max said softly.

"Your unbelief doesn't change the facts, Max," Vladimir commented as softly. "It will just put you in the lake of fire. In Revelation 21:8, God says, 'The unbelieving . . . shall have their part in the lake which burneth with fire and brimstone: which is the second death.' In John chapter 3, it says, 'For God sent not his Son into the world to condemn the world; but that the world through him might be saved. He that believeth on him is not condemned: but he that believeth not is condemned already, because he hath not believed in the name of the only begotten Son of God.' Did you hear that? Your unbelief has you already condemned, Max. And once again, Scripture says it is only through Jesus that you can be saved. You must repent of your sin of unbelief, or die in your sins and spend eternity in the lake of fire.

"The Bible says that all of us are sinners. We all need to be saved. If you will repent and believe the gospel and simply call on Jesus to save you, He will do it. The Bible says, 'For whosoever shall call upon the name of the Lord shall be saved.' The difference is eternal heaven or eternal hell."

As Max was shaking his head, about to say something, Ivan said, "Max, I was once as hard against God and the Bible as you are, but Vladimir's father showed me with Scripture how wrong I was. God dealt with my heart, and I called on Jesus to save me. He did. And I've never been sorry I became a Christian. I won't be sorry that I did when I die, either. I'll be in heaven with Jesus."

Max shook his head stubbornly again and came back with some Nietzsche philosophy, which both men calmly refuted with Scripture. Max was stumped.

Seeing it, Vladimir said, "Max, I want you to think about what has been said here. Ivan and I have given you lots of Scripture to think about. And you have not given us reasonable and sensible answers to what we have just given you. Be honest with yourself. God's Word does make sense. Nietzsche's philosophy doesn't. Let me put it to you like this: If you're right and when we die, that's the end of us, what have we lost by putting our faith in Jesus Christ?"

Max shrugged. "You've lost nothing."

"Right. But if we are right and you are wrong, what have you lost?"

"Everything," said Max, his face expressionless.

Laying a friendly hand on Max's shoulder, Vladimir said, "Think on that, and we'll talk again soon."

Twenty-two

When Barny Kaluga arrived in Rotterdam, he immediately rode through the city, looking at church buildings. He was glad to find that the church signs were written both in Dutch and English. He attributed this to the fact that England was relatively close, just across the English Channel. At any given time there were many British people visiting Rotterdam. Some of the signs, in brief, indicated the basic beliefs of the churches.

Late in the afternoon of his first day in Rotterdam, he came upon a church whose sign attested that the true gospel of Jesus Christ was preached there without mixture of religious rites and human works. Upon meeting the pastor, he was pleased to find that the man was readily conversant in English, and he was even more pleased after a brief conversation to learn that, indeed, it was the right kind of church.

As Barny began telling his story and mentioned the name of Olecia Petrovna, the pastor's eyes lit up. He told Barny that the Petrovnas, the Tambovs, and Alekin Kolpino attended his church during their stay in Rotterdam. He knew Olecia was grieving over the loss of the young man she loved, who had sacrificed his life to spare them from being captured and executed by the Cossacks. He was elated to know that Barny was the young man. He then explained that the group had embarked for America on the Dutch ship, *Willem Bilderdijk*, on September 15.

The pastor told Barny there was a man and wife in the church who were in their late forties. Their only son had died several months ago, and he was just a year or two younger than Barny. He was sure they would let him stay in their home until he could get on a ship for America.

When the pastor brought Barny and the couple together and they heard his story, their hearts went out to him, and they welcomed him to stay in their home saying they thought Olecia was such a nice girl. They talked about how surprised and happy she would be when she found out he was alive.

The people of the church helped Barny in every way they could. A man who owned a grocery store gave Barny a job for as long as he would be in Rotterdam. Once he had enough money, Barny went to the shipping dock and purchased a ticket to go to America on a ship that would leave December 1.

Each day as Barny worked in the store, his mind was often on Olecia and he prayed that God, in His own wonderful way would lead him to her, wherever she had gone in America.

On Monday, October 25, the *Willem Bilderdijk* was rolling gently over and through the waves, steaming its way closer to America's northeast coast. Billows of black smoke curled skyward from the dual smokestacks.

Word was spread by white-uniformed crewmen that the captain wanted a meeting with all the passengers at ten o'clock that morning. They were to gather on the three decks, and he would address them from the bridge.

The crewmen would be there to translate the captain's English into Dutch, German, Polish, and Russian.

At precisely ten o'clock, Captain Ernst van Deuningen came out of his office just behind the pilot's cabin and putting a megaphone to his mouth, said loudly, "Good morning, everyone!"

Using megaphones, themselves, the crewmen rapidly made their translations.

The excited passengers responded by calling back the greeting.

"I wanted to inform all of you that our navigator tells me that barring any storms, we will arrive in New York harbor this coming Thursday, October 28."

The crowd applauded and cheered, and the captain dismissed the meeting.

From where Vladimir stood with his family on the second deck, he could see Max Hillgruber on the top deck, leaning on the rail and looking out over the sea. Turning to Sasha, he said, "It's time for me to have my talk with Max. He's had long enough for the Holy Spirit to do His work with the Scriptures Ivan and I planted in his heart."

"I'll be praying, darling," said Sasha, rising on her tiptoes to kiss his cheek.

Having heard Vladimir's words, Murom said, "I wish I could go with you, but it's probably best that you deal with him alone."

"I believe you're right," said Vladimir. "All of you be praying, please."

The rest of them assured him they would, and Vladimir headed for the stairs that led up to the third deck.

The two men had chatted on a few occasions since the day Vladimir and Ivan had talked to Max about his need to be saved, but Vladimir had purposely refrained from pressing him so as not to drive him away.

As he reached the top deck, Max saw him and smiled, heading toward him.

"Looks like we have an excited bunch," said Max as they came face to face.

"I'll say," said Vladimir. "I can almost smell the sweet air in New York harbor now."

Max chuckled. "Yes. Me too."

"You know what it makes me think of?"

"What's that?"

"There's going to be real joy when this ship arrives in New York harbor on Thursday."

"That's for sure," agreed Max.

"I was just thinking what joy there always is in heaven when a saved earthly sojourner takes his last breath on earth and arrives in that heavenly harbor."

Max's jaw muscles were working under the skin, but he did not comment.

"In Luke 16, Max, Jesus tells what it's like for the lost earthly sojourner when he dies. He tells about a rich man who died lost and instantly lifted up his eyes in hell. He begged for water, crying that he was tormented in the flame. But there was no water and no relief from his torment. There was no joy for him."

Suddenly, Max's face contorted, reddened, and his eyes filled with tears. "Vladimir," he said, "you told me to think on those things that you and Ivan quoted to me from the Bible. Let me tell you . . . I haven't been able to get them out of my mind. I've had nightmares about standing before God, facing my record, then being cast into the lake of fire. I've pictured Jesus dying on that cross for me, and I realize how much He loves this guilty sinner."

Vladimir's heart was aflutter.

Wiping tears from his eyes with the back of his hand, Max said, "I see now that Nietzsche's philosophy is empty and offers no hope to the human soul. You told me that God would make Himself known to me, and He has! I know that God is most certainly alive . . . as is His Son, and I want to be saved."

Fighting his own tears, Vladimir thanked the Lord in his heart, laid a hand on the weeping man's shoulder and said, "Let's go to your cabin, Max."

As they sat down in Max's cabin, Vladimir said, "Let me remind you that Jesus said for you to repent and believe the gospel."

Max said, "You don't have to remind me.

It has gone through my mind a thousand times."

Vladimir then explained to him that Jesus said, "Except a man be born again, he cannot see the kingdom of God." He quoted John 1:12 and Ephesians 3:17, making sure Max understood that it was receiving Jesus into his heart that would give him the new birth and make him a child of God. He quoted Romans 10:13 once more, explaining that it was by calling on the Lord that he would receive Jesus into his heart and be born again.

Then and there, Vladimir Petrovna had the joy of leading Max Hillgruber from Friedrich Nietzsche to the Lord Jesus Christ.

Vladimir then took Max to his family, and when Max told them he had become a born-again child of God, there was great rejoicing.

On Wednesday morning, October 27, the Petrovnas, the Tambovs, Alekin Kolpino, Ivan and Ridna Chikov, and Max Hillgruber met in the men's cabin on the second level for Bible study and prayer time, which was led by Vladimir.

Max was full of questions wanting to learn as much Bible as he could. After the

Bible study, he began firing questions and the group was pleased to see him so hungry to learn.

When Vladimir and Murom had answered them all, Max shook his head in wonderment and said, "I am amazed at how blind I was to the truth. I was so foolish to believe Nietzsche's godless philosophy."

Ivan smiled at Max and said, "I know exactly how you feel. I didn't follow the teachings of some rank infidel, but I was raised to believe that the Bible was just another book, and though it had some good principles it was not the Word of God. I was taught by my parents that man made his own heaven or hell right here on earth, and when he died, that was the end of him. Oh, how wrong I was to believe such a false idea."

"Well," said Murom, "it's prayer time. Ivan, would you lead us?"

"Certainly."

"Ah . . . could I ask you to pray for my wife, Marlena, Ivan?" asked Max. "I want her to be saved."

"Praise the Lord!" said Vladimir. "I'm glad to hear you say that, Max. One of the first signs that a person has really gotten saved is that they have a concern for the salvation of others, especially their loved ones."

Ivan said, "All right. Let's pray." Heads were bowed, and Ivan prayed for Marlena Hillgruber's salvation; for Olecia in the grief she still carried over the loss of Barny; for the spiritual growth of everyone in the cabin; and for safety and guidance as all of them began their new life in America.

Just as Ivan said his amen, a loud voice came through a megaphone for the passengers to gather on the decks for a meeting with the captain.

When the crowd was assembled, the crewmen were on the bridge, megaphones in hand, ready to translate. Captain Ernst van Deuningen stepped out of his office, carrying his own megaphone. Putting it to his mouth, he lifted his voice and said, "My navigator tells me we have stayed on schedule since I spoke to you on Monday. We will be pulling into New York harbor early tomorrow afternoon!"

There was cheering and whistling from the happy crowd.

The captain explained the procedure those who were not American citizens would face in being processed at Castle Island. They would be examined by medical doctors first. Anyone who was rejected for health reasons would be put back on the ship to return to Rotterdam.

Many hearts were filled with fear upon hearing the captain's dire words, especially those who were traveling in steerage. No one had prepared them for such news. If they were refused entrance into America, all their plans would be destroyed. What did the physical examination require?

A number of them had suffered sea sickness during the storm and had lost weight. They still were pale and gaunt. Some of the steerage passengers had come down with dysentery during the journey. Their bodies were emaciated, their faces wan and pallid.

They began to murmur among themselves, and Captain van Deuningen had to call for quiet.

As the murmuring abated, an elderly woman dressed in a black, threadbare coat looked up at the captain as tears slid down her seamed and sunken cheeks. She stood with her thin, gnarled hands pressed against her wildly beating heart and said to the young man who stood beside her, "We have come so far and endured untold hardships in order to make this trip."

He put a frail arm around her bony shoulders. "It's all right, Grandma. God will make a way for us. He will see that we aren't turned away."

The careworn woman palmed tears from

her wrinkled face and nodded. "Yes, Willie," she remarked quietly, her faith taking control of her fears. "Yes. God will do that."

When the crowd was silent again, the captain explained that those who passed the medical examinations would then be interviewed by government workers. If the questions were answered properly, they would be allowed into the country. He hastened to add that since ships carrying immigrants from all over Europe and other parts of the world were continuously entering New York harbor, it might be a few days before all the immigrants aboard the *Willem Bilderdijk* could be processed.

"Now, there is something else I would like to explain to you," said the captain. "When we enter New York harbor tomorrow, you are going to see a gigantic statue towering over a small island. The people of France have recently given this statue to the American people to demonstrate the harmonious relationship between the two countries and to honor the American spirit of freedom that has inspired the world.

"The statue was actually built in France, then dismantled and shipped to New York harbor in large sections aboard several ships and has been erected on the small island, which is called Bedloe's Island. My crew and I have come and gone across the Atlantic four times since they began to erect the statue on Bedloe's Island. You will find it fascinating."

The captain took a folded sheet of paper from his coat pocket, opened it, and said, "Let me give you some facts about the statue. This great structure was built with a skeleton of iron, sinews of rivets and beams, and a skin of glowing copper. The French people had called it the statue of 'Liberty Enlightening the World.' The Americans now call it the 'Statue of Liberty.' The statue, including its huge pedestal, stands 302 feet high. It is a woman who is holding a torch high above her head in her right hand, symbolizing that America is the land of liberty. There is a tablet in her left hand, bearing the date July 4, 1776, proclaiming the freedom that was purchased at the price of blood and lives in the Revolutionary War.

"You immigrants who are allowed to make your new home in America will definitely be living in the land of the free."

Captain van Deuningen went on to explain that upon his last journey to America, he had learned that the statue was to be publicly dedicated in an afternoon ceremony led by President Grover Cleveland on Thursday, October 28, 1886.

"As you all know," he said, "that is to-morrow. My navigator has given me hope that we will make it into New York harbor in time to observe the ceremony."

A wave of joy swept over the crowd. Happy faces beamed as applause filled the air.

The captain said, "Let me tell you about the poem that is inscribed on the statue's pedestal. The words are supposed to be coming from the lips of the Statue of Liberty herself. It was written by a lady named Emma Lazarus, who is a resident of New York City, and is entitled, 'The New Colossus.' The word 'colossus' means something of great size or scope."

Looking at the paper in his hand again, he said, "Let me read it to you:

'Give me your tired, your poor:
Your huddled masses yearning to breathe free,
The wretched refuse of your teeming shore.
Send these, the homeless, the tempest-tossed
*   to me,*
I lift up my lamp beside the golden door!' "

Vladimir Petrovna and his group were wiping tears as they thought of the atrocities they had faced in Russia under the despotism and iron hands of the czars.

Max Hillgruber stood with them, looking on, and wiping his own tears as Vladimir said to his family and Alekin, "Praise the Lord! We are going to live in the 'land of the free'! True liberty will be ours after we pass under the shadow of the Statue of Liberty."

"Yes," said Max. "And believe me, it is true liberty." His features took on a glow and a gleam filled his eyes. "But I must praise God for the freedom I now have from the bondage of sin and Satan because of my faith in the Lord Jesus Christ! He bought me eternal liberty when He shed His precious blood on the cross, died for me, and rose again to give me salvation."

"Praise His name!" Vladimir said, sniffling and wiping tears.

The rest of the group joined in, praising the Lord together.

It was an hour past noon the next day when the ship from Rotterdam left the Atlantic Ocean and glided into New York harbor under a flawless blue sky.

Aboard the ship, there had been little sleep the night before and all were up early, gathering their belongings together and making their families as presentable as possible. Even those who had been ill during the crossing of the Atlantic looked stronger and more robust on that day. The thrill of arriving at their long-awaited destination at last had put roses in the palest of cheeks. Happy children were running about, calling to each other. Babies could be heard crying as they, too, felt the strange emotions of their parents and siblings.

The mingling of trepidation and excitement was almost palpable among the immigrants as they stared in awe at the skyline of New York City.

"Look!" a man shouted, pointing past the bow of the ship. "It's the Statue of Liberty!"

They all looked to the magnificent statue in the distance, towering over the harbor, casting her shadow on the rippling waters.

As the ship steamed deeper into the harbor, the passengers' attention was also drawn to the imposing shoreline. Many were pointing out the Brooklyn Bridge, while others were captivated by the lofty structures of Staten Island, Brooklyn, and Manhattan.

Kadyn Petrovna pointed at the skyline and said, "Papa! Mama! Look at the tall buildings!"

"They're tall, all right," said Max. "Over here on Staten Island and there in Brooklyn, the tallest ones are five and six stories high. In Manhattan — straight ahead of us —

some of them are eight and ten stories high. When I came through on my way to Frankfurt this time, I was told they are building one in Manhattan that will stand eleven floors in the air!"

"I don't know how they keep them from toppling over," said Sasha.

"Me either," said Oksana. "Modern miracles of engineering. Aren't they something!"

"They sure are!" said Ivan Chikov. "I have never seen anything like this!"

Soon they were drawing near the Statue of Liberty. Several small boats and a couple of ocean liners were positioned in a half circle near Bedloe's Island.

From the bridge, Captain van Deuningen called out through his megaphone for all passengers to gather on the port side of the ship so they could get a good view of the statue. The crewmen followed by translating for him.

While the passengers were collecting on the port side as directed, the *Willem Bilderdijk* moved up close to Bedloe's Island. Below Miss Liberty's left foot, set into a grassy bank separating the harbor walk from the pedestal of the statue, was a metal grid thirty feet long and six feet wide. The grid was barely visible because of the great crowd that was gathered at the foot of the statue. A military band marched onto the island from a boat that had just pulled up to the small dock on the island's west side. Two soldiers each carried an American flag on a pole.

The entrance to the statue through the pedestal was situated on the front side, and in keeping with the beauty of the awesome structure were two bronze doors, twenty feet in height. A group of dignitaries was being seated on wooden chairs near the doors.

The band filed up near the dignitaries and under the direction of their leader, took their usual formation, standing at attention. The flag bearers held the flags high as they flapped dramatically in the breeze. The band instantly struck up a rousing tune.

Captain van Deuningen was pleased that they had arrived in time to take in the entire ceremony and sent a command to the engine room. As the engines were cut and the ship came to a halt, a hush fell over the passengers. All chatter ceased, even that of the children. Not one baby was crying.

Every eye on the ship was trained on the glorious statue and every ear attuned to the exhilarating sounds coming from the island where Miss Liberty stood proudly, welcoming one and all to the protection of her shores.

Standing with his new Russian friends at the railing on the second level, Max Hillgruber noted the joyful look on their faces as they listened to the lilting music and looked up at the statue as she held the torch of freedom high. It was easy for him to imagine the impact Miss Liberty would have, seen from weary and hopeful eyes in need of new dreams.

When the band ended its tune, one of the dignitaries left his chair, stepped to the rostrum that had been placed in the forefront, and introduced himself as George Monroe, the mayor of Manhattan. He called for the flag bearers to step forward, and when they did, the band struck up Francis Scott Key's "Star Spangled Banner." Every man sitting down behind the rostrum was instantly on his feet.

At the close of the song, Monroe came back to the rostrum and introduced President Grover Cleveland. There was a special thrill in the hearts of the immigrants as Cleveland spoke of the wondrous gift the people of France had given his country. He then welcomed four French government leaders who had traversed the Atlantic for the ceremony and had each man give a brief word about his feelings for the people of America, and his admiration for the country because of its spirit of freedom that had inspired the world.

President Cleveland then introduced a fifth man who had come from France for the ceremony: sculptor Frederic Auguste Bartholdi, who had designed and led in the construction of the Statue of Liberty. While the band played, applause and cheers came from the crowd on the island.

Bartholdi spoke of his admiration for the spirit of freedom in the American people and was loudly cheered and applauded again as he took his seat.

President Cleveland then made his speech, in which he sincerely expressed the gratitude of the American people and himself for France's marvelous gift. He closed by saying all Americans must pray that God would help their nation to always be known as the land of the free and that it would ever inspire the world with its spirit of freedom.

After much applause, a large man stepped to the rostrum, and with the military band backing him, sang through a megaphone with his deep, resonant voice:

My country 'tis of thee,
Sweet land of liberty,
Of thee I sing:
Land where my fathers died,
Land of the pilgrims' pride,
From every mountain side
Let freedom ring!

Tears were streaming down Vladimir Petrovna's cheeks as he turned to his little group — who were also weeping — and said, "Yes! Sweet land of liberty! Let freedom ring!"

As the ship pulled away with the sound of the military band playing another rousing tune, Max told Vladimir and the others that when the ship docked, he would be taking a hired buggy to the railroad station. He must catch a train for Chicago, where he would board another one for Minneapolis, then board another train that would take him home. He explained that the officials on Castle Island would instruct them how to obtain their railroad tickets. He would see them when they arrived in Grand Forks in a few days.

Max told Ivan and Ridna good-bye, then embraced Vladimir, thanking him for caring enough about his lost soul to give him the gospel.

Patting Max's back with both hands,

Vladimir said, "I'm just so glad you got saved. I'll look forward to helping you get established in church. My family and I will be praying for Marlena."

When the *Willem Bilderdijk* drew within five hundred yards of Castle Island, there were several other ships ahead of them. Captain Ernst van Deuningen had his crewmen drop anchor and went in a lifeboat to the island. When he returned, he explained to the immigrants that with so many ships ahead of them, the officials told him it would be three days at the most before they could be processed. The government officials and the medical doctors were working long hours and were processing some five thousand people per day. Those aboard who were United States citizens would be going ashore immediately in a ferryboat that was on its way.

The days of waiting aboard ship seemed to drag on interminably. The Petrovnas, the Tambovs, the Chikovs, and Alekin Kolpino spent hours on the decks together, looking longingly toward the island where their future rested.

Olecia tried valiantly to enter into the anticipation of starting a new life in this new land where all men were free and had equal opportunity, but her heart was still held captive by thoughts of Barny. The memory of him grew stronger in her heart each day as she thought of how he had given his life so she and her family could live free in America.

As they watched people on the ships ahead of them being taken by ferryboats to Castle Island, they all felt they were reasonably healthy and of sound mind, but there was always a tiny nagging fear at the back of their minds that the doctors would find some reason to refuse them entrance into the country.

On Sunday morning, October 31, the Chikovs were taken from the ship in the first group that went to Castle Island. An hour later, the Petrovnas, the Tambovs, and Alekin were put aboard a ferryboat and soon set foot on solid land. With a bit of fear and trembling they were processed one by one by the doctors and the officials who asked their usual questions, but each one passed. An immigration official gave papers to Murom for the group, including instructions for purchasing railroad tickets for Dakota Territory.

From there, they were taken to one of Castle Island's docks where they found Ivan and Ridna waiting to board a ferryboat with them along with some two hundred other happy immigrants from the *Willem Bilderdijk*. The ferry would take them to Manhattan Island.

While the ferry was crossing the bay toward the Manhattan docks, the Chikovs explained that they would take a train from Grand Central Station to Atlantic City, New Jersey. Ridna's relatives would meet them there and take them to McKee City, where they would make their new home.

Vladimir told the Chikovs that they were set to do as Max did — take a train to Chicago, another to Minneapolis, and another to Grand Forks.

Soon the Chikovs found themselves saying good-bye to their Christian friends in Grand Central Station. Ivan's last words were about Vladimir's father, and how much he was looking forward to meeting him in heaven.

Twenty-three

Early in the afternoon on Wednesday, November 3, the train from Minneapolis chugged into the depot at Grand Forks.

When the Petrovnas, Tambovs, and Alekin Kolpino alighted from the train and carried their luggage out of the terminal building to hire a carriage to take them to a hotel, it was spitting snow and a cold wind was blowing.

Kadyn felt the cold blast and said, "Hey, everybody! It is just like Russia! I feel at home already!"

Everybody laughed.

Murom hailed a carriage driver and asked him what was the best hotel in town. The driver told him there were only two, but he recommended the Red River Hotel because it was kept up better and the people were friendlier.

Twenty minutes later the men were placing the women's luggage in their room. When that was done, they took their own luggage to their room across the hall. Vladimir and Murom had agreed that the first thing they would do was find Hillgruber's Clothiers and let Max know they were in town.

Leaving Alekin and Kadyn to unpack, the two men told the women where they were going and went down the stairs to the desk. They learned that the store was only two blocks down the same street.

The snow was still falling lightly, but the wind was dying down when Vladimir and Murom entered Hillgruber's Clothiers. Both male clerks were waiting on customers at the counter but took the time to smile at them. One of them said, "We'll be with you shortly, gentlemen."

The Russians both smiled at him, then looked around the store while they waited. They were amazed at how well stocked the store was. They had never seen so many racks displaying men's and women's clothing and shelves so loaded with socks, underwear, stockings, gloves, scarves, caps, and hats.

The clerk who had spoken earlier came up from behind them and said, "I don't recall seeing you gentlemen before. You must be new in the area."

Vladimir explained that they had just

come from Russia and were going to buy farmland; then he introduced Murom and himself. The clerk shook their hands, welcoming them, told them his name was James Garvey, then said, "I know about you gentlemen and your families. Mr. Hillgruber told us he met you on the ship, and that he talked you into coming here to live. He said you would probably be here before he got back. He's in Minnesota right now, checking on his stores over there. He'll be back next Tuesday."

Vladimir thanked Garvey for the information, telling him when Mr. Hillgruber returned to let him know they were in town and staying at the Red River Hotel. Garvey assured them he would, and they went back into the snow and the diminishing wind.

The next morning, Vladimir and Murom stopped at the hotel desk after the family had eaten breakfast together and asked if the clerk had a list of the churches in town. They were given the list of six churches, and as they looked it over with the rest of the group when they were back upstairs, Vladimir reminded them that Max had told him on the day the two of them first met that Grand Forks had one Bible-preaching church. Max no doubt knew which church preached the doctrines that bothered him the most.

Since Max was not there to tell them which church it was, they would have to find it on their own. They quickly eliminated four of the churches, knowing their doctrines were steeped in religious tradition rather than founded on the Word of God.

"All right, Murom," said Vladimir, "let's you and I go check out these other two."

Getting directions from people on the street, Vladimir and Murom soon came upon the first church of the two. They were pleased to see a salvation verse written on the sign beneath the name of the church. The pastor's name was Ben Packard.

Knocking on the door of the parsonage, which was adjacent to the church building, they were greeted warmly by Shirley Packard. She told them her husband was in his study at the church and led them to him.

They found Pastor Ben Packard a warm-hearted man, and as they talked to him about his doctrines it took only a few minutes to know that they had found the right church. They told the pastor they would be there on Sunday.

When the Petrovnas, the Tambovs, and Alekin attended the services on Sunday, they all loved it and knew they would be happy in the church.

During announcement time in the morning service, Pastor Packard had the new group from Russia stand up and publicly welcomed them. He then explained to the congregation that they were looking for farms to purchase. After the service, they were welcomed by the people, some who were immigrants from many European countries.

On Tuesday morning, the whole group decided to walk to the clothing store from the hotel and see if Max was there. When they entered the store, Max was at the counter talking to James Garvey, who said, "Well, they've saved you a trip to the hotel. Here they are."

Max pivoted, set his eyes on them and smiled. "Hello! James and I were just talking about you! I was about to bring Marlena to the hotel to meet all of you." Turning toward the back of the store, he called, "Marlena!"

"Yes, darling!" came a quick reply.

"My Russian friends are here!"

"I'll be right out!" she called back.

Max then began introducing James to those who had not met him, and just as he was finishing, Marlena appeared. Lovely and nicely dressed, Marlena welcomed her husband's friends. She embraced the women as each one was introduced to her by Max and extended her hand to the men and Kadyn.

A man and woman came in. James excused himself and went to wait on them.

Putting an arm around Marlena's shoulders, Max said to the group, "I've been talking to her about my faith in Jesus Christ, and she is very interested."

"Yes, I am," Marlena said quickly. "I want to learn more. I have a brand-new husband. Of course I loved him before, but his being born again has made him so much easier to live with. He's always smiling."

Max shrugged. "The Nietzsche philosophy didn't give me anything to smile about."

Sasha set compassionate eyes on Marlena. "I am glad you want to learn more."

"We want both of you to come to church with us next Sunday," said Vladimir. "Pastor Packard keeps a stock of new Bibles at the church. Anyone who visits and doesn't have a Bible gets one as a gift the first time he comes. You both need to have a Bible."

"I can't wait," said Max.

"It would help you a lot to hear some good Bible preaching, Mrs. Hillgruber," said Oksana.

"Right," said Vladimir, "and as I told you, Max, you need to make a public profession of faith and be baptized."

"I certainly will," said Max. "Both of us will be there Sunday."

The next day, Murom learned of a large wheat farm that had just come up for sale some five miles south of town. He rented a buggy and took Oksana with him to look at it. When they returned, they told the others they loved the place and had told the owner they would buy it, along with the horses and the farm equipment. The deal would be closed in the office of Grand Forks' land agent on Monday. Murom explained that the house had four bedrooms and that there was a small house on the place which had been the home of the hired hand and his wife. He asked Alekin if he would like to be their hired hand, and thrilled at the offer, Alekin accepted the job. Murom told him he could move into the small house as soon as they took possession of the farm, which would be next Wednesday. He then told the Petrovnas that since the house was plenty big enough, they could stay with them until they had their own farm.

The Petrovnas were happy to accept, and there was joy over the way the Lord was working in their lives.

On Sunday, Max walked the aisle during the invitation and presented himself for baptism. The baptistry water was already heated up for two other people who had come prepared to be baptized. Max made the third.

Marlena was a bit overwhelmed by it all since she had never been in a church service, but told Pastor Packard and his wife and Max's new friends that she wanted to come back and hear more about Jesus Christ.

On Wednesday the Tambovs took possession of the farm, and the group moved in. Alekin was thrilled with his house, and gave Zoya a personal tour. They discussed their future while standing in the house and agreed they would talk to Pastor Packard soon about a wedding date. Zoya already had ideas about redecorating the house.

The women were so used to working together by then that they quickly fell into a pattern of daily chores with each one doing her part. While they worked, they sang songs of praise that had been of necessity held in their hearts when in Russia, but now, with no fear of reprisal, they lifted their voices in thanksgiving to their heavenly Father for His manifold blessings.

On Thursday afternoon, while the men were helping Murom build a new toolshed, the women went into town and paid a visit to Marlena Hillgruber. They were warmly received, and while enjoying tea together, they answered many questions Marlena had about the Bible and salvation. By the time they left, they could see that she was getting close to opening her heart to Jesus.

In the morning service on the following Sunday, Marlena responded to the invitation at the close of the sermon, walked the aisle, and was led to Christ by Shirley Packard. Max was overjoyed and wept openly when Marlena gave her testimony. She was baptized in the evening service.

On Monday morning, November 15, Vladimir drove into town alone to pick up a load of oats and barley for feeding the horses. After helping the owner of the feed store load the heavy gunnysacks, Vladimir was climbing up to the wagon seat when he heard a male voice call his name from the boardwalk. A man named Steve Gentry — who was a member of the church — hurried up to him and said, "I was just about to ride out to the Tambov farm to see you, Vladimir."

The Russian grinned. "Well, I guess I saved you a trip. What did you want to see me about, Steve?"

"I wanted to tell you about a potato and sugar beet farm that has just gone up for sale. The farmer is a Norwegian — Lars Agder. Lars is getting too old to handle the farm, so he's going to sell it and move to Minneapolis, where he will live with his son and daughter-in-law. His wife died about a year ago. It's ninety acres and has made Lars a good living for forty years. I'm sure he will sell it for a reasonable price. You'll like the location too. It's less than a mile from Murom's place."

A grin spread across Vladimir's face. "Well, ninety acres isn't as much ground as Murom's hundred and sixty acres, but that's more than I had in Russia. I'm sure I can make a good living on it. I'd like to take a look at it."

"Lars hired Grand Forks' land agent, Bob Becker, to handle the sale for him. In fact it was Bob who told me about it some ten minutes ago. I told him I'd drive out to the Tambov place and tell you about it. He will take you out and show it to you. Do you know where his office is?"

"Yes. Next door to the bank. I'll go talk to him right now."

The women were putting hot potato soup on the kitchen table for lunch as Murom, Alekin, and Kadyn came in from the barn, where they had been repairing feed troughs.

"Sure smells good!" said Kadyn.

Looking around as he was taking off his hat and coat, Murom said, "I wonder what's keeping Vladimir. He should've been back a couple of hours ago."

"He probably got to talking to someone in town," said Sasha. "You know how he is about that."

Murom grinned. "Yes. He —"

"There's Papa now," said Olecia, looking out the kitchen's side window.

They all glanced out the window to see Vladimir driving the wagon past the side of the house, loaded with grain sacks.

"He'll be in shortly," said Sasha. "You men get washed up."

Moments later, Vladimir came into the kitchen, his face reddened from the cold. The smile on his lips told them he had something good to tell them.

"All right, Papa," said Zoya. "What is it? You look superbly happy."

Removing his gloves, Vladimir stuffed them in his coat pocket and hung his hat on a peg. As he was unbuttoning his coat, he said, "The Petrovna family has a ninety-acre potato and sugar beet farm, if Mrs. Petrovna and the offspring approve of it."

Eyes widened among the group at Vladimir's words as Sasha said, "You're serious?"

"Yes, sweetheart. I just took a look at it. The horses and farm equipment go with the place, and the house, barn, and outbuildings are in good condition. The furniture also stays, as well as dishes, pots, pans, and eating utensils in the kitchen. The house is not as large as this one, but it has two stories and three bedrooms. The price is very reasonable, and the land agent who is handling the sale told me if we could come up with a four hundred dollar down payment, we can pay the balance over a period of five years. Murom has five hundred dollars set aside to loan us for the down payment, so I don't see why we can't make the annual payments. The farm has been quite productive for forty years. The owner is an elderly man, and he left for Minneapolis early this morning. If we want it, we can move in tomorrow."

"Well, praise the Lord!" said Murom. "You can give us all the details while we eat lunch."

An hour later the group climbed out of the wagon as they let their eyes rove over the farmhouse. It had a wide front porch, and Sasha immediately fell in love with it. Vladimir led them inside, holding Sasha's hand. The house had been well cared for, and though it was not elaborate, all agreed it was very serviceable and quite livable.

The rooms were plain and simply laid out, but a feeling of warmth and welcome permeated each one, and Sasha's mind was already busy making plans. Smiling up at her husband, she said, "Darling, it's beautiful! It will do just fine."

Zoya, Olecia, and Kadyn agreed. Murom and Oksana were happy that such a place had come up for sale.

While Vladimir was showing the men the barn and outbuildings, the women slowly walked through the house a second time with Sasha. A satisfied smile tugged at the corners of her mouth as she spoke of plans for each room.

The Petrovnas moved into their newly purchased home the next afternoon.

That night, while Zoya and Alekin were downstairs in the parlor with Vladimir and Kadyn talking about their upcoming wedding, Sasha and Olecia entered the girls' room. Sasha was explaining what she wanted to do to the room after Zoya was married and it was Olecia's room.

"I like your ideas, Mama," said Olecia. "I guess I'd better like them. I may be living here a long time. Probably till you and Papa get tired of having this old maid around and tell me to get a place of my own."

"We're not going to ever get tired of having you around, sweetheart," said Sasha, putting her arms around her. "And I doubt you will be an old maid. The Lord has someone all picked out for you."

Olecia eased back in her mother's embrace, looked her in the eye, and said, "But, Mama, my heart belongs only to Barny . . . even though he is in heaven and I am on earth. There will never be anyone else for me. But this is God's will for me, so I will follow His will with an obedient heart and let Him show me just what His plans are for my life. I have claimed Psalm 138:8 ever since I got a grip on my emotions over Barny's death: 'The LORD will perfect that which concerneth me.' He has given me peace about it."

Sasha smiled, looking deep into her daughter's eyes. The calmness on Olecia's countenance was proof that God's grace had proven sufficient. A happy sigh escaped Sasha's lips, and again, she drew Olecia into her arms, a silent prayer of thanksgiving flowing from her heart.

On Christmas Eve, Alekin and Zoya stood before Pastor Ben Packard at the altar in the church. It was a very simple ceremony, but beautiful in its simplicity.

As the vows were being said, Olecia sat between Murom and Oksana. Her heart was touched as she thought of the wedding she and Barny would never have and silent tears began to course down her cheeks. Quickly, she gained control of herself lest she break into sobs. Alekin and Zoya would turn around in a few moments, and she did not want to mar the happiness of the young couple who had traveled so far to come to this time and place in their lives.

The next morning, everyone gathered at the Petrovna house. After a luscious breakfast prepared by Sasha and Olecia, the family went together into the parlor.

It was rather a modest Christmas since no one had had much time to prepare for it, what with getting settled in new homes in a new country.

Funds were low and must be kept aside for purchasing supplies for the farms so they would be ready for spring planting when the time came.

Still there was joy as each one opened the few gifts that had been placed under a tree decorated with strings of popcorn and gingerbread men, tied on the limbs with red ribbons.

They were happily showing off their gifts and thanking each other when there was a knock at the front door. Jumping up, Kadyn said, "I'll see who it is."

The happy chatter went on in the parlor as Kadyn stepped into the hall, crossed the foyer, and opened the door. Suddenly, he stood awestruck and frozen in place, eyes widened in shocked disbelief.

A smiling Barny Kaluga said, "Hello, Kadyn. Is Olecia here?"

The boy was struggling to free his tongue as he nodded.

"May I come in?"

"S-sure. C-come in."

As Barny stepped in, a pallid-faced Kadyn Petrovna closed the door.

The happy chatter could be heard coming from the parlor. Gripping Barny's arm, the boy whispered, "It's you! It's really you!"

Barny nodded.

Calling over his shoulder with his eyes fixed on Barny, Kadyn said, "Olecia! Olecia! Come here, quick!"

There was no response for a few seconds,

then they heard Sasha say, "Olecia, go see what your brother wants."

Kadyn called again, "Hurry, Olecia!"

Steady footsteps were heard from the parlor. Just before she reached the hall, Olecia was saying, "Kadyn, whatever are you so excited ab—" She was now in the hall, her bulging eyes fixed on the man she had thought was dead, and her lungs devoid of breath. Her legs and feet were like lead. Her lovely face had become a caricature of stunned, mind-boggling amazement.

Barny and Olecia looked at each other for a long, timeless moment; then smiling, he rushed to her, folded her in his arms, and planted a tender kiss on her lips.

Vladimir called, "What's going on out there? Kadyn, who knocked at the door?"

Olecia stared into Barny's eyes with tears misting her own. In that moment of silence, Vladimir appeared at the parlor door and gasped. The others quickly gathered behind him, and suddenly found themselves standing like statues, hardly able to believe their eyes or get their lungs to function.

Easing back in Barny's arms, Olecia let her tears fall as she looked up at him and ran her hands over his beloved face. "Oh, please tell me I'm not dreaming," she said, barely above a whisper. "I've had this same vision in my mind's eye so many times."

Reaching up and grasping her hands in his, Barny said in a steady voice, "You're not dreaming, my darling Olecia. This is real. I, too, have played this moment over and over in my mind. But the reality of it is so much better than I ever imagined."

Like sleepwalkers the rest of the family moved toward the happy couple. Arms around each other, Barny and Olecia turned to face them with Kadyn stepping up to flank them.

Suddenly Sasha said, "Praise the Lord!"

With smiles beaming on every face, everybody embraced Barny, asking how he lived through the battle with the Cossacks.

"Let's all go in the parlor, and he can tell us," said Vladimir.

Everybody sat down in the parlor, and with Olecia next to him gripping his hand, Barny told his story. Periodically as he spoke, they asked him questions, and quite often Barny's words were overridden by someone lifting up their voice to praise God.

With the story of his seemingly impossible journey completed, Barny explained that he was booked to embark from Rotterdam on December 1, but that the shipping company had been informed by the

United States government immigration officials that they could bring an earlier shipload, so they left on November 10.

"Barny," said Alekin, "how were you able to find us? It seems it would be impossible to do, since you had no idea where we were going when we arrived in America."

Barny grinned. "You're right, Alekin. It would be impossible to do, except we serve the God of the impossible. I had prayed so hard that He would work the miracle that was needed, for without it, I would never find you . . . I would never be able to let Olecia know I was still alive. We could never have our life together."

Everyone sat with bated breath, waiting to hear how God had done it.

"It happened like this," said Barny. "When I was being checked through Castle Island, I was being questioned by an official like everyone else. He asked me where I was going to live in America. I started explaining my story, telling him I was going to do everything I could to find Olecia and her family. When I told him your last name, the official in the next booth overheard it. He left his chair, came to me, and said there was a Russian family by that name who had checked through Castle Island several weeks previously. They were going to Grand

Forks, Dakota Territory, and the reason he remembered it was because he is from this area."

Heads were being shaken in wonderment.

Grinning, Barny said, "Once I arrived in Grand Forks this morning, I asked a man who was meeting family members at the depot if he knew where the Petrovnas and the Tambovs lived. His name was Bob Becker. He gave me directions immediately."

Tears streamed down cheeks as they all saw how God had not only saved Barny's life but had guided him straight to Olecia. Right in front of everybody, Barny asked Olecia if she would marry him when he had found a job and could support her, and she quickly agreed. He then asked her parents if it was all right with them, and they gave their consent.

Olecia wrapped her arms around Barny and said, "Darling, you are the best Christmas present I have ever had!"

There was laughter all around.

Before the new year arrived, Barny had a job at Hillgruber's Clothiers in Grand Forks.

Time passed quickly, and on Sunday afternoon, March 27, 1887, Barny and Olecia were married in a beautiful ceremony conducted by Pastor Ben Packard.

There was snow on the ground. The sky was a brittle blue, and a cold, brisk north wind was blowing outside the church building, but only warmth and happiness was felt by all those attending this most joyous occasion.

The light of heaven was on Olecia's lovely face as Barny looked into her eyes and repeated his vows as guided by Pastor Packard. Barny's own face reflected that light as Olecia then spoke her vows to her cherished groom. The ceremony for this couple who had loved and lost each other, only by God's grace to find one another again, was a breathtaking sight for all to behold.

When prayer had been offered by the pastor after the vows were completed, he told Barny he could kiss his bride. Many tears of joy were shed among the guests.

The couple then turned to face the crowd. The pastor introduced them as Mr. and Mrs. Barny Kaluga; then as planned, Olecia looked up into her husband's eyes and repeated the age-old passage from the book of Ruth: "Whither thou goest, I will go; and where thou lodgest, I will lodge: thy people shall be my people, and thy God my God."

A hush hovered over the congregation as

they witnessed this most touching, holy moment.

The happy couple took up residence in a small house Barny had rented in January, a few blocks from the store.

On Saturday, April 2, Vladimir was working alone in his barn, spreading fresh straw in one of the horse stalls, when he heard the big barn door squeak on its hinges, and turned to see a stranger enter.

The man was in his late fifties and dressed in suit and tie. "Mr. Petrovna, your wife said I would find you here. My name is Wayne Millett. I'm from the Grand Forks County tax assessor's office."

The look on Millett's face told Vladimir he was uneasy. Leaning the pitchfork against the wall, he stepped through the gate of the stall and extended his hand. "Glad to meet you, Mr. Millett." As they shook hands, Vladimir said, "What can I do for you, sir?"

With trembling hand, Millett reached inside his suit coat and produced a folded sheet of paper. Handing it to Vladimir, he said, "This is a bill for back taxes on your farm, Mr. Petrovna."

Vladimir's head bobbed. Blinking, he said, "Back taxes?"

"Yes, sir. The taxes haven't been paid on this place for four years."

"But I only bought the place in November."

"I know, sir. It's right there on the bill. But Lars Agder sold it to you with the taxes due from 1883. The county has been very lax in collecting its taxes for the past eight years. But now, with the new administration voted in by the people in the November election, it is going to be different. Everybody's taxes will, of necessity, be somewhat higher."

Vladimir unfolded the bill, examined it, then looked at Millett and said, "These taxes are not high at all, compared to the taxes in Russia. But still, sir, our funds are very low right now, and will be until we can bring in a crop next fall. There's no way we can pay these back taxes."

"I feel bad about this, Mr. Petrovna," said Millett, "but it is the law in Dakota Territory that when you buy property, you also buy whatever tax debt is owed on it. The administration will make no exceptions. This bill has been owed for a long time, and as you can see on the bill, the new administration has declared the taxes due and payable by April 15 and there will be no leniency."

Vladimir's face was a dull, brick red. "Your office won't understand that I didn't know about the tax debt when I bought the farm? They won't defer the due date until I can bring in a crop?"

"No, sir. I'm very sorry. I wish I didn't have to be the one to bring you the bill, but if the tax debt is not paid by April 15, the county will confiscate the farm."

Vladimir sighed and rubbed the back of his neck. "You're just doing your job, Mr. Millett. I understand that."

"Thank you, sir. Well, I'll be going now."

With nothing more to say, Vladimir watched Wayne Millett walk to the barn door and open it. Millett was surprised to see Sasha standing there, tears in her eyes. He told her he was sorry and hurried toward his buggy, which was parked at the rear of the house.

Vladimir and Sasha rushed to each other. As he folded her in his arms, she said, sniffling, "I heard every word. I didn't hear the amount, but I did hear you say we can't pay it."

"No, we can't."

"Maybe Murom and Oksana —"

"They can't help us, sweetheart. They've put their spare money into more farm equipment and building that toolshed."

Sasha sniffed. "Then . . . we are going to lose the farm."

"Unless the Lord comes up with a miracle, we will lose the farm. We must leave it in His hands."

Twenty-four

Vladimir Petrovna held Sasha in his arms another moment, then said, "I'm almost through putting the straw in the stall. Is Kadyn finished with the job you gave him in the pantry?"

Sasha wiped tears from her cheeks. "He was almost finished when I left the kitchen. I told him to stay there."

"Well, we need to hurry into town and get the groceries. I'll finish up in a couple of minutes, then hitch the team to the wagon."

Sasha nodded. "All right."

As she turned to leave the barn, Vladimir took hold of her arm. "Sweetheart, don't let this tax thing get you down. The Lord still has some miracles on His shelf in heaven."

Forcing a smile, Sasha said, "Of course. See you in a few minutes."

Moments later, as they drove toward town with Kadyn riding in the seat on the other side of his mother, Vladimir explained to the boy that the man from the tax assessor's office had presented him with the bill for the back taxes.

When Kadyn understood the amount due, and that it had to be paid by April 15 or the county would confiscate the farm, he looked at both parents and said, "Papa, Mama, the Lord brought us to Grand Forks. He will provide the tax money for us somehow. He won't let us lose the farm."

"We're not giving up, son," said Vladimir.

Sasha cleared her throat gently. "We can't give up."

"Of course not," said the boy. "The God who stopped the storm for us on the sea and kept Barny alive and led him to Olecia can see that our back taxes are paid."

Both parents were proud of their son for his unwavering faith in the Lord's ability to take care of His children but silently found their own faith a bit weaker.

Soon they pulled into Grand Forks, and as the Petrovna wagon approached the town square they saw a large crowd, and a man was addressing the gathering. When they were closer, Vladimir said, "It's Will Barkley who's talking to the crowd. You know him, don't you? He has that big wheat farm south of town on the road to Fargo."

"Yes," said Sasha. "I've talked to his wife a few times at the market."

"Let's see what's going on," said Vladimir, guiding the wagon to the side of the street.

"Look!" said Kadyn, pointing into the midst of the crowd. "Zoya and Alekin and Barny and Olecia are here."

As Vladimir, Sasha, and Kadyn wove their way through the press to join the four family members, farmer Will Barkley was making a loud speech against the raise in property taxes and most of the crowd was cheering him.

When the trio closed in, Barny said in a low voice, "Big protest here about the tax raise. Some folks are really angry about it."

"I can tell," said Vladimir.

The Petrovnas, the Kolpinos, and the Kalugas noted that the crowd was growing in size while Will Barkley was issuing his angry tirade against the government and the majority showed they agreed with him.

After some twenty minutes, Barkley stopped shouting, and breathing hard, looked at another prominent farmer and said, "Jess, you look like you've got something to say."

"I sure do!" Jess Williams said, stomping to the forefront. Immediately, he began lambasting the county officials for daring to raise the property taxes, saying they were already too high. He was shouting so loud, people heard him two blocks away.

Vladimir's family noticed the deep frown on his face as Williams went on, with people shouting their agreement.

Moments later, another farmer — Joseph Horning — followed Williams, unleashing a fierce diatribe on the government. Men were waving their hats, urging him on. Horning kept it up for some ten minutes, then stepped aside.

Vladimir's family saw the crimson color of his face and neck as he suddenly threaded his way through the crowd to the front. While he was doing so, Sasha quickly told her daughters and sons-in-law about Wayne Millett's visit to the farm that morning, the bill for the back taxes, and the potential loss of the farm. Shock showed on their faces.

Before anyone else could step up, Vladimir planted himself where the other three had stood while making their angry speeches, lifted his voice, told his name, and said, "I would like to say something!"

Knowing Vladimir was fairly new in the area and in the country, the people applauded and cheered him. Sasha and her small group looked on, wondering what was going to come from Vladimir's mouth.

Speaking loud enough for all to hear,

Vladimir said, "I cannot believe what I am hearing here! Don't you people realize how very fortunate you are to live in this wonderful country? America has the greatest government on this earth. Do you not understand that it takes money to build and maintain schools? To build roads and keep them in good repair? To build bridges across our streams and rivers so we can cross them conveniently?"

A hush fell over the crowd.

Vladimir proceeded to tell them the story of what happened to him and his family in Russia, and how they had to flee the country for their lives because they could not pay the extremely high taxes.

While the crowd looked on, wide-eyed and silent, Vladimir told them what the taxes were on his farm in Russia, which made the Grand Forks County taxes infinitesimal in comparison.

When the people heard it, they began looking at each other sheepishly. Vladimir went on to give details of government oppression in Russia, and the longer he talked about the suffering and dying of Russian citizens who couldn't pay their taxes, the more sheepish the crowd became.

Having everyone's rapt attention, Vladimir told them about his visit from

Wayne Millett that morning, and being served the bill for four years' back taxes on his recently-purchased farm. "Ladies and gentlemen," he went on, "my family and I cannot pay that tax debt. We do not have the money, and Mr. Millett made it clear that there will be no leniency. I am not blaming him. He was only stating the fact. So . . . the Petrovnas stand to lose our farm."

The silence over the crowd was akin to that of a tomb.

Running his gaze over the sea of faces, Vladimir said, "Even though it looks like we will lose our farm, that doesn't change how we feel toward our government. We love this land of the free, and we are going to stay. And somehow, we will buy another farm someday."

By that time some of the people were shedding silent tears.

"Like I said a moment ago," Vladimir went on, "you people are fortunate to live in this country. In Russia, only the rich can go to school. In America, everybody can. This wonderful country made it through the Revolutionary War and the Civil War and I know it will go on to be a greater country yet.

"This great country has freedoms that are denied people in other countries . . .

freedom to have meetings like this one, freedom of speech so Mr. Barkley, Mr. Williams, and Mr. Horning could stand up without fear of government reprisal and launch their tirades against that very government."

The three men Vladimir had just mentioned, lowered their heads, staring at the ground.

Vladimir went on. "This wonderful America has freedom of the press, a freedom not enjoyed in a multitude of other countries on this earth. And best of all, freedom of worship."

Vladimir took the time to tell them about the underground churches in Russia and the penalty that would be exacted on the worshipers if they were caught. He was wiping tears as he said, "In this country, my family and I can go to church without fearing for our lives, or at least spending the rest of our time on earth in prison."

More heads were drooping.

"In Russia, the taxes are not for schools, roads, and bridges, but for the pockets of the czar and his cabinet. If a man does not pay his property taxes on time, the Cossacks come and take him away. He is never seen or heard from again, and his family no longer has a home."

Shock showed on faces, and the majority were hanging their heads in shame for having complained about their taxes.

"Ladies and gentlemen," said Vladimir, "let me tell you about the day the Dutch ship brought us into New York harbor at the very moment the Statue of Liberty was being dedicated by President Grover Cleveland, October 28, 1886. Our ship captain had us as close as possible to Bedloe's Island so we could see and hear the dedication ceremony. A song was sung beautifully that day that brought tears to my eyes and a lump to my throat. You've heard it. It's called 'America.' The first verse goes like this:

My country 'tis of thee,
Sweet land of liberty,
Of thee I sing:
Land where my fathers died,
Land of the pilgrims' pride,
From every mountain side
Let freedom ring!

"I love every word of it, ladies and gentlemen, but those last three words have a solid grip on my heart: Let freedom ring!"

There was sudden applause, accompanied by loud cheering and people crying out, "God bless you, Vladimir! God bless you!"

As Vladimir thumbed tears from his eyes, he set his gaze on Sasha, who was applauding vigorously. Suddenly he saw a familiar face weaving through the crowd from the right side. It was Max Hillgruber. Everyone knew Max and watched as he stepped up to Vladimir and put an arm around his shoulder.

Sasha and her little group were transfixed by the scene before them, wondering what Max was going to do.

The crowd was quiet once again as Max said so all could hear, "Vladimir, I have been here since the crowd first began to form. I heard all four speeches, and I want to go on record that I agree 100 percent with your attitude about this great country."

There were cheers and shouts, as well as applause. When it died down, Max said, "Vladimir, you are not going to lose your farm. I am going to pay those back taxes for you."

The crowd stood in absolute silence.

With a lump in his throat, Vladimir said, "Max, I can't let you do that."

Max set his jaw with a twinkle in his eye. "Oh yes, you can. I am going to do it. It is my way of thanking the Lord for saving me from the devil's bondage and setting me free. It was you who cared enough about my soul to witness to me aboard ship and bring me to Jesus. I have been set free from the bondage of sin, and you, my dear friend, will be set free from the bondage of back taxes."

In the crowd, Sasha burst into joyful sobs and immediately was in the arms of her daughters while Kadyn, Alekin, and Barny looked on.

Vladimir wiped tears from his cheeks and thanked Max as the crowd observed the scene in amazement.

Max embraced Vladimir, and as they held each other tightly, said, "Let freedom ring!"

With fresh tears streaming down his face, Vladimir cried, "Yes! Let freedom ring!"